Praise for Anne Hope's
Broken Angels

"The tension mounts as clues reveal a villain who turns out to be someone quite unexpected. There is a sense of family that grows throughout the novel and is supported by a well-developed cast of characters. Fast pacing adds another dimension to the story."
~ *Romantic Times Book Reviews*

"Buckle up and get ready for the ride of your life with this nail-biting, edge-of-your-seat, romantic suspense thriller. If you like the writing of Lisa Jackson, Lisa Gardner or J.T. Ellison you will love Anne Hope."
~ *Long and Short Reviews*

"When Rebecca and Zach finally give in to their desire and love, it's nothing short of explosive.... A thoroughly enjoyable read."
~ *Fallen Angel Reviews*

"I was so pleasantly surprised with Broken Angels.... I really enjoyed Zach—his total confusion on how to handle three small children is cute and his slow seduction of Rebecca works really well in this story."
~ *Smexy Books Romance Reviews*

"His (Zach's) devotion to Rebecca is very touching, and I found myself grinning at the changes that overcame him throughout the book. This is the first time I have read one of Ms. Hope's stories and I can say that she did a really nice job. The way she wrote the plot is very well done, she kept me reading to figure out the villain and, boy, was I surprised."
~ *Literary Nymphs Reviews*

"Broken Angels is a story about healing, redemption, hope and rebuilding of lives through some tragic circumstances. I liked the message about happiness and grabbing hold of it with all your might and never letting go; live with no regrets."
~ *Joyfully Reviewed*

Look for these titles by
Anne Hope

Now Available:

Where Dreams Are Made

Broken Angels

Anne Hope

SAMHAIN
PUBLISHING

Samhain Publishing, Ltd.
11821 Mason Montgomery Rd., 4B
Cincinnati, OH 45249
www.samhainpublishing.com

Broken Angels
Copyright © 2011 by Anne Hope
Print ISBN: 978-1-60928-171-7
Digital ISBN: 978-1-60928-158-8

Editing by Imogen Howson
Cover by Scott Carpenter

First Samhain Publishing, Ltd. electronic publication: August 2010
First Samhain Publishing, Ltd. print publication: August 2011

Dedication

I dedicate this book to my children for their relentless squabbles, their fierce devotion to each other and their refusal to do anything I ask of them. But most of all, I thank them for reminding me every day what it means to be a parent and for teaching me just how deeply the heart can love.

A very special thank you to Deborah Nemeth for her guidance and to Imogen Howson for making *Broken Angels* shine.

Prologue

Evil has many faces. Even that of a loved one, a friend.

Liam Birch sensed time was running out. The shadows were closing in on him, the darkness drawing nearer. He wouldn't be able to keep the pretense up much longer. Shock, horror and repugnance were not easy feelings to mask, and he suspected he'd already given himself away.

Still, he'd waited before going to the cops because deep down he'd hoped his hunch was wrong. He should have known better than to question his instincts. All his doubts had been put to rest this morning when he'd taken a trip to Martha's Vineyard. Now he had all the evidence he needed to act.

But first he had to back up the files, just in case.

He'd already downloaded the photographs he'd snapped in a mad rush. Photographs of important documents he'd found in a secret location, deep in the woods, hidden beneath a cover of innocence. Now all that was left to do was copy the hard drive he'd stolen.

His hands shook as he attached the device to his home computer. He clicked open the files, and the children's faces flashed on the screen. Sad, lost, terrified faces. As a lawyer he observed the dark corruption of society on a daily basis, but not like this. Never like this. There were many kinds of predators in the world, but none as loathsome as this one.

A leaden weight crushed his lungs. Why hadn't he seen it sooner?

Because he'd trusted the man, had secretly looked up to him. *Idiot.*

All that had changed when the bastard had targeted his family. Now the gloves were off, and the son of a bitch was going down.

"I need to know what's going on."

He jolted at the sound of Lindsay's voice. She stood in the doorway, looking so intense his stomach clamped. They would be married eleven years next month. It felt like only yesterday he'd watched her glide down the aisle toward him, draped in silly flowers and white silk. The memory only fueled his knee-weakening desire to protect her and the kids.

He pressed Save and minimized the screen to hide the snapshots. "Have you finished packing?"

"No. And I won't until you tell me what we're running from." She approached him, almost floated into the room. Lindsay never made a sound when she walked.

Bitterness lumped in his throat. He didn't have the energy to fight with her again. "You need to trust me."

"Not until you trust me enough to tell me the truth. Why do you want me to take the kids to Ireland tomorrow?"

When he didn't answer, she fell to her knees and grabbed hold of his hands. "Liam, please. You're scaring me."

Desperation and defeat tugged at his shoulders. Maybe he was wrong to shut her out. He couldn't keep her in the dark forever. She needed to know what they were up against if she was to be on guard.

So he told her.

When he was done, the same shock and disgust that had twined inside him when he'd first realized what was going on shone in her eyes. Dread rolled off her in sheets. "I don't believe this."

"Believe it." He unhooked the drive, shut off the computer, then stood and pulled her to her feet. They had little time to waste.

Lindsay shook her head in silent denial. "He's always been so good to us, to the kids..." She lifted her gaze to his face. "Does he know you know?"

"I'm not sure. But I'm not taking any chances. I've gotta act. Fast. But I can't until you and the kids are safe."

She nodded feebly, buried her face in the crook of his neck. Her hair brushed his cheek, a soft, comforting caress. "What if he comes after you?"

"Don't worry about me. Just get the kids as far away from here as possible."

Lindsay stepped back but seemed reluctant to let go. "I'll go pack." After a lengthy pause, she finally released his shirt and headed for the door.

She never made it out. Someone sprang from the shadows, blocked her way. Before Liam could react, the dark figure grabbed her and dug the black barrel of a gun—equipped with a silencer—into her forehead.

Liam instinctively took a step forward, but the man stopped him with a quelling look, tightening his hold on the trigger. "No sudden moves or she bleeds," he threatened in the smooth voice of a schoolteacher. "I'd really hate to have her bleed all over me. I don't like blood. The stench is practically impossible to wash off."

He wasn't wearing a mask, which convinced Liam he had no

intention of sparing them. His round, boyish face was oddly familiar. Where had he seen him before?

Then he remembered, Ringgold Park, the rendezvous point. No one else had been there that day, apart from a bunch of teenagers shooting hoops.

Liam's heart hammered a steady beat against his ribcage. Suddenly, he knew precisely who had sent him. This was no random break-in. "Let her go, and I'll give you what you want."

The man smiled, unnerving in his calmness. "And what do I want?"

He showed him the hard drive. "This."

"Hand it over. Slowly."

Lindsay begged him with her eyes not to give in, but her terrified expression shattered his resolve and left him broken inside. He'd do anything to protect his family—even let a monster go—so he did as he was told.

The man approached, with his thick arm still fastened around Lindsay, and reached for the drive. The moment his fingers closed around the device, he shoved Lindsay to the ground, then shot her, point-blank, in the heart. A scream rose in Liam's throat, but he swallowed it. He couldn't risk waking the kids. Red-hot agony speared through him. With a burst of fury, he lunged, intending to tackle the murderous bastard. He'd barely taken a step when the bullet struck him hard in the chest. A numbing haze enfolded him, cold and silky, like Lindsay's wedding gown.

Darkness danced along the edges of his vision as he slumped to the ground. He should have felt pain when he hit the floor, but he didn't. He felt only weakness. Weakness and an intense sadness...for his children, for the children he'd failed to save. Seconds before the black shroud of death descended upon him, he heard a thumping sound and feared his kids had awakened. He tried to call out to them, to tell them to run, but the only thing that spilled from his mouth was blood.

Then he saw them—three pale white silhouettes shimmering in the darkness, reaching for him—and two words, sharper than a metal blade, sliced through his mind.

Broken Angels.

Part One

Broken

A simple child,
That lightly draws its breath,
And feels its life in every limb,
What should it know of death?

William Wordsworth, "We Are Seven"

Chapter One

Three children.

Was the universe playing some cruel joke on her? Rebecca wanted to laugh at the absurdity of it, but all humor evaded her. Instead, she stared dumbly at the stern-looking, gray-haired attorney in the expensive Hugo Boss suit, fighting an onslaught of symptoms she hadn't experienced in months—the damp palms, the erratic heartbeat, the all-too-familiar stabbing sensation beneath her ribs. They gripped her with steel claws as she sat on the comfortable brown leather couch next to the man she'd sworn to love a lifetime.

A lifetime that had lasted but eight sweet, miserable years.

His familiar scent wafted toward her—that musky fragrance of mint and rain, peppered with a dash of aftershave. It strangled her almost as much as the word *children* had.

"There must be some mistake." She hardly recognized her own voice. It was hoarse and held a barely noticeable trace of terror that only someone who knew her well could detect.

Of course, Zach caught it. Sympathy sped across his face, and she wanted to scream. She didn't want his pity. She didn't want anything from him anymore. He'd walked out on her when she'd needed him the most. He'd discarded her like a defective piece of merchandise. He'd left her to wallow in a sea of pain and misery so deep she'd nearly drowned.

But she hadn't. She'd taken all the hope in her heart and locked it away in that dark little box where all her demons dwelled. Then she'd picked herself up and learned to move on and live again. Two long, hard years she'd worked to regain her sanity and accept the blow fate had dealt her. Two long, grueling years.

And after all was said and done, it took only that dreadful word, *children*, to make it all come crashing down on her again. And Zach just sat there, looking at her as if he understood all too well how she felt.

"I assure you, Mrs. Ryler—"

"James." The word popped out before she could stop it.

Confusion pleated the attorney's bushy brows. "Excuse me?"

"My name is Rebecca James. Mr. Ryler and I are divorced." She could almost feel Zach flinch beside her. She angled a glance his way, noted the sharpness of his features, the way his lips tightened and his dark blue eyes suddenly refused to meet hers. Had she intentionally said that to hurt him? A part of her—the part he'd torn to shreds when he'd walked out on her—probably had.

He looked thin, drawn. His usually tanned skin was pale beneath the harsh glare of the fluorescent overhead lighting, his midnight-black hair—although still as thick as the day she'd met him—laced with gray at the temples. Grief had taken its toll on him, but he would rather swallow a glassful of nails than show it.

His ability to bottle up his emotions, to take control of a situation and accept life's twists and turns with grace and a humbling sense of self-discipline had always driven her crazy. Why wasn't he shaking his fists at the sky, screaming bloody murder at the heavens? His baby sister and brother-in-law had just been shot to death, leaving his niece and two nephews orphaned. That should have been enough to send even Gandhi over the edge, but not him. Nothing shook Zach Ryler. Not death, not heartache and certainly not the slow, devastating loss of a dream.

Sensing the tension between them, the attorney—Neil Hopkins, or was it Hawkins?—cleared his throat and continued. "I assure you, Ms. James, there's no mistake. I had the benefit of working with Liam for over ten years. I deeply hope he saw me not only as his boss, but as his friend." He paused, took a second to compose himself.

"What I'm trying to say is that I knew Liam on a personal level, and he and Lindsay made their wishes very clear. You and your husband—ex-husband—" he corrected, "have been named legal guardians of their three children." Errant sunbeams trickled in from the window and gilded the smooth surface of the mahogany desk that dominated the room. Behind it, the lawyer sat, looking aggrieved.

Panic expanded inside her. *Get a grip. Don't lose it.*

"I'll take care of my niece and nephews on my own." Zach's voice scraped the air like sandpaper. This was the first time he'd spoken since they'd entered the stifling office in the downtown Boston highrise. "I don't want or need Rebecca's help."

Why did his dismissal cut her so deep? He was giving her what she wanted—a way out. She should've been thrilled. Instead, a wrenching ache blossomed in her chest.

"Social services may take issue with that," the lawyer replied. "A man raising three young children on his own—"

"Widowed and divorced fathers do it all the time." He leaned forward and propped his elbows on his knees, his hands fisted between them. She recognized the non-negotiable stance, noted the square set of his shoulders and the slight spasm in his jaw. He was digging in his heels, literally and figuratively. His eyes, however, remained shuttered—as clear and flat as a calm sea on a windless day.

Fighting to keep her wits about her, Rebecca rose. Her nails dug painfully into her palms. "I'm sorry." She slanted a beseeching look Zach's way. "I loved Lindsay like a sister—you know that—but I can't do this. I just can't."

The lawyer looked stunned and, for the first time since he'd called them into the leather-scented office, at a loss for words.

Zach simply nodded. "I know."

Rebecca steeled her heart and broke the unsettling eye contact, then shot out the door. It slammed behind her, a loud, hollow reminder of what a coward she was. She was an expert at slamming doors. She'd slammed the door on her marriage, she'd slammed the door on all her dreams of home and family, and now she'd just slammed the door on the second chance fate had seen fit to grant her.

The thought of letting Lindsay down gnawed at her. Lindsay wasn't only her sister-in-law but her lifelong best friend. Or she had been until Rebecca turned her back on her. Ever since she'd separated from Zach, she'd been unable to bear being around Lindsay anymore. Lindsay—with her perfect marriage and three beautiful children—had been a reminder of everything she'd never have. Just thinking of her had jammed painful needles in her gut, had driven in her failures with the force of a sledgehammer.

Instead of facing the pain, she'd opted to hide from it, and in the process she'd not only lost a best friend but a sister.

She'd missed her these past two years. Loneliness was an insidious thing, sharp-toothed and pervasive. It had slowly eaten away at her until she was hollow inside, a frail shell encompassing nothing.

For months she'd been meaning to call her, but every time she picked up the phone she'd lose her nerve. Now it was too late. Lindsay was dead, and Rebecca could never tell her how sorry she was.

Perhaps she shouldn't have walked out just now. She owed it to Lindsay to make sure her children were okay. She had to put her personal feelings aside and do what was right.

Her heart pounded louder than a symphony of drums at the thought. The walls of her throat swelled. With a growing sense of urgency, she rammed her finger against the elevator button harder than was required. The urge to escape strangled her. *Dear God, what's wrong with me?*

She'd thought she'd finally gotten a handle on her emotions. Had she just spent the last two years fooling herself?

No, she couldn't accept that. She was solid now, on her way to finally being whole again. This little lapse in her self-control was perfectly understandable. She was still reeling from Lindsay's death, was coping with feelings of pain and loss, layered with guilt.

"I'm sorry, Becca." Zach's voice pierced the heavy mist smothering her brain. She hadn't heard him creep up behind her. "I had no idea. I would have expected Lindsay and Liam to change their will after the divorce."

She wanted to tell him to leave her alone, to let her wallow in her despondency the way he had two years ago, but the words remained trapped in her throat.

"Are you all right?" Zach anchored her by placing his hand on her lower back. Whether it was habit or a desire to touch her that impelled him to do so, she couldn't be sure.

Rebecca tensed in response. Part of her wanted to recoil, her flesh scorched by yet another reminder of all that was lost to her forever. But another part of her—the traitorous part—wanted to lean into his embrace, to let him comfort and support her.

Great solace could be found in the familiar, and Zach's touch was like the comfortable sweater you'd had since you were a teen or the house you'd lived in all your life—full of memories and feelings, both good and bad, but always a soothing balm to a bruised spirit.

"I meant what I said in there. I'll take care of those kids on my own. So you can breathe easy."

His heat branded her, made her body flush and her heart crash. The lump blocking her windpipe thickened. "I'm sorry— I can't—"

A high-pitched *ding* rent the air, and the elevator doors slid open. Desperate to sever the physical contact, Rebecca dove into the cab. Seconds later the doors glided closed, shutting out the image of Zach's beautiful face, pinched with disappointment and a sobering dose of acceptance.

Rebecca wasn't sure how long she sat in her car. She estimated close to ten minutes, but it felt more like an hour. She kept willing herself to turn the key, put the car into drive and rocket down the street, away from this place and the man who'd broken her heart so many times she'd lost count. Instead she just idled behind the wheel, jumbled thoughts roiling in her mind as sunlight painted yellow streaks across her windshield.

As much as she tried, she couldn't chase Zach's parting expression from her head. She was used to seeing disappointment on his face, but the acceptance had cut deeper than it should have. She'd believed he'd given up on her when their marriage had ended. Now she wondered if that moment hadn't come till today. The possibility rankled.

"Go ahead," she told herself. "Get the hell out of here before you're tempted to go back in there."

Zach Ryler was her greatest weakness. One she'd struggled for two years to overcome. If she spent another minute in his presence, she feared she'd fall all over again. She couldn't risk living through that kind of pain again.

She gripped the key but failed to start the engine. *He needs you*, a tiny voice whispered.

"Where was he when I needed him?"

Her subconscious didn't answer. Instead, it chose to show her the image of his bedraggled face yet again.

"Damn it." She withdrew the key from the ignition and stepped out of her Camry. Then, knowing full well she'd live to regret it, she made a beeline for the very building she'd just fled.

When she returned to Neil Hopkins' office, Zach stood alone at the window, nothing but a dark silhouette against a pale backdrop of light.

"You're still here." Relief trembled in her voice, underscored by anxiety.

The slight inclination of his head was the only indication he'd heard her. "I didn't expect you to come back," he said after a short pause.

She refrained from telling him she'd never been too good at staying away from him. "Where's the lawyer?"

"He went to get some documents for me to sign concerning Liam and Lindsay's estate. He should be back any minute." Zach finally turned to look at her, and she wished he hadn't. The sight of his eyes made her heart ache. They were tired, filled with sorrow, despite his best efforts to conceal it.

The old impulse to reach out to him—to nurture and soothe—reared within her, but she fought it. It wasn't her job to comfort him any longer. He was on his own, just as she was. She fisted her hands and ventured deeper into the room.

"Why are you here, Becca?"

"I wish I knew."

A whisper of a smile fluttered over his lips. She'd always loved his smile. It brightened his whole face, made his eyes sparkle and long grooves dimple his cheeks. But today it was half-hearted, strained.

Rebecca wet her lips. "I'd like to apologize for the way I reacted earlier. I don't know what came over me."

"I do." He walked toward her, his gait smooth, his body lean and square. She was aware of every muscle his gray cotton shirt concealed, was intimately acquainted with the wide curve of his shoulder, the springy whorls of hair on his chest, the powerful arc of his back. Her fingers still burned with the feel of his flesh beneath them. Why did the

17

body—the heart—remember, even as the mind struggled to forget?

"I'm past that now."

"Yeah? Then how come the mere thought of kids has you running for the nearest exit?"

He was right, of course, but there was no way she'd admit it. Just the idea of children—other people's children—crippled her. It wasn't that she didn't love kids. On the contrary, she loved them too much. Loved them so desperately she'd made herself sick with yearning. She couldn't allow that yearning to take root within her again. This time it would destroy her. Hope was a double-edged sword, as sharp as it was seductive. She'd learned that the hard way.

"It was just a shock to my system," she said in her own defense. "I never expected to have any children, let alone three at once."

He nodded, his gaze so piercing she felt it all the way down to the marrow of her bones. She tried not to squirm, but failed. Butterflies brushed silken wings against the walls of her stomach. "Could you please—" She faltered. "Could you please tell me about the shooting?" She'd wanted to ask him about it when she'd seen him at the funeral two weeks ago, but it hadn't seemed appropriate at the time. Everything had been so new then, the wounds still shockingly fresh. "Did the children see—" She couldn't bring herself to say the words. *Did they see their parents murdered?*

Zach sat on the edge of the gleaming desk, as if he'd suddenly grown so weary he needed the support it offered. "No. They were in bed when—" He released a thin stream of air that was half sigh, half snort. "When the son of a bitch broke in."

A shadow passed behind his eyes. "No one heard a thing. He probably had a silencer."

"Who discovered them?"

"The next-door neighbor." A lengthy pause followed. "The police think she probably scared the killer off. That's why the children were spared. She took the kids to her place while the cops worked, so they wouldn't see—" His voice trailed off.

She raised her fingers to her lips, gently shook her head. "How could something like this happen? Why?"

She didn't expect an answer, but he answered just the same. "Because some junkie was looking for his next fix and was short on cash. Because some nut job wanted to try out his new gun. Because the world has just gone crazy. Take your pick."

Something arctic-cold and lethal blew across his face. "My sister was shot in the heart. Death was so instantaneous she hardly bled. Liam's death was a little slower. He must have realized what was happening." He clutched his hands, wrapped his palm around his fist in a steel clamp. "That's all it takes. One shot and you're out." The latter was spoken so softly she barely heard it. "Now I've got three brokenhearted kids and no idea what to do about it."

Something inside her shattered. "I can only imagine how Noah and Kristen felt when they found out. Who told them?"

Zach's gaze latched onto hers, and she read the words before he spoke them. "I did."

"Oh, Zach." She lost the battle and went to him, but stopped herself before she reached for his hand. It seemed so natural to touch him, even though a chasm of time now gaped between them.

"Noah just turned nine, so he understands what death means. He took the news like a man." His Adam's apple bobbed as he swallowed. "That's what worries me. He didn't react at all. No shock, no pain. He has to let himself grieve like a child, but he won't.

"Kristen is just the opposite. She refuses to believe her parents are gone. Death is an abstract concept to a five-year-old. She's convinced they're just sleeping and they'll come home once they wake up. No one ever dies in cartoons, right?" His voice dripped with bitterness.

"And Will," he continued, "he's barely walking, so he doesn't understand much at all. All he knows is that his mother isn't there to hug him or rock him to sleep, and he thinks if he cries hard enough she'll hear him and come to him. The other night he chewed on his fist so hard, he gnawed the skin off."

Rebecca inhaled a sharp, deep breath that rattled in her chest. As much as she fought it, the overwhelming urge to draw that baby into her arms and hold him until his tears dried and peace befell him seized her.

Her demons awakened, reached long, scaly limbs through her veins. She battled to subdue them, all the while knowing what she had to do. Those children needed her. It was time she stopped wallowing in her misery and did the only thing her conscience allowed.

"I'm going to do it." Her voice was firm and resolute, void of the tremor that passed through her.

Zach arched two puzzled brows.

"I'm going to help you take care of those kids if it kills me."

And she meant it.

Chapter Two

On the outside, the four-bedroom, redbrick, bowfront townhouse with the high steps facing Union Park was the picture of architectural brilliance. On the inside, it looked like it had been hit by an earthquake. And not a small earthquake. This one would have measured at least eight on the Richter scale. Maybe even ten. Every toy these kids owned had been pulled off the shelves. A mountain of stuffed animals carpeted the faded hardwood floor. In the center of the living room, about a thousand microscopic Lego pieces lay scattered, and Zach couldn't help but wonder if someone had set off a bomb in here while he'd been busy making lunch.

He wouldn't have heard it over the racket these three were making. Noah and Kristen were arguing over the ugliest stuffed animal he'd ever seen. It was some kind of googly-eyed monkey that would have given him nightmares when he was a kid. Hell, it would probably give him nightmares now.

From his highchair, Will wailed at the top of his lungs, loud enough to give a fire engine a serious run for its money.

"It's mine." Noah shoved his sister, tugging on the monkey.

"I had it first." Tears welled in Kristen's blue eyes, her bottom lip trembled, but nothing short of a set of vise-grip pliers would pry the blasted thing from her tiny hands.

"Give it a rest, guys. Noah, let your sister have the goddamned thing." He realized he'd sworn in front of the kids and ran rough fingers through his hair.

Behind him, baby Will continued practicing his siren impersonation. The pungent smell of smoke filled the kitchen, and for a second Zach thought he was hearing a fire truck after all. Then he remembered he'd forgotten the grilled-cheese sandwiches on the burner.

A groan rumbled in his throat. He grabbed the pan, nearly singeing his flesh, and tossed the blackened sandwiches into the trash.

Above him, the fire detector let out a trill even soprano Will couldn't match. The children released the monkey and covered their small ears with their palms. Will howled louder, his face turning a downright scary shade of red.

Zach tried to open the window over the sink, but the fucking thing refused to budge. "Christ."

Old buildings.

He grabbed a kitchen towel, began swatting at the smoke. But all he managed to do was spread it through the room until he couldn't see two feet in front of him.

Just when he thought things couldn't get any worse, Kristen decided to join Will in an ear-splitting operetta that would have made Pavarotti proud.

Zach propped his ass on the kitchen table, his shoulders heavy with defeat. As an account executive for Ad Edge, one of the most prestigious advertising agencies in Boston, he was accustomed to stressful situations. He was often required to meet impossible deadlines, to put out fires in the figurative sense, to deal with conflict and appease hard-nosed business executives whenever they threw a tantrum. For nearly a decade he'd handled each situation life tossed his way like a pro football player avoiding a tackle, his eye always trained on the goal. His co-workers had nicknamed him the Iceberg, thanks to his ability to stay cool and collected no matter what.

And now it had taken these kids but two weeks to turn him into a complete moron. He thought of all the terms of endearment people used to describe children—little darlings, sweethearts, angels. Like hell they were. Devils in disguise was more like it. They pulled the wool over your eyes with their sugary smiles and puppy-dog expressions, all the while plotting to blindside you when you least expected it.

"Aren't you going to turn that thing off?" Noah's question cut through the cloud of smoke enveloping them.

"It'll stop on its own in a few seconds." Zach barely recognized his own voice. It was gravelly, flat and resigned.

A sharp snort punctured the air. "Loser." The smoke dissipated a tad, and Zach caught sight of Noah bending over. The insolent child swiped the monkey, then took off at a run.

"Noah," his sister bellowed. "Give it back! I want it!"

Zach pitched aside the towel and went in search of another window he could pry open. A bitter taste spread through his mouth. He was messing this up, big-time. His eldest nephew didn't respect him, his niece didn't know what to make of him and the baby cried like a banshee whenever he got within three feet of him.

He tried the window by the fridge, managed to crank it open a notch, and a warm gush of fresh air trickled in.

Will's cries settled into a miserable whimper interspersed with hiccups. Noah and Kristen raced up the stairs, stomping and arguing the whole way.

Zach leaned on the sill and let the clean air fill his lungs. Maybe Becca was right. He couldn't do this alone, no matter how badly he wanted to. The plan—her plan—was for her to move in next week, after she took care of a few things.

He still wasn't convinced it was a good idea. How could they possibly live together given their history? They'd tear each other apart, or worse, end up in bed together.

That couldn't happen. He wouldn't let it. He'd rather take his chances with the three sugar-smiled devils than risk going down that old road again.

She hated him now. He saw it in her eyes, heard it in her icy tone, and that irrefutable truth stung like a bitch. She thought he'd abandoned her, that he hadn't wanted her because she'd failed to bear him children. That was total bullshit. All he'd ever needed was her, but she'd been too busy beating herself up to see it.

If she ever realized he still wanted her, everything he'd accomplished by leaving her would be lost. She'd torture herself with impossible fantasies again, and he'd have to helplessly sit by and watch the woman he loved slowly tear herself apart. He'd be damned if he'd put her—or himself—through that again.

He had to call her and tell her the deal was off.

He never should have agreed in the first place. Not that it would have made a difference. When Becca had her mind set on something, she was like a runaway train. There was no stopping her. It was this single-minded focus that had cost them their marriage and nearly destroyed her.

The alarm stopped shrieking. Finally. He glanced over at a now unnaturally quiet Will. The boy watched him with an accusing glare that oozed disappointment.

"Sorry, buddy." Zach reached for the phone. "Trust me. It's for the best." He'd dialed the first three numbers when the doorbell rang. "Probably one of the neighbors wondering if I've burnt the place to the ground yet."

The baby furrowed his brows in a way that made Zach feel like the worst kind of fool. Unlike his older brother, Will couldn't voice the word *loser*, but he didn't have to. It was written all over his pudgy, tear-stained face.

Embarrassment saturated Zach's bloodstream as he took in the war zone around him. "I'll be surprised if they don't report me."

The doorbell rang a second time. Zach slanted another glance at Will. "Something tells me they're not going away."

Hiccup. Drool. Chest-heaving sigh.

The kid was no help whatsoever.

Zach bit the bullet and went to answer. Another earthquake

struck the moment he swung the door open. The ground beneath his feet shifted. Something inside him cringed and rejoiced in one painful heartbeat.

Becca stood on the doorstep, looking shy and provocative as hell. Sunlight poured over her, a golden flood that made her hair shimmer like aged brandy. An odd prickle hopped along his spine. The wind blew, sent those wicked curls rioting around her face. His body stiffened in more ways than one.

Her eyes met his, distant, guarded. On either side of her, two large suitcases lay propped at her feet—both a threat and a tantalizing promise.

Chapter Three

Rebecca tried to smile but managed nothing more than a twitch of the lips. Her stomach wrung at the sight of Zach looking so harried. His dark hair was wild and mussed, as if he'd just crawled out of bed, but the tired lines around his eyes told her he hadn't gotten much sleep. Long grooves carved deep trenches in his cheeks, giving him a tough, angular look. Alarm leapt across his face upon seeing her.

"Hi," she managed to squeeze out.

"What are you doing here?"

His words crushed any compassion his disheveled appearance had triggered within her. "Great to see you, too."

"Sorry." He ran his palm over his face, inhaled slow and steady. "I didn't mean that the way it sounded. I just wasn't expecting you till next week."

She forced a smile again and almost succeeded this time. Above her, a tall elm brushed the sky with green-tipped fingers. It shivered in the breeze, and from one of its bristly branches a song sparrow happily serenaded the warm summer day.

"I wrapped everything up early," she explained. "Sent the article to the magazine this morning, so I'm all yours." She winced at her choice of words.

Briefly his gaze met hers, dark and stormy. Something churned within them—pain, regret and a well of yearning so deep it turned her bones to dust. Then the shutters closed, and she convinced herself she'd imagined the whole thing.

Reluctantly, he moved aside to admit her, but she could tell his heart wasn't in it. He didn't want her here; that was as clear as the day was bright.

Ignoring the sharp stab of disappointment that skewered her, she bent to retrieve her suitcases. Zach had the same idea, and his fingers grazed hers, sending small electrical sparks ricocheting along her nerve endings. She looked up. His face was only inches from hers. Instant heat crawled through her veins. His gaze tangled up her insides until she had no choice but to jerk away.

She hastened into the townhouse and gladly left him to haul her bags in after her. The first thing that struck her was the smell. "Is something burning?"

"Not anymore," came his clipped reply.

She scrunched her brows and took a few more tentative steps forward. Wispy threads of smoke curled overhead. Heaps of toys littered the floor. From the kitchen, a heartrending whimper punctuated the air, followed by a hiccup.

"What happened here?"

Zach dropped her bags in the hall and quickly latched the door. "Didn't you hear the tornado warning?"

"Tornado warning?"

"Yeah, three to be exact. Two did most of the damage. The third—" he angled his head toward the kitchen, "—was in charge of sound effects."

The ceiling above her head quaked, and angry howls shattered any illusion of tranquility this place might have at some time possessed. Seconds later, two scruffy-haired kids came barreling down the stairs, tugging and shoving each other the whole way.

"I told you two to cut it out," Zach warned in that stiff tone she recognized all too well. He didn't lose his patience often, but when he did, his voice grew strained, rough, like a taut rope just beginning to fray at the edges.

The kids ignored him and bulldozed their way into the living room, their small feet sending Lego pieces skittering across the weathered floor. They wrestled over a stuffed baboon. At least she thought it was a baboon.

For the first time since she'd known him Zach appeared lost, defeated. An aura of hopelessness encompassed him, and it tugged at her heartstrings despite herself.

He'd lost weight. He'd always been lean, but now he was nothing but muscle and bone. At six-foot-three he should have looked lanky, but he didn't. His square shoulders, wide chest and sinewy arms gave him a swimmer's build, though he wasn't much of a swimmer. He'd nearly drowned when he was a kid, and even now he had an irrational aversion to water. He much preferred biking, hiking and running. Back in school he'd been the track and field champion. She'd never missed an opportunity to watch him run. Those long, muscular legs of his coated in a sheen of sweat, bulging and straining as he'd leapt across the track, had captivated her, left her dry-mouthed and tongue-tied.

Of course, she was three years younger than he, and back then he hadn't spared her a glance. To him, she'd been nothing more than his little sister's nerdy best friend. To her, he'd been the sun around which her whole world had revolved.

Anne Hope

Everything has changed, and nothing.

Once again he couldn't care less about her, and yet her heart still betrayed her with a painful series of thuds whenever he drew near.

Noah and Kristen vaulted over the couch, still playing tug-of-war with the baboon. The material sundered under the pressure, and the stuffed animal's arm tore off, sending Kristen toppling backward. She landed on an end table, where a porcelain lamp sat. The lamp tottered, then crashed to the ground. Simultaneously, the baby let out a yowl loud enough to wake the dead.

"Look what you did!" Noah roared. "It's all your fault."

His sister's bottom lip quivered as tears gathered in her clear blue eyes.

Rebecca had seen enough. Ignoring the knot of unease that twined in her gut, she cut through the mess to confront the kids. "What are you two doing? Look at this place."

Two pairs of stunned eyes turned her way. "Aunt Becca," Noah cried. "I didn't know you were here."

"Obviously." She picked up the severed arm of the toy.

"Can you fix it?" a thin voice whispered. "Mommy always sews our stuff when they tear." Kristen's dampened gaze sparkled like diamonds on snow. A tender ache coiled in Rebecca's chest. Her fingers itched to stroke the girl's sunny blond hair, to soothe her with a comforting touch or a bolstering hug, but she couldn't bring herself to lift her arm. It felt heavy, weighed down by the merciless sum of her regrets.

Instead, she nodded. "I'll try."

In the kitchen, Will's howls escalated. With an oath, Zach stomped out of the living room. Moments later he returned with an inconsolable Will tucked in the crook of his arm. The baby kicked and screamed, gasping, a red flush staining his round cheeks.

Zach cooed and made funny faces, all the while trying to mask his panic and failing miserably. He looked so awkward, so terrified, she couldn't help the amusement that tickled her throat. Before she knew it, she'd laughed out loud.

"What's so darn funny?"

"You've got *the look*."

He arched two puzzled brows. "The look?"

"Yeah, *the look*. The one you get whenever you'd rather chew on broken glass than do whatever it is you're doing."

Denial spiced with indignation sparked in his eyes. "I don't have *the look*. The kids and I are getting along just fine. Aren't we, kids?"

Will stopped bawling, and a victorious smile bounced across Zach's full mouth. His triumph, however, was short-lived. The baby nestled his face in Zach's shoulder, then violently hurled all over him.

Horror soaked Zach's features when he saw the long streak of white vomit trickling down the front of his black T-shirt. "Shit."

26

Rebecca bit her lower lip to keep from laughing again. "No, puke."

He watched her through narrowed slits, his expression downright murderous.

That was when it struck her. Zach Ryler didn't want her, but maybe—just maybe—for once in his life he needed her. And that simple thought made this whole ordeal somewhat bearable.

It took several hours before some semblance of peace settled over the townhouse again. While Rebecca boiled a pot of spaghetti, Zach and the kids worked to tidy the place up. Everyone was then rewarded with a nice meal, some orange juice and a box of Oreos. After lunch Zach put Will down for his nap, and Kristen and Noah snuggled on the couch to watch their favorite cartoon, *Spongebob Squarepants*.

As Rebecca finished washing the dishes, Zach collapsed in a chair, propping his elbows on the kitchen table and supporting his head with the heel of his palms.

"You look exhausted." She turned off the faucet and went to join him at the table. "Why don't you go get some rest? I'll hold down the fort for a while."

"I'm fine."

"When's the last time you slept?"

He shrugged. "Couple of weeks ago. Can't seem to drift off even when I try. Too many thoughts in my head."

She understood. The mind could be a cruel, unforgiving thing, unwilling to grant you even a few hours of respite.

"I'm guessing you're taking some time off work?" Throughout their marriage Zach had been obsessed with his career, often working seventy-hour weeks, but she couldn't remember ever having seen him this weary.

"I had six weeks of vacation time saved up. I haven't had much reason to use it these past two years." He raised his head and their eyes locked. Something hot and gripping passed between them, laden with meaning. She could've sworn she caught a note of remorse in his voice, heightened by a trace of loneliness that perfectly matched her own.

She averted her gaze; she had to. "What are you going to do with your place in Beacon Hill?" she asked, changing the subject.

"Sublet it. It's a nice area. I'm sure it won't take me long to find another tenant."

She glanced out the window at Union Park, where trees fluttered in the wind, fountains gushed amidst lush green grass and neat rows of Victorian townhouses stood framed by quaint brick streets. She thought of the higher-end Beacon Hill with its Federal-style rowhouses and its narrow, gas-lit sidewalks, only a stone's throw from downtown

Boston. "And you'll be happy living in the South End?"

"Why not? It's the kids' home. They're more comfortable here, despite what happened. Took them to my apartment for a few days while this place was being cleaned up. All they cared about was going back home." He rubbed his temples as if to relieve some invisible weight. "Plus, this area has kinda grown on me. It's metropolitan, close enough to downtown and still kid-friendly. Did you know there are eleven parks here?"

Her mouth curled despite herself. "Something tells me you've become acquainted with each and every one of them."

"You betcha." The quiet resignation on his face, coupled with that boyish grin of his, reminded her why she'd once been so infatuated with him. "Kristen knows them all by name. She strong-arms me into taking her to a different one each day."

She swallowed to wash away the syrupy emotion pooling in her throat. "That doesn't surprise me. She has her mother's memory. And her uncle's bullheadedness."

"Now there's the pot calling the kettle black."

She quirked a brow. "Are you saying I'm bullheaded?"

"I don't think bullheaded is strong enough to describe you. You've got a one-track mind. Once you get fixated on something, there's no derailing you."

They were heading down an old, familiar path, and at the end of it only heartache dwelled. "There's nothing wrong with being persistent."

"There is if it slowly tears you apart."

She eyed him steadily, accusingly. "When something's really important to me, I'd rather die trying than give up." She never would have quit on their marriage the way he had.

He flinched, and too late she realized her words had scratched open an old wound. "You almost did," he said flatly.

She didn't want to discuss that again. They'd gone over *the incident* so many times it made her head spin just thinking about it. "I told you that was an accident."

He didn't answer, and she was seized by the desire to shake him. Why did he refuse to believe her? "Is that why you walked out on me? Because you didn't want to be married to a basket case?" she asked instead.

His jaw clenched. A muscle twitched below his cheekbone. "After all these months you still don't get it." He shook his head as if he were the injured party instead of her. "If it makes you happy to think of me as a coward and a quitter, go right ahead. I'm too tired to argue."

She wanted to tell him that it didn't make her happy. She hadn't been happy in years. Happiness was as tangible as air, as evasive as water. Whenever she tried to close her fingers around it, it melted from her grasp. Maybe people weren't really meant to hold on to it. Maybe it was simply a promise, hovering just beyond their reach, tempting and seducing them with the possibilities it offered. Just another way to keep them forging ahead, as tantalizing and as deceptive as hope.

She stood and walked to the window. The sun gilded all it touched, made the water spraying from the fountain glow silver and gold. Above, white-winged clouds floated across a yawning blue sky. "There's nothing left to argue about," she finally said. "Sometimes things just end. There's no going back."

The problem was, she still didn't know how to move forward. For as long as she could remember, Zach had been a part of her life. She'd met Lindsay in middle school, and from that day forward Zach had been there—the embodiment of all her desires wrapped in a most seductive package.

Over time she'd grown to love him, hate him and eventually lose him. Now he was back in her life again, and she didn't know what to do with him, didn't know where he fit anymore. They could never be lovers again, but with any luck maybe they could learn to be friends again. They had no choice. Three kids depended on them.

The chair scraped the linoleum floor as he rose. "I think I'll take you up on your offer." He refused to meet her gaze. "I could use a shower. I still smell like puke."

She watched him leave, happy to have some time to herself. Zach's presence unsettled her. Something about him slipped past her carefully erected defenses and filled her with bitterness, a weakening sense of loss and, worst of all, the one feeling she'd sworn she'd never allow into her heart again—hope.

Chapter Four

Rebecca pulled out her laptop, tapped into the WiFi network and began searching the Web. With any luck her efforts would trigger an idea for her next story. She worked for a magazine called *Women Today*, and once a month she submitted an article dealing with issues the modern woman faced—career, family, health and so forth. She didn't have much to say about family, but career and health she could usually gush about for pages upon pages.

Writing her last article, however, had been an ordeal. As much as she'd tried, her mind had kept drifting to Lindsay, to the unspeakable circumstances of her death. She found it no less difficult to concentrate here in her home, where reminders of her best friend were everywhere. The watercolor she'd painted back in high school hung in the hallway. Wedding pictures of her and Liam, with Rebecca and Zach standing vigil on either side of them, adorned end tables and bookcases. A small pewter frame boasted the image of Lindsay holding a newborn Noah in her arms. Rebecca hadn't been able to bring herself to look at that photograph in years.

It sat on the kitchen counter now. Sunlight poured through the window in white sheets to kiss the brushed silver. The glare of the glass taunted her, constantly pried her gaze from her computer screen until she felt compelled to stand up and walk toward it. She reached out, closed her fingers around the cold metal.

For the first time she forced herself to really look at the snapshot. She noted the exhaustion on her friend's face, the limpness of her hair, her widened hips and bloated belly. In all the years Rebecca had known her, Lindsay had never looked worse...or happier. The way she held that baby as if he were a natural extension of herself, the tenderness soaking her features as she gazed at his dozing face, hit Rebecca like a punch to the gut. The small frame suddenly felt heavy in her palm, so she placed it back on the counter and turned away.

Decisively, she walked to the table and shut off her computer. There was no way she'd get any work done today. She was far too distracted and far too emotional. If there was one thing she'd learned, it was to write with her brain, not her heart.

Her heart was erratic, undependable, and more often than not led her down the wrong path. Her mind, on the other hand, was a compass, keeping her focused, pointing her in the right direction.

And right now it was telling her to go check on the kids. They were way too quiet for her liking.

Noah stood outside his dad's home office, trying to find the guts to walk in. He hadn't stepped into this room since that night—the night his parents died—and he was tired of feeling like a coward. If only he hadn't been such a chicken that night, maybe...

A fist tightened in his throat. He was such a loser.

His aunt thought he was watching TV, but some dumb baby show had come on and the computer was here, so he figured he'd have a lot more fun playing one of his games.

If only he could open the stupid door.

He wrapped his hand around the handle. It was cold, like the weight in his chest. Slowly, he turned it, inched the door open. The hinges creaked, and he nearly lost his nerve.

Stop being such a baby. Nothing's in there.

Nothing but the images in his head. Images he just couldn't erase, no matter how hard he tried.

He took a deep breath, a small step forward, then another. Before he knew it, he was inside.

See, that wasn't so bad.

The room didn't look much different. The carpet was gone, but that was about it. It was hard to believe his parents had died here. But they had.

All his insides stung as if something was trying to rip the flesh from his bones. He hunched his shoulders to hold in the pain, to keep it from devouring him. It didn't work. It just tied him up in knots and made his belly ache.

So he did what he always did when he wanted to forget how much life sucked—he ran to his dad's computer. He hadn't gone on Falcon World in weeks, ever since he and his dad had that nasty scrap and he'd forbidden him from ever logging onto his favorite site again, which was totally unfair. Still, he felt guilty for disobeying him, even though his dad wasn't around anymore. Maybe it was because he was in this room, where his parents had been shot.

The pain returned—a sharp, burning sword slashing through him—so he turned the computer on. What did it matter if he played a game or two with one of his online friends? What was the big deal, anyway? He tossed a glance over his shoulder as he waited for the lousy machine to boot up. It seemed to take forever.

Finally, color exploded on the screen. Using his parents' e-mail address, Noah quickly reactivated the account his dad had blocked, then went to the login page. He knew his way around a computer, and that pleased him. It was cool to be good at something, especially computers. He typed in his screen name, Raptor100, followed by his password. Anyone who signed up had to use the name of a bird. That was the way things worked at Falcon World. He didn't recognize any of the other players, but he hung out with them for a while just the same.

Then Night-Owl came on. He always seemed to be around when Noah was there, so they'd become friends. They chatted about all sorts of things—mainly the latest games and how annoying adults were.

Noah loved the talks he had with Night-Owl. It was great to speak to someone who actually listened for a change.

"Hey, Raptor WB. WU?" *Welcome back. What's up?*

Noah didn't feel like going into the whole ugly story, so he wrote: "Nothing much. My life blows."

"Y?"

"NVM." *Never mind.*

"Glad you're back. This place sucks without U."

Warmth spread through him, numbed the hurt. It felt good to know that someone actually wanted him around. Normally, people just wanted him gone.

"Wanna play Checkers?" That was the game he and Night-Owl always played on Falcon World, so Noah suggested it, partly because he wanted to change the subject and partly because he was looking for something to help him forget.

"K."

When the game came on, all Noah could see was the gun, that long barrel with the squares carved into it. It blurred his vision, made his brain go blank. He tried to push the images aside and focus on the game, but they refused to go away.

So much for forgetting.

After Night-Owl beat him three times, Noah decided to give up. "EIE!" *Enough is enough.*

Night-Owl sent him a laughing face. "ROFL. Sore loser."

"BM." *Bite me.*

"Wait till we meet F2F." Then, "Why didn't you show up last time?"

Embarrassment singed his cheeks. "My dad grounded me."

"IDGI. Y?"

Noah didn't get it, either, so he wasn't sure how to explain it to Night-Owl. "Long story," he typed.

"Wanna come over tomorrow? I got DSI."

Excitement shot through Noah. DSI had cooler games than his Game Boy. It would be awesome to play some of them with Night-Owl, but his dad would be royally pissed. Then it hit him again, like a hammer to the brain. His dad was dead. Uncle Zach and Aunt Becca were in charge now.

Maybe they wouldn't mind letting him visit his buddy. Night-Owl was all right. He was twelve and lived in Boston. He loved video games, just like him. He had a crazy cat named Ralph. He couldn't see why Uncle Zach and Aunt Becca would have a problem letting him meet Ralph.

Then again, maybe they would. He couldn't chance telling them.

From the kitchen came the sound of footsteps. His aunt was up and about. Noah's heart pounded a ferocious beat against his ribs. "PAH. BBL." *Parent at home,* he typed. *Be back later.*

He quickly shut off the computer, then raced back to the living room. Kristen was nowhere in sight. An episode of *Dora the Explorer* flashed on the television screen. Backpack was singing a silly song about having everything you need.

He flipped the channel and popped in a PlayStation game. Then, settling himself on the couch, he grabbed the controller and adopted his bored, innocent, couldn't-care-less expression.

Noah slumped on the couch, playing some animated video game when Rebecca entered the living room. He was alone. An unsettling hush hung in the air, disrupted only by the occasional beep of Noah's game.

"Where's your sister?"

"Don't know." The boy's eyes refused to stray from the screen.

"How can you not know? She was sitting right next to you a few minutes ago."

He shrugged evasively. The television set let out a victorious jingle, and Noah howled in triumph.

Realizing she was getting nowhere, she decided to search the house. The girl couldn't have gone far. She was probably upstairs in her room playing.

Rebecca mounted the steps. The pitter-patter of the shower echoed from across the hall. The image of Zach standing naked beneath the jets, surrounded by steam, his skin glistening as water sluiced over him, flashed in her mind. There was a time she would have shed her clothing and joined him. Now she just tamped down the thick lump of yearning clogging her windpipe and kept walking.

She stopped to check on Will. He lay in his crib, fast asleep, his tiny hand clutching a yellow blanket. An aura of peace enveloped him. For a moment she stood in the doorway, absorbing the sight of his little face slackened by sleep as blades of light knifed through the horizontal blinds and streaked his skin gold. A different kind of yearning gripped her, and again she walked away.

Kristen's room was at the end of the hall. She thought back to the day Lindsay had first shown it to her. Her friend had been so excited energy had rippled from her and made the air around her pulse. All Rebecca had managed in response was a stiff smile and the words: "It's nice. Very...girlie."

The room hadn't changed. Gauzy white curtains with pink ribbons hung from the windows. Framed pictures of various Disney princesses adorned the walls. A white canopy bed with pastel-pink linens stretched over a joyful rug sprinkled with tiny flowers. A fuzzy brown teddy bear sat in a miniature wooden rocking chair, surrounded by a slew of stuffed animals of every size, shape and color.

But one thing—or more precisely, person—was missing. Kristen.

Alarm and self-disgust leapt through her. She'd barely been here two hours and she'd already lost one of the children. Where could the girl have gone?

Urgency nipping at her heels, she bolted from the room and scrambled down the stairs. Seconds later she burst into the living room, where Noah still sat, thoroughly enthralled by his game.

"Noah, tell me where your sister went."

The aggravating boy ignored her.

"Noah!" Worry and frustration spiked her voice.

A pair of annoyed eyes, the same penetrating blue as his uncle's, looked up at her. "I don't know. She takes off sometimes."

Rebecca shook her head, dismayed. "I would have heard the door—"

"She goes out the back. She's real sneaky. Probably went to visit Mrs. Petrakis again."

"Who's Mrs. Petrakis?"

"She lives next door." Noah gestured to the far-left wall with his head, then promptly got back to his game.

With an exasperated huff, Rebecca darted outside and raced down the front steps. Without stopping to catch her breath, she climbed the neighboring stairs and banged on the door. She'd always wondered how Lindsay had managed to lose all the weight she'd gained with each of her pregnancies so fast. Now she knew. The secret was a hefty measure of fear mixed with adrenaline, coupled with a regular running regime.

The door inched inward, held in place by a security chain, and a friendly looking woman in her early fifties peeked out. "Yes?"

Rebecca wasted no time on niceties. "Is Kristen here?"

"Who would like to know?"

It took all of her self-control not to slide her arm through the crack and shake the woman. "Her aunt. I'm her guardian now. Is she here?"

The neighbor seemed to take an inordinate amount of time to answer. "How do I know you're telling me the truth?"

"Sorry," Rebecca said through gritted teeth, "I seem to have left my ID in the house. Look, she was on the couch watching *Spongebob* five minutes ago. Now I can't find her. Noah said she probably came to visit you. You are Mrs. Petrakis, right?"

The woman slammed the door in Rebecca's face, and the blood drained from her cheeks. She clenched her hand and raised it to knock again, when the door swung open.

"She loves *Spongebob*," Mrs. Petrakis raved. "It's her favorite show. She has talked of nothing else since she got here."

Relief washed over her. She closed her eyes and released the breath she'd been holding. "Thank God."

"Come in." Mrs. Petrakis moved aside and extended her arm in welcome. Her home smelled delicious, the air redolent with butter and vanilla. It was obvious that she'd been baking.

She guided Rebecca to the kitchen, where Kristen sat dunking a cookie in an enormous glass of milk. "Hi, Aunt Becca," the girl said past a mouthful of sodden crumbs.

"Kristen, why did you take off like that? You scared me half to death."

"I wanted to see Voula."

Rebecca was momentarily confused. She looked at Mrs. Petrakis, who smiled, her chocolate-brown eyes twinkling. "That's me. My name is really Paraskevi, which means Friday. But that's too complicated for most people, so I use the short version, Voula, instead."

Rebecca couldn't for the life of her fathom how Voula could be short for a name like Paraskevi, but she took the woman at her word.

"Please let me know before you visit Voula next time," she admonished the child, who shoved another cookie into her mouth and chased it down with a long gulp of milk.

"Would you like to join us?" Voula offered.

"I'm not sure I can—"

"Of course you can. I was just about to make some coffee." The neighbor pulled out an ornate cherrywood chair and insisted that she take it.

Rebecca reluctantly folded her body into its gleaming lap, praying Noah would stay put and Will wouldn't wake up while she was busy socializing with the neighbor.

Voula scurried off and returned with another plate layered with an impressive mound of cookies, which she placed in front of Rebecca as though she expected her to eat every last bite herself. "Try one of my koulourakia," she urged. "They're Greek vanilla cookies. Kristen absolutely loves them. She always knows when I'm baking them. I think she can smell them through the wall."

She trailed soft fingers down Kristen's hair, bent down and kissed her on the crown of her head with grandmotherly affection. Then the elfin woman scampered off again. That was the only way Rebecca could describe her—elfin. She was petite, no taller than five feet in height, with olive skin and hair the same rich brown as her eyes. She wore a white apron over a pair of beige slacks and a floral-print shirt, all the while flashing a radiant smile that was as welcoming as her sweet-smelling kitchen. There was something very inviting about her, homey and comforting.

Rebecca understood why Kristen liked to seek refuge here. It seemed like nothing bad could happen in this house, where the air was laced with the aroma of freshly baked cookies and this jovial woman hopped about with the energy of a certain pink bunny. Where else could a little girl go to forget her whole world had just come crashing down around her? Where else could she find a ready smile, a soothing touch, a slow, lingering kiss?

She felt guilty for not being the one who could give Kristen the affection she craved, the solace she so desperately needed. What kind of person was she, when she couldn't bring herself to reach out to a sad little girl in need? There was a time she would have known exactly what to do. A time when these children would have gravitated toward her like moths to a flame. Now she felt awkward around them, so charred inside she could no longer find that special glow within her that would draw them to her.

But Voula had it. She simply radiated with it.

The spirited woman dumped spoonful after spoonful of coffee grains into the percolator as though she were expecting a houseful of guests. Soon the rich, fragrant aroma of coffee mingled with the smell of vanilla and wafted toward Rebecca, making her feel as if she were sitting in some exotic café. For the first time in two weeks the unforgiving tension that clutched her loosened its hold, and she almost relaxed.

Tentatively she picked up one of the cookies and brought it to her lips. It crumbled on her tongue the instant she bit into it. The sweet, buttery flavor that filled her mouth nearly wrenched a contented moan from her. She gazed at the mountain in front of her and realized with growing alarm that she could probably empty the whole plate given half the chance. Her thighs would never forgive her, but her taste buds would dance a happy jig and sing their praises to the heavens.

"Aren't they yummy?" A milk mustache dripped from Kristen's top lip.

Rebecca couldn't help but smile at the child's enthusiasm. "They're delicious."

"Voula makes the best cookies."

Right on cue, Voula returned with two steaming mugs of coffee. "You say that because you never tasted my mother's. All the neighborhood kids would gather in her kitchen for a taste of her cookies. We never had an empty house." Pride and a hint of wistfulness tinged her words.

"Cream and sugar?" she asked Rebecca.

"Just cream, please."

Voula added a splash of cream to one of the mugs and handed it to her. Rebecca took a hearty swallow, hoping the bitter liquid would wash away the sweet taste in her mouth before she was tempted to snatch another cookie.

Draining the last of her milk, Kristen leapt to her feet. "Can I go play with Kanela now?"

"All right," Voula replied. "But be careful she doesn't scratch you."

"I will." Kristen bulleted out of the kitchen, soaring on the invisible wings of anticipation.

"Kanela is my cat," the woman explained. "A beautiful reddish-brown tabby. She was a stray. Every day she came to my door begging for food, so I adopted her. Or should I say she adopted me?"

Voula sank into the opposite chair and took a sip of her coffee after sweetening it with two heaping spoonfuls of sugar. A frown pleated her brows. "Maybe you should get the children a pet. It may help them deal with their loss. Pets have a way of filling the empty spaces in our hearts."

Rebecca nodded. "That's not a bad idea. They need to focus their energy on something positive."

Voula's jovial expression vanished. "I still can't believe Lindsay and Liam are gone. I keep thinking, if only I'd knocked on the door a few minutes earlier..."

"You're the neighbor? The one who interrupted the break-in?"

The woman nodded. "The kids were over at my place earlier that day. Kristen forgot her favorite teddy bear. I figured she might have trouble falling asleep, so I brought it over. I knocked and knocked, but no one answered. I became worried, so I got the spare key Lindsay had given me in case of an emergency.

"I realize now that wasn't the smartest thing for me to do. I should have just called the police. But I never imagined..." Her voice broke.

Rebecca understood the woman's pain. She couldn't chase the what ifs from her brain either. She took a sip of her coffee, suddenly wishing she'd added some sugar to the bitter blend.

"I found them," Voula confided after a lengthy pause.

A rock fell to settle at the pit of Rebecca's stomach. "I'm sorry you had to see that."

Voula blinked away tears. "I'm just glad I was there for the children until their uncle came. They had no idea what was going on, and I couldn't bring myself to tell them. Noah was so quiet it broke my heart."

A flood of grief invaded Rebecca's system, and she closed her eyes to hold it at bay. "I just don't understand it. Why them?" Liam and Lindsay lived comfortably, but they weren't rich by any means. "With all the choices out there, why would someone target their home to rob?"

"He wasn't there to rob them. He was there to kill them." The certainty with which Voula spoke chilled Rebecca to the bone.

She stiffened. "Why would you think something like that?"

The small woman wrapped her hand around her coffee mug. "I'm sorry. I don't mean to upset you. My husband says I watch too many movies, but I can't shake this feeling I have." She raised the mug, then reconsidered and put it back down without taking a sip. "I think Liam may have gotten himself into some kind of trouble. He was acting very strangely before he died. He was very...uptight."

Nostalgia tugged at Rebecca's heartstrings. "Liam was born uptight." They'd often teased him for being so serious, bordering on neurotic.

"More than usual. Especially after the car accident."

"What car accident?"

"You don't know? A week before the break-in, one of Liam's tires blew. He nearly died."

No, she wouldn't have known because she'd stopped talking to Lindsay ages ago. The guilt returned, hot and blistering.

"Lindsay was worried about him," Voula continued, oblivious to Rebecca's inner turmoil. "She and I were friends, so she confided in me. She was concerned her husband may have stumbled into something dangerous. He was quiet, evasive, edgy..."

She tapped her square fingernails nervously against the table. "At first I thought she was deluding herself. Chances were he was having an affair."

"Impossible. Liam would never cheat on Lindsay."

The woman nodded. "I know that now. He wasn't feeling guilty. He was scared."

"Scared of what?"

"Of something happening to his children. A few weeks ago he came to see me. He told me if the kids were here and anyone came knocking on my door, I shouldn't let them in, even if I recognized them. That's why I was so reluctant to open the door to you."

That didn't sound like an unusual request coming from Liam. As a lawyer he'd been trained to be suspicious. The world could be a treacherous place. It seemed perfectly natural for a father to be concerned.

"They argued on the day they were killed," Voula admitted after a short pause. "That's why the kids were over at my place. Kristen told me her dad wanted her mom to take them to visit his parents in Ireland. He'd bought the tickets without asking her, and her mom didn't want to go."

Rebecca's interest was piqued. "What else did Kristen say?"

Voula peered over her shoulder to make sure the girl was out of earshot. "That her mom was mad because her dad was keeping secrets."

Something slimy slithered up Rebecca's spine. The tiny buds of suspicion Voula had planted within her entered full bloom. She didn't know what to think. Was Voula one of those paranoid neighbors who saw conspiracies everywhere, or was there a chance she was right? Had someone purposely set out to murder Lindsay and Liam? But for what reason? They were just a regular couple, living a simple life, toiling to raise their children in an increasingly hectic world. Things like this didn't happen to ordinary people. Or did they?

Kristen zipped through the kitchen, chasing the fattest cat Rebecca had ever seen. She giggled and sprinted, momentarily forgetting that her parents no longer waited for her in the safe bosom of her home. But Rebecca couldn't forget even if she tried, and now, after everything Voula had told her, it haunted her thoughts more than ever. A dark mist closed around her, darkening her mood. Questions reeled inside her head, as distressing as they were puzzling.

With a defeated sigh, she grabbed another cookie and resigned herself to the depressing fact that the truth, like happiness and skinny thighs, would most likely forever evade her.

Chapter Five

When Zach emerged from the shower, he felt like a new man. He couldn't remember the last time he'd had a decent shower. His mornings were more hectic than ever, filled with endless requests, numerous fights to break up and a baby to coddle and feed. He barely had enough time to hop under the jets, scrub, rinse and hop right out again.

So today he'd indulged, letting the steam build around him, enjoying the way the hot water pummeled his body and massaged his skin. He felt revitalized, almost human again.

Briefly, he wondered how Becca was faring with the kids. He could barely believe she was here at all. Given her history, it took a hell of a lot of courage to do what she was doing, and he couldn't help but admire her for it. Maybe she'd gotten past her self-destructive obsession. Maybe there was still hope...

He snickered as he slipped into a new shirt. This was precisely what he'd feared would happen. Just a few hours with her and he was already looking for reasons to give this thing between them another shot.

"There's no going back." Wasn't that what she'd said?

Well, she was right, and it was high time he accepted it.

He dried his hair, flung the towel over a chair. This wasn't going to work. They couldn't live together again. And even if they did, it couldn't last. At some point they'd have to go their separate ways. What would happen to the kids then? He wrapped his hands over the back of the chair, clenched his fists around the smooth oak finish. This situation had disaster written all over it.

But what could he possibly do to make her leave? He contemplated his options, then decided he might not have to do anything. With any luck, she wouldn't be able to hack it. She had no idea what she'd gotten herself into, but he did. He'd lived it for two weeks straight, and raising these three made the cutthroat world of advertising look like a day at the beach. It was only a matter of time before she caved under the pressure.

Doubt gnawed at him. Her words rang in his mind, as clear as glass: *"I'd rather die trying than give up. I'm not a quitter."*

A groan rumbled in his chest. Who was he kidding? Becca didn't quit. Ever. She'd bash her head into the same brick wall over and over again until she bled to death rather than give in.

So how on earth was he going to get rid of her?

The baby monitor chimed with a joyful squeal. Will was awake, and for once he wasn't crying. Of course, that could change on a dime the second Zach walked into the room. He filled his lungs with a bolstering breath, straightened his back and prepared for battle.

When he entered Will's bedroom, the baby was standing in his crib, chewing on the railing. His cheeks were flushed, and a thin rivulet of drool crawled along his chin—both of which, Zach had quickly come to learn, were symptoms of teething. Thankfully, the boy looked rested and relatively happy.

Emboldened, he inched closer. To his great surprise, Will didn't let loose an ear-splitting scream but a giggle, and a grin tugged at Zach's mouth. Things were finally looking up.

Gathering his courage, he lifted the squirming baby, half expecting the melt. The melt was that thing Will did when he didn't want to be picked up. The little rug rat had the uncanny ability to turn his bones to rubber and somehow make himself as easy to grasp as a wad of half-set Jell-O.

Will didn't engage in the melt. He actually smiled as if he was happy to see him, then wrapped his tiny arms around Zach's neck. A funny sensation swelled in his chest, tingling in his throat. He'd never realized how comforting a baby's hug could be. The sense of acceptance, of complete trust reached deep inside him and squeezed.

"Feeling a little better?" He barely recognized his own voice. It sounded gruff, yet softer somehow.

The baby cooed, then squealed again.

"Let's go see what your brother and sister are up to. What do you say, buddy?"

Will answered by blowing a spit bubble.

With a heartfelt chuckle, Zach hastened downstairs. He found Noah in the living room, frying his brain in front of the screen again. He was playing some war game on PlayStation 3. The rapid sound of gunfire thundered from the speakers.

"Aren't you too young to be playing this game?"

Noah didn't take his eyes off the television set. "Nope. Dad always let me play it."

He shook his head. "Where's your sister?"

The infuriating kid didn't answer, so Zach did the only thing a self-respecting uncle and guardian could do—he shut off the game.

Noah exploded in a fit of rage. "Why'd you do that? I was winning!" His body was wired tighter than a guitar, his shoulders hunched forward, his hands balled into fists. Anger bled from every pore.

"Next time, please answer me when I ask you a question."

"Why does everyone keep asking me about Kristen? I don't know where my stupid sister went."

Will sensed the tension, and his little body stiffened. Zach rubbed his back in an effort to soothe. "Watch your mouth," he told Noah.

The boy scoffed and kicked at the couch. Fury contorted his features. Zach sensed the kid was trying very hard not to tackle him. He almost wished he would. Maybe then they'd make some progress. There was nothing healthy about bottling up pain. It ate you up and left you empty. He'd experienced it firsthand when he'd lost his mother to cancer five years ago. Watching her battle that unforgiving disease, then slowly fade away—piled on top of the problems he was having with Becca at the time—had been one of the greatest challenges of his life.

If Phyllis Ryler were here, she would have known what to do. She would have known exactly how to console these kids, how to make the tears come. That was what Noah needed—a good cry. But he was a boy, and boys were taught at a very young age that tears were for babies and girls.

If anyone could have convinced him that it was all right to cry and that no one would think he was a sissy, it was Phyllis. Zach had never missed his mother as much as he did now, with his sister gone and her three kids looking to him for guidance. Then again, maybe it was a blessing that she hadn't lived long enough to see her daughter murdered.

Noah grabbed the couch cushions and flung them, one by one, on the floor. A thick cloud of rage pulsated around him. Will watched his brother with round, startled eyes, as if he wasn't sure whether he should laugh or bawl.

After Noah finished assaulting the furniture, he stood amidst the wreckage, panting.

Zach cocked a brow and reined in his own temper. "Are you done?"

The boy shrugged, then nodded.

"Good. Now you can clean this mess up," he said, his tone far calmer than he felt.

The boy narrowed his eyes and wrapped his arms across his chest. Defiance rolled off him in aggravating waves. "Only if you put my game back on."

"I don't think you're in any position to negotiate. Clean this mess up or you won't play for a week."

Their gazes locked, Noah's brimming with resentment, Zach's firm and resolute. He sensed his nephew was sizing him up, trying to determine whether he had any intention of following through with his threat.

"I don't have to listen to you." The boy stood his ground. His arms flexed as he squeezed his thin, lanky body. "You're not my father."

Zach had been expecting that statement sooner or later, and it didn't cut as deep as he'd thought. He had no intention of replacing Liam. He didn't want these kids to ever forget their parents. He just wanted to do the best he could by them, and maybe, just maybe, if he played his cards right he might carve his own place in their lives...and hearts.

"No," he replied, "but I am your guardian. And yes, you do have to listen to me. At least for the next decade or so."

Noah hunched his shoulders and kicked the hand-knit rug blanketing the floor. "This isn't fair." Despite his protests, he bent over and carelessly threw the cushions back on the sofa.

It wasn't an ideal job, but Zach was satisfied. He placed his thumb on the power button and prepared to turn the boy's game back on. "One more question before I let you play. Where's your Aunt Becca?"

Noah huffed. "She went after Kristen, all right? I think they're at Mrs. Petrakis's house."

Zach smiled. "Much better. Thank you." Then he fired up the game and let the boy shoot away his frustrations.

When Rebecca returned from Voula's with Kristen practically fused to her hip, she found Zach sitting on the living room rug next to Will, building castles out of colorful blocks. For a brief wedge of time before he realized she was there, she just watched him. Watched the way he helped the baby stack the blocks, the tenderness on his face, the calm fluidity of his movements, the way his strong hands cupped and guided Will's. She listened to his soft words of encouragement, his quiet whispers of praise, and shocked herself by admiring the very patience she'd once found annoying.

Even as affection washed over her, her sense of failure returned to hammer her. Somehow she'd always known he'd be good with children, the way you know when the sun's about to pierce through the clouds or a raindrop's about to fall. She'd felt it deep down within her, in that place where instinct and consciousness merged. And that had only made her inability to conceive all the more gut-wrenching.

Seeing the proof before her now shook her, drilled a hole straight through her and left her hollow. It only drove in what she'd always known to be true. He was born to have the one thing she could never give him. No wonder he'd cut her loose.

He sensed her presence and looked up, flashing the wry grin that had always turned her knees to water. Some things never changed.

"Look, Will," he said in that upbeat voice people tend to adopt when addressing a baby. "The girls are back. I was starting to worry."

"We were visiting with the next-door neighbor," she explained. "Kristen took off without saying anything."

The girl looked at her shoes, squirming.

"She does that sometimes." Zach stacked another block. The tower quivered, then stilled.

"So I heard. She scared the living daylights out of me."

He directed an admonishing stare at his niece. "Kristen, please tell us next time before you take off."

Kristen pouted and her eyes misted. "I wanted to play with Kanela."

Zach stood, closed the distance between them and crouched beside the child. "I know you like visiting Voula. I'm not telling you not to go. But it's important that you tell us where you are so we don't worry." He took her small, pale hand in his large one.

The girl nodded, pouting so hard her lower lip covered her top one. "Where's Noah?" she asked.

"Upstairs in his room," Zach replied.

"Can I go play with him?"

He hesitated. "Sure. But the minute you two start fighting, I'm splitting you up."

Kristen hardly heard him. She bulleted up the stairs in search of her big brother, her body so taut with anticipation one would think she hadn't seen him in weeks.

Rebecca raised two curious brows. "I thought they didn't get along."

"It's a love-hate thing." He stood and stretched. Muscles rippled over his arms and chest, tapering down to a washboard stomach, then wending their way across a pair of strong, sinewy legs.

Rebecca's mouth went dry. He smelled so good—like soap and man, spiced with a hint of that musky aftershave. She fought the urge to lean forward and breathe him in.

Will giggled and cooed, sending his blocks toppling to the floor.

"Things look...calmer around here," she observed.

He massaged the nape of his neck, as if to relieve the tension that coiled there. "Enjoy it while it lasts." His words dripped with resignation, underscored by dread.

She took a few hesitant steps toward the baby, realizing she hardly knew him at all. He'd been born after the divorce, and she'd only seen him once, briefly when he was an infant. She'd visited Lindsay in the hospital with a generic gift and nothing inspiring to say.

He looked very different now, plumper, with wide eyes as crystal blue as his sister's and blond hair that curled at the ends. Both Kristen and Will had inherited their father's pale looks, but Noah was the spitting image of Zach. His hair was so dark it was almost black, and his navy blue eyes were deep and every bit as unreadable as his uncle's.

Will glanced up at her and smiled, a shiny coat of drool on his chin.

She forced herself to smile back, even as unease snaked through her. "He seems happier now."

"He always is after his nap. But the minute he gets hungry, or tired, or bored, all hell will break loose again."

If she didn't know any better, she would have sworn he was trying to scare her.

"We need to talk." He took her by the elbow and led her to the couch. Her skin sparked and hummed at his touch, but she ignored it. Instead she lowered herself onto the sofa, as far away from him as possible.

He raked his fingers through his hair, his favorite gesture when he was upset or edgy. "You and I living together again," he said after a long, nerve-rattling pause, "it can't possibly work."

So that was it. He hated the idea of living with her. His words shouldn't have stung, but they did. "We managed all right for eight years," came her biting reply. "Surely we can endure each other's presence long enough to help these kids through this difficult time."

"Which brings me to my next question." He met and held her gaze. "How long do you plan on staying?"

"Until I'm convinced you—" embarrassment flooded her cheeks, "—they don't need me anymore." She studied Will, who'd abandoned stacking the blocks in favor of chewing on them. Insecurity instantly swelled to strangle her. What made her think she could do this? How could she possibly help these kids when she couldn't even bring herself to touch them? "Look, I know I'm not the best person for the job. Far from it. But I'm the one Lindsay chose." Her friend's wedding picture towered over the fireplace, and Rebecca couldn't help but feel that—wherever she was—she was watching her. "I won't let her down again. I can't."

Zach's face mirrored exasperation and frustration, but at the same time his lips slackened with acceptance. In his eyes she caught a gleam that hadn't been there before. Was it admiration or outright terror?

"Then we have one more thing to sort out." He buried his fingers in his hair again. "The sleeping arrangements."

Noah sat on his bed, playing Pokémon. Uncle Zach thought he'd spent enough time in front of the television set, so he'd told him to go find something else to do. Noah hadn't bothered arguing. Instead, he'd trudged to his room and fished out his Game Boy. The fact that Uncle Zach had no idea he was still playing video games filled him with satisfaction.

Who did he think he was, anyway, moving into his house and telling him what to do? Noah didn't have to take his uncle's crap...or his aunt's for that matter. As if having Uncle Zach here wasn't bad enough, now Aunt Becca had to come live with them, too. He hadn't seen her since he was seven, and all of a sudden, here she was, moving into their house.

He didn't get it. She didn't even like kids; he could tell. Every time she smiled she looked like she was sucking on a lemon. She reminded him of his grade one teacher, Mrs. Reid. She didn't like kids, either, which was weird 'cause she was a teacher and had to hang around kids all the time. It made no sense, like Aunt Becca moving in.

The door swung open, startling him. Noah shoved his Game Boy under his sheets, but it was Kristen who came crashing in, not Uncle Zach.

"What do you want?" he grunted, getting back to his game.

"I played tag with Kanela." His sister hopped onto his bed. "I won."

Noah shrugged, not even bothering to look at her. He had to keep his eyes on the game or he'd lose. "Big deal. That cat is so fat she can barely run."

"Not true! She's very fast, but I'm faster."

He snorted. "Who cares anyway?"

"You're so mean!"

"And you're such a baby."

His sister gave him a nice hard shove. He missed his next move, ended up getting killed. "What'd you do that for?"

"Don't call me a baby." She folded her arms over her chest and frowned. "Mommy and Daddy hate it when you call me that. When they wake up—"

Noah had had enough. "They're not going to wake up! Don't you get it? They're dead." His throat thickened so much it hurt, like he'd swallowed a sourball and it had lodged itself in his esophagus. That's what it was called, an esophagus. He'd learned it at school last year.

Kristen didn't know what an esophagus was, just like she was too dumb to understand their parents weren't coming back—ever.

All because of me.

"Don't say that." Her bottom lip quivered, and she started breathing real funny. "The witch—" she panted. "The witch put a spell on them—"

She stopped talking. Her skin turned a frightful shade of blue. His own breath hitched. "Crap." Noah shot to his feet and sped to the door.

"Uncle Zach," he hollered. "It's Kristen. She's having an asthma attack."

Not bothering to wait for his uncle, he rushed to her bedroom in search of her pump. He found it on the dresser, snatched it and darted back to his room, where his sister lay gasping on his bed.

Don't die, please don't die.

He lifted her head, forced her to breathe as he pumped the medicine into her mouth.

Then, fighting tears, he nestled next to her, held her hand and prayed with every inch of his heart.

Chapter Six

The minute Noah called him, Zach's blood turned to ice water. Kristen suffered from a severe case of asthma. She didn't get attacks too often, but when she did, they were sudden and brutal.

"Watch Will." He vaulted off the couch and took the steps two by two, leaving Becca with the baby.

When he got to Noah's room, he found the kids lying side by side. Kristen rested her head on her brother's shoulder while he tenderly stroked her hair. She was so still fear sank pointed hooks in his gut. He couldn't tell whether or not she was breathing. The asthma pump rested on the bed next to Noah, and he realized the boy had acted quickly.

Thank God.

"Kristen?"

Noah released his sister and bulleted out of bed, adopting his usual I-couldn't-give-a-damn expression.

Kristen opened her eyes, turned her head toward Zach. She looked exhausted, but her skin was rosy and her breathing slow and even. Relief submerged him. He sat beside her, the twin mattress sinking beneath his weight. "How are you feeling, kiddo?"

"Okay." Her voice was gravelly. "Noah got—" She cleared her throat as mucus rose to clatter in her windpipe. "Noah got my pump."

He captured his nephew's gaze, held it briefly. "Nice going. You acted instead of panicking. Probably saved your sister's life."

The boy shrugged, staring at the floor. "Didn't want her croaking in my bed."

Zach didn't buy his act for a second. The kid looked terrified. His skin was pale, his hands jittery, his voice thin and winded. He wanted to shake him, hug him, knock some sense into him. There was nothing wrong with being afraid...or caring.

He grabbed the pump and placed it in Kristen's limp hand. "I want you to have this on you at all times. Understand?"

The girl nodded weakly. "I forgot it."

Regret swept through him. "So did I." Was he ever going to get a handle on this parenting thing?

On the edge of the bed Noah's Game Boy idled, beeping and blinking. Zach shook his head. So much for the boy not playing video games.

Following Zach's gaze, Noah grabbed the device and turned it off. Color swamped his cheeks. At least he had enough sense to feel bad about trying to deceive him.

"How about you rest a little?" Zach told Kristen. "Would you like me to take you to your room?"

She wagged her head with as much passion as she could muster. "I want to stay with Noah."

Zach turned an assessing stare toward his nephew. The boy nodded noncommittally. "She can stay, as long as she promises not to be too annoying."

"I won't," she whispered. "Be annoying," she explained.

Zach bit back a smile, knowing that—despite all his grumblings—his nephew would watch over his sister like a hawk. There was a time when he'd been the same with Lindsay—aloof, condescending, but always the protective older brother, ready to sacrifice life and limb for his younger sibling.

He saw a lot of himself in Noah. That was what scared him.

"I'll be downstairs if you need me. I left Becca alone with Will."

"Better hurry," Noah scoffed. "She might eat him."

Zach didn't like the tone in the boy's voice. "I better not catch you being rude to your aunt or there'll be hell to pay."

Thoroughly chastened, Noah retreated to the far corner of his room, where an impressive Lego collection waited.

With a sigh, Zach headed to the door, wondering not whether Becca had eaten the baby, but whether the baby had eaten Becca.

Oh, God. He was crawling her way, giggling and flashing a toothless grin. Well, technically, it wasn't completely toothless, just partially toothless. Four front pearl-white teeth glistened with saliva. He looked like a rabbit about to bite into a juicy carrot.

The fifteen-month-old stood with the help of the coffee table, then waddled toward her. It was obvious he hadn't been walking very long. More often than not, he preferred to crawl.

He watched her expectantly as he approached. What was she supposed to do with him now? Pick him up? What if he didn't want her to?

She flashed her most honeyed grin. "Nice baby."

Will shrieked. Was that a laugh or a cry? She couldn't be sure. He shuffled closer, grabbed hold of her leg. Panic doused her, and she froze, afraid to move. The baby bent forward, then greedily started chewing on her knee. Drool spread over her white silk slacks. She made a mental note to wear only jeans and sweats from now on.

His small, pointy teeth pinched her skin, but she fought not to move. If she disturbed him, he might start crying, and then what would she do?

"Easy there, little one," she cooed, but only managed to sound constipated. The baby squealed, bit harder.

She jolted. "Ouch!"

"I was afraid of this." Zach's voice rolled over her like a cool breeze on a hot day. He snatched Will up as if he weighed no more than a feather. "I walk away for a few minutes and you let him drool all over you."

"Anything to keep him from screaming." She stood in an attempt to chase the tension from her limbs. "How's Kristen?"

"Better. She suffers from asthma. It hits her every now and then. That's why it's important that she have her pump on her at all times. Otherwise, it could be fatal."

Rebecca nodded. "It's a good thing you told me. I'll make it a point to remind her."

Will began gnawing on Zach's shoulder. "He's teething," he explained. "He'll chew on anything he can find."

"Yeah, I kinda figured that." She looked down at her damp pants. "I better go change into something more comfortable." Heat flashed in his eyes, and something equally hot flared in her belly, dancing along her nerve endings. "I mean more appropriate," she amended. "Where did you put my suitcases?"

"In the master bedroom."

Alarm gripped her. "Isn't that where you're sleeping?"

"Not anymore. There's an extra mattress in Will's room. Lindsay used to sleep there whenever he was sick or teething. I'll bunk with him."

"Are you sure?"

The air thickened. Something hot and electric thrummed between them. "Yeah. He wakes up every couple of hours. I spend most of the night there anyway."

"All right." Her fingers twitched. She clenched them at her sides and struggled not to fidget. "I'll head on up then."

"Take your time."

She walked away, making a conscious effort not to sprint, all the while feeling the intensity of his gaze sear her back. Anxiety pulsed through her, and for the umpteenth time she wondered what on earth had possessed her to do this.

The house finally slept, bathed in silence and shadows. The only light came from a blue and white Chinese porcelain lamp with a silver-threaded shade in the living room, which sat opposite the one the kids had shattered earlier. It had taken Zach longer than usual to get the little imps to bed. Their nervous energy had been palpable. Not that he could blame them for being hyper. It had been a pretty wild day. In fact, he highly doubted he was going to get any sleep tonight, either. Especially with Becca just a door away.

He entered the living room to find her sitting on the edge of the blue couch, sewing by the pale yellow lamplight. The soft glow gilded her skin, made her hair shimmer with bronze sparks. She looked so soft, so damn appealing he had to stop and catch his breath. He wanted to touch her, to taste her again. Wanted it with a fierceness that made his heart hurt.

She lifted her chin, latched her gaze onto his face, and something hot and sultry tightened in his chest. For a second the last two years fell away. He almost convinced himself she was still his wife, waiting for him to come home after a hard day at the office.

You're an idiot, he told himself. *A flaming idiot. She's not your wife and never will be again. Accept it.*

"What are you up to?" he asked. Maybe if he struck up a conversation, he'd keep his thoughts from venturing into dangerous territory.

"Sewing a baboon." She showed him the monkey.

"Don't bother. That thing is butt ugly."

"I promised Kristen." She sank the needle into the fabric, pulled it back out again. "I always keep my promises."

Was that another jab for his benefit? She seemed to draw immeasurable pleasure from driving in the fact that he'd failed her, almost with the same zeal with which she plunged the needle into the toy.

He sat in the armchair across from her, leaning against the backrest and letting his head fall backward. He closed his lids, drew solace from the darkness. In the dark he couldn't see the bitter accusation in her eyes, the rigid set of her shoulders, the disappointment thinning her lush, sexy mouth. Silence stretched between them.

"Voula said something today that got me thinking." Her voice was hesitant, as heavy as the silence it pierced. He opened his eyes and looked at her, anxious to hear what was on her mind.

"Are you sure—" She pricked her finger, brought it to her mouth and sucked on it.

The blood in his veins pumped faster, rushed straight to his crotch. He remembered the feel of that mouth, the heat of it.

"Are you sure the shooting was a random break-in and not a hit?" Her words shattered the mood as effectively as a bucket of ice chips.

Tension twined and snapped inside him. "Course I'm sure. A hit—" he shook his head, "—that's damn crazy."

Small furrows formed between her brows. "What if you're wrong? Liam was a lawyer. He interacted with people on the wrong side of the law on a daily basis. What if he got involved in something he shouldn't have or knew something someone was desperate to keep quiet?"

"Don't go there, Becca." He didn't mean to be short-tempered, but this was a sore subject for him. She was adding salt to an open wound, scraping it until it bled again. "It's hard enough knowing that my sister and her husband were murdered for no good reason, now you want me to believe someone intentionally gunned them down?"

"I just want you to acknowledge that it's a possibility. Voula said Liam was acting edgy lately. Apparently, he and Lindsay argued on the day they were killed. He wanted to ship her and the kids off to his parents' place in Ireland, but Lindsay refused to go. She was angry because he was keeping secrets from her."

"Voula's just a busybody with nothing better to do than stick her nose in other people's business."

"I don't think so. She didn't strike me as a gossip."

She was doing it again—looking to make sense of a senseless situation, the way she had when she'd realized she couldn't get pregnant. She'd dragged him to doctor after doctor, subjected them both to a slew of tests that had left them drained, frustrated and embittered. And for what? Nothing but pain had come of it.

Still, he understood her need for answers. When he first heard about the shooting, he'd wanted an explanation, too. But the truth was, finding someone to blame for a tragedy didn't lessen the sting of it. All it did was fuel the anger.

He leaned forward and clasped his hands between his spread knees. "Look, no one wants to catch this bastard more than I do." If he could, he'd tear the son of a bitch apart limb by limb for what he'd done to his sister. "If I had a lead, any lead, I'd be all over it like a dog on a bone. But all we've got are theories."

A leaden sigh blasted from his throat. "I know you want answers. So do I. But letting this Voula character fill your head with delusions isn't going to do anyone any good. Sometimes we just have to accept things for what they are and move on."

Fire flashed in her eyes, deepened them to a glittering shade of rust. "The way you did when our marriage fell apart?"

The blade fell, slashing through him, cutting him deep. He thought of all the nights he'd lain awake aching for her, all the times he'd rushed home after landing an account to share the news with her only to find she wasn't there, all the regrets that plagued him even as he told himself he'd had no choice.

He took in the condemnation twisting her features, the pain no amount of resentment could mask, and spoke the first honest words he'd spoken to her in years. "Who says I moved on?"

Chapter Seven

Who says I moved on?

Those words had bounced inside Rebecca's head all evening. Like nervous grasshoppers, they whizzed through her, stopping only long enough to tie knots in every organ they encountered along the way.

What had he meant by that?

She'd never gotten a chance to ask him. Will had chosen that moment to start fussing, and Zach had rushed off, leaving her with nothing but unvoiced questions and a funny feeling festering in the pit of her stomach.

Now, hours later, as she changed into her pajamas and prepared for bed, she still couldn't quell the jittery excitement his statement had elicited. She'd always believed he'd walked away from their marriage without as much as a backward glance. While she'd been busy trying to reassemble the broken pieces of her heart, he'd gone on with his life with the same cool self-possession for which he was renowned. While she'd lain in bed at night, her eyes painfully dry, her cheeks stinging from all the tears she'd shed, she'd imagined him with some other woman. One who could give him everything he wanted, be everything he needed.

Not once since the breakup had he called or dropped by for a visit, so she'd naturally assumed he'd been glad to wash his hands of her. Even the divorce had been handled through a lawyer Liam had recommended, with as little personal contact as possible.

She applied her face cream, checking—as she always did—for the telltale sign of wrinkles. She was only thirty-four, young by anyone's standard, but she still couldn't help but feel time evaporating around her. Her youth was slipping away, gently, imperceptibly. One day she'd look in the mirror at a face she barely recognized and ask herself what she'd accomplished. Her failures would snarl at her with vivid clarity—no husband, no children, just loneliness and a gaping emptiness that simply couldn't be filled.

It seemed unfair that Lindsay—who had everything to live for—no longer existed, while Rebecca continued to forge ahead, building nothing. Nothing that lasted.

Maybe this was her chance to change that.

The stuffed animal she'd sewn sat on the nightstand, staring at her with bulging eyes. She went to it, gathered it in her arms and cradled it as if it were a baby. Maybe if she practiced, one of these days she'd be able to hold Will, hug Kristen or take Noah's hand in hers without experiencing that plummeting sensation in her abdomen.

With a sigh, she wandered into the darkened corridor and walked to Kristen's room. Across the hall, Will's door stood closed. From behind the thick wooden divider Zach's presence called to her, connected with that secret corner of her being that was still intimately aware of his every move, his every breath.

Who says I moved on?

Warmth inundated her, made her pulse trip and her heart crash.

She shook her head at her stupidity and swallowed a snort. Decisively, she pushed open Kristen's door and entered. A nightlight cast a thin, shivering glow through the room. The curtains were parted and moon-silvered shadows danced on the walls. Beyond the glass, winking stars salted the black cloak of night.

Rebecca approached the bed, where the girl lay in a tangle of sheets, her hair draped over her forehead like fallen straw. She looked serene, almost angelic.

Peace was infectious, hypnotic. It made you want to believe it would last forever. But it couldn't. Reality wouldn't allow it. Even now it hovered in the air, as pervasive as it was invisible, waiting to awaken with the sun.

In her arms the girl clutched something white. At first Rebecca thought it was a blanket. Upon closer inspection, however, she realized it was a sweater. She recognized it because she'd given it to Lindsay for her twenty-eighth birthday, a short six years ago. She'd picked it for its warmth and softness. No wonder Kristen favored it. It didn't hurt that the garment probably still carried the scent of her mom's perfume.

Rebecca reached out, assailed by the sudden urge to brush Kristen's hair from her face, to stroke her dimpled cheek. Instead, she placed the stuffed animal at her side.

"Sweet dreams," she whispered.

Then, with a last lingering glance at the girl's dozing face, she left the softly lit room and slipped into the waiting embrace of night, where regrets dimmed and her failures didn't clang quite so loudly.

Something boomed. A shrill cacophony slithered into her consciousness and yanked her from a dreamless sleep. Rebecca moaned and covered her head with a pillow, but nothing short of deafness could block out the racket pummeling her brain like a jackhammer. What was all the commotion?

She crawled out of bed and dragged herself to the door, half expecting to find the house on fire. Maybe Zach had decided to cook again. He was adept at many things, but cooking wasn't one of them. Once, on their anniversary, he'd decided to bring her hash browns and scrambled eggs in bed. She had a sneaking suspicion that he'd unwittingly broken the yolks and tried to cover his blunder by insisting he'd intended to scramble them all along. Whatever the case, he'd forgotten to turn off the burner, while failing to remove the oily pan from the stove. When they'd come down quite some time later—she blushed recalling the heated love they'd made on that rain-swept morning so many years ago—the pungent smell of hot oil had burned their nostrils.

Instantly, the neglected pan had ignited in a burst of orange flames. Zach, always ready to take charge of a situation, had rushed in and attempted to extinguish the blaze with a glass of water. Big mistake. He'd nearly incinerated his eyebrows.

It hadn't been funny at the time, but now the memory made Rebecca's lips quirk with amusement. She'd never loved him more than she had at that moment, when complete ineptness had afflicted him and left him cursing.

She grabbed the baby-blue robe she'd left on the dresser by the door and ventured outside. No inferno raged. No flames crackled and roared with deadly intent, yet the house still simmered with a furious undercurrent of energy. Noah and Kristen whizzed past her, howling like injured wolves. For a second she wondered if they were in pain, then realized they were only playing.

From his room, Will hollered.

Blinking to chase the cobwebs of sleep from her eyes, she hurried to see what all the fuss was about. The door to Will's bedroom was open, so she stole a glimpse inside. The sight she beheld made a smile spread through her. Zach was on the floor, wrestling with Will. He clutched a diaper in one hand while struggling to pin the baby down with the other. Will kicked, screamed and writhed. Tiny feet and fists flailed.

"Sit still, you little rug rat," he muttered between oaths.

Again, Rebecca had a vision of him tossing a glass of water onto a flaming pan. There were many kinds of fire, and this was definitely one of them.

She edged into the room. "Need some help?" she offered.

He started at the sound of her voice. His gaze rose to her face, then glided over her in a slow sweep that made a rush of self-consciousness roll through her. She knew exactly how she looked in the morning. Her hair was a wild tangle of untamed curls that brought to mind clumps of Spanish moss. Her skin was pale without the benefit of blush, her eyes slightly swollen and misted by sleep.

"No one ever told me that dressing a kid was more exhausting than an Olympic marathon," he grumbled. "I'd take a five-thousand-meter run any day over this."

He tried to slide the diaper under the baby, but Will kicked it away. "First he pulled the melt on me," he explained. "Now he's doing the jiggle."

"The jiggle?"

"Stick around long enough and you'll know what I'm talking about." Will managed to wriggle free from Zach's grasp. Not bothering to waste time trying to stand, he made a dash for the door on all fours, zipping across the room with the speed of a jackrabbit. Rebecca never would have believed anyone could crawl that fast.

"Don't let him escape," Zach yelled.

She hastened into the room and shut the door behind her. Zach ran and scooped up the baby, then placed him back in the crib. Will let out a whoop of indignation so loud, it made her ears ring.

"Come here and hold him down for me," he said.

She did as he asked, grabbing the baby's legs as Zach struggled to attach the diaper. The kid was surprisingly strong for one so small. She was barely able to keep him still long enough for Zach to dress him. Like a contortionist drenched in Vaseline, he turned onto his stomach and slid out of her grip.

Her eyes rounded with surprise, but Zach just smiled knowingly. "The jiggle," he said.

"At least you got the diaper on him." Relieved, she took a step away from the crib and inched toward the door.

"Not so fast." Zach walked to the dresser and pulled a pair of shorts and a T-shirt from the drawers. He flashed an unsettling grin that made dread congeal in her veins. "We're not done yet. Not even close."

The morning went a little smoother than usual, maybe because Becca was here. Noah and Kristen were behaving surprisingly well, playing as if they were the best of friends. Even Will refrained from practicing his falsetto. Overall, life was good.

Zach looked across the kitchen table at Becca, who nibbled on a piece of toast as if taking a real bite would cause her to balloon on the spot. She'd always been overly concerned with her weight, even though she had the most incredible figure he'd ever seen. True, she wasn't on the skinny side. Her hips were wide and round, her breasts full. In today's society, where anorexic runway models ruled, women like Becca were made to feel self-conscious about their bodies, which was a damn shame. To Zach she was the ideal woman, firm and voluptuous, curved in all the right places.

"What's the plan for today?" she asked between bites.

"Divide and conquer."

She aimed a confused stare his way.

"A great strategy in both war and parenting," he explained. "Together, they'll wipe us out. Split them up and we actually stand a chance."

"Okay, commando, so what do you suggest?" Her tousled hair fell in a silken cascade over her forehead.

He'd always loved the way she looked in the morning, fresh and soft with just a hint of wildness. Long-forgotten cravings swam to the surface, made him acutely aware of her every gesture, her every sigh and sound. The way she smacked her lips together, wetting them with the tip of her pink tongue. The way she brushed the piece of toast against her mouth right before she took a bite. The soft whisper of fabric scraping her skin as she bent forward and reached for her coffee mug. Her pale blue satin robe parted, exposing the smooth swell of her breast.

Need pummeled him with iron fists. It took all his self-control not to glide his hand beneath her tank top and explore the tempting curve of her creamy white skin. He knew just how she'd feel in his palm, soft and supple and hot enough to scorch his flesh. He could all too easily imagine her eyes growing smoky as her nipple puckered beneath his thumb...

All the more reason to divide and conquer. He couldn't bear to spend another minute in this house with her.

"For starters, you can take Kristen to ballet class." His voice sounded gruff, roughened by desire. Thankfully, she didn't catch the change in him.

"I didn't know she attended ballet." She lifted her coffee mug and took a sip. The warm liquid glazed her lips, made them glisten in the sunlight.

Zach pried his gaze away from her mouth. "Every Saturday at ten. Lindsay insists—insisted—that her daughter inherited her talent for dance."

When she was a kid, Lindsay had always spun around the house, usually dressed in a silly tutu that had made him snicker and roll his eyes. The going joke was that she'd been born with a pair of ballet slippers on her feet. For a while he'd almost believed it. He wasn't sure Kristen was as gifted a dancer, but Lindsay had somehow convinced herself that she was.

"Ten?" She shot a glance at her watch, and a frantic expression dashed across her face. "It's almost nine. I haven't even showered yet."

"Then you better get a move on."

She inhaled the rest of her toast, forced it down with a couple of mouthfuls of coffee, then bolted to her feet. Within seconds she was sprinting up the stairs.

A smile tugged at the corner of his mouth.

Welcome to the land of parenthood.

He wondered how the reality of it measured up to the fantasy she'd always harbored. To Becca, being a parent had always meant long strolls through the park, shared laughter and games, cozy hugs and kisses. She'd never anticipated sleepless nights, an endless battle of wills and nerve-shattering noise levels that set your teeth on edge.

If these last two weeks had taught him anything, it was that she was in for a rude awakening. One that was long overdue.

The Movement and Dance Studio was located in a beautifully renovated building on Harvard Street in Brookline, a short ten-minute drive away. Ms. Orloff, the owner and dance instructor, had once trained with the Russian ballet. She was a tall, lithe woman, with soft, fluid movements and the kind of innate grace that made goose bumps spring from one's pores. She glided across the shiny hardwood floor as if on invisible skates, perfectly in tune with her body and the world around her.

Rebecca envied her. From the time she was old enough to walk, she'd longed for grace, composure and the kind of self-assurance that had always come so naturally to Zach and Lindsay. When Lindsay had been performing in dance recitals and Zach had been awarded medal after medal, Rebecca had sat in the shadows, silently cheering them on. She'd been so proud of them both, even as she'd secretly ached for something of her own—a talent, a passion, a smidgen of success.

She'd been the geek through and through. Sure, she'd aced all her tests and won the best short story award in high school, but athletically speaking, she'd been a nobody—the last kid ever picked in gym class, the invisible one, the one no one ever bothered to acknowledge with a pass or a pat on the back.

At seventeen she'd decided to change that. She'd joined a gym, had pushed herself to work out even as her muscles screamed in protest. After a year of training, her body had grown firm and supple, strong and defined. She'd been so pleased with the results that she'd never stopped working out. Even now she tried to go to the gym at least twice a week.

So, although she wasn't willowy like Ms. Orloff and did not possess a fraction of her grace, she was still in relatively good shape and hoped to keep it that way.

Ms. Orloff demonstrated a pirouette. Eleven little girls in pink tights followed her lead. Kristen didn't. She spun the wrong way, lost her balance and fell. Ms. Orloff frowned and pinched her mouth in a way that reminded Rebecca of a plucked ostrich. Kristen cowered and slowly dragged herself to her feet.

The mother sitting beside Rebecca clucked her tongue disapprovingly, and Rebecca shot her a withering look.

"Chassé," Ms. Orloff instructed, skating across the dance floor. Eleven little girls floated through the room, as graceful as swans. Kristen moved a little too fast and crashed into the girl beside her. Ms. Orloff's chest heaved with an exasperated sigh. The same mother snickered and shook her head.

Rebecca angled a glance her way. "Is there a problem?"

"That girl's got two left feet," she said, unaware that Rebecca was Kristen's aunt. "She'll never be a dancer. I don't know why her mother keeps bringing her."

She leaned closer, whispered conspiratorially, "I haven't seen her around these past few weeks. Maybe she's too embarrassed to stay and watch."

Rebecca wanted nothing more than to wipe that self-satisfied smirk from her face. What a wretched, wretched woman. "That's because she was shot to death two weeks ago," she informed her. "I'm Kristen's guardian now."

The woman's features fell. Purple blotches blossomed on her cheeks. "I'm sorry— I had no idea— I didn't mean—"

Rebecca noted the despair on Kristen's face, the way she inched away from the group and stared at her pink slippers as if they were the source of all her misery. She felt her pain. Her embarrassment was her own. It would probably take years for this little girl to find herself, and when she did, it most certainly would not be here in this stodgy studio.

"You're right," she agreed. "Kristen may never learn to be a ballet dancer, but at five she's already learned compassion, decency and common courtesy." She shot the woman an accusing look infused with bitter meaning. "Things so many adults still fail to grasp."

The woman's lips parted with an unvoiced protest, but Rebecca didn't wait for her reply. She stood and tore into the classroom, not caring that she was interrupting the lesson. She walked up to her niece and crouched beside her. "Are you having fun?"

"Excuse me," Ms. Orloff reprimanded with a hint of haughtiness, "we're in the middle of a lesson."

Rebecca ignored her. "Sweetie, are you having fun?" she asked again.

The girl shrugged. "I'm no good. I can't dance." Self-reproof shimmered in her bruised irises, making her look far older than her years. She was too young to know of failure, of loss, of death. Too young to know anything but joy.

"That's not what I asked you. I asked you if you were enjoying yourself."

With a wary look at her teacher, Kristen reluctantly wagged her head.

"That settles it then. We're blowing this pop stand."

"You cannot leave in the middle of a lesson—"

With no hesitation at all, Rebecca took hold of Kristen's hand and stalked past the dried-up old prune of an instructor. She no longer envied her willowy charms or pretentious grace. Without stopping to look back, she barreled past the startled mothers—who watched her as if she were a couple of baskets short of a picnic—raced down the stairs and burst out the front door.

The hot July sun welcomed them, sprinkled kisses along their skin as a warm breeze caressed their faces. The thick wooden door swung shut behind them with an angry clunk. In the street, cars whizzed by at breakneck speed, the drivers hardly noticing the cotton-tailed clouds chugging across a cornflower-blue sky or the way newly planted trees saluted them with a wild flutter of leaves. In a few months those leaves would be mottled with orange and gold before they slowly abandoned the safety of their branches in favor of an icy grave. But for now a stunning burst of color streaked the day.

Rebecca cradled Kristen's small hand in hers and walked away from the redbrick building with its impeccably polished floors and stone-hearted inhabitants. The lost little girl gazed up at her tentatively, her expression brimming with confusion and something else—trust.

Rebecca's heart swelled until it could barely beat. The strangest feeling came upon her. A feeling more powerful than despair, more paralyzing than self-recrimination, more gripping than longing. It was one of purpose, and it brought with it a bone-deep conviction that made her insides shake. She would help these damaged children heal, grow and find their place in the world...and God have mercy on anyone who dared get in her way.

"Finally. U came," Night-Owl wrote the moment Noah logged on to Falcon World. "I'm bored."

"Yeah, me 2." With Kristen gone and Uncle Zach busy taking care of Will, Noah was completely on his own. Being alone sucked. He'd made a few drawings for the comic book he was working on, but now he was sick of drawing. He'd called up his friend Jason to see if he wanted to get together at the park or something, but no one had answered.

So he'd snuck into his dad's office, turned off the speaker on the computer and stepped into Falcon World. Being in this room still made a swarm of bees buzz around in his stomach, but he fought to ignore them.

Chicken-shit.

He was happy that Night-Owl was here. "Still glad school's out," he added.

"KWUM." *Know what you mean,* Night-Owl typed. "Rather be bored at home than in some dumb classroom."

"School is total B/S."

"Total." There was a short pause. "What R U doin this summer?"

"BTSOOM." *Beats the shit out of me.* "It's up to my aunt and uncle." As soon as Noah pressed Enter, he regretted it. He hadn't told Night-Owl about his parents dying. The last thing he wanted was to have to explain. Just thinking about the shooting made the bees in his belly angry enough to sting.

"How come?"

A thick, wet knot rose to clog his throat. He couldn't bring himself to answer. The words were all tangled up in the ugly images in his head.

"Raptor, R U there?"

"I'm here. Wanna play a game?" he wrote instead.

"Checkers?"

"No. How bout Chess?"

"K."

So they played and Night-Owl didn't ask him any more questions about his parents. For a few minutes Noah forgot they were gone. Forgot the shiny black gun with the long barrel that had taken them from him. Forgot how shitty the world could be.

He was just a kid again, having fun with a friend, and he liked it.

Chapter Eight

Becca and Kristen should have been back over an hour ago. Zach had tried calling to see what was holding them up, but Becca's cell phone was off. He told himself it was too early to worry, but he couldn't help it. After what had happened to Liam and Lindsay, he saw disaster around every corner. A truck could have rammed into Becca's car, crumpled the metal and trapped them inside. A distracted driver might have passed a red light as they crossed the street, flattening them on the pavement. Even now, a strung-out gang member could be roaming the streets with a loaded gun in hand, determined to use pedestrians for target practice. Danger was a shadow, barely visible yet ever present, waiting for the perfect opportunity to bury you.

He tried to distract himself by entertaining Will, but it didn't work. The grandfather clock in the living room kept catching his eye. Every damn tick was torture. When the doorbell rang, relief flooded his veins. He didn't bother asking himself why Becca would ring the doorbell when he'd given her one of the spare keys that morning. He simply rushed to open it.

Disappointment sliced through him when he found Martin Birch standing on the front porch instead.

"Hey, Zach," he greeted, squeezing in past him.

Martin was Liam's older brother, a slick financial advisor with more arrogance than common sense. Zach had never liked him much. There was something about his perfect row of pearl-white teeth and icy blue gaze that left a greasy feeling in Zach's gut.

"We weren't expecting you," Zach said a little too curtly. "I thought you were out of town."

"I was. Sorry I missed the reading of the will, but I had a seven-digit deal to close and couldn't get out of it."

Of course, what could be more important than a million-dollar deal? Certainly not the fate of his niece and nephews. Zach thanked God Lindsay and Liam had had the good sense not to appoint Martin as guardian. He was single, emotionally crippled, and marked each new day on the calendar with a dollar sign.

"How are the kids doing?"

Zach wanted to say, *"What do you care?"*

Instead, he tamped down his bitterness and followed Martin to the living room. "As well as can be expected. They need a little time to adapt."

"I bet they do." Martin bent his body at midriff, placed his hands on his knees and flashed an exaggerated grin at Will, who sat on the rug chewing on a carrot. Zach had read somewhere that it helped with the teething.

"Where are the others?"

"Noah's upstairs in his room. Kristen's at dance class."

"Business as usual, huh?"

"I'm trying to keep their routine as normal as possible." He didn't like having to explain himself, especially to the likes of Liam's snake-oil salesman of a brother.

"Sounds fair enough." Martin swaggered to the couch, dropped into it and stretched out his arms like a king staking a claim on his throne. Dressed in a pair of crisp black slacks, a designer shirt and Italian loafers, he looked like he should be on the cover of *Business Week.* "Have you gotten around to clearing out Liam and Lindsay's things yet?"

Anguish serpentined around Zach's chest, a hungry python that squeezed him until his lungs hurt. "No," he said a little too adamantly. "Haven't found the time."

"If you need help, give me a ring. I don't mind lending a hand." He glanced at the wedding picture hanging over the fireplace and had the decency to look remorseful. "I still can't believe my baby brother's gone."

For once, Zach had to agree with him. He understood Kristen's refusal to accept her parents' death. Hell, he could barely wrap his brain around it himself.

"If you need a break, I can take them over the weekend," Martin offered. "Now that the big deal's behind me, I've got some down time."

"Thanks, but Becca moved in yesterday. She's assuming some of the responsibilities, so things have gotten a lot easier."

Something dark and predatory flared in Martin's cool gaze, but he quickly subdued it. "How's that working out?"

"Sorry?"

"It's gotta be weird, living with your ex again."

Zach bristled. Becca had always been a sore subject for them. "We're both adults. We can be civil to each other. The kids have to come first."

A humorless chuckle resonated in Martin's throat. "If I ever moved in with one of my exes, she'd skin me alive. You know what they say about a woman scorned."

"Becca's different."

"Sure she is. Bet she's never fantasized about raking you over burning coals."

You wish. He fought to tamp down his growing irritation. Martin had the annoying habit of assuming he knew his wife better than he did, and as hard as he tried Zach couldn't squelch the prickling fear that the jerk might be right.

Noah ambled into the living room, an iPod clipped to his belt. The moment he saw Martin, he pulled the plugs from his ears. "Hi, Uncle Martin. Are you moving in, too? 'Cause if you are, we need a bigger house."

Martin's face lit up at the sight of his eldest nephew, and he laughed. "No, bud. I'm not moving in." He patted the couch cushion, invited Noah to come sit beside him. When the boy complied, Martin wrapped an arm around him and drew him hard against his side. "So how you holding up?"

Noah gave one of his trademark shrugs and wriggled free from the man's grasp. He was old enough for open displays of affection to make him uncomfortable. "I'm fine. But Will whines all the time and Kristen's a pain in the ass—"

Zach skewered the boy with a quelling look. "How many times have I told you to watch your mouth?"

"What's the big deal?" He slid his thumbs through his belt hoops and slumped back in the couch. "You swear all the time."

Martin watched Zach with a reproachful look that made him want to ball his hands into fists. What right did the cocky son of a bitch have to judge him? While Martin was off wheeling and dealing, Zach was here rolling with the punches, trying his damnedest to keep this family together. He had to put aside his own ambitions, bury his pain even as it struggled to eat him from the inside out and work to mend the three young lives tragedy had left in shambles. The way he saw it, he was damn well entitled to a swear word or two.

"So, bud," Martin said after a short pause, "are you still a fiend for video games?"

Noah's belligerent expression vanished, replaced by excitement. "What do you think?"

Martin laughed. "Then I'm sure you're gonna love what I've got in my car for you."

The boy rocketed to his feet. "DSI?"

As if the kid needed another handheld device he could hide under his sheets.

"Not exactly. Come take a look." Noah needed no further incentive to follow his uncle outside.

When they returned a few minutes later, Noah had his hands

wrapped around a brand new video game. "Look." He showed Zach the game. "Uncle Martin got me *G.I. Joe: Rise of the Cobra* for PlayStation 3!"

Great. Now the kid would spend the next five hours glued to the television set. "Are you old enough to play that game?" he asked, since he was the only responsible adult in the room.

"You're never too young for G.I. Joe." Martin gave Noah a playful punch on the arm. Noah beamed.

Zach shook his head and swallowed a grunt. This was going to be a very long afternoon.

In line with his thoughts, the clock chimed the hour. The pendulum swung on well-oiled hinges as the small hand fell to rest upon the one. Kristen's dance class had ended two hours ago. The python tightened its hold on him, baring hungry fangs.

What the hell was keeping Becca?

There was a surefire way to brighten a girl's mood when she was feeling down, and Rebecca knew exactly what that was—shopping. Coolidge Corner, located at the intersection of Harvard and Beacon, was home to many small independent boutiques and retail chain stores. So instead of heading home after the fiasco at The Movement and Dance Studio, she decided to take Kristen for a little stroll down Harvard Street. They stopped at a coffee shop and fortified themselves with some delicious beverages—cold coffee for Rebecca, juice for Kristen—then the marathon was on.

They visited store after store, as zealous in their quest as any crusader, attacking the racks with unmasked gusto. Rebecca purchased the most adorable outfit for Kristen, an embroidered jean skirt with a matching blouse and a pair of colorful tights. She'd never realized what an incredible selection stores boasted for girls. She usually avoided the children's section with a passion that bordered on obsession. The mere sight of these doll-like outfits, with their frilly socks and miniature hats, displayed on mannequins or hangers, sent a shrill ache resonating through her. Whenever she happened to cross one of these displays, she quickly averted her gaze, hoping to spare herself the pain.

Today, however, she welcomed the quiet throb in her chest that told her she still had the capacity to feel. It wasn't nearly as sharp as it had once been, just a mild flutter of longing overshadowed by excitement. After she finished shopping for Kristen, she selected a one-piece jumpsuit for Will and a pair of shorts and a T-shirt for Noah. With the packages safely secured in her arms and Kristen's small hand buried in hers, she walked into the blinding bright day, feeling surprisingly invigorated. In some small way she'd faced one of her demons today and won. She'd looked directly into its slime-green eyes and successfully stared it into submission.

"Aunt Becca," Kristen whispered timidly, "can we do this every Saturday instead of going to dance class?"

Rebecca laughed. "You betcha, kiddo." She glanced at her watch. It was just shy of one in the afternoon. "How about we stop for lunch?" she suggested. "You must be starving. I know I am."

Kristen nodded emphatically. "Can I have a chocolate milkshake?"

"Sure, but only if you have some food to go with it."

They stopped at the Coolidge Corner Clubhouse, a sports bar with a diverse menu and a laid-back ambience. Colorful sports photos, cartoons and posters of all sizes decorated the walls. Twenty strategically placed LCD screens displayed a Celtics game. A group of college jocks huddled in a distant corner, cheering their idols on. Every so often a whoop of pleasure rent the air, sometimes closely followed by cries of indignation and disgruntled boos.

They sat at a small wooden table, Kristen curiously watching one of the screens as Rebecca perused the menu. Practically every dish was named after a famous figure. She ended up ordering the Wade Bogg, a salad topped with teriyaki chicken. Kristen decided to play it safe and chose the grilled-cheese sandwich with a side order of fries, and a chocolate milkshake, of course.

They ate in companionable silence, a temporary escape from the dark reality that had befallen them. For a few short hours they allowed pure fun to add balm to their internal bruises, to dull the pain and soothe their spirits.

It was nearly two when they started their long trek back to the car. Along the way Rebecca noticed Kristen was no longer following her and glanced back. The girl stood staring through the window of a pet shop. From the other side of the glass, a beagle saluted her with a lolling tongue and an overactive tail. Kristen was mesmerized.

"Can we go in and see it?" she begged, adopting a puppy-dog look that would have made any canine proud.

Rebecca hesitated. On some instinctive level she knew this meant trouble. Still, she didn't have the heart to disappoint the child. "Only for a few minutes," she said. Zach was probably starting to worry, and she couldn't even call to appease him because she'd forgotten to charge her cell phone last night.

Once inside, the beagle pulled every trick in the book. Rebecca wondered if the animal had been trained to lure and seduce or if it came naturally to the breed. He sprinkled wet kisses over Kristen's hand, hopped, rolled and drooled with absolute joy. Pleading brown eyes sparkled with devotion as he wagged his tail like a windshield wiper on overdrive.

"Would you like to hold him?" the saleslady asked.

Rebecca began to shake her head, but Kristen flashed the most radiant smile. "Can I?"

Despite her better judgment, Rebecca reluctantly nodded.

As soon as the saleslady placed the puppy in Kristen's arms, any hope of walking out of this store empty-handed turned to cinders and floated away on the nonexistent wind. The beagle slapped Kristen's face with a long wet tongue while it quaked, thrilled by the embrace. Kristen giggled and beamed with the kind of happiness that had died along with her parents. Rebecca's resolve crumbled.

"If you're interested," the sly, underhanded, totally manipulative saleslady told her, "I can tell you about the sale we're having this week."

"Sure," she heard herself say. "I'd love to hear all about it."

Martin prattled on for a good hour before he realized he had better things to do than hang out at suburb central. He ruffled Noah's hair, flashed Will another phony grin, then pranced out the door.

Zach, happy to be left alone with his anxiety, decided to try Becca's cell phone one more time…and got her voice mail again. He cursed. Where the hell had the woman gone?

He dialed The Movement and Dance Studio—Lindsay had penned the number in the address book next to the kitchen phone—and promptly got an earful from Ms. Orloff. Apparently, Becca had disrupted her class by dragging Kristen off halfway through the lesson. Ms. Orloff's knickers were in an awful twist. Never before had something like this happened at her dance studio. She'd been thoroughly embarrassed in front of all her clients, feared the reputation of her school had suffered irreparable damage.

He tried his best to appease her, but there was no consoling the woman. She ended the call by emphatically stating that she never wanted to see Kristen back there again, and she was perfectly willing to reimburse them their fees to ensure that she didn't.

Zach hung up the phone and filled his lungs with a badly needed dose of oxygen. Becca would always be Becca. She was impulsive, more emotional than rational and loyal to a fault. Although her approach often lacked finesse, her heart was always in the right place. So if Becca had pulled Kristen out of class, he was willing to bet a kidney she'd had a darn good reason to do it.

Still, he was no closer to answering the question that had harassed him for hours. If the girls had left The Movement and Dance Studio early, why weren't they home yet?

Something crashed in the living room, punctuated by Noah's outraged cry. Zach rushed to see what all the fuss was about and found Will surrounded by broken glass. It looked like he'd dropped a picture frame.

Noah kneeled beside his brother, cradling the photograph like some precious artifact. "He broke it," he spat. Beneath thick layers of anger, pain trembled. "It's ruined now."

Zach swept Will into his arms before the toddler could cut himself. The picture was a family snapshot. From the looks of it, his sister had been pregnant with Will when it was taken. "We'll just get a new frame," he told his eldest nephew.

"Won't make a difference. The photo's scratched." The boy looked like he was trying very hard not to cry.

Zach placed a comforting hand on the nape of Noah's neck. "How about I go through your dad's computer and put an album together? I can send the files out and have a stack of photos printed. Would you like that?"

Noah shrugged noncommittally, but Zach caught a flicker of interest in his shuttered eyes. Behind all that bravado, all that forced maturity, the heart of a child still beat. And it was every bit as broken as the frame on the floor.

"I've got to clean this mess up before someone gets hurt." Zach stood and went to place Will in his playpen.

When he returned, he found Noah sweeping up the glass. He stood frozen, watched.

Well, I'll be damned.

A smile yanked at Zach's mouth. For the first time in weeks he felt hopeful.

Then a key jingled in the lock and a slobbering beast tumbled in, vaulting across the couch, claiming every corner of the house as its own. The animal sampled a taste of Noah, then sniffed Zach's leg, all the while watching him with a dumb expression that said "I'm all yours". Becca and Kristen followed at its heels, Kristen chattering up a storm. He hadn't heard such a stream of words spill from her lips in weeks.

Noah forgot his distress over the photograph and hopped to attention, joining his sister in her excitement. Together they chased the beagle, laughing wholeheartedly, as if they'd suddenly remembered how to be children again.

Becca studied him with apologetic eyes as she deposited an armful of bags on the floor. "I couldn't say no," she voiced thinly.

Zach rammed his fingers through his hair. "What are we supposed to do with a dog?"

"Feed it, walk it, clean up its poop."

He stifled a moan. "Great. Sounds like another kid."

"Except for one big difference. This one won't talk back." Her eyes twinkled. She looked different, almost happy. He couldn't remember the last time he'd seen her happy. Her smile was potent, addictive. One look and he was hooked again.

A crazy kind of joy filled the house. Zach couldn't believe something as simple as a puppy could bring about such a turnaround. The beagle curled around his legs and licked his feet, as if begging him to let it stay. Zach's reservations slowly dissolved and vanished.

What the hell. If that was what it took to hear the kids laugh and see Becca smile, then he'd gladly clean up the poop. He was already neck deep in it anyway.

"I guess we better give him a name," he muttered.

"Bolt!" Kristen piped up. "He's a super dog!"

"No he's not. He just thinks he is. He's an actor."

Zach and Becca exchanged confused glances. "Is that a show?" she asked.

"A movie," Noah clarified.

Kristen scrambled through the living room, enthusiasm punctuating her every word. "He's super strong and super fast and has a super bark..."

"No he doesn't," Noah insisted. "He just *thinks* he does!"

"So you don't like the name Bolt, Noah?" Becca probed.

"Sure I do. It's a great name. But he's *not* a super dog."

Kristen stopped running and balled her hands on her hips. "Is too."

"Is not."

"Is too."

Zach rolled his eyes. *Here we go again.*

"Let's stay focused." Becca squatted next to the dog and scratched it behind the ears. The dog's eyes went dreamy. Zach could relate. "What do you think, puppy? How do you like the name Bolt?"

An excited bark rent the air. Becca laughed. "It's settled then. We've got a dog named Bolt."

The kids cheered. From his playpen in the corner of the living room, Will released an indignant yowl, insisting he be let in on the fun. Zach freed him from his prison, and the toddler instantly began to chase the beagle. The animal ran for dear life. Not that Zach could blame him. Will had no notion of his strength and would happily tug on Bolt's ears or tail given half the chance. He prayed to God the creature was as affable as he looked. The last thing they needed was a dog with a super *bite*.

The day had overflowed with unbridled excitement sprinkled with a hefty dose of chaos. Children and dog had bonded over a series of leaps and bounds, followed by several hours of Fetch. Finally exhausted, the little ones had gone to bed, leaving Rebecca with an over-stimulated puppy to settle down. With the help of an old blanket and a laundry basket, she fashioned a comfortable bed for him in a cozy corner of the basement.

Bolt would have none of it. He much preferred the couch or one of the mattresses instead. Every time she brought him downstairs he dashed right back up again. She tried locking him in, but he just whimpered until she succumbed to his pleas and released him. She finally gave up—praying to God he was housebroken, fully expecting that he wasn't—and left him curled at the foot of her bed, while she went in search of Zach.

The stars were dull tonight, set against a backdrop of smoky gray. A thin slice of moon scarred the dark underbelly of the sky, casting elongated shadows on the walls. Rebecca softly padded down the stairs, careful not to wake the children. She'd quickly come to appreciate these precious hours between dusk and midnight. An unnatural hush hovered over the house, a lulling mist, almost loud in its stillness.

She found Zach in the den, which Liam had converted into a home office. He sat at the desk, his face illuminated only by the flicker of the computer screen and the pale, silver sheen of moon and stars. For a moment she absorbed the sight of him. Admired the way the fluorescent light caressed him, the way it softened the creases around his mouth and dulled the worry lines permanently etched between his brows. In that instant before he realized she was there, the years fell away. He looked exactly like the boy she'd fallen in love with a lifetime ago.

Then he turned to gaze at her, and the illusion of innocence faded into the night as surely as did any remnants of the dying sun. Before her sat a man hardened by life, no stranger to loss or pain, yet somehow graced with the strength to rise above it.

"I thought you'd gone to bed," he said.

"It's barely nine o'clock."

His glance darted back to the screen. "Is it? It feels later."

"Probably because you're exhausted." She fought the urge to bridge the distance between them and massage his shoulders as she would have done so effortlessly in the past. She no longer had the right to touch him, and that only heightened her desire to do so.

"What are you up to?" she asked instead.

"I told Noah I'd put a photo album together. Have some prints made. I've already sent some shots off to Walmart. Now I'm downloading the files onto Noah's iPod. I figure he'll like having access to them whenever he's missing his parents, which I'm guessing is pretty much all the time."

A warm, languid feeling unfurled silky wings beneath her breastbone. "That's a great idea. I'm sure it will please him."

"He's hurting, Becca." His eyes fastened onto hers, deep and dark and troubled. "He's hurting but he refuses to let it show. And it's killing him."

"Why does he keep it all inside?" If anyone could answer that question, it would be Zach.

He shook his head. "I wish I knew. Something's eating him up—I can tell. But he doesn't trust me enough yet to tell me what it is."

"Give it time." She walked toward him, buried her hands in her pant pockets to keep from sliding her palms over his wide shoulders and down the length of his sinewy arms. "He just lost his parents."

"I know." He bent his head forward and rubbed his eyelids to wipe the stress away. "Damn it, I know. I just feel so useless."

"You can't fix everything, Zach." Losing the battle, she brought her fingers to his temple. Spiky threads of black twined with silver to scrape her fingertips. Something sparked in his gaze, dark and hot and gripping. It shocked her, branded her flesh with the force of an electrical charge, and she withdrew her hand.

"Some things just have to run their course," she added in an effort to distract herself. "There's no magic cure for grief. Every heart heals at its own pace."

She took a step away from him, but he clasped her hand. The heat of those long, strong fingers wrapped around hers seeped into her system, a startling surge that flooded her chest.

"Has yours healed, Becca?"

She tried to pry her hand from his, but he refused to release her. She had no choice but to look into his beautiful face as her traitorous heart continued to tap-dance against her ribcage. Pretense fell away. All that remained was honesty. "I don't know. I didn't believe it ever would. But today I did something I never thought I'd have the courage to do. I shopped for the kids.

"I walked into the children's section, looked at all those adorable little outfits, and you know what? I didn't fall apart. So who knows? Maybe it will. Maybe it already has."

He wanted to believe her. She could tell by the flicker of interest in his eyes, by the glimmer of hope that struggled to break through.

"I'm glad you're here," he whispered.

Oh, that was low. So low. Those simple words tangled up her insides until she felt as if a contortionist had crawled into her abdomen to perform his tricks. She'd never been very good at resisting him, but when he looked at her that way, when his voice took on that silky quality, all her defenses collapsed and left her needy, completely at his mercy.

He leaned forward, drew her closer. His thumb stroked the underside of her wrist. For one thunderous heartbeat she forgot herself and narrowed the distance between them. She still remembered the intoxicating feel of his mouth on hers, secretly hungered to taste it again. And here he was, so close, glazed by starlight and watching her with a glittering intensity that flattened her resolve and made her belly ache.

Then, like a sudden draft sweeping in to banish the heat, he severed all physical contact, and the insanity melted away.

"The kids need a woman around."

She was a fool. An honest-to-God fool. How many times did she have to get rejected before she learned her lesson?

She walked to the window, desperate to place a safe distance between her and the man who'd been toying with her heart ever since she'd been unlucky enough to grow boobs. "Glad to help." She sounded bitter, but she didn't care. She was tired of pining after Zach Ryler.

"Did you get the dog settled in?" He stood, placed his hands on his lower back, and stretched. The thin cotton fabric of his black T-shirt reached across his chest, outlining every delicious muscle. Long, lean, jean-clad legs just begged to be noticed.

Refusing to give them the satisfaction, she looked away. "I made a nice little area for him downstairs, but I think he prefers my bed."

"Can't say that I blame him."

She pinned him with a startled gaze.

"Who wouldn't prefer a soft mattress to a hard floor?" he clarified.

"For your information, I made him a bed. He's just being difficult. Luckily, I'm used to dealing with difficult males."

"You've known quite a few of them, have you?" Was that a note of jealousy she caught in his voice? Had he spent the last two years wondering, the way she had, who was warming her bed at night?

She was tempted to put him out of his misery and tell him Bolt was the first since he'd left her, but revenge was far too sweet. "Wouldn't you just love to know?"

A cryptic smile curved her lips at the proprietary look that fell to darken his features. Maybe he did care after all. Or maybe he didn't like the idea of someone else taking what was his. Some men were like that. Even though they didn't want a woman, they hated the thought of anyone else having her.

She glanced past the glass at the hazy sky. Boiling clouds smothered the stars, bringing with them the promise of rain. Come to think of it, the air itself smelled musty, cool and damp as it trickled in to fill her lungs.

"Looks like it's going to rain," she said, hoping to pierce the sudden silence that enveloped them.

He came to stand behind her, leaned over her shoulder and stole a glimpse of what lay beyond the window. Energy surged between them, made her skin prickle and a shiver glide along her spine. Swallowing a sigh, she embraced herself and rubbed away the stubborn goose bumps that had risen to pebble her flesh.

He moved in closer and slid his hands up her arms. "Are you cold?" His touch enfolded her like a pocket of sunshine, set off tiny explosions along her nerve endings. She closed her eyes and sank into it, powerless to resist its lure. Her back sought support from his chest as a thrilling current swept in to fuse their bodies together. He was hard and warm and familiar. He was everything she'd ever wanted and everything she could never have.

The sharp pain that lanced through her brought her back to her senses. She jerked out of his arms and nearly sped out of the room. "I should get some work done now that the kids are asleep." She sounded winded.

"Don't stay up too late. I know how you get when you start writing."

She edged to the door, reluctance pulling at her heels. It would have been so easy to stay here with him and let the memories devour her. So easy to fall right back into that old destructive pattern, full of fire and quiet desperation, rapture and heartache.

His loneliness sang to her, beat in perfect tune with her own, but she didn't allow its lovely strains to seduce her. She left him standing at the window, surrounded by navy blue shadows, with only the suffocating moon to light his face.

Part Two

Surrender

Ah, when to the heart of man
Was it ever less than a treason
To go with the drift of things,
To yield with a grace to reason,
And bow and accept the end
Of a love or a season?

Robert Frost, "Reluctance"

Chapter Nine

Raymond York wasn't one to ask questions. He did as he was told, followed the directives he was given with the cool detachment of a machine. He wasn't burdened by something as cumbersome as a conscience, didn't spend hours pondering things like ethical behavior or moral responsibility. He got the job done, pure and simple, and his employer always rewarded him with a thick wad of crisp hundred-dollar bills.

When his cell phone rang, he answered immediately. His last assignment had been one of those rare occasions when things hadn't gone according to plan, and he was eager to make it up to his boss. In his line of work, mistakes didn't get you a pink slip—they got you a bullet to the brain. If you were lucky.

"It's time," the man told him in a familiar voice that was both cultured and chilling. "I need that backup."

A sliver of apprehension lanced through Raymond, and he tightened his grip on the phone. "Are you sure he made one? Birch panicked when he saw me. He surrendered the information before I even asked for it."

"That's how I know he made a backup. Liam wouldn't have given in that easily, even for the sake of his wife." Silence stretched between them, thick and stifling. Then, "We wouldn't be in this bind if you'd done things right the first time."

Ice crusted along Raymond's spine. "I didn't have a choice. The neighbor showed up before I could search the place. If I hadn't left when I did, she would've discovered me."

"And if she had? You could have shot her, too."

True, he could have. But all that blood had turned his stomach. He'd been crippled by the overwhelming compulsion to race home and wash the unsavory stench from his flesh. Raymond usually made it a point to keep his intense aversion to blood a secret, even from his employer. Especially from his employer. He'd only divulged his particular weakness to the Birches because he'd known he was about to shoot them. With the wife, his aim had been dead on. Her heart had stopped instantly, stemming the flow of blood. The husband had been a different story.

Raymond thought fast. "I was afraid she called the cops when she ran back to her place to get the key—"

"Enough excuses. Stop wasting my time. Just get the job done."

With agile fingers, Raymond holstered his gun—the 9mm SIG he'd used to terminate the Birches. "When?"

"Tonight."

"And the kid?"

"Not yet. I don't want anyone to know you broke in. The last thing I need is for some gung-ho vigilante to start digging again."

Raymond understood. He wouldn't mess up this time. He couldn't.

His life depended on it.

The night was as deep as Zach's sleep was restless. Every so often, lightning flared beyond the bedroom window, but no rain pounded against the rooftop. Will slept soundly, temporarily spared from the teething pain that afflicted him more often than not.

Zach wasn't nearly as lucky.

Thoughts of Becca continued to torture him. He could still feel the imprint of her soft curves, the arousing fragrance of lavender and sage tickling his nostrils, the feathering caress of her fingers in his hair. His body had come alive, absorbing the sensations the way the earth absorbs water after a long drought, and now it was drunk with need.

For two years he'd denied himself the pleasure of a woman's body. He'd remained true to Becca even after the divorce was finalized. It didn't make one iota of a difference how many papers he signed. In his heart he was still married to her, and he always would be.

At first he'd missed her with a fierceness that bordered on physical pain. But in time his body had grown numb, and he'd slowly learned to live without her. Now, long-forgotten yearnings stirred within him, red-hot and insistent. All he could think about was going to her, slipping into her bed, touching her the way he knew she liked to be touched. It wouldn't be all that difficult to seduce her. He just had to glide his hand up the nape of her neck, massage the base of her skull, sprinkle moist kisses along the curve of her cheek and throat...

The taste of her filled him, the memory of it burning brighter than the sizzling blades of light cleaving the sky, and that snapped him back to reality quicker than a sharp slap. He was treading on dangerous ground, going places he'd sworn he'd never go again.

Had he made a mistake staying true to her? It wasn't that opportunities hadn't presented themselves. He'd had his share of seductive glances and heated innuendoes, not to mention overt offers, over the past two years. If he'd acted on one or more of them, would it have made it easier to move on? Maybe then he wouldn't be so tempted to do the very thing that could destroy the one woman he'd do anything to protect.

Cutting her loose had been the best gift he'd ever given her. He'd realized that, if nothing else, tonight. She'd said it herself; her heart was finally healing. If he gave in to temptation and made love to her, he risked breaking it all over again. Nothing was powerful enough to compel him to do that. Not even the pounding need inside him, screaming to be appeased.

He turned over in bed, tried to get comfortable even as desire fought to ensure he didn't. Outside, thunder boomed. Lightning lacerated the bruised sky. In the crib beside him, Will softly snored. And a few doors down the hall, barely a heartbeat away, the woman he ached for lay sleeping, oblivious to his torment.

The townhouse slept, swathed in gray gloom, the windows dark, save for the intermittent slash of lightning reflected in the glass. Behind him the night yawned, bottomless and hungry. With the help of his LAT-17 snap gun, Raymond disengaged the lock and crept inside, happy the new occupants hadn't had the good sense to install an alarm. Not that an alarm would have dissuaded him. Breaking and entering was his specialty. Still, no matter how adept he was at this sort of thing, he didn't consider himself a thief. Those days were behind him. Now he was a facilitator, the middleman. He got the job done, no matter how dirty, and in the process he kept his employer's hands clean.

Around him, silence pulsed like a living creature holding its breath. Oily shadows stretched across the floor and ceiling. His 9mm SIG was strapped to his belt, within easy reach should trouble arise, though he hoped not to have to use it. Another break-in would be sure to raise some eyebrows, and the last thing his boss wanted was for the cops to start connecting the dots.

There had been too many incidents already. First was the death of Adrien Gorski, the computer geek who had assisted Birch in his investigation. Raymond had learned that Gorski suffered from a heart condition and was on a drug called Digoxin. A few weeks ago he'd broken into the guy's house and made him ingest five times the recommended dose. Gorski had died of a heart attack that very night. Since the cause of death was obvious and given Gorski's medical history, the authorities hadn't bothered with an autopsy.

Then there had been the first attempt on Birch's life. When Raymond had gotten his orders, he'd devised a plan to get rid of the target without having to personally spill any blood. He'd punctured one of the tires on Birch's fully equipped Volvo sedan. The car had been new from the looks of it, the black paint gleaming in the morning sun, without a nick on it. It obviously paid to be a lawyer in Boston. But not as much as it paid to be a middleman.

Unfortunately, Birch had survived the car crash and had become more determined than ever to find the person behind it. If he'd been smart, he would have backed off. But he hadn't. The trip to Martha's Vineyard had sealed his fate...and that of his wife.

But three deaths were enough for one month. More bloodshed was sure to raise suspicion, so Raymond worked extra hard to be invisible. He wasn't the kind of man people normally noticed. He was of average height and build, with boyish features and a prominent forehead. There was nothing threatening or extraordinary about him, and that very commonness was what made him special. He could melt into a crowd as effectively as ice cream on a sunny day. That was the reason he was so good at what he did. When a crime was committed, no one spared him a second glance because he looked like any middle-aged accountant, someone's next-door neighbor, a dad or an uncle.

Tonight he was a ghost. He made no noise as he slid across the hardwood floor. The fabric of his pants didn't sigh when it brushed his legs. His breath was steady and silent.

So he couldn't help the surprise that rocked him when the sky thundered, and the house erupted in a fit of barking.

All of Raymond's instincts sharpened. Adrenaline coursed through him and, although he loathed the thought of using it, he drew great comfort from the reassuring weight of his gun.

Rebecca jolted awake. Her drowsy brain swam toward awareness. At the foot of her bed, Bolt barked up a storm, then bounded to the floor and scratched at the door.

Reluctantly crawling out of bed, she fought the irritation that swept over her. "Shh, you'll wake the children. It's just thunder."

A predatory growl rumbled in his throat.

With a sigh, she padded across the room and released him. Instantly, the animal lunged into the darkness and nearly flew down the stairs. She was about to return to bed when a thought struck her. What if nature called? The last thing she wanted was to have to clean up a puddle of pee or worse come morning.

Swiping her sleep-tousled hair from her face, she ignored the bed's beckoning call and followed the puppy downstairs.

Raymond didn't like surprises. He liked dogs even less. For some reason, as dumb as they looked, they weren't fooled by his boyish cheeks and winning smile. Most of them growled whenever they crossed his path, as if they could smell the stench of blood forever imprinted in his skin. They made him feel tainted, dirty, and if there was one thing Raymond couldn't stand, it was feeling unclean. He showered three times a day, sometimes more. He was obsessed with cleanliness and couldn't abide some stinking mutt looking down its snout at him.

Still, he had no intention of shooting the animal, no matter how much the worthless creature deserved it. That would leave an awful mess behind and draw undue attention to him.

"I don't want anyone to know you broke in," his employer had said. Raymond always followed orders. Except for the times when he had no choice but to improvise. He feared this might very well be one of those occasions.

A prickle of frustration needled his gut. Anywhere he hid, the canine was sure to sniff him out. His best bet was to make a speedy exit and leave the search for another day.

But the mutt had other ideas. It came tunneling down the stairs at the speed of a hurricane. Raymond had no choice but to seek refuge in the very room he'd come to search—Birch's home office. The walls seemed to narrow, swallow him whole. He could still smell the nauseating stench of death, see it spill to saturate the carpet, then slowly trickle toward the window...

A thin film of sweat formed on his brow. With the back of his hand, he swiped it away before it could leak into his eyes.

Keep it together. You have a job to do.

In the dark he made out the black silhouette of a desk, the back of a chair, a bookcase lining the far wall. From the heart of the room the twenty-four-inch computer monitor beckoned him. If Birch had made a backup of the hard drive he'd stolen, this is where he would have stored it. But would he have time to locate the information before the dog caught a whiff of his scent and alerted the new residents?

A bark exploded outside the door, followed by the persistent hiss of claws scraping wood.

It didn't look like it.

Rebecca had expected Bolt to make a beeline for the back door. Instead, she found him in front of the den. The fur on his back bristled, and a low, menacing snarl thrummed through his body.

Annoyance tumbled into alarm. What if a thief was in there? Or worse, what if Lindsay and Liam's killer had come back to finish the job he'd started? Ice-cold fear doused her. Voula's words echoed in her head: *"He wasn't there to rob them. He was there to kill them."*

She placed her ear to the door, heard nothing but her own ragged breathing.

You're being paranoid, she told herself. *Only an idiot would return to the scene of the crime.*

Unless he'd failed to get his hands on what he'd wanted the first time around.

Decisively, she inched away from the door. There was only one thing to do. Imitating Lindsay's quiet-as-a-mouse walk, she tiptoed to the kitchen, grabbed the phone and began to dial nine-one-one.

Chapter Ten

Zach awakened to the drilling sound of barking, drowned by the occasional bout of thunder. With a grunt, he dragged himself out of bed, checked on Will to find the baby still sound asleep, then trudged to the door. The racket was coming from downstairs.

"Damn dog." As if three kids didn't make enough of a ruckus. Now he had furball to contend with. If the mangy beast woke the kids, he'd have his balls sliced off.

He found the puppy barking and whimpering outside the office. Exasperated, he scooped the frantic animal in his arms, marched to the back door and tossed him outside.

He knew he couldn't very well leave him out there for long. It was bound to start raining at any minute. Still, he reveled in the temporary silence that settled over the house. Even the illusion of peace was better than none at all.

Rubbing the slumber from his eyes with his thumb and forefinger, he headed to the kitchen for a glass of water, hoping to wash the dryness from his mouth. That was when he saw Becca standing in a puddle of moonlight, clutching the phone.

"Who are you calling at this hour?"

She started, dropped the phone and spun around to face him. A mouthful of air whooshed out of her upon seeing him. "Don't sneak up on me like that. You scared me half to death." She shot a curious look at the door. "What happened to Bolt?"

"I put him outside. He was going to wake the kids with all that caterwauling."

She bent over and retrieved the phone, giving him a nice view of her backside. The desire that had battered him for hours before he'd finally drifted off to sleep returned full-force to clobber him.

"I think there's an intruder in the house. I'm trying to call nine-one-one, but all I'm getting is static."

"Let's not be hasty. Let me check it out—"

Her hand clamped over his arm. "Don't."

She'd forgotten to put on her robe. The thin cotton tank top she wore clung to her breasts, outlining every delicious curve, straining over her nipples. Heat lanced through him.

He pried his gaze away before he was tempted to reach out and touch. "I'm sure everything's in order. The dog probably freaked because of the storm."

"What if you're wrong? There's no reason to chance it." She tapped the numeric keypad, then grunted in frustration. "Why is this phone not working?"

"It's the weather. Ever since the bastard cut the line, it hasn't worked right. When humidity gets in, it goes down. I haven't gotten around to calling the phone company so they can service it again."

"Give me your cell phone. I still haven't charged mine."

"It's in the office—"

"Forget it. He's in there."

"Who's in there?"

"The burglar."

Zach rolled his eyes. "Did you have one of your vivid dreams again?"

She punched him on the arm, hard. "This is no time to kid around. What if Lindsay and Liam's killer came back?"

Her words shocked the humor right out of him. "What kind of moron breaks into the same house twice?"

"This one, apparently." Dismay raced across her face. "Oh, no. The kids are alone upstairs. I have to go check on them." She flung open a drawer and withdrew a scary-looking knife that made the hairs on the nape of Zach's neck bristle.

Paranoia was obviously contagious. A million-and-one chilling scenarios raced across his mind. He was a damn idiot not to have had that alarm system installed. He'd gotten quotes weeks ago, but with the funeral to plan and the children to look after, he hadn't gotten around to scheduling anything. "We'll check on them together," he said.

Becca led the way, her arm stretched out in front of her, the long blade slicing the air as she advanced. They made their way to all three bedrooms and ensured that all three children lay safe and snug in their beds.

"See, everything's fine," he told her. "There's no one in the house apart from us." He wasn't sure who he was trying to reassure—her or himself.

She didn't look convinced. A frown creased her forehead. "There's one room we still haven't checked." Her freckled nose puckered with distaste. "The office."

"I'll do it. You stay up here and keep an eye on the kids."

She bit her lower lip in alarm. "Wait. Take the knife."

"You need it more than I do."

"But what if he's armed?"

"Then I'll just have to disarm him."

A dubious expression drenched her features. "With what?"

"With these." He showed her his hands. "They may look harmless, but don't let that fool you. These babies are lethal weapons."

She snorted a laugh. "You're a runner, not a kung fu master."

If he weren't so tired, he would have been offended by her obvious lack of faith in his strength and virility. "Then you've got nothing to worry about. If push comes to shove, I can always outrun him."

Raymond lovingly ran his palm over the computer monitor. The dog had stopped barking, and he briefly allowed himself to hope that the threat of discovery had passed. He attached his zip drive to the USB port and punched in a few keys. Within minutes he would have a copy of Liam Birch's entire hard drive. That way his boss would know for sure that Raymond had found Birch's backup, if indeed one existed. His boss had asked him to wipe the drive clean, but he had a better idea. He'd simulate a system crash instead. The next time someone tried to access the computer, all they'd get would be a blank screen.

With any luck, he'd be out of here soon, away from the blood-tainted room and the sickening memories it triggered. His skin prickled at the thought. He couldn't wait to get home and shower. Once he scrubbed the pervasive stench away, he'd change into his silk pajamas and sleep, smelling of citrus and sandalwood.

The tempting thought scratched at his patience. His glance darted to the screen. Only twenty-five percent of the files had been downloaded. Footsteps echoed outside, accompanied by the hushed drone of conversation. Anticipation tangled with frustration to irritate his ulcer. If the machine didn't speed up, he'd surely be discovered. Then he'd have to shoot his way out, which did little to comfort him.

At least the dog was gone. He didn't know if he was fast enough to shoot a dog. A German Shepherd had jumped him once, and he still had the scars to prove it.

Thirty percent and climbing.

"Come on," he muttered under his breath. "Speed up, you worthless piece of junk."

Outside, rain began to fall, a slow drizzle that pitter-pattered on the glass. Soon water would bullet toward the earth with the force of a machine gun. He'd most likely get soaked walking the two blocks to his car. He didn't mind getting wet. What he minded was getting dirty. Rain was polluted, riddled with germs and chemicals and all kinds of unthinkable things.

Forty percent.

At this rate he'd be here all night.

The storm roared. Lightning flashed beyond the glass. Somewhere in the distance the dog barked. Raymond fisted his hands against his thighs, swallowed his impatience and waited.

As if reacting to a sudden electrical surge, the computer sped up.

Just as he was about to rejoice, the whisper of footsteps resonated beyond the door. Raymond's fingers unclenched and swiftly rose to settle on the butt of his SIG.

Chapter Eleven

Silence stretched, thick and palpable, and that only made the thunder louder when it boomed. The walls themselves seemed to shake, as if a giant hand fought to pry the house from the ground. Zach grabbed a baseball bat from the hall closet and approached the office door. He knew a bat was no match for a semi-automatic, but he figured he had the element of surprise on his side. Plus, he had a pretty good arm. If he managed to swing before the son of a bitch pulled the trigger, he actually stood a chance.

He put his head to the door, listened for the telltale signs of an intruder. Then, raising the bat, he pushed the door open and lunged into the room, ready to strike.

Inky darkness greeted him. He could've sworn he'd left the computer on, but the monitor sat on the desk blacker than death. Maybe they'd experienced a brief power outage while they'd slept.

He turned on the lights, inched farther into the room. Everything seemed in order. No drawers had been opened, no furniture overturned or papers scattered. He searched every corner of the den to find it deserted.

The tension drained from his limbs. He'd been right all along. No one had slunk into the house in the middle of the night. The dog had simply reacted to the thunderstorm.

Rain tap-danced on the window sill. The damp scent of humidity tickled his nose, just as a draft planted an icy kiss on the nape of his neck. Zach turned to find the window wide open. He rushed to close it, unable to recall if he'd shut it before going to bed. He couldn't imagine leaving it open with a storm brewing. Then again, a lot of things seemed to be slipping his mind lately.

He left the office, reassured yet slightly uneasy, and hastened to the back door to let the dog in. As soon as Bolt entered the house, he sprinted to the office and sniffed at the floor. How the animal managed to smell anything past the odor of dog and rain that clung to his shiny wet coat was a mystery.

"Come on, furball." The puppy whined as Zach hooked an arm under his belly and lifted him off his feet. "Time for bed."

He placed the dog in the basket Becca had fashioned for him, then closed the door to the basement so he couldn't escape. Next, he checked the rest of the house, made sure all the locks were engaged and the windows shut. When he was convinced he'd taken care of everything, he rubbed the strain from his neck and trudged upstairs, happy another crisis had been averted.

Two blocks away, Raymond York made a phone call. "I've got it." Water pelted on his windshield, reminding him he was soaked, covered in germs. The same germs now rolled off him to contaminate his car. He'd have to have the interior shampooed again.

"Good." His employer's relief resonated in Raymond's ear. "Did you wipe the hard drive clean?"

"Better. I crashed the system."

An unsettling pause followed. "That's not what I asked you to do." The reproach in his boss's voice was unmistakable.

Raymond's hackles rose. "If I'd erased all the files, they would have gotten suspicious. This way is better. There's a thunderstorm tonight. They'll just blame the crash on a power surge."

His boss didn't respond, but Raymond felt the other man's frustration rippling through the line as surely as the white flashes slicing the sky. "Bring me the files."

That was the last thing he said before the phone went dead.

"So," Becca asked the moment Zach made his way upstairs, "was someone there?"

"Nope. Just an open window and some rain."

She didn't look convinced. "Are you sure?"

Weariness slowly seeped in to replace adrenaline. "I went through the whole place with a fine-toothed comb. Trust me, everything's fine." The open window still nagged at him, but he decided to attribute his restlessness to paranoia and a bad case of fatigue and leave it at that.

"Did you let Bolt in?"

"I locked him in the basement. Where he'll spend the rest of the night," he added in the event she entertained the notion of springing him. "The last thing we need is for his *super bark* to wake the kids. I'm surprised they slept through all this racket."

Becca nodded her acquiescence. "What now?"

"Now we go to bed."

Heat flickered in her eyes, and his gaze couldn't help but wander downward. He took in the sight of her full breasts—barely concealed by that tiny top—her flat belly, the gentle flare of her hips, and an altogether different kind of tension crawled through his veins. He hadn't meant to suggest they go to bed together, but the implication was there, hovering like a tangible mist between them.

She cleared her throat, took a step away from him. "I'll just head back to my room then." Was that a note of hesitation in her voice?

"See you in the morning," he replied before he was tempted to join her.

"Sure. In the morning." With a quirk of the lips, which he interpreted as an attempt at a smile, she inched toward her bedroom.

When the door closed behind her, his shoulders slumped in relief. Things were getting way too complicated for his liking.

As exhaustion and desire dueled inside him, he sought the safe comfort of his own room. He'd barely managed to stretch out on the twin mattress and close his eyes when the door opened and Becca sailed in.

"Zach," she intoned so softly he barely heard her. "Are you awake?"

"That seems to be a permanent state with me."

The mattress sagged as she sat beside him. A long, unsettling pause followed. He was aware of each inhalation she drew, the whisper of her pajama bottoms as they brushed his sheets. Her familiar fragrance wafted toward him, soothed and enfolded him like a long-lost friend. "I'm glad you weren't hurt," she finally confessed.

All the feelings he'd crammed into a ball and buried deep within him unraveled all at once. It had been so long since someone had worried about him, since someone had sat at his bedside and whispered softly to him. His resolve ruptured from the weight of his loneliness, until only need and tenderness remained.

"Ah, Becca..." He reached up and cupped her cheek, let his fingers venture into the sinful web of hair on her head to settle at the base of her skull. Then he drew her to him.

Their lips met in a furious explosion of fire and need. She tasted the same—sweet and seductive, moist and inviting. Kissing her was like coming home. He couldn't get enough of her mouth, her tongue, the feel of those fire-kissed curls caressing his arm. He was lost, adrift in an ocean where desire ruled, where thought ceased to be and only sensation mattered.

The past blurred. Nothing existed but this moment. He trailed his fingers down her throat, slid them over her shoulder. His blood pounded to the rhythm of his heart, fast and furious. The hunger to savor and possess, to cherish and devour assailed him. He hooked his thumb beneath the strap of her tank top and yanked it down, exposing a perfect white breast.

She sucked in a breath, broke the kiss. "Zach, what are we doing?" Her voice was throaty, short and winded.

"I don't know." He ran his mouth over her cheek, kissed the sensitive spot behind her ear, traced the curve of her neck with his lips. "All I know is that I don't want to stop."

She sighed and went liquid against him. Heat thrummed between them—a living, breathing thing that screamed to be acknowledged. A groan vibrated deep in his throat, and he palmed her breast, loving the weight of it, the warmth of it as it filled his hand. He wanted to draw her nipple into his mouth, to bury himself in her hot, tight folds and drown in her softness. He wanted it so bad every inch of him ached.

In one smooth sweep he spun her on the bed beneath him. She was warm and supple and willing. Fervency shone in her eyes as she raised her chin to kiss him. He trapped her lower lip between his teeth, nipped and tugged at it lightly. She made a sound that was thin and eager and entirely feminine, then arched her hips against his, only stoking the flames consuming him.

"Lord, I've missed you," he mumbled against her mouth. Desperate to feel flesh on flesh, heat on heat, he reached down, began to peel off her pajama bottoms...

Then a shrill wail rang out and snapped them out of their daze.

Will was awake.

A string of choice curses zipped through Zach's brain, but he refrained from voicing them. With a pained grunt, he eased himself off the bed, took a minute or two to quiet the roar of his pulse, then turned his back to the bewitching woman wrapped in his sheets. He needed to get a hold of himself, and gazing down at her swollen lips and exposed breasts wasn't the way to do it. A cold shower would do the trick, but he doubted Will would be that patient.

When his blood cooled, settling from scorching hot to a slow simmer, he made his way to the crib and lifted the crying toddler.

The baby kicked and punched at him, nearly choking on his sobs. "Mama, Mama, Mama..."

This was nothing new. Will often awoke in a state of panic, calling for his mother. Sometimes it took nearly an hour to soothe him and get him back to sleep. Zach tamped down his exhaustion and prepared for another sleepless night.

Becca, who'd straightened her clothing and crawled out of bed, came to stand beside him. She watched Will with unmasked distress. "Why is he so upset? Is he sick?"

"Yeah." Zach cradled Will, even as the baby fought to break free. "Heartsick." He held him close to his chest and comforted him as best he could, knowing full well it wasn't his comfort the toddler craved.

She said nothing, but he felt her anguish, saw it in the way she raised her fingers to her lips and in the soft shimmer that came into her eyes. "Can I hold him?"

Her words nearly knocked him off his feet. "Are you sure?"

She nodded meekly. "I want to try."

Reluctantly, he passed her the child. She held him awkwardly at first, as if she didn't quite know what to do with him. Will struggled against her, shoved her away with his small fists, used his feet to climb up her ribs and push with all his might. Still, she held on, gently stroking his back. She walked to the rocking chair, which squatted at the far corner of the room, and sank into it with the baby safely tucked in her arms. Then she began to rock him, humming softly. Peace descended upon the house, silent and glorious. Will relaxed and closed his eyes, but even after he fell asleep, Becca continued to hold him next to her heart.

From across the room Zach watched her. He noted how naturally the child fit in the crook of her elbow, how his head nested against her shoulder and his legs curled over hers. They looked like one being, fused by tenderness, two pieces of a puzzle merging to find completion.

And for the first time, he understood.

He understood her pain, her longing, her emptiness, the senseless despair that had gripped her, and something inside him died a small death. Never before had he wished so ardently that he could give her everything she wanted, everything she needed to be whole. All he'd ever given her were false reassurances and a truckload of grief.

Crushed by the weight of his regret, he ate up the distance between them and fell to his knees beside her. Her eyelids were closed, but he knew she was awake because fresh tears glistened on her cheeks. Words rarely evaded him as they did now. Maybe there weren't any words to express how he felt. Instead, he simply rested his head in her lap.

She meshed her fingers in his hair and caressed him the way she had the baby. Zach closed his eyes and allowed her touch to heal the wounds inflicted by loss, the thin scars of remorse he would forever bear. A lulling serenity settled over him, and he, too, drifted effortlessly to sleep.

They stayed like that well into the night—man, woman and child joined as one—until the pale rays of dawn spilled into the room and the sun peeked over the clouds to shed its milky light.

Chapter Twelve

The violent rainfall had ended, but humidity lingered, speckling the trees with dew. Grass and flower petals shimmered in the early morning sun, despite the thin haze that clung to the ground. Everything appeared new, cleansed and reborn.

Rebecca sat on the back porch, sipping her coffee as she watched the children play with Bolt. A brisk breeze made the trees shiver, and she drew the sides of her jacket closer together. The day would warm up eventually, but now a biting chill still hovered in the air.

After last night she should have been exhausted. Instead, a strange energy coursed through her. Memories of Zach's touch, Zach's kisses, fueled a firestorm deep inside her. Every inch of her skin burned. She hadn't felt anything like this in years, and she didn't quite know what to do with it. Emotions she'd never expected to experience again saturated her bloodstream, tied her up in knots.

She felt like a teenager—awkward, antsy, ruled by hormones and impossible fantasies. She didn't want to go down that path again. She'd walked it many times before, and at the end, only pain awaited her. It was dangerous to love a man too much. It gave him the power to raise you to unrivaled heights of bliss and the power to destroy you. There was no happy medium, no safety net. Only pulse-pounding highs and soul-shattering lows. She'd had more than her share of disappointments and heartbreaks. She didn't think she could survive another.

Will hobbled toward her and grabbed hold of her leg for support, then gave her a drool-drenched smile. The knots in her belly tightened. She still couldn't believe she'd held him last night, rocked him to sleep. The fact that he'd actually found her embrace soothing filled her with pride.

If the truth be told, she'd drawn as much comfort from the act as he. His soft cheek snuggled against her breast, the feel of his little body going boneless in her arms had warmed her like a blanket on a cold winter's day. Twin blades of joy and pain had knifed through her, making the experience as bitter as it was sweet. She desperately wanted to open her heart to these children, to give them all the love she'd stored up for the ones she'd never have, and yet she was terrified to do so.

She wasn't their mother and never would be. What if they didn't return her love? What if she lost them? She knew she couldn't live with Zach forever. Sooner or later she'd have to move out. Then she'd have no choice but to walk away from the kids as well. She didn't think she was strong enough to live with that kind of loss. Her best bet was to keep her heart out of it.

Will cooed and raised his arms to her. She bit her lower lip as her resolve disintegrated. Reluctantly, she reached for him and drew him onto her lap. Liquid warmth swam through her veins. Before she could stop herself, she feathered a kiss over the scraggy yellow mop on his head.

She closed her eyes to block out the glaring light of the sun, but it continued to dance along her eyelids. She snickered at the irony. Shutting these kids out of her heart was about as futile as hiding from the light...or quelling her love for their uncle.

Zach walked onto the porch, a hot cup of coffee clasped between his fingers. Barks, yowls and giggles greeted him. Noah and Kristen were playing ball with the dog. He couldn't help but smile at the sight. These last couple of days were the first he'd seen them happy in weeks. He didn't know how long it would last. The novelty of the puppy would wear off eventually, and reality would creep in to steal their joy again. Helplessness was a bitter pill to swallow. There was nothing he wouldn't give to preserve their innocence, but he couldn't. Tragedy had found them and stolen it from them. Particularly Noah.

"You look refreshed." Becca's voice jarred him out of his thoughts. He hadn't noticed her sitting on the porch with Will in her lap.

"Considering the night we had, I feel pretty invigorated."

"Must be the rain. It has a way of renewing everything." Will tugged at her hair, then placed the lock in his mouth. Becca flinched and slowly pried it free from his gums.

"Still letting him slobber all over you, I see."

"What can I say? I'm a sucker for a dreamy pair of blue eyes and a toothless grin."

Zach smiled. "Remind me never to get dentures." Again, he was struck by the image of Becca with the baby in her arms. It reminded him of last night, of the way he'd fallen asleep with his head buried in her lap and her fingers twined in his hair.

Heat trickled down his neck to pool in his chest. He couldn't remember the last time he'd slept so peacefully, even with his legs folded awkwardly beneath him and his body half sprawled across the floor. He should've felt like a total wreck this morning, but he didn't. He felt better than he had in years.

"You two seem to have hit it off."

She graced him with a wobbly smile. "I think the fact that I'm scared out of my wits makes me less intimidating."

Laughter scratched at his throat. "Then why does he scream bloody murder every time I get within two feet of him?"

"Maybe you're trying too hard. You're so determined to do everything right you're shooting yourself in the foot."

Her statement floored him. He'd never looked at it that way before.

She traced the curve of Will's ear with unmasked tenderness, then leaned back in her chair. "You have to let them come to you."

Defeat weighed heavy on his shoulders. "What if they never do?"

"Then you'll just have to accept it." A glance, laden with meaning, passed between them. "Who ever said love was easy?"

She had him there. In his experience, love brought nothing but grief. Still, the heart kept right on loving. There was no organ more self-destructive, more addicted to pain. He'd proven that last night when he'd kissed her. He should have known better, he should have kept his hands off her, but fatigue and loneliness had conspired against him. Now he couldn't get the taste of her out of his mouth.

As if sensing his thoughts, she averted her gaze. Trembling sunlight spilled over her, set her curls on fire. She'd always hated the copper highlights in her hair. Once, ages ago, she'd gone and dyed it a nasty shade of mousy brown. He'd been mad as hell. Spent the better part of the year harassing her until she'd given in and gone back to her natural shade. Thankfully, she hadn't messed with it again after that.

"It's my turn," Kristen's voice rang out. "Give it to me."

"You throw like a girl." Noah tauntingly dangled the ball over his sister's head, while Kristen struggled to grasp it. She rose on the tips of her toes, jumped several times to no avail. Then the exasperating boy flung it across the yard. At lightning speed, the dog scampered over the lawn in eager pursuit.

"Not fair," the girl screamed. "It was my turn."

Both children galloped after the animal. Wagging his tail, Bolt dropped the ball. Noah and Kristen simultaneously lunged for it, tripping over each other to wrestle in the damp grass.

A sparrow screeched from one of the trees above as a fat cloud scuttled across the sun. Below, the two children kicked and screamed. The dog stood beside them, round-eyed, his tongue lolling while he followed the ball with his gaze. Fed up with being ignored, he released an indignant bark.

Zach gulped down his coffee, took a second to savor it, then plowed across the lawn to break up the fight.

Another day had officially begun.

Noah hated being treated like a kid. He was nine years old—big enough to make his own decisions. Tomorrow Uncle Zach was forcing him to go back to summer camp, when all he wanted to do was stay home and play his video games. Why did he have to go to stupid summer camp anyway? The truth was, his aunt and uncle wanted to get rid of him.

And why wouldn't they?

His own parents hadn't wanted him around. He was too much trouble, too loud, always scrapping it out with Kristen. He argued, refused to do as he was told. He tried to be good, he really did, but his true nature always got the better of him. He wished he could be sweet like Kristen or cute like Will. He wished he could make people smile. Instead, all he seemed to do was make everyone angry.

He was angry, too, all the time. Everyone got on his nerves, especially his douche bag sister. Uncle Zach had sent him to his room for fighting with Kristen again. Now he was bored out of his wits. His uncle had forced him to turn over his Game Boy, so he had nothing but Lego and stuffed animals to help pass the time. He was too old for stuffed animals, and he'd had his fill of Lego for the day.

He shuffled to the door and peeked outside. Nothing but silence greeted him. Maybe Uncle Zach and Aunt Becca were still out in the yard. He took a few tentative steps into the corridor, closed his bedroom door behind him and stole a look over the railing. The house seemed empty.

All the better for him.

Quietly, he scurried down the stairs and sneaked into his dad's office, where the computer—and Night-Owl—waited. Night-Owl would understand why he was so bummed. Unlike him, his friend got to play on the computer all day long. He didn't have to go to stupid summer camp. He could do whatever he wanted. Night-Owl's parents were way cooler than his own had been, way cooler than Uncle Zach and Aunt Becca.

Feeling guilty for thinking this way, Noah peered over his shoulder, booted up the computer, then settled into the chair. Nothing happened. The screen seemed to be dead. All he got was an endless sea of blue.

Panic screamed through him. Before he could stop it, a shrill cry blasted from his mouth. "Uncle Zach!"

Noah's scream tumbled from the open window, and Zach jackknifed to his feet. With long strides he bridged the distance to the house and hastened inside, expecting a disaster of inordinate proportions. Maybe the kid had cut himself, broken a leg or set the house on fire. Anything was possible with Noah. Instead he found him in the office in a state of panic, slapping the computer screen and knocking the mouse on the desk.

Frustration nibbled at his patience. "What are you doing in here?"

"The computer. It's dead. I can't get it to work." The tears he fought not to shed trembled in his voice.

Zach approached the boy and assessed the blank screen. "What did you do?"

"Nothing. I just booted it up. It's not my fault!"

Zach struggled to stay calm. "Move aside. Let me take a look at it." For once Noah listened.

Zach fiddled with the keypad, then tried rebooting the machine with zero success. "I think it crashed." The power outage they'd had last night was probably to blame. That was why the computer had been off, when he specifically recalled leaving it on. An electrical surge could have easily fried the hard drive.

"But everything's in there. My games, all the pictures—" His voice hitched. A sob quivered in the boy's chest.

Suddenly, he understood the source of his nephew's distress. If he'd reacted so passionately to a broken picture frame, how would he react to losing every snapshot ever taken of his parents? Zach's heart withered at the thought.

"I sent out a bunch of shots yesterday to be developed," he reassured him. "I even downloaded a handful of them on your iPod." He opened the desk drawer and withdrew the device in question.

The boy's face instantly brightened. For a second Zach thought he was going to hug him. Instead, he reached for the iPod, holding it with such care one would think it was made of fine crystal. His fingers shook as he turned it on. Zach leaned in and promptly showed him where he'd saved the files.

A weak smile throbbed on Noah's lips when the pictures appeared on the small screen. "They're not gone," he whispered.

Zach tenderly squeezed his nephew's shoulder. "No, they're not gone."

The office building was exceptionally quiet, empty save for one man sitting at his desk. Cars sped below, but he was too high up to hear the roar of motors revving beneath their hoods, the shriek of brakes or the occasional honking of a horn. Beyond his window, the city yawned, vibrant and alive, yet he failed to see any of it.

His gaze was riveted to his computer monitor, across which all his secrets stretched like a goddamn exposé—names, dates, even faces. A spool of anger threaded with admiration unfurled inside him. Liam had been nothing if not thorough.

He'd made one mistake, and the bastard had rounded on him like a bloodhound on the hunt. The traitor had dug up everything he'd spent years cleverly concealing. And here it was, contaminating his screen, every sordid detail that could earn him life in prison and bring down the intricate global network that was his livelihood.

But luck had been on his side. He'd intercepted a phone call meant for Liam and had put two and two together before any serious damage was done.

He should've known better than to underestimate Liam, should've stuck to his game plan. But after years of avoiding discovery, he'd grown confident, hungry for a challenge.

He'd gotten his wish. Liam had proved a more formidable opponent than he'd ever anticipated. Now that that particular thorn in his side was gone, he felt empty, void of purpose. Especially since York had decided to fry Liam's hard drive.

He told himself it was for the best. The smartest thing to do was to walk away and never look back. There were other challenges to be had.

Swiveling around in his chair, he stared out at the bustling city below. A bitter burn spread to coat the walls of his stomach. Why then was it so difficult to let go?

Chapter Thirteen

The next few days were uneventful, quiet except for the odd scuffle between the kids. Noah and Kristen returned to summer camp after a two-week sabbatical, giving Zach enough time to take care of some of the things he'd neglected—including packing up Lindsay's and Liam's belongings. He hadn't wanted to undertake the painful task while the kids were at home. He could only imagine how traumatic it would be for them to watch him get rid of their parents' stuff, especially for Kristen, who fully expected them to return one day.

Hell, it was traumatic for him. Every item he touched reminded him of his sister—the red jersey dress she'd worn last Christmas, the cashmere sweater and matching scarf he'd given her for her birthday, the scruffy slippers she'd had since she was a teen because she just couldn't bear to part with them. Each item told a story. Each was a testament to the short life she'd led. Each carried the faint hint of her perfume.

He didn't understand how scent had such power to evoke emotion and dredge up old memories. How it slid long-reaching fingers inside him and somehow turned back the hands of time. The medley of aromas in his mother's kitchen still haunted him. To this day he couldn't smell waffles and coffee without being reduced to childhood.

He placed sweaters, slacks, shoes and any other item his sister had seen fit to crowd in her closet into a nondescript cardboard box. This was what life was ultimately reduced to—a cardboard box. The thought depressed him. There was nothing like death to put everything into perspective and remind you just how pointless life was. All the hours he'd wasted stressing over a campaign gone wrong, losing sleep over a bad print job or a poorly executed ad, pointless. He was a damned moron. He should have found a way to make every second matter. Especially the years he'd had with Becca.

In answer to his thoughts, she padded into the bedroom. The expression on her face was as grim as his musings.

"Did you get Will to sleep?" he asked.

She nodded. "It took a while. I think he's teething." She shuffled closer and kneeled beside him. "How are things coming along in here?"

"As well as can be expected. I'm almost done packing up Lindsay's things." His voice rang flat, void of the turmoil raging within him.

She reached into the box, pulled out an alligator pump. A nostalgic mist rolled over her eyes. "I was with her when she bought these. She always wanted alligator pumps, but they were too expensive. Then she found these. They're imitations, but you can't really tell." Her throat worked as she swallowed. "God, it was so long ago, but it feels like yesterday."

She tenderly placed the shoe back in the box, shook her head. "We don't realize how quickly time flies, how fragile life is."

"I was just thinking the same thing. We gotta make every minute count." His gaze settled on her face. "Life is a gift, even when it feels like a burden."

She met his stare, and an unspoken memory slid between them— the day he'd come home to find her passed out in bed with a bottle of sleeping pills on her nightstand and a blanket slung across her hips. She'd been pale as death, completely unresponsive. If he hadn't gotten her to the hospital in time...

The thought was too black to even contemplate. A world without Becca was like a world without light. He'd realized two things that day: leaving her was the only way to save her, and he loved her enough to let her go.

"You still don't believe that it was an accident," she said, her voice made husky by disappointment. "That I didn't try to kill myself."

When she'd awakened she'd explained to him and the doctors that she'd been having trouble sleeping. No sedative had been strong enough to dull the sharp edge of her anxiety. So she'd tripled the recommended dose.

"I never meant for things to turn out that way," she insisted. "I just wanted to sleep."

He would have liked nothing more than to take her word for it, but he couldn't help but think that on a subconscious level she'd wanted to end things. That was how deep she'd sunk into depression.

She watched him, waiting for a reaction he couldn't give. Then her shoulders sagged with defeat and she dug into the box again. She withdrew an old college T-shirt and hugged it the way she would a person, with both arms crossed over her chest.

"I wasted so much time hurting," she said, "being angry. I pushed everyone that ever mattered to me away. I just wish—" Her voice faltered. "I wish I could tell her how sorry I am."

He slid his hand up her back. "You don't have to. Lindsay knew how you felt about her. That's why she entrusted you with her children. Every time you smile at Noah or take Kristen's hand or rock

Will to sleep, you're making amends."

With a jerky nod, she lowered the T-shirt onto her lap and folded it. "Do you mind if I keep this?"

"Go right ahead. I kept several things myself. I even put some aside for the kids."

She traced the college emblem with her index finger. "Kristen sleeps with Lindsay's favorite sweater."

"I know." His sides throbbed, as if he'd just taken a swift jab to the ribs. "I've seen her."

She closed her eyes, inhaled deep and hard. "How will they ever survive this?"

Zach let his arm fall away. Bitterness slid down his throat to burn a hole in his stomach. "They just will. They don't have a choice."

Rebecca never realized how loud children could be, especially in the small confines of a car. She'd just picked up Noah and Kristen from summer camp, and they hadn't clammed up for a second. Every scream echoed off the glass and ceiling to pummel her brain. Every whine nudged her anxiety up to a perilous high.

"Look, Aunt Becca," Kristen's excited voice trilled from the backseat. "I've got wak in my ear."

In the rearview mirror, Rebecca saw Noah roll his eyes. "It's wax, not wak."

His sister ignored him and dug her pinkie into her ear canal for another scrumptious find. "Look, more wak."

"Wax!" Noah insisted.

"Is wak bad for you?"

"Yeah," her brother piped up. "It makes you deaf. I told you it's called wax." He then leaned over and knocked her across the head. "That's a whack."

At which point Kristen let out a howl that made the car shake and Rebecca's head throb. She made a mental note to pick up a lifetime supply of Advil the next time she was at a drugstore.

When they finally got to the townhouse, an insane rush of relief flooded her system. Bolt greeted them at the door with a wet tongue and a frantic wag of his tail. The children, ecstatic to see their new pet, took off at a dash, apparently having forgotten their little disagreement in the car.

If only life could be that simple for adults.

Rebecca dragged herself to the living room and collapsed into the nearest armchair. Seconds later Zach popped in to say hi, with a drooling Will perched in the crook of his arm.

"How was pick-up duty?" he asked.

"I think I'd rather schedule a root canal tomorrow."

He laughed, and the walls of her heart gave way at the seams. She'd always loved his laugh. It was deep and gravelly and soulful. The mere sound of it made her body grow warm and molten.

She dug into her bag to distract herself. "I picked up the pictures at Walmart." She withdrew several thick stacks from her purse. "How many did you have developed?"

"Almost all of them."

"I figured as much. They gave me over twenty envelopes. I barely managed to fit them in my purse."

He placed Will on the rug, and the toddler wasted no time staggering to his feet. "Really? I would've bet good money you could fit an entire filing cabinet in there."

"Very funny." She dropped the envelopes on the coffee table, then selected one and began rifling through the prints. "You actually went through all these photos? There are hundreds of them."

"I didn't open each and every file. I just selected a bunch of them and sent them off. Knowing Liam, I figured he would have deleted anything not worth printing."

She couldn't help but smile at that. "He was pretty anal, wasn't he?"

A lopsided grin tugged at his sensual mouth. "He preferred the term *organized.*"

"Yes, of course. That's precisely what I meant. Organized."

Will hobbled to the coffee table, grabbed one of the thick envelopes, and began chewing on it. Zach snatched it from his eager little fingers. "Oh, no you don't. Chew on this instead." He handed him a fat carrot. Will wailed in frustration and pitched the vegetable. It spiraled through the air and landed in Rebecca's lap.

"He's got quite an arm," she quipped. "I see baseball in his future."

"Not to mention a food fight or two."

The lighthearted banter felt good. It had been years since they'd been at ease with each other. There was a time when she could talk to Zach about anything. They hadn't only been lovers, but friends. After they'd separated, that friendship was one of the things she'd missed the most.

He crept up beside her and glanced over her shoulder at the snapshots. Silence congealed around them as they both gazed down at happier times. Most of the photographs were of the children, but once in a while Lindsay's or Liam's face would smile up at them. It was hard to look at them, but she forced herself to do just that. She never wanted to forget her best friend or the times they'd shared, no matter how much it hurt to remember.

She tossed the pictures back into the envelope and selected

another one. This stack held a few older shots. There was one of her and Zach taken a few Christmases ago. Her fingers curled around the edges of the photograph as she absorbed the sight of herself snuggled against the husband she'd adored. Funny, from the way he was looking at her, she almost believed he'd loved her, too.

"We always did look good together." His words made the air above her head shiver.

"It takes more than looking good together to make a marriage work." Bitterness slid into her voice. "A lot more."

"If I remember correctly, we had it all for a while."

Her fingers stilled. She tilted her chin upward to look at him. "Did we?"

"I always thought so...until—" He paused.

"Until I ruined everything by wanting children?"

"No, until you decided to throw it all away by swallowing a mouthful of pills." There was steel in his tone, peppered with disappointment and an unvoiced whisper of anger.

"So we're back to that again." She threw the pictures onto the table, but her aim was off and they fluttered to the ground. "What will it take for you to believe me?"

"It doesn't matter what your intentions were. The result was the same. You nearly died...in my arms."

Rebecca fell to her knees and began gathering the photographs she'd dropped. The task kept her hands occupied, but most importantly, it kept her from seeing the unmasked recrimination in Zach's gaze. "I didn't."

"You could have. If I'd gotten home a few minutes later—"

"I made an error in judgment. How long are you going to punish me for it?" Her insides shook with pain and rage.

He squatted beside her, gripped her by the shoulders and forced her to look at him. "Is that what you think I'm doing? Punishing you? Goddammit, Becca, I saved you."

Pure bafflement swept through her. "Saved me how?"

"I set you free. As long as we stayed married, you would have longed for something that could never be. It would have destroyed you. Hell, it almost did. So I crushed the dream before it could swallow you." His expression darkened, and the truth glimmered in the ocean-blue depths of his eyes. "And after all is said and done, you still have no idea what it cost me."

Shock erupted inside her. He really believed what he was telling her. Had he actually abandoned her out of some idiotic sense of valor? How could he have convinced himself that pulverizing her heart would save her? The stupid, stupid man.

He palmed her cheek, stroked her with his thumb. This was one of those rare times when naked vulnerability shone on his face. The thin thread of restraint inside her snapped. Tossing the pictures aside, she bracketed his jaw and kissed him. She kissed him long and hard and tender. She kissed him until he stopped fighting the crazy attraction between them and kissed her back.

He tumbled to his knees as he continued drinking from her mouth. His arm swooped around her waist, and he drew her hard against him. She felt the outline of every delicious muscle on his chest, the rippled surface of his abdomen, the tremor of desire that speared through him. His hands explored her back, the length of her arm, the curve of her butt. Years of pent-up need buffeted them, and they forgot all but the fire consuming them.

His hips fused with hers, and the insistent bulge of his erection dug into her belly. Somewhere in the muddled haze of her mind she knew they had to stop, otherwise they'd end up naked on the living room floor. But she couldn't bring herself to stop kissing him. For the first time in years she felt alive. Frissons of pleasure danced across her skin. Like a flower unfurling its petals to the sun, her defenses crumpled, leaving her wide open and frightfully exposed.

He tasted like mint and Zach, like everything she'd denied herself for so long. She wanted more. She wanted everything she'd lost. She wanted him naked, at her mercy, crying out her name...

"Uh, guys?" At the sound of Noah's voice, they both jerked apart. "Will's eating the remote control."

Rebecca's glance darted to the toddler. She hastened to straighten her clothing, then patted down her hair and rose. With as much dignity as she could muster, she walked across the living room and took the remote from Will.

Behind her, she sensed Zach get to his feet as well. "Anything else we should know about?" he asked Noah. A note of frustration tinkled in his voice.

"Yeah," the boy replied. "Bolt just crapped on the kitchen floor."

Needless to say, the mood was blown.

Chapter Fourteen

Zach was playing a perilous game. Becca hadn't been here a week and he'd already kissed her twice. He'd nearly made love to her. If he didn't pull himself together soon, he'd do something they'd both regret. The moment they had sex, she'd start obsessing about getting pregnant again. She'd start timing her cycle—even if she didn't openly admit it. She'd die a little more inside every time she got her period. He couldn't put her—or himself—through that again. But how was he going to keep his hands off her?

He considered spending a few nights at his condo, but that would mean leaving Becca alone with the kids. He wasn't sure she was ready for that yet. Plus, the whole breaking-and-entering thing still had him a little on edge. He'd had an alarm installed the previous day while the kids were at camp, but it still failed to reassure him.

Like it or not, he was stuck here...with her. Guess it was time to exercise that iron will of his. He hadn't been nicknamed the Iceberg for nothing. He could cool things down between them, even if it killed him.

The kids were all asleep, so he went to the kitchen and indulged in a beer. He didn't drink alcohol often, but tonight he needed it. His nerves were bunched so tight nothing short of a miracle would loosen them. Maybe he should do the guy thing—drink beer and watch a football game. Becca never could stand football. If there was anything that would compel her to make herself scarce, it was that.

He strolled into the living room. She kneeled on the rug, organizing the photographs. Ignoring her, he dropped into the couch and began channel flipping. The only thing on the sports channel was the PGA Championship. Golf wasn't his thing, but what the hell.

He felt her gaze drill through him, so he pretended to be riveted by the game.

"Since when do you watch golf?"

He took a swig of his beer. "Since always," was his muffled reply. "Great sport. It's all about strategy and precision."

She watched him dubiously. "Uh huh. How exciting."

She returned her attention to the thick pile in her lap. Her fingers worked quickly and efficiently. She had great hands—strong and competent, yet soft and feminine. Erotic images of those hands on his body flared in his mind. She'd always known just how to touch him, just how to please him and drive him insane. He'd give anything to feel those hands on him one more time.

Downing another mouthful of beer, he tried to focus on the golf game...and failed. His gaze kept straying to Becca. Try as he might, he couldn't help but notice the way her hair brushed the soft swell of her breasts. The way she suckled her lower lip, made it gleam like honey. And those hands—he could all too easily picture them closing around him, stroking...

Jesus, he was losing it. Two years of abstinence could do that to a man. He needed to get out of this house. He stood decisively and slammed the beer can on the table so hard it startled her.

"What's wrong?"

"Nothing. I'm just going to go for a drive."

A frown tugged at her brows. "At this hour?"

"Would you rather I go when the kids are up?" The need to escape suffocated him. "I'm going stir-crazy in here." And with that, he barreled out of the living room, yanked on his shoes and, grabbing his keys from the console by the door, shot out into the warm, balmy night.

Rebecca figured her ex-husband had finally gone and lost his mind. First golf, and now this. Granted men didn't take too well to confinement, but this display of cabin fever was a little over the top, especially for him. Zach didn't lose his cool, and yet he seemed to be doing just that lately.

With a shrug, she switched the television channel, settling on a rerun of *Desperate Housewives*. She only half-watched the episode, preferring to flip through the photographs instead. Bolt curled into a ball beside her and dropped his furry head in her lap.

"Guess it's just you and me," she said to her scruffy companion.

The puppy whined, so she scratched him behind the ear. His expression went hazy and he leaned into her palm. "So you like that, huh?" She swallowed a chuckle. "So does Uncle Zach."

Thoughts of what he'd revealed to her earlier today continued to trouble her. She'd spent the last two years convinced that he'd walked away from their marriage because he didn't love her enough. Now she wondered if maybe he'd walked out on her because he loved her too much. Life had a way of throwing you a curveball when you least expected it, and she wasn't quite sure how to react to this unexpected revelation. Part of her wanted to jump right back into the game, to put her marriage back together and fix what was broken. But another—the part that still suffered from the sting of rejection—was scared witless. What if they failed to make it work the second time around the way they had the first? What if her heart shattered all over again?

"Who ever said love was easy?" she reminded herself. "The question is, is it worth the risk?"

Bolt gazed up at her with adoring brown eyes. A whimper sounded deep in his throat. Rebecca smiled and began to slide the photographs into the envelope when something caught her eye. One of the prints wasn't a picture at all, but a document. It looked like some kind of birth certificate, only it didn't belong to anyone she knew. Perplexed, she rifled through some more snapshots to find several others like this one. Then she came across a list of names, contacts for some organization called the Broken Angels.

Probably related to Liam's work, she thought. She withdrew the peculiar shots from the stack and shoved the rest in the envelope.

"Guess Liam wasn't as organized as we thought," she told her long-eared pal.

She stood and carried the pictures to the office, where she placed them on the desk. Directing another curious look at the prints she'd withdrawn, she tossed them into the trash.

Then she headed back to the living room to cuddle with the dog and finish watching what was left of *Desperate Housewives.*

When Zach returned that evening, Becca was in bed, probably fast asleep. A hollow quiescence filled the house, peaceful yet unnatural. He'd become so accustomed to the cheers and yells of the kids, the chime of Becca's voice, the intermittent barking of the dog that silence now seemed odd to him, lonely and stifling.

As if to appease him, Bolt yipped from behind the closed basement door, so Zach crept downstairs to give the dog a chance to greet him and hopefully settle down. He scratched the puppy on the rump, and the animal wagged his butt with the gusto of a hula dancer.

"Goodnight, fleabag." He gave Bolt a final pat, then mounted the steps to his room.

He hadn't planned on stopping outside Becca's door, but as he passed her room, it seemed as if gravity suddenly grew so fierce it nailed him to the floor. Fighting the urge to turn the handle and enter, he pictured her lying in bed. He knew exactly how he'd find her—on her side, the sheet pressed to her chest like some kind of shield. Even in sleep she refused to let her guard down. Becca was always waiting for the other shoe to fall. She'd never placed much faith in herself, or in life. That was one of the things that had ultimately broken her—her lack of faith, her unwavering belief that the universe was out to get her.

When he'd left here tonight, he'd gone to his favorite Irish pub, where he'd nursed the same beer for four hours and contemplated all the reasons their marriage had fallen apart. Becca's fatalistic attitude had topped the list, along with his inability to understand and comfort her. He doubted anything had changed.

Sure, they still had loads of chemistry, but that had never been one of their problems. The attraction between them had always been nothing less than explosive. That was what originally compelled him to ignore the warning voice of caution and jump, head first, into the yawning mouth of the volcano.

He'd known even then that the consequences could prove disastrous. Most relationships went down in flames, and in this particular case the ramifications stretched far and wide. By loving Becca, he'd cost his baby sister her best friend. She'd never gotten over that loss, and he would bear the stain of that on his conscience for the rest of his days.

But they'd been happy for a while. They'd been a family, even though Becca hadn't seen it that way. He generally didn't like dwelling on the past. Those days were gone. Time had swept in and wiped them away with a wet rag. Still, a part of him couldn't help but wonder what would have happened if he hadn't walked out on her. Would they have found a way to be happy again? Or would he have lost her to despair?

Damned if he knew. Or ever would for that matter.

With a sound that was half snort, half sigh, he turned away from Becca's door and strode down the corridor. He stopped by Noah's room, then Kristen's, ensuring both children were properly tucked in. His last stop was Will's room, where his own mattress awaited him beneath a messy tangle of sheets. He never could remember to make the bed, now less than ever. After covering Will, who had a habit of always kicking off his blanket, Zach crashed into bed and, shockingly enough, fell instantly asleep.

Rebecca was in the kitchen making breakfast when Zach stumbled in the next morning. Kristen and Noah were playing tag around the kitchen table with the dog, while Will sat complaining in his high chair. The delicious aromas of bacon and coffee lingered in the air, yet she still caught a whiff of Zach's mint-scented soap as he approached.

"Enjoy your shower?" she asked him, not bothering to glance his way.

"You bet."

She herself had awakened early and lazed in the tub while everyone was still asleep. After the restless night she'd had, she'd needed it. Despite the bath and a hefty dose of caffeine, she still felt as though she had a head full of wool. Resentment needled her gut at the sight of Zach looking so refreshed, especially since it was his fault she felt like crap.

"You look rested." She tossed a few plates—heaped with bacon and eggs—onto the table. They clattered for an instant, then settled into silence. "It's surprising, considering how late you were out last night." A cool draft blew in from the open window, matching the chill in her voice.

She'd lain awake for hours the previous night waiting for him to come home. It wasn't before one in the morning that she'd finally heard him skulking outside her door.

Zach grabbed a piece of bacon from one of the plates and popped it into his mouth. "Are you keeping tabs on me now?"

"Of course not," she replied a little too passionately. "We're divorced. You're free to do as you please. Stay out all night for all I care."

Kristen, who never seemed to look where she was going, collided with a chair. It rocked on its hind legs, then smashed to the ground. The sudden burst of sound startled Bolt, who let loose a thunderous bark. A frightened Will began to cry.

"If you don't care, why do you look so pissed off?" Zach righted the chair, then gathered Will in his arms.

"I'm not pissed off. You're as free as a bird now. You can go out whenever you wish with whomever you wish."

Bolt clamped his teeth around Noah's pants and tugged. The boy stumbled and fell. His sister rushed to his aid, yanking the fabric from the steel clasp of the dog's jaw.

"Is that what all this is about?" Zach asked, an amused look on his face. "You think I was out with some woman? Good God, Becca, don't I have enough on my plate?"

She wanted to believe him, but a part of her—the part that had never quite felt she was good enough for him—refused to yield. Of course there would be women. There had to be. Zach had always been a passionate man. She couldn't possibly expect him to lead the life of a monk. She just hadn't considered how difficult it would be to sit in the sidelines and watch.

An unforgiving fist clenched in her abdomen. This arrangement wasn't going to work. What had ever compelled her to agree to do this? "I think I made a mistake moving in."

All humor drained from his features. Anger hardened the stubborn set of his jaw. "No one's forcing you to stay. Go ahead. Run away, from me, from the kids. Hell, from life."

Noah and Kristen stopped playing. Will quieted down. Even the dog stood statue still, watching them with curious round eyes.

"You're the track and field champion, not me." Last time she checked, he was the one running...right out the door. It was becoming a pattern with him.

He didn't seem to agree. "Physically speaking, sure. But emotionally, you take the prize, sweetheart."

Did he actually have the gall to be angry with *her*? "You pompous, arrogant, hypocritical...ass!"

"Why don't you both leave?" Noah's cry punctured the tension snowballing around them. Anger and disappointment contorted his youthful face into a grimace that made him look old and hard. "I don't want either one of you here." Then, shoving a chair aside, he stomped out of the kitchen, muttering something under his breath that sounded oddly like "losers".

Kristen's lower lip trembled as water puddled in her eyes. Suddenly, she sprinted toward Rebecca and hugged her leg with a passion that rocked her. "Don't go." She sniffed. "Please."

That simple gesture humbled her beyond words. What had possessed her to argue with Zach in front of the kids? How could she threaten to leave when they'd just lost their parents in the worst possible way? God, Noah was right. She was a loser.

"It's okay, Kristen," she reassured her, awkwardly bringing her hand to rest upon her sunny blond head. "I'm not going anywhere. I promise."

Still, the girl refused to let go of her leg. Perhaps she believed if she held on hard enough she wouldn't lose another person she cared about.

Rebecca struggled to subdue the current of anxiety ripping through her. "Here," she said, pulling out a chair. "Sit down and have your breakfast. You can't go to summer camp hungry."

Kristen reluctantly let go of Rebecca's leg and climbed into the chair, but she didn't seem to have much of an appetite. She stared at her plate for a while, then moved her food around with her fork before finally taking a bite.

Zach placed Will back in his high chair, looking as harried as she felt. The toddler shoved a few handfuls of food into his mouth, but decided halfway through that it was far more fun to throw the scrambled eggs at the dog instead. Bolt didn't complain. He was all too happy to lick the floor clean.

"What do we do about Noah?" she asked Zach.

He shrugged noncommittally, displaying a belligerence befitting his eldest nephew. "I'll get him."

Back straight, shoulders taut, he plowed out of the kitchen, while she remained behind to stew in her frustration and foolishness.

Chapter Fifteen

When it rains it pours.

Why was it that whenever a day started off on the wrong foot, everything that followed seemed to go wrong? First, the kids were late for summer camp. Then Will decided to throw a crying fit that lasted no less than an hour. After which, Zach conveniently told her he had to go to Ad Edge to sort out some crisis, even though he was officially on holiday. Rebecca didn't want to be paranoid, but she got the distinct impression her ex-husband was doing his best to avoid her. Heck, even the weather wasn't cooperating. Boiling clouds gathered in the sky, once again promising rain. But the crowning glory was a phone call from her editor, informing her that her deadline had just been moved up by a week. She hadn't had a moment to gather her thoughts, let alone write.

All in all, this was shaping up to be a pretty lousy day.

While Will napped, Rebecca tried to work, but inspiration insisted on eluding her. The best title she'd come up with was: "A Pedicure a Month Keeps Away Fungus".

Great, her career was on the line and all she could write about were mushrooms. Granted, women often did ignore their feet, but she doubted this was the type of article her editor, Carol, had in mind. Rebecca was already walking a tightrope with her.

"You always used to know how to get to the heart of a matter," Carol had told her after she'd submitted her last article. "That's what I loved about you. I couldn't read one of your pieces without tearing up. But these past two years you've been writing nothing but fluff."

"I don't write fluff," Rebecca had argued. "I write about issues that deeply impact women's lives."

Carol hadn't bought it. In fact, she'd used the title of Rebecca's latest article to prove her point. "Red is the New Black?"

"Fashion's important," she'd voiced meekly. "The way other people perceive a woman influences the way she perceives herself. And I'm right. Fall fashions have already started hitting the shelves, and red is in."

Her editor's disapproval had all but sizzled through the phone line. "Give me something I can really sink my teeth into," she'd stated decisively before hanging up.

Rebecca sighed. Maybe she should write about hamburgers. Nutrition was an important health factor. Which reminded her, she hadn't had lunch. That could explain why her brain refused to cooperate. Snapping her laptop shut, she headed to the kitchen.

She'd just finished making herself a sandwich when the phone rang. It was Noah and Kristen's summer camp counselor, and she didn't sound pleased. "Noah's been in a fight," the woman told her in a clipped tone. "He punched one of the campers. This type of behavior is not accepted here. We need you to come pick him up right away."

Rebecca tried to get more details out of her, but the counselor refused to elaborate. "We'll talk when you get here," she said with an unmistakable note of finality.

Could anything else go wrong today? With a discouraged shake of her head, she took a few quick bites of her sandwich, then hastened upstairs to get Will, knowing full well he wouldn't take too kindly to being awakened in the middle of his nap. Where was Zach when she needed him?

As she expected, Will threw a one-boy concert loud enough to scare the neighbors. By the time she got the toddler dressed and ready, her nerves were rubbed raw and her patience was all but depleted. The last thing she needed was another phone call, and yet the phone screeched again. She seriously contemplated letting the machine get it, but then decided to answer it in case it concerned the kids. For all she knew, Noah had gone and decked the counselor as well.

Thankfully, it wasn't anyone from summer camp, but that attorney—Liam's old boss, Neil Hopkins. "I've got some papers for you and Mr. Ryler to sign concerning the guardianship," he advised her. "I was hoping you could drop by today—"

"I'm sorry, Mr. Hopkins, but that won't be possible. Zach had to go to the office and I've got to go pick up the kids at summer camp. Noah was in some kind of fight."

A brief silence followed. "I'm sorry to hear that." Static slunk into the line, and Rebecca realized a light drizzle had begun to fall. "Nobody was hurt, I hope."

"I'm not sure. The camp counselor was really tight-lipped. That's why I've got to hurry over there. I'm sorry. I don't mean to be rude—"

"No, no, you go right ahead. I'm meeting a client in your area tomorrow. Why don't I just drop off the papers then?"

"Sure. Sounds great." She thanked the attorney and hung up the phone just as the line went dead again. She really had to remember to call the phone company and get that little problem fixed.

With a whining Will secured in one arm and her purse tucked under the other, she shot out the door, all the while psyching herself for the tongue-lashing she was sure to receive.

Will fell asleep in the car. When she got to the building that housed the kids' camp, she was able to successfully transfer him to his stroller without waking him. The elation that crested within her at such a small feat was shocking to say the least. One would think she'd just negotiated a treaty that ensured world peace. Maybe in a small way she had.

She took the elevator to the second floor, where a receptionist directed her to a closed office. A swarm of butterflies battered her ribs as she knocked. The door immediately swung open, and a tall woman with cat-green eyes and a short crop of black hair filled the doorway. She wore a T-shirt with the camp's name and logo, a pair of gym pants, and an expression that could freeze the sun. Inside, Noah sulked in a chair beside a boy with an impressive bruise beneath his right eye.

"As you can see," the woman said, indicating the injured boy, "we have a serious problem. This type of behavior will not be tolerated."

"Hello to you, too," Rebecca replied flippantly, then instantly regretted it upon seeing the dark scowl that twisted the woman's features.

"Do you think this is funny? You are this boy's guardian, are you not?"

"Yes, to the second question. No, to the first. I'm Rebecca James." She extended her hand.

The woman ignored her and continued her tirade. "I run a peaceful establishment here. That's why people entrust their children to me. I can't have campers going around punching other campers. It just isn't acceptable."

"We've already established that," Rebecca said. She'd never liked getting lectured. The counselor's self-righteous tone made irritation flare in her veins and awakened all her protective instincts. "If you don't mind, I'd like to take a moment to hear Noah's explanation."

Noah's eyes flashed to hers, and she could've sworn she saw a flicker of gratitude pierce through the misery.

"So you condone this behavior?" Whatever veneer of civility the counselor struggled to maintain cracked.

"I never said that. I just want to hear what happened. Did you even bother asking him?"

"Several times," the woman informed her frostily. "He refuses to speak."

Rebecca looked pointedly at her nephew. "Noah?"

He shrugged, shot a nervous glance at his counselor. "He was picking on my sister."

The injured boy stuck out his lower lip in an impressive pout. "Not true," he cried.

"He called her a baby," Noah insisted. His voice resonated with a surprising measure of steel for someone so young. "He even shoved her a couple of times, made her cry. I told him to stop, but he just laughed at me and shoved me, too, so I punched him."

"He's lying," the other boy yelled. "I didn't shove nobody."

"It's okay," the counselor soothed him. "I believe you."

A black cloud of fury rolled across Noah's face. He opened his mouth to speak, but Rebecca silenced him with a quelling look.

"Why don't we get Kristen in here?" she told the counselor. "Perhaps she can shed some light on the situation."

"She will only side with her brother."

"The way you're siding with your son?" Noah challenged.

Shock and indignation rushed through Rebecca. "This boy is your son?" she asked.

The counselor tangled her arms across her chest and sat at the corner of the desk. "As a matter of fact, he is."

"That strikes me as a conflict of interest."

"No shit." Noah interjected.

"Noah!" The boy was not helping his case. She turned her attention back to the counselor. "How is this allowed?"

"Are you questioning my judgment, Mrs. James?"

"It's Ms. James, and I most definitely am. Your son is sitting here with a black eye. How can you possibly be objective?"

The woman looked as if she was about to explode. Her cheeks turned a frightful shade of tomato red. "I've had enough of this. No wonder the boy is such a problem case. With this kind of over-indulgence—"

Rebecca reined in her temper. "Can I speak with you in private please?"

She waited till both boys were shepherded out into the corridor before letting the counselor have it. "Over-indulgence?" she repeated. "Do you not know that that boy just lost his parents? Are you completely heartless? How is he over-indulged?"

"And do you not know that by defending a child's actions you unwittingly give him permission to continue the bad behavior?"

"The way you just did with your son?"

The counselor's eyes widened with disbelief. "Get out of my office," she spat. "You are a detriment to those children. You should be reported."

"I think you've got it wrong," Rebecca voiced calmly. "The only person here who should be reported is you." With that, she spun on her heels, opened the door and clumsily wheeled out the stroller, where Will lay, thankfully still asleep. "Noah, get your sister," she commanded. "We're going home."

For once, the boy happily complied. The counselor tore out of the office, grabbed her son by the hand and escorted him back to the gym, where a handful of campers were engaged in a soccer game. Through the window Rebecca saw Noah zero in on his sister and whisper something to her. Kristen dutifully followed her brother as a dozen or so heads swiveled curiously in their direction.

"Is Noah in trouble?" Kristen asked the second she saw Rebecca.

"I'm not sure." Rebecca shot an assessing stare Noah's way.

"He was only defending me," Kristen quickly corroborated her brother's story. "That boy was being mean to me."

"Did you tell the counselor?" she asked her.

"Yes, but she didn't do anything, so Noah punched him to make him stop."

As upset as she was by this whole wretched situation, Rebecca couldn't help but experience a swell of warmth at Noah's protective nature toward his sister. He could call her a million names, push her around till judgment day, but woe befall anyone else who dared pick on her. Siblings were funny creatures. She had none herself and couldn't quite understand the dynamic that existed between these two.

"Still, fighting is wrong," she told Noah. "No matter the reason."

"You didn't seem to think so this morning," he threw back at her without a thread of remorse.

Whatever patience she had left began to wane. "Is that what all this is about? You're getting even with your uncle and me for losing our tempers? We made a mistake. That doesn't mean you need to go out there and repeat it the first chance you get."

"I wasn't. I told you the jerk picked on Kristen."

Rebecca tamped down her frustration. She realized she was getting nowhere. "Come on," she told them. "Let's get out of here before they kick us out again."

Minutes later everyone was strapped safely into her Camry. An unnatural silence filled the metal shell of her car as she drove home. She glanced in the rearview mirror to see Noah staring pensively out the window as the highway streaked by. The blistering sorrow she caught in his eyes made a slow burn spread inside her.

She couldn't find it in her heart to scold him, and yet she knew she had to try. "I know you're having a tough time with all this." His eyes met hers in the rearview mirror. "We all are. But we have to make an effort to get along with each other and the people around us. Lashing out isn't going to do anyone any good."

His expression was mutinous. "Why not? I'm sick of rules. Someone can hit my sister, but I can't hit back. Someone can shoot my parents and get away with it, but I can't give that little creep a black eye. Rules suck. Nothing's fair."

Kristen began to sniffle. Will stirred in his car seat.

"You're right," Rebecca answered. "Life's not fair. And most of the time, it does suck. But you have to learn to rise above it. Because every bad thing that happens to you makes you stronger—wiser—so that when happiness finally does come your way, you'll recognize it. And if you're smart, you'll grab it with all your might and never let go."

"The way you did?"

The question threw her. For a second she forgot she was talking to a nine-year-old. An old sadness overtook her, drowned her in a sea of regret. "I never said I was smart."

Maybe Zach had been right all along. Maybe she really had thrown away her chance at happiness by dwelling on the unfair hand she'd been dealt. Right now she saw herself clearly in Noah's sizzling stare, heard her own bitterness in the resentment that bubbled in his voice.

It wasn't too late for him, she reassured herself. She could still help him.

If only she could figure out how.

Chapter Sixteen

When Zach finally got out of Ad Edge, the day had grown gray and drab. Humidity hung heavy in the air and the wind carried a hint of fog. Still, he felt more energized than he had in weeks. In the cutthroat world of advertising, where adrenaline washed over him in buckets and the pace never slowed, he was in his element. He knew just what to do, just what to say. He could handle any crisis without shedding a single drop of sweat.

At home he was a different person—edgy, unsure how to act, constantly struggling to keep it together. He didn't like the loss of control or the jumble of emotions he was experiencing. It was so much easier to have a bunch of executives counting on him than it was to have children. Children expected you to be a better person, to rise above your weaknesses, to be wise and strong and well-rounded. Each mistake you made could impact their lives, their future. The pressure was tremendous, as was the desire to do right by them. It seemed the more he struggled to be the person they looked up to, the more he messed up.

Then there was Becca, who just last week hadn't been able to hear the word *children* without panicking. And yet the kids seemed to have bonded with her on sight. Well, at least Kristen and Will had. Noah was a much tougher nut to crack. Becca somehow understood them. She felt their pain and—unlike him—instinctively knew what they needed. Maybe she was right. Maybe he was trying too hard.

As he drove up to the house, dread rolled through him. The weight of his responsibility crushed him. Still, he mounted the steps and turned the key, surprisingly anxious to see his family.

His family.

The words sounded odd, but unexpectedly comforting. Familiar sounds greeted him. The dog barked and nearly ran him over. Will fussed from somewhere in the living room as a cartoon blared in the background. In the kitchen, pots and pans clanged beneath the rush of water.

A delicious aroma wafted toward him, and he removed his shoes and followed it to the kitchen, where Becca stood washing the dishes. The sight of her was so domestic it cut him off at the knees. He remembered a time when he would have crept up behind her, wrapped his arms around her middle and brushed a kiss on the side of her neck. He fought the overwhelming urge to do just that, even as a part of his brain wondered why he bothered. Maybe he should just give in, try to make it work with Becca again. Things could be different this time. There came a point in every guy's life when he just had to swallow his doubts and take the plunge. Problem was, he wasn't sure he could swim, and if he failed to tread water then he risked drowning them both.

She sensed his presence. He could tell by the way she angled her head, right before she shut off the faucet.

"How was work?"

It took him a second to focus on her question. "One of my clients threw a tantrum. Apparently, the campaign turned out all wrong. They needed me to help pacify him."

"So you were babysitting again?"

"You could put it that way."

She turned around to face him. Her hair fell in uneven strands across her forehead to brush her skin like threads of silk. She grabbed a dish towel and nervously wiped her hands. "I made lasagna. I kept a plate warm for you in the oven."

"Thanks." He walked over to the stove and opened the oven door, retrieving his dinner. "How were things around here?"

She hesitated, and alarm inched into his bones. The guilty look on her face set his teeth on edge.

"Becca?" he said in his most probing tone.

"I had to pull the kids out of summer camp," she confessed in a wild rush.

He closed his eyes and bit back an oath. "What did you do?"

Indignation flitted across her features. "Why do you automatically assume it was my fault?"

"Because I've known you from the time you wore a training bra." He placed the plate of lasagna on the table, then dropped into a chair. "Spill it."

Her fingers wrung the dishrag until soft spirals distorted the checkered fabric. "Noah got into a fight. He gave one of the other campers a black eye."

He shook his head, exasperated. "You know, the saddest part is that I'm not the least bit surprised. That kid's been itching for a fight for weeks. What was his excuse?"

Becca joined him at the table. "He said the boy picked on Kristen, then shoved him."

"Why didn't he just tell the counselor?" He dug into his meal, though he wasn't sure why. His appetite was slowly dwindling.

"Kristen did, but the counselor ignored her. It turns out she's the boy's mother."

Zach paused, the fork halfway to his mouth. "Is that allowed?"

"That's what I asked her. She didn't seem to appreciate the question."

"So you had it out with her." He let the fork drop back into his plate without taking a bite.

"I didn't have a choice. She was being totally biased. It wasn't fair to Noah...or to Kristen for that matter."

Rubbing his throbbing temples, he stood and walked to the window, where a sprinkle of raindrops battered the glass. "You can't pull them out of their activities every time something goes wrong. There's bound to be trouble, particularly with Noah. What happens when they start school in September? Are you going to decide to home school them at the first sign of trouble?"

"What would you have me do?" She pitched the towel aside, not attempting to mask her frustration. "Send those kids back there after what happened? You didn't see the shiner on that boy, Zach. Do you think the instructor will ever forgive Noah for that?"

He sighed. Defeat tugged at his shoulders. "No, I suppose not. But how the hell are we going to keep them entertained for the rest of the summer?"

She smiled a wobbly smile. "We'll figure something out."

"We better, or they'll have us for breakfast."

Becca's laughter filled the small kitchen. It was warm and heartfelt, as smooth as honey and just as sweet. The tension gripping him seeped away, and he returned to his seat to finish his dinner.

"I almost forgot—that lawyer called."

"Neil?"

"Yeah, he says he has some documents for us to sign to finalize the guardianship. He offered to drop them off tomorrow."

Zach took a bite. A medley of delicious spices spread through his mouth, and he realized he was hungrier than he'd thought. "Sounds good," he said between mouthfuls. "I wanna get this settled as soon as possible." Then, lifting a pair of inquisitive eyes her way, he asked, "Are you still on board?" It stunned him, how badly he was anticipating her answer.

"Of course I am. How can you ask me something like that?"

The pleasure he drew from her fervent reply delivered an even greater shock to his system. He'd convinced himself he wanted her to leave, yet the mere thought of not having her around filled him with a disappointment so bitter it seared his stomach.

"I just thought— After what happened this morning—"

"That I may have changed my mind?" Her brows rode high on her forehead. "Look, Zach, we haven't lived together in two years. It's going to take some getting used to. We're bound to tick each other off every now and then."

One corner of his mouth inched upward. "If I remember correctly, we did that a lot when we were married. Things between us were always very—"

"Passionate?" she finished for him.

His last bite lodged in his throat. "I was going to say interesting." He tugged at the collar of his shirt. "Did you close the windows? It's kinda warm in here."

A knowing smile bounded across her lips. "It's raining."

"Right." Their gazes locked. He could've sworn a silent challenge flickered in her rust-colored eyes. One thing was certain; she wasn't mad at him anymore. In fact, what he caught in her heated glance was far more unsettling...and far riskier.

"You're not leaving, are you, Aunt Becca?" Kristen gazed up at Rebecca, her curious eyes fringed with worry. Dwarfed by her pink and white canopy bed, she appeared small and fragile, like an angel floating on a fluffy cloud.

"No, kiddo, I'm not leaving." She seemed to be getting that question a lot today.

Kristen didn't look reassured. She reached for Lindsay's sweater and clasped it tightly in her arms. A long pause ensued, in which the child immobilized her with her hesitant stare. Worry lines crinkled her smooth brows. "Aunt Becca?"

"Yes?"

"When are my mommy and daddy coming home?"

The innocent query nearly knocked Rebecca to the ground. Her knees weakened, and she lowered her body onto the bed beside Kristen. She had no idea what to say to the child. Was it wise to lie to her, to keep the delusion alive? Or was it best to tell her the truth? If so, how did one shatter a little girl's hopes and live with oneself?

"I'm not sure, sweetie," was all she managed to say.

Kristen hugged the sweater harder, and a light went out in her eyes. "Noah says they're never coming back." A cough shook her small chest, and Rebecca couldn't help but worry that another asthma attack was imminent. She had to calm the girl before things got out of hand.

"Boys always think they know everything." She struggled to infuse some levity in her voice. "But we know better, don't we?"

Kristen nearly smiled. To Rebecca's great relief, her breathing eased a tad. After smoothing out the sheets she urged the girl to lie down. Kristen complied, and Rebecca tenderly tucked her in. She wished she could comfort her in a more significant way—wished she could ease her pain and chase the dark cloud of grief from her face— but only time could accomplish that. All she could do was help these kids get through each and every day, distract them to the best of her abilities, until the memories lost color and the harsh ache in their hearts settled into a weak throb.

Kristen turned on her side and closed her eyes. Rebecca slowly rose to her feet and prepared to leave.

"Aunt Becca," the girl called again, "could you sleep with me a little? I don't like being alone."

Anxiety tingled along her spine, but she reluctantly nodded. She stretched out beside Kristen and gently gathered her in her arms. Lindsay's flower-scented perfume enfolded her, made her heart ache and a flood of memories rush in. She closed her eyes, listened to the silence, until the soft drone banished all thought and sleep finally swept in to anesthetize her mind.

Zach closed Will's door behind him, happy the toddler was asleep at last. The rain had stopped. All he heard was the gentle rasp of his feet as he made his way to Noah's room. The boy sat in bed, playing his Game Boy with the volume off. When he caught sight of Zach, he stashed the device behind his back.

Zach pretended not to have noticed. "Still awake?"

"Can't sleep." Noah watched him warily, like a rabbit eyeing a wolf.

Various drawings littered the nightstand, all dark and bloody. Zach picked one up. The image of some kind of monster running a spike through another's heart glared up at him. "What are these?"

The boy shrugged. "I'm making a comic book."

Zach put the violent drawing aside. Concern congealed in his gut. "I hear there was some trouble at summer camp today."

"Yeah, so?" Noah averted his gaze. Somehow he managed to look ashamed and annoyed all at once.

"Wanna tell me about it?"

"Not really. I already told Aunt Becca. Didn't she tell you everything?"

"Yeah, but I want to hear it from you." Zach sat on the corner of Noah's bed, letting him know in no uncertain terms that he wasn't going anywhere until they had it out. "What happened?"

The boy shrugged again—his favorite gesture, apparently. "This kid picked on Kristen. I told him to stop, but he wouldn't listen. Then he shoved me, so I decked him."

Zach dug deep inside him, hoping to find some fatherly wisdom he could impart. "Lots of people are going to say and do things you don't like. You're going to have to learn to control your temper. You can't raise your fists every time someone annoys you."

"Why not?"

The question stumped him. "Because violence isn't the answer."

"So it's okay for him to call my sister names and push me, but it's not okay for me to hit back?"

"That's not what I said. What he did was wrong. There's no question about that. But there are other ways to handle things—"

"Like what?"

Hell, he wasn't sure. Maybe Noah really had given the little creep what he deserved, but he couldn't very well tell him that. He was his nephew's guardian now. He had to give him the right advice, whatever that may be.

"You could've just ignored him."

Noah snorted. "Yeah, right. That would've worked." The sarcasm in his voice was unmistakable.

"All I'm saying is that violence should be the last resort. Just because you're stronger than someone doesn't mean you have to flatten them."

"Fine. Whatever you say." Noah slid down in bed, pulling the covers to his chin. Zach got the distinct feeling his nephew was silently telling him to get lost.

Realizing he wasn't going to make any inroads tonight, he stood and shuffled to the door. "Get some sleep," he told him. "Tomorrow's a new day."

The boy turned his back to him. Defeat siphoned what remained of Zach's energy. With lethargic fingers he turned off the light. "Good night," he whispered as he slipped out of the bedroom.

Noah didn't bother to reply.

Chapter Seventeen

"I see you took my advice," came an unexpected voice from beyond the shrubs. Rebecca gazed over the fence to find Voula beaming at her. The neighbor pointed to the children, who were playing with Bolt. "You got them a dog."

"I sort of got suckered into it," she confessed. "It seems I have a problem saying no to them."

Warmth glazed the woman's features. "They look happy. I haven't seen them this happy since—" She faltered. "Well, I can barely remember. Everything that happened before is unclear, like a dream."

"I know what you mean." Memories dulled over time, lost definition. She feared one day she'd wake up and Lindsay's face would be nothing more than a washed-out photograph in her mind.

"The baby's gotten so big." Voula observed Will as he tried to climb onto the puppy's back. Bolt dashed off, and Will fell on his backside. His shrill wail instantly rose to the heavens, loud enough to shock the wings off the angels.

"He's convinced the dog's a pony," Rebecca told her with a smile. "Keeps trying to ride him."

Voula laughed. "I can see that." Her gaze strayed to Kristen and Noah, who were ecstatic not to have to go to summer camp this morning. "How are Noah and Kristen getting along?"

"Better. They haven't fought once today. I take it as a good sign."

"Don't let their squabbles fool you," she whispered conspiratorially. "They're the best of friends. There's nothing that boy wouldn't do for his sister. He may like to torment her, but he's always watching out for her."

Rebecca nodded. "I'm starting to get that."

Voula's cat lazily strayed into the yard, oblivious to the fact that a dog had now marked it as his territory. As soon as Bolt sensed her, his ears perked up and his body stretched in an unmistakable hunting stance. Barely a heartbeat later he sprinted after the unsuspecting feline. The cat hissed and scampered away, surprisingly fast for her hefty build.

The children guffawed with laughter. "Told you Kanela was fast." Kristen gloated.

"Bolt's faster," Noah challenged. "The cat just got away because she was able to crawl under the fence."

"Not true." Kristen pouted.

"Is too."

"Not true."

"Is too."

"Enough of that, kids," Rebecca quickly interjected before things got out of hand. "Look, Bolt wants to play Fetch."

The puppy watched the children with a pleading look, a ball clasped between his teeth. Within moments Kristen and Noah were arguing over who would get to throw the ball first.

Rebecca rolled her eyes and sighed. "Here we go again. I knew their sudden truce was too good to last."

"Enjoy it," the neighbor advised. "They grow up so fast. I was only blessed with one daughter, and in a blink she was gone."

"She moved away?"

Regret stole the sparkle from Voula's eyes. "She lives in California now. She's an anchorwoman for NBC."

Rebecca was impressed. "Wow, you must be proud."

"I'm happy she's living her dream," Voula replied, "but I'd much rather have her close to home."

Rebecca understood the woman's loneliness, that quiet ache inside to have a person you love close to you. Her own mother had recently remarried and moved to North Carolina. Granted, it wasn't as far as California, but far enough to make seeing her on a daily basis impossible. While Rebecca had been growing up, her mom had been the only steadfast presence in her life, the one person she'd always turned to for comfort. Her dad had left when she was too little to remember him. As far as she was concerned, she'd always had but one parent. She would have loved to turn to her mom for help right now, but a phone call was the best she could hope for.

"Kristen's birthday is coming up," Voula said, brightening. "Are you planning a party for her?"

"I hadn't thought about it."

"You should. A birthday celebration is a wonderful distraction."

Rebecca frowned. "I don't even know who her friends are."

"It doesn't have to be big. Family will do. I'll bake a cake." The woman radiated with energy.

"I don't want to put you to any trouble—"

"It's no trouble at all. You invite the guests. I'll handle everything else."

"If you really don't mind," Rebecca reluctantly agreed.

"Nonsense. Why would I mind? These kids are like family to me." Her expression brimmed with wistfulness. "My daughter is so career-minded she insists she'll never have kids." She gazed at the children, smiling with tender warmth. "So these three are the only grandkids I'll ever have. It makes no difference that we're not related. They're my grandchildren in every way that counts."

Something about Voula's quiet yearning sang to her own. She envied the woman's ability to accept what she would never have and her willingness to open her heart to three children who needed the affection only a grandmother could provide. Zach and Lindsay's mother had sadly passed away five years ago, and since Liam's parents lived abroad, the children only got to see them a couple of times a year. Rebecca was happy Voula's presence filled a void in their lives, especially given all the losses they'd recently suffered.

The dog went splashing around in a puddle of mud, then jumped on Noah and Kristen with unbridled excitement, staining their clothing with a set of muddy prints.

"Oh, no," Rebecca groaned.

Kristen and Noah laughed at her horror-struck expression.

"There are two things every self-respecting mother or guardian should have." Voula grinned. "A good stain-remover and plenty of bleach."

It was nearly two in the afternoon when Neil Hopkins arrived, a leather briefcase gripped in one hand and a bottle of wine in the other. "Hope it's not a bad time," he said, as Zach moved aside to admit him.

"Not at all. We've been expecting you."

Becca strolled into the vestibule and came to stand beside Zach. "Hello, Mr. Hopkins."

"Ms. James." The attorney handed her the wine. "A small gift to mark this special occasion. It's from my own personal collection. A Cabernet Sauvignon."

Becca took the bottle from him. "Thank you."

"It's a wonderfully textured wine," he added, "woodsy and spicy, with just a hint of cherry and mint. Trust me when I tell you you're going to love it. Grew up on a vineyard, so I know what I'm talking about."

"Sounds delicious." An appreciative smile skipped across her mouth. "But it really wasn't necessary."

"Nonsense. Becoming a parent is an event that should be celebrated, regardless of the circumstances."

Zach watched Becca for a reaction, noting the way her shoulders stiffened and her fingers tightened around the neck of the bottle. Her face, however, gave none of her anxiety away. "Isn't it a little premature?" he asked the lawyer, hoping he didn't sound too ungrateful. "I thought we had to have some kind of hearing first—"

Hopkins waved his concerns away with a perfectly manicured hand. "Just a technicality. Those three are as good as yours." His sharp gaze swept through the house. "It's pretty quiet in here. I'm guessing the kids are at camp."

"No, they're at the neighbor's," Becca clarified. "We figured it was best if they were out of the house when..." She fumbled. "When we signed the documents."

"Of course. Good thinking. No use upsetting them further. God knows they've been through enough."

"How 'bout we head to the living room?" Zach tossed in. "Get this show on the road?"

His own anxiety was creeping up on him. Just a few weeks ago he was the single, career-minded uncle. Someone who dropped by with the occasional gift and a carefree smile. Now he was about to become a father, with all the responsibilities that came with it. There was no learning curve for him, no time to adapt, no room for errors. It was all or nothing. Sink or swim. Fly or crash and burn.

The second he signed on the dotted line, his fate—and Becca's—would be sealed forever.

Becca dropped the wine off in the kitchen, then joined them on the couch. Her skin was pale, her hands a nervous tangle in her lap.

Neil saw none of it. He was too busy pulling a stack of papers from his briefcase. "Everything you need to establish guardianship is right here." He handed Zach the documents. "I've filled in all the particulars. Nothing left for you two to do but sign."

Zach studied the forms, tension snaking through his limbs. Still, the overpowering desire to do right by his sister blasted away all his misgivings and had him anxiously grabbing the pen the attorney held out to him. Without a second's hesitation, he scribbled his name at the bottom of the last page. Then he gave the pen to Becca.

Their fingers brushed as she took it from him. Her gaze met his, and he saw everything he felt, every question that tortured him, reflected in her eyes. She examined the documents for an unnervingly long time.

Zach sensed the lawyer's impatience. "I assure you, Mrs. Ry—Ms. James, everything's in order."

She gave a weak nod. "I'm sure it is." Then, with a burst of courage Zach couldn't help but admire, she swallowed her doubts and signed the form.

"Wonderful. We're all set then." Neil Hopkins stood and retrieved the papers, then carefully placed them in his briefcase. "The next step is for me to file the documents. Once I do, a hearing will be scheduled.

You'll have to appear before a judge in a couple of weeks or so, but no worries. Like I said, it's just a technicality."

Zach and Rebecca quietly escorted him to the door. "Thank you, Mr. Hopkins," she said. "For the wine and the house call."

"My pleasure. Liam was like a son to me. Nothing I want more than to see his kids settled."

Zach shook the man's hand, then shut the door behind him. An unnatural hush hung over the house as he turned to Becca. "Are you really ready for this?"

The question seemed to take her by surprise. "Of course I am. I have no reservations as far as the children are concerned."

A leaden ball carved a slow, burning path to his gut. "I guess any reservations you have are about me." The implication cut deeper than he cared to admit, even to himself.

She turned and stalked back to the living room, where she stared long and hard at a framed photograph taken at their wedding. "Let's be honest, Zach. Things are complicated between us. We're divorced. We can't exactly live together forever."

Why not? dangled on the tip of his tongue, but he refrained from voicing it. The truth was, he'd gotten used to having her around again. The thought of not seeing her face every night before he went to sleep and every morning when he awoke left him hollow and ashen inside.

"There are tons of divorced couples with kids. If they can make it work, so can we."

She was quiet for a long time. Then, "You're right. We owe it to those kids to at least try."

Anger blistered beneath his skin. "Was it so awful, being married to me?" The question popped out before he could stop it. He knew he hadn't done a great job comforting her when she'd needed it. He hadn't known the right words to say, the right things to do to ease her pain. But he'd loved her with every inch of his soul. Didn't that count for something?

She looked at him as though he'd just landed from Mars. "I think I should be asking you that question. I'm not the one who left, remember?"

So they were back to that again. "I left because I wasn't what you needed."

"Did you bother asking me?"

"No point. I knew you'd be better off if I ended things between us. The grief was killing you."

She shook her head, made an exasperated mewling sound deep in her throat. "Do you ever stop to think that maybe you can't fix everything, that some things just have to sort themselves out over time? There's no on/off switch for grief. I don't think you ever really got that."

Irritation melted into defeat. "I get it now."

Her expression softening, she reached out and took his hand in hers. "Sometimes it's all right to do nothing. You don't have to play hero all the time."

Her heat sank into his flesh, thawed the ice in his blood and made longing throb in his veins. He would have easily surrendered right there and then, drawn her into his arms and let the past fall away and a new future rise to redefine them. But still he held back.

Damned if he knew why.

As if stung by the rejection, she briskly withdrew her hand and changed the subject. "I was thinking we could take the kids up to the summer house for a week or two."

It had been years since he'd last stayed at his father's beach house in Cape Cod. Ever since the divorce he'd steered clear of it with a passion.

"I'm not sure that's such a great idea."

"Why not? Lindsay always said the kids had fun there."

He fisted the hand she'd touched to keep from reaching for her again. "Too many memories." That was where he'd first admitted to her—to himself—that he wanted her, where they'd made love for the first time.

Quiet understanding passed between them. Her eyes went molten as they rose to settle on his face. "For them or for you?"

He didn't get a chance to answer. The phone rang, and he was spared the embarrassment of confessing how often he thought of that stormy night when he'd claimed her as his, despite his better judgment. He'd known even then what a mistake it was to touch her, and yet he hadn't been able to keep his hands off her.

He grabbed the cordless phone, which sat at the corner of the coffee table, and pressed the talk button. "Yeah?" He wasn't in the mood to be formal today.

"Zach, it's Martin."

Great. Just what he needed. "What's up?"

"The kids have been on my mind a lot lately, thought I'd call to check on them."

"The kids are great," he replied curtly.

Becca watched him curiously, and he silently mouthed the name *Martin*. A small smile fluttered over her lips. She knew he'd never had much use for Liam's older brother, and she knew the reason why.

Zach had always suspected Martin had a thing for Becca. There was something in the way he looked at her, like a hungry coyote eyeing a chicken. What had transpired on their wedding day had only cemented his suspicions...and his resentment.

"You sure?" The doubt and accusation in Martin's voice only served to heighten his aggravation.

"Are you calling me a liar?"

Becca gestured that he take it easy. Zach ignored her.

"It's just..." Martin paused, searching for his words. "Do you know Mrs. O'Donnell?"

"Nope."

"She's one of my clients. Her son goes to day camp with Noah and Kristen. When she dropped by my office today, she happened to mention the kids were kicked out. She said Noah punched one of the other campers."

Zach stifled a groan. "There was a slight disagreement. Becca decided it was best to pull the kids out."

Martin's heavy-hearted sigh hummed through the phone line. "I get the feeling Noah's not coping too well."

Perceptive bastard, wasn't he? "There's no on/off switch for grief." He winked at Becca. "Some things just need to sort themselves out over time."

"I know, but I can't help but feel I should be doing more. I'd like to spend some time with the kids. Liam was my brother. I owe it to him to help."

For eight years Martin had shown absolutely no interest in his brother's children, and all of a sudden he couldn't wait to play uncle. What was the deal with that?

"I was thinking I could take Noah and Kristen for a boat ride this weekend," he added. "Spend some time at my place in Edgartown."

A couple of years ago Martin had decided to spoil himself. He'd gone and bought himself a miniature yacht and a mansion on a bluff in Martha's Vineyard.

Pretentious prick.

Zach's first impulse was to say, "No chance in hell," especially about the boat part, but he fought it. Martin had as much right to spend time with Kristen and Noah as he did. Still, he couldn't picture the cocky playboy playing in the sand with a couple of rowdy kids. His clothing was too sleek, his shoes too shiny.

"That won't be possible," he told him. "Becca and I just decided to take the kids to my dad's place down at the Cape. We leave tomorrow."

Becca arched two puzzled brows. Zach shrugged.

"Oh." Martin's dissatisfaction was palpable. "I hope you guys enjoy yourselves. Another time then."

"Sure, another time," he muttered a little too smugly.

When he hung up, relief momentarily engulfed him. Then he caught the unbridled excitement on Becca's face. "So we're going to the summer house after all," she said, beaming.

Zach cringed at the thought, but he couldn't bring himself to disappoint her. "Guess so."

The laptop sat on the kitchen table in silent invitation. Noah knew he probably shouldn't mess with his aunt's computer, but she was busy packing, and here it was, calling out his name. There was no telling when he'd get another chance like this one. So he made sure no one was around, then ran and flipped open the screen. Instantly, it came to life. She'd forgotten to turn it off, which made things a heck of a lot easier for him.

He logged on to Falcon World, played a quick game of Chess. No more Checkers for him. After a few minutes, when Night-Owl didn't come on and join him, he decided to send him a note.

"Stupid computer crashed. G2 my grandpa's place in Chatham tomorrow. Dunno how long I'll be gone. I'll try 2 log on from there. CWYL."

He wasn't sure how he felt about going to the Cape. He loved it there, no question about that, but it would be weird to be there without his parents. That was the place they always went to spend time together, where his mom baked chocolate-chip cookies and his dad took him out in the canoe, all the way to the National Seashore sometimes, where they spent hours exploring the dunes.

They always had loads of fun there...or they used to. Now the place would be empty, dead like his parents. Part of him didn't want to go, but another wanted to get out of this house, away from the black images in his head. Maybe if he went to the Cape, the memories would fade, and he'd stop hearing the popping sound the gun had made when it released the bullets that killed his mom and dad.

His eyes suddenly stung. He didn't understand why tears burned so much when they were just water. But they did. They burned like fire. He wiped them away, swallowed the sour gumball in his throat and stood. The sound of footsteps on the stairs had him quickly logging off and folding the screen shut again.

Then, with a quietness he'd inherited from his mom, he slunk to the sink, poured himself a glass of water and headed for his room.

He met his aunt along the way. "I thought you were in bed," she said.

"Just getting some water." He showed her the glass, tried to look innocent.

She obviously bought it because she smiled that stiff smile of hers. "Are you excited about going to the Cape tomorrow?"

"Sure. Whatever." And with that, he sped past her and disappeared in the safe circle of his room, where the scary images melted into the shadows and he almost remembered what it felt like to be safe.

Chapter Eighteen

Gentle swells rolled across the sand, frothing and melting, leaving a smattering of broken seashells and clams behind. The sun reflected off the water, a trembling beacon of light that cleaved the heavens and made the harbor's glassy surface shimmer.

Rebecca stood barefoot on the small spit of beach that hemmed in the summer house, enjoying the way the wind spilled across her face and threaded through her hair. The day was unnaturally hot, so the cool breeze was a welcome relief. She'd applied handfuls of sunscreen to the whole family, herself included, but she could already feel her skin baking.

Beside her, Will splashed happily on the shore, while Kristen and Noah swam nearby. The water was cold, even in late July, thanks to the icy Labrador currents streaming in from the north. Still, the kids didn't seem to mind.

An osprey had built a nest on one of the posts bracketing the beach house, and the hatchlings' hungry cries punctuated the salt-laden air. Bolt stood vigil at the foot of the post, scratching at the wood, his excited barks forming a discordant chorus with the birds.

Rebecca smiled. She loved this place.

The yelps and barks and shrieks failed to crush the peaceful feeling that unfurled inside her. The beach was small, strewn with seaweed, littered with patches of grass and crabs that had been dismembered, then tossed onto the sandy shore by the forceful tide. The air was thick, peppered with must, the surrounding trees and rooftops carpeted by moss.

Still, to Rebecca, this was paradise. Life was slow and easy at the Cape, uncomplicated. Happiness didn't seem as elusive here, where deer and cottontails roamed free in your backyard and cool, silky whitecaps tickled your toes. Even hope somehow lost its sharp edges.

She heard footsteps and glanced over her shoulder. The pale gray house with the cobalt-blue roof and shutters sat on a rocky ridge to protect it from erosion. A thin trail bordered by shrubs led to the beach below. It was on this path that Zach trekked, narrowing the distance between them, dressed in a white T-shirt and a pair of jean cutoffs. His muscular legs glinted gold in the sunlight, reminded her of the old days when she'd watched him run with a snag in her heart and a lump the size of a grapefruit trapped in her windpipe. Shadows danced across the flat planes of his face, heightening the dramatic blue of his eyes and deepening the grooves on his cheeks. Everything about him was long and lean and hard. Her mouth went dry. For several pulse-pounding seconds, nothing existed but him.

His gaze traveled down the length of her body, over her thin cotton sundress, all the way down to her bare feet. As always, her stomach folded with a painful thud. Nearly a lifetime later nothing had changed. She was just as affected by him now as she'd been on that cold winter's night so many years ago, when she'd finally cut through his defenses and crept into his heart.

Maybe that was the reason this place was so dear to her. It made no difference that it had taken a near-death experience to get him to admit he had feelings for her. All that mattered was that he had.

He came to stand beside her, staring out at the rippling water, where Kristen and Noah dove in search of seashells.

"Should they be doing that?" His face was an impassive mask, but she sensed the anxiety churning beneath the surface. She wondered if he'd ever learn to feel comfortable around the sea.

"They're good swimmers," she reassured him. "Lindsay had them taking lessons when they were still in diapers. But you know that."

"Yeah." A worried frown pleated his brows. "Still, there could be a riptide—"

"Maybe out in the Atlantic, but not here in the harbor."

Will clambered away, then clumsily climbed into the canoe that sat tethered to a post on the beach. The toddler squealed with delight, and Rebecca couldn't help but smile. "They're really enjoying themselves."

"Maybe this wasn't such a bad idea after all," he grudgingly conceded.

Triumph pressed against the walls of her chest. "Told you."

Silver sunbeams glanced off the waves. Rebecca closed her eyes and sighed.

She felt Zach's gaze upon her, and her lids sprang open again. The intensity with which he watched her unsettled her. Her pulse took off at a gallop. "What?"

"You look—" he shook his head as if at a loss for words, "—serene."

A laugh vibrated in her throat. "You sound surprised."

"I haven't seen you like this in a very long time. You're different, that's all. It's like...you're *you* again."

Remnants of the old bitterness returned to dampen her mood. "As opposed to the crazy woman who inhabited my body for a while?"

He shrugged. "She *was* kinda scary." The boyish hitch of his shoulder coupled with the crooked grin tugging at one corner of his mouth made amusement bloom in her belly, despite her best efforts to feel offended.

"Aunt Becca! Uncle Zach! Look what I found." Kristen clomped onto the beach, water dripping from her hair and body, an unbroken crab clasped between her eager fingers.

Rebecca leaned in for a closer look. "Is that thing still alive? Careful it doesn't pinch you."

"It's just a shell." The girl sparkled with pride. "Isn't it beautiful?"

"Sure is." Zach clasped one of her wet locks.

Bolt abandoned his position beneath the ospreys and padded to Kristen's side. As if to show his approval, he proceeded to lick the salt water from her legs. "That tickles." She giggled.

Noah swam to the shore, his own hands full. He dropped his shells in a bucket, then shook the water from his hair in a way reminiscent of the dog. Seconds later, his gaze latched onto his brother and he sprinted across the beach to the canoe.

"Will's got something in his mouth." His voice was pitched, laced with panic.

By the time Zach and Rebecca made it over there, Noah had already pried the object free from the toddler's clenched gums. The boy studied it for a second or two, then palmed it and walked to the edge of the harbor, where he crouched in the sand, his expression far too serious, far too pensive for a nine-year-old. He seemed to see nothing but the foam licking his feet, hear nothing but the clamor of waves and gulls.

Zach studied him, and the look on his face perfectly matched his nephew's. Both appeared rigid, carved in flesh-toned marble. Two statues—still and composed—with a tempest brewing inside. How long could they contain it? she wondered. How long before the storm broke?

"What do you have there?" Zach tried to infuse some levity into his voice as he squatted beside his nephew.

The boy didn't answer.

"Noah?" Zach persisted.

Slowly, Noah uncurled his fingers. In his palm lay an elaborate silver band. Zach reached for it, but Noah made a tight fist around it. "It's my dad's," he explained. "He lost it last summer."

"That's what Will was chewing on?"

Noah nodded. "He could've choked."

"Let me see." Kristen flew to her brother's side, but he refused to open his hand.

"It's mine now," he spat.

"I just want to see it." She tugged persistently at his fingers.

Noah shot to his feet. "No." Briefly, the marble cracked and his young face reflected a well of pain too deep even for anger to conceal. "I told you it's mine."

Then, wrapping his arms around his torso as if to hold himself together, the boy bulleted across the beach and disappeared into the house.

The sense of victory Rebecca had felt earlier was short-lived. Now she questioned how wise it was to have come here. Maybe Zach was right. Maybe this place did indeed harbor too many memories. Every item was imbued with meaning. The cast-stone fireplace, where Zach had lit a fire to chase the chill from her bones after she'd nearly died in a blizzard. The hand-knit, blue and white afghan they'd huddled under on countless occasions. The down-filled leather sofa, where they'd made love for the very first time...

She remembered that night as if it had been yesterday. She and Lindsay had vowed to spend Valentine's Day here at the Cape, swearing off men and drowning their sorrows in ice-cream. Then, at the last second, Lindsay had changed her mind, and Rebecca had driven to the beach house on her own. She'd discounted the snowstorm, the icy pellets crashing onto her windshield, the warning whistle of the wind. All that had mattered was getting away from Boston and the man who'd owned her heart from the moment she first laid eyes on him.

She hadn't expected her car to break down or to have to trudge through two miles of knee-deep snow. But more importantly, she hadn't expected Zach to show up and haul her over his shoulder and into the heated cocoon of his Jeep.

What had come afterward still felt like a dream. She recalled the taste of his intoxicating kisses, the tenderness of his touch, the delicious warmth of his body against hers. She could still feel that slow, seductive tingle in her center, the way it had stretched to surround her heart. She knew without a doubt that, given the chance, she would endure it all again—the hypothermia, the tumultuous marriage, even the heartache. The years she'd spent with Zach were the best—and worst—of her life.

Reluctantly, she approached the couch and sank into its welcoming folds. The leather was soft and cool, as familiar as an old friend. She ran her palm over its smooth surface, then reached for the afghan and pulled it up to her chin, even though the evening was warm. She liked the smell of it, the feel of it. *Welcome home*, it seemed to say.

Zach chose that instant to walk into the room. His eyes were shadowed, his expression grim...until he caught sight of her. Then an altogether different expression washed over his face. Need slow-danced with tenderness, wrapped in dread. She saw her own memories reflected in his smoldering gaze and knew he struggled with the same questions that plagued her. Would they be able to resist the pull this time? Did they really want to? Were they destined to repeat the same mistakes over and over again until it ultimately destroyed them? Even so, wasn't it better to know happiness, however brief, than to live with this unrelenting emptiness?

He approached her in unsteady steps, stopping a few feet from the couch, as if this small measure of distance could somehow protect him from the strange energy that had always existed between them. The tension around him was so thick she could almost reach out and touch it.

"How's Noah?" she asked.

"Asleep. Finally." He dropped onto the sofa, his back stiff.

"Finding that ring really upset him."

"Any reminder of his parents would upset him right now. Unfortunately, there's no way to escape memories."

Their gazes locked, simmering with everything that remained unspoken between them. "Especially here," he added, and she knew exactly to which memories he alluded.

Heat flooded her system. It shot from her scalp all the way to her toes. "This place hasn't changed at all."

"Dad isn't really into decorating. That was always my mother's job."

The mention of Phyllis brought on that familiar throb beneath her breastbone. Zach's mother had been an amazing woman, always welcoming, with a heart as big as her smile. She was the glue that had held the Rylers together. Rebecca had always admired their close-knit family, the sense of belonging they each enjoyed, the shared history. All she'd ever wanted was to be part of that, and thanks to Zach and Lindsay she'd gotten her wish—for a while, anyway.

Nostalgia flickered across his face, and she read the pain in his eyes. Instinctively, she knew what he was thinking. Both of the Ryler women were gone. Only he and his dad remained. The family had been split down the middle, and it was incomplete now, forever damaged. He'd had the one thing she'd always wanted and he'd lost it. Which was worse, she wondered, never experiencing that sense of togetherness or having it stolen from you?

She needed to distract him, draw his mind away from morbid thoughts of a past he couldn't change and a future he had yet to figure out.

"I think I know just what you need." She stood and shuffled to the kitchen, then returned with two wine glasses and the bottle of

Cabernet Sauvignon Neil Hopkins had given them, glad she'd thought to bring it along.

She poured him a glass, then one for herself.

"Is that the bottle Hopkins brought us?"

"Sure is." She sat down beside him and handed him his wine. "Let's see if it's as good as he claims." With a flick of the wrist, she tipped her glass toward his. "To new beginnings."

A slow, lazy smile crawled across his full mouth. "To staying sane."

"That too."

They both took a hearty sip. Rebecca let the full-bodied beverage rest on her tongue for a second or two before swallowing. "I taste currant," she said. "And cherries. How about you?"

He reflected, then sampled the wine again. "Oak, vanilla and a twist of mint."

Settling deeper into the couch, she allowed the alcohol to soothe her frayed nerves and calm the rush of her pulse. "Guess Neil Hopkins really does know his wine."

"Guess so." He downed the glass.

She shook her head. "You're supposed to savor it."

"I savored it just fine."

She grabbed the bottle, topped off his glass again.

Zach watched her warily. "Are you trying to get me drunk?" The humor in his glance offset the suspicion in his voice.

"Maybe. You look really stressed out."

"That's because I am. Neck's killing me."

Whenever Zach was tense, pain coiled at the base of his skull, delivering smarting lashes down his nape and across his shoulders. Ignoring the warning that screeched in her head, she placed her glass on the coffee table, reached across the space that divided them, and massaged his neck.

His muscles stiffened beneath her fingertips. "You don't have to do this," he rasped.

"I know. I want to make you feel better."

The sound he made was between a laugh and a growl. Everything feminine inside her responded to it. Maybe it was this place or the wine or the sweet, balmy night, but she realized with a surge of excitement that she wanted to seduce him. It made no difference that he'd probably break her heart all over again. She wanted this man. She always had. She didn't care if she had a lifetime with him or one night. She just wanted him, any way she could have him.

She edged in closer, made her movements softer, more sensual. Her fingers feathered across his collarbone, traced a line up his neck to tangle themselves in the short crop of his hair. Then she massaged his scalp—gently, deliberately.

His eyes drifted shut. His head grew heavy in her palm. Encouraged, she took the wine from him and deepened her caress. Slowly, the strain ebbed away and his body shifted. Any minute now he would reach for her, the way he had that night so long ago. The thought made a swarm of butterflies uncurl silky wings inside her.

He fell toward her. His arm slid across her abdomen—warm and languid.

"Zach." His name escaped her lips in a husky breath as every inch of her skin came alive.

His only reply was a sharp snore. The fantasy disintegrated like a soap bubble. Rebecca laughed past her disappointment. She was a natural at this. A real temptress, she mused. Maybe if she was lucky, he'd dream about her.

With a defeated sigh, she wrapped her arm around him and threw the afghan over his legs. It barely covered half his body. Snuggling close, she buried herself in the warm shelter of his embrace, lulled by the gentle whoosh of the wind brushing the treetops. Beyond the window, the crescent moon glowed silver, a fissure of light scarring the blackened sky.

Zach's familiar heat wrapped unforgiving shackles around her, binding her to him in ways she couldn't even begin to comprehend, speaking to a part of her spirit she'd thought was long dead.

Welcome home, it seemed to say.

Chapter Nineteen

Bolt's excited barks woke Rebecca the next morning. With a grunt, she stumbled out of bed and squinted at the blinding rush of light that streamed through the window. Once again Zach had insisted that she take the master bedroom. It was just as well that he'd fallen asleep on the couch. That was where he'd planned on sleeping anyway. Noah and Kristen were sharing the king-sized bed in the only other room, with Will sleeping in his playpen a few feet away.

After taking a moment to stretch, she dragged herself to the front door to let the dog out. She had no choice but to pass through the living room, where Zach lay sprawled across the sofa, his lean body way too long even for a three-seater. The blanket she'd thrown over him sometime during the night had fallen to the floor.

Bolt let out another succession of barks. Zach twitched and threw his arm over his head to block out the irritating noise. His entire face contorted into a scowl. He looked murderous, and yet he was still lost in sleep. Amusement yanked at the corners of her mouth. She'd forgotten how expressive he could be when he was unconscious.

With renewed urgency, she swung the door open before the anxious beagle woke the whole household.

There was something extremely precious about being the first one to awaken. To be able to sip her coffee silently while the haze of slumber still hovered over the house. To have the luxury of admiring the sun's gentle climb over the horizon while it softly chased away the darkness with an invisible paintbrush and made everything it touched glow.

When Rebecca stepped onto the porch, she expected to hear nothing but the hungry cries of the ospreys, the clamor of the surf, so it was a jolt to her system when the trill of children's laughter pierced the bright morning. For a second she wondered if the kids had crawled out of bed without her noticing. Then she realized the children in question—a boy and a girl roughly the same ages as Noah and Kristen—were strangers. They hovered on the edge of the water, trying to outrun the waves.

"Jason! Amy!" a woman called from the neighboring porch. "I told you it's too early to go swimming. The water's freezing."

Rebecca inclined her head toward the house next door. The friendly looking blonde met her gaze and smiled. There was something familiar about her, but she couldn't quite place her.

"Good morning," the neighbor greeted, her pale green eyes twinkling.

"Good morning." Rebecca returned her smile.

"I wasn't expecting anyone to be here." The woman secured a short curl behind her ear. "Are you renting the Rylers' place?"

"Not exactly. I'm Rebecca James, the kids' aunt. Well, guardian actually."

Understanding made the neighbor's mouth pucker in a silent *oh*. Rebecca realized she must know about the tragedy that had befallen Liam and Lindsay. Then it came to her, where she'd seen her before. "You were at the funeral."

She nodded. "Liam and Patrick—my husband—were practically brothers. They studied at Harvard together. I'm Tess, by the way."

"Nice to meet you."

Another musical laugh rose from the beach. "Jason! Amy!" their mother yelled again. "Stay out of Daddy's boat." The children ignored her, hopping into the small craft that was attached to a buoy near the shore. Bolt, too skittish to follow them, began to bark up a storm.

Tess groaned. "I swear all I am is background noise to them. They have absolutely no trouble tuning me out."

Rebecca bit back a grin. She wondered how long it would take before she became background noise.

"Are the kids with you?" Tess asked.

"Yes, they're inside sleeping."

"Wonderful. Jason and Amy will be pleased to hear that. They always have a great time together. When Pat suggested we spend a couple of weeks at the Cape, I wasn't exactly sold on the idea. My husband loves to go fishing," she explained. "With the old dinghy, he wouldn't go too far. Since he bought the speedboat, he can be gone all day." The neighbor didn't attempt to hide her frustration.

"To be honest, I'm not much of a nature enthusiast myself," she confessed. "I'm a city girl through and through. But now that you guys are here, I'm glad we came."

Rebecca, too, was happy the kids would have some company. Perhaps this was exactly the distraction they needed. Jason and Amy seemed every bit as spirited as Noah and Kristen. They ran circles around the puppy, trying to catch him. Bolt wagged his tail and barked each time he gave them the slip.

"They're going to drive your dog crazy," Tess stated with a shake of her head.

"Don't worry about it. He's used to it. Will is always trying to ride him."

The woman laughed wholeheartedly. "That explains why he's a master at evasion."

"He's named after some super dog. Or, I should say, a dog that thinks he's a super dog."

"Not *Bolt*?"

"You've heard of him?"

Tess rolled her eyes. "My kids watch nothing else. They think it's the greatest thing since *SpongeBob*."

A loud splash cut the conversation short. Amy emerged from beneath the waves, giggling, her clothing drenched. Tess sprinted across the beach to gather her daughter. Rebecca couldn't help but wonder if that level of speed came naturally as soon as a woman gave birth or if it was an acquired skill. If the latter were true, she'd be able to outrun Zach in no time.

"See you later," Tess called as she hauled both her kids into the house to change and feed them.

Rebecca tossed a wave her way, then leaned over the porch railing. The morning was cool, but sunny enough to promise some heat in the afternoon. Cotton clouds wafted softly overhead, across a sky so blue it looked like a painting. Sparkling waves lapped across the pebbled sand, bubbling at the tips. Nature painted a beautiful canvas, perfect and peaceful.

Then the house came alive. Will's cry tumbled out the open window, overriding the screech of gulls and ospreys.

"Shut up," Noah and Kristen screamed simultaneously.

From the living room, Zach cursed.

Rebecca swallowed a mouthful of salty air and reluctantly crawled back into the house. It was time to start practicing her sprint.

Zach wasn't sure he was happy to have company. It was nice to see the kids having fun, but he wasn't feeling particularly sociable lately. Still, the neighbors kept his mind off Becca, so in a way it was a good thing. As long as Patrick Jenkins—Liam's old college buddy and assistant district attorney, kept chatting up a storm—Zach wouldn't be as inclined to notice the way Becca's smile made her whole face glow. He wouldn't dwell on the appealing way her swimsuit clung to her soft curves, especially when it was wet. He wouldn't pay much heed to the smattering of freckles across her nose, which only grew more pronounced as her tan deepened.

Not with Patrick here beside him, droning on about his latest case as he flipped burgers on the grill. "The defendant insisted his girlfriend was his alibi, but one of my sources told me she was seen at some club with another guy that night. Blew the defense's case right out of the water," he stated proudly.

Zach plastered on a grin and nodded in approval because he figured that was what Patrick expected of him. It seemed to have the desired effect. Smiling like a frog that had just nabbed a juicy fly, the ADA performed another one of his fancy wrist flips and dropped a patty onto a bun, which he handed to Zach.

"Only fair that you should have first dibs," he said.

"Since you have to endure Pat's stories," his wife finished, placing a large salad bowl on the teak garden table.

"Hey, people would pay good money to hear my stories. I should write a book."

Tess released a chest-heaving sigh. "Here we go again."

At Zach's legs, Bolt sat drooling, his brown eyes two large saucers riveted on the meat patty. When Pat wasn't looking, Zach tossed the dog a bite. Bolt licked his chops, then whimpered, begging for more.

"Time for lunch, kids," Tess called.

A symphony of protests echoed from the beach, where all five children splashed under Becca's supervision.

It took some effort, but eventually they succeeded in rounding everyone up and getting some food into them. Zach wondered who polished off the majority of the burgers, the kids or the dog.

One minute, Kristen's plate was full. The next, there was nothing on it but crumbs. "Look," she said, "I finished my booger."

Everyone exploded with laughter. All except for Will, who was too busy shoving chunks of bread up his nose.

"It's *burger*," Noah snorted.

Kristen's brows bunched into a frown. "That's what I said."

"No, it's not. You said booger."

"I said burger."

"Booger."

"Burger."

"All right, kids," Becca interjected before things got out of hand. "Why don't you go play on the swings while we finish up?"

With a teeth-jarring victory cry, the four of them scattered, nearly tipping over their chairs as they made a beeline for the Jenkinses' swing set. It didn't take long for Noah and Kristen to start arguing again, this time over who would go first. The others rushed to join in. Zach muffled an oath.

Tess moaned. "Where do they get their energy?"

"From my burgers," Pat gloated.

"What they ate of them," she clarified. "I don't think anyone enjoyed your burgers more than *superdog* over there." She angled her head toward Bolt, who lay sprawled at Becca's feet, too full even to wag his tail.

Pat feigned indignation. "That beagle knows a good thing when he smells it."

A soft smile hung around the edges of Becca's mouth as she listened to the exchange. She was a vision, all tanned skin and wild hair streaked with gold. Zach's gut gave a swift kick. He could sit here for hours and just watch her.

She sensed his stare and turned his way. His heart dropped into his stomach as a slow languid heat reached through him. He'd forgotten how wonderful it was to be held captive by Becca's cinnamon-flecked eyes.

"So how have you two been handling things?" Pat's question jarred him back to reality. For a second he'd almost forgotten the neighbors were there.

"It's been a challenge," Becca answered. "The kids still haven't come to terms with what happened to their parents. Noah especially. It breaks my heart to see them suffering like this."

The peace was shattered like glass on stone. Heaviness settled over them.

"They'll be all right," Zach added. "They're tough, all three of them."

The Jenkinses didn't look convinced.

"I can't believe the bastard who shot them got away." Pat's jaw clenched. "If I had him in my courtroom, I'd make sure he got thirty to life. Too bad the State of Massachusetts doesn't believe in the death penalty."

"That wouldn't bring Liam and Lindsay back," his wife uttered.

"Maybe, but it would make me feel a hell of a lot better. Liam was the closest thing to a brother I had." A shadow passed behind his eyes. "I kept meaning to call him," he confessed. "Ask him to go out for a couple of beers or something. But I just didn't get around to it. Never thought I'd run out of time. We think we got all the days in the world, you know?"

Zach caught the pained look on Becca's face and knew she understood, better than anyone.

"What's done is done," Zach pitched in. "Lindsay and Liam were aware of how people felt about them. They valued their friends and family and knew how much their friends and family valued them. Not everyone is as lucky."

"Their luck ran out in the end, though, didn't it?" Pat slumped in his chair, looking suddenly drained. "Now those kids are stuck paying the price."

After lunch Rebecca offered to help Tess with the dishes. It only seemed appropriate, seeing as she and her husband had gone through the trouble of feeding them. Pat and Zach took over babysitting duty, and the women retreated inside the house. Pat and Tess's summer home was similar to Zach's, with the exception of a more flamboyant décor—from the pastel palette they obviously favored to the floral-print overstuffed couches and chairs. Vivid throws added even more color, as did the Oriental rug in the living room.

Figurines of all shapes and sizes lined the bookcase facing the stone hearth.

"They're Pat's," Tess explained, noticing where Rebecca's gaze had fallen. "He's had them since he was a kid."

"They're pretty," she said, although she couldn't understand why a boy—or a grown man for that matter—would collect porcelain figures.

"They were his mother's," Tess said in response to Rebecca's unvoiced query. "She gave them to him right before she took off. Pat was twelve at the time. It's all he's got left of her."

Suddenly, she understood. She knew exactly how it felt to be a child left behind. She understood the isolation, the desperation to fit in, the yearning to hold on to anything that made you feel connected to something greater than yourself. For her, that had been Zach and his family and the children she wasn't able to have. For Pat, it was these figurines.

"How long have you owned this place?" she asked Tess as they proceeded to the kitchen.

"Only two years. Liam let us know as soon as it was put on the market. Pat wasted no time picking it up."

"You said Liam and Pat met at Harvard?"

"Yes, they were roommates."

"It's funny that our paths never crossed before now. Lindsay and I grew up together. I was married to Zach for eight years."

"Pat took a job in New York right after he graduated. We only moved back to Boston three years ago."

That explained it. During the last year of her marriage, Rebecca had lived in a bubble. She'd shied away from all family events or public gatherings, too lost in her disappointment and grief to find joy in anything. Happiness had become painful to watch.

"The first thing Pat did when he got here was reconnect with Liam," Tess continued. "They never lost touch."

She wished she could claim the same with Lindsay. Losing touch with her best friend was one of her greatest regrets.

They both unloaded the plates they held, and Tess hurried to fill the sink with suds. "Did I tell you Amy has taken a fancy to helping me with the dishes?"

Rebecca shook her head, dropped a handful of dirty utensils into the sink.

"The other day she left the faucet on. There were bubbles everywhere, counters, floor, even inside the toaster. I nearly blew a fuse. The kids thought it was Christmas in July, rolling around in the suds like it was a pile of snow."

A whisper of a smile yanked at Rebecca's lips. There was a time when she would have found some excuse to escape. Anything so as not to have to listen to Tess drone on about her kids with that note of possessiveness in her voice, that soft sigh of affection that somehow scraped away at the annoyance. She was pleased when the need to run didn't assail her, thrilled that she found it in her to be amused.

For the first time in a long while, she thought, *I'm going to be all right.* What shocked her was that she actually believed it.

Between the two of them, they finished washing and drying the dishes in no time at all.

Rebecca busied herself putting the utensils away while Tess focused on the leftovers. She heard a clunk, turned to find Tess cursing while dabbing at her pink T-shirt with a napkin.

"Dropped the ketchup bottle," Tess said sheepishly, then hurried to clean up the mess she'd made. "Better go change." She blew out an exasperated sigh. "And rinse out this shirt before it stains."

"I heard salt works wonders," Rebecca offered.

"I've got about a gallon of Spray and Wash in the laundry room. Be right back."

Deciding to pick up where Tess left off, Rebecca grabbed a few Tupperware containers and began placing them in the fridge. The house was still, peaceful, the silence broken only by the hum of the refrigerator and the occasional giggle or scream that trickled in from the open window.

The sudden sound of Pat's voice coming from the living room startled her, and she nearly tipped over the orange juice. One more inch and she would have needed some of Tess's Spray and Wash, too. "You know I'm vacationing with the family right now," he said. "You promised to back off and give me some time to regroup."

Obviously, he wasn't talking to his wife or Zach, for that matter. Probably on his cell, she reasoned.

His footsteps thundered as he approached the kitchen. "I've done everything I can. I've been working with Interpol and the OSCE—" There was a long pause. "'Course I care about the kids. I got two of my own. But these sons of bitches are about as slippery as mud. The only witness we had turned up face down in the harbor." Another pause. "I understand. I'll do my best. But without another witness or some kind of lead, I'm just spinning my wheels."

She heard his cellular slam shut right before he barreled into the kitchen. "That Dan's got a brick up his ass. He expects me to crack this case wide open while he sits in his office sipping goddamn martinis and playing with his dick."

Rebecca closed the refrigerator door, turned to look at Pat. His sunburned skin was flushed with anger. The moment he caught sight of her, his already ruddy complexion turned an even deeper shade of red. "Sorry, I thought you were Tess."

"She went to change. I'm just finishing up here."

Pat cleared his throat. Embarrassment had him staring at her feet. "About what I just said—"

"Don't worry about it. I was married to Zach for eight years. I'm used to a swear word or two." She smiled, hoping to defuse the situation and ease his discomfort.

Before the tension could escalate further, Kristen slunk in, her hands clenched in front of her, her eyes downcast. She crept up to Rebecca, tugged on her sarong and mumbled something.

"I didn't hear you, sweetie."

Rebecca leaned down so the girl could whisper in her ear. "I need to use the potty."

"Sure. Come, I'll take you." She excused herself. Taking Kristen by the hand, she bolted from the kitchen and happily left Pat to his privacy.

Dusk came, slow and steady, with a streak of red so brilliant it set the sky on fire and turned the harbor a deep, shimmering rose. Rebecca watched the small waves from the window as she tucked Kristen into bed. She'd go for a late-night swim, she decided, get a few laps in before she called it a night. She didn't have the benefit of a gym here, so she had to get her exercise any way she could.

Will was teething, so Zach was in the other room with him, trying to calm him. Once the baby settled, Zach would place him in his playpen, which was set up in Noah and Kristen's room. Hopefully, Noah and Kristen would already be asleep by then. Though, judging by the way Noah sat in the armchair across the room playing with his Game Boy, she highly doubted it.

"Aren't you coming to bed?" she asked.

"Not tired yet."

"It's late."

"I'm nine," he argued. "I can stay up later than my baby sister."

"I'm not a baby," Kristen tossed in, obviously offended. "If Noah can stay up, I can, too."

Rebecca closed her eyes and sighed. "All I know is that you better be in bed when your uncle brings Will in, or there'll be hell to pay."

Noah ignored her. Kristen on the other hand sank into bed and pulled the sheet up to her chin. She looked troubled, pensive, as she had ever since she'd walked into the Jenkinses' kitchen earlier today. Rebecca had been meaning to ask her what was wrong, but hadn't known how to go about it. She wasn't sure the girl felt comfortable enough to confide in her yet. But she had to try. "Did you have fun today?"

The girl gave a feeble nod. "I like playing with Jason and Amy."

"So no one did anything to upset you? One of the kids, maybe—"

Kristen wagged her head.

"You're sure?"

She nodded again.

Concern strained Rebecca's brows, and she realized with a twinge of alarm she'd probably just given herself another wrinkle...and a few gray hairs to go along with it. She really wished she had some idea what she was doing. Wished she knew how to get Noah to make eye contact and Kristen to share her worries. But she didn't. She was as lost as the thin wisp of a girl buried in the king-sized bed.

Defeated, she stood to leave.

"Aunt Becca," Kristen called as Rebecca reached the door. "Am I going to disappear, like my mommy and daddy?"

Rebecca's pulse gave a nice, swift kick. "Of course not. Where did you get an idea like that?"

Kristen shrugged. From across the room, Noah snorted. "Probably from one of her dumb baby shows."

"I'm not a baby!"

"Noah, please." Rebecca begged the boy to be quiet, not caring if she sounded pathetic. She returned to the girl's bedside, reached out to grip her small hand. "You're not going to disappear."

Kristen bit her lower lip until it turned white. "But Amy's dad said the children are disappearing because the angels are broken."

Confusion streamed in to crowd out distress. "Pat? When?"

"I heard him when I went to use the potty. He was screaming in the phone." The lip she stopped worrying trembled dangerously. "Is it true? Are the angels broken?"

"No." Rebecca lifted her hand, allowed it to stroke the child's hair, surprised when the act didn't sting. "The angels aren't broken. They're strong and they're whole and they're watching over you. Every day and every night, they're watching over us all."

She lifted her gaze to rest on Noah, and this time his eyes locked with hers. There was anger and pain in them, but hope, too. In his turbulent stare she sensed a desperate need to believe that the bad really could be kept at bay.

Kristen hugged Lindsay's sweater. Pulling her favorite teddy bear close with her other arm, she turned on her side. "I don't want to disappear," she muttered into the brown fur.

145

Rebecca shocked herself by doing something she didn't believe she was capable of doing. She leaned over and brushed a kiss on the girl's forehead. "You won't," she promised. "I won't let it happen. Ever."

She didn't know who Pat had been talking with on the phone or why he'd gotten so angry. But she knew one thing—an adult always had to be on guard around children, because they listened, and they heard, even when they didn't seem to be paying attention. Every inadvertent word spoken had the potential to plant doubt and the power to devastate.

She waited until Kristen drifted off to sleep and Noah finally decided to climb into bed. Then—her heart heavy yet full—she tiptoed out of the room, down the stairs and out into the cool night, where the sea beckoned her.

So they'd gotten through another day. That was how Zach measured success now—not in terms of award-winning advertising campaigns or multi-million-dollar accounts, but in terms of meals consumed, games played and a minimum number of tears shed.

The sun had set over an hour ago. The sky was a deep indigo spattered with stars. Silver moon shadows hopped along the edges of the water, making it pulse with a neon-blue glow. Normally, he didn't have much use for the ocean. It was a death trap, if you asked him. Still, he liked the sound the waves made when they slapped the shore. He listened to that sound, let it soothe him, while he sat on the porch steps staring into the black void of night.

Life looked so simple from this vantage point, and he almost convinced himself everything would sort itself out. He was probably a fool to think they could all start over, but he didn't give a shit. He wanted to savor this strange peace that had fallen over him.

The kids were safe, healthy, able to smile occasionally. That was something, he guessed. Yeah, they were torn to shreds inside, but that would right itself in time. It had to. The body had a self-preservation mechanism that forced you to survive, whether you wanted to or not.

Take Becca, for instance. She was living proof that time healed all wounds. He could see the change in her. There was something solid and composed about her that hadn't been there before. Something that told him maybe history didn't have to repeat itself. She could smile through her pain, wrap her arms around a crying baby, listen to a mother talk about her children without shriveling inside. And that gave him hope. Maybe she'd learned to accept what she couldn't change. Maybe she'd finally made peace with fate.

Just the same, he couldn't help but wonder if she could ever really be happy with their makeshift family or if she'd always feel cheated, always crave the one thing he couldn't give her.

The harbor shivered, and from its depths a figure sprang. She walked toward him, bathed in starlight, her body glistening, her hair streaming wet and wild down her back.

Zach's next breath snagged in his throat.

A siren, he thought. A mythical creature rising from the sea to seduce him.

His lungs felt crushed, deprived of air. The walls of his throat narrowed as an electrical charge pulsed across his nerve endings.

Then he realized the siren was Becca. She'd gone for an evening swim. She loved swimming at night because the water was always warmer then. Shadows played along her curves, making her hips rounder, her stomach flatter, her breasts fuller. Her hair was a deep bronze, her skin a translucent ivory in the pale light of the moon.

His body instantly responded to the sight of her, hardening, aching, until he couldn't remember why he'd vowed to keep his hands off her. None of it seemed to matter anymore.

She grabbed a towel from the porch railing and swathed it around her figure, and it took all of his self-control to bite back the protest that scratched at his throat.

"I was wondering where you disappeared to," he muttered instead. His voice sounded gruff.

"After I tucked Noah and Kristen in, I decided to go for a swim. You were busy with Will, and I can always use the exercise." She lowered her body next to his, smelling of the sun and the sea. Water dripped from her hair. Rivulets trickled over her shoulders and slid down her arms.

Unable to stop himself, he captured one of the drops with the back of his index finger. It was cool against her warm skin, silky. Their gazes locked, and awareness sizzled between them.

"Did Will go to sleep okay?" Her question pierced the cloud of lust enveloping him.

"Yeah." He let his hand fall away before he was tempted to explore more of her. "He was exhausted after all that crying."

"Not to mention all that fun in the sun." A hazy smile ghosted across her lips. "We had a pretty full day. The kids were really excited, weren't they?" The tenderness on her face shook him. It was the same look Lindsay always used to get whenever she spoke of the kids.

He eyed her steadily. An image of her playing in the waves with the pack earlier today flashed through his mind. "You're really something with them." He couldn't suppress the note of wonder in his voice. "I never expected it."

She gave a self-deprecating chuckle. "Half the time—correction, most of the time—I feel like I'm in way over my head." Bolt ambled onto the porch to sit beside her, and she stroked him absently. Zach's gaze was drawn to the gentle rhythm of her fingers as she threaded them through the dog's lustrous coat. He remembered how those hands had felt on his body when she'd massaged him last night, the way they'd twined in his hair and chased the tension from his limbs.

"But I understand them. Understand how they feel," she added, oblivious to the dangerous path his thoughts were taking. "I get Noah's anger, Kristen's totally delusional hope, Will's tantrums."

Zach made a sound that was half laugh, half snort. "At least one of us does."

"You're being too hard on yourself as usual. You're great with them. I can see how much they look up to you."

"That's because I'm tall."

Her heartfelt laughter filled the night. God, he'd missed hearing her laugh. The sound of it made a strange energy pulsate in his pores and burrow deep within the marrow of his bones. It took all his self-control not to reach out and touch her again. Instead, he clasped his hands together and let them hang between his knees.

"Can you answer a question for me?" He stared at his joined fingers, unable to look her in the eyes for fear of what he would see there.

"Sure."

"When I suggested adoption, why did you refuse? I thought maybe you believed you couldn't love a child that wasn't biologically ours. But now that I see you with these kids I can't help but wonder—"

"You thought I couldn't love a child I didn't give birth to?" She sounded offended.

He ventured a glance in her direction. Even in the dark he couldn't miss the indignation that flamed in her cheeks.

"I didn't know what to think," he answered honestly. "You were so set against it."

"Because I was angry. Because if I couldn't have what I wanted, then I wanted nothing at all. It was the injustice of it, the unfairness. Why should I be deprived the joy of feeling my child grow inside me when it came so naturally to everyone else? Adoption felt like acceptance, like throwing in the towel."

"Would that have been so bad?"

"At the time, yes."

"And now?"

She hesitated. The light breeze lifted her wet curls from her shoulders, sent them rioting around her face. "It doesn't really matter anymore," she whispered. "The choice is no longer mine to make." He barely heard her past the whoosh of the waves.

"That sounds oddly like acceptance."

"Maybe it is. Even I have to give up sometime." Her inflection held a hint of amusement, but he wasn't buying the flippancy.

"Is that what this feels like to you, giving up?"

She was quiet for a long time. The waxing moon haloed her head and made her eyes sparkle like liquid gold.

"No," she answered with more conviction than he'd expected. "It feels like family."

Vulnerability sparkled in her eyes, more potent than her glistening skin, her clingy swimsuit, the small towel wrapped around her breasts and hips. Zach lost the battle and extended his hand to cup her face. Her skin was soft, an odd blend of velvet and satin. It tickled his palm as a strange current traveled up his arm and thrummed along his flesh.

He never should have allowed himself to touch her. Now the need to kiss her blinded him. It was a physical ache, sharp and insistent. She turned her cheek into his palm, moved closer...

"Becca—" Her name tore from his throat, both a desperate plea and a growl. In the same heartbeat, his mouth crushed hers. Fire shot through his veins, sent his resolve straight to hell. Need raged through him, and every minute he'd spent without her only seemed to stoke the blaze.

Her lips parted to receive him. He wasn't sure whether the sound she made was a gasp or a sigh, and to be honest he didn't give a damn. He just wanted to taste her. Her mouth was moist, inviting, as he slid his tongue in to mate with hers. She brought her palms to his abdomen, let them glide across his ribs and around his back, and he knew she wouldn't put up a fight. A part of him was hoping she would because, right about now, he wasn't exactly thinking with his head. Not the one on his shoulders, anyway.

She had no intention of making this easy for him—the way the movements of her lips matched his, the way she edged in closer and flattened her breasts against his chest.

She had no idea what she was doing to him. Or maybe she did. He couldn't be sure. He tasted boldness on her tongue. Boldness and a trace of desperation.

All of a sudden he wanted more. He wanted to feel every inch of her, to recapture what he'd lost, to once again anchor himself to the one woman who could keep him rooted. She was his purpose. A man had to have purpose or he drifted, got swept away by the tide.

Decisively, he stood and pulled her to her feet so the length of her damp body pressed against his. He felt every hot curve, every sea-scented curl, the wild tempo of her heart as it galloped in perfect beat with his own.

There was no more room for doubt. With a groan, he clumsily pushed open the door, and they stumbled into the house. He tugged at the straps of her swimsuit, his mouth traveling down her neck and over her shoulder as the unrelenting agony in his groin sharpened. The towel slid to the ground. His hand found her breast, yanked it free. She moaned and dug her hips into his until he thought he'd explode. He wanted to tell her to take it easy, but he couldn't find his voice. All he managed was a grunt.

Then he was lifting her off her feet and carrying her to the bedroom, with nothing but the moon and stars to light his path.

Chapter Twenty

Rebecca's senses swam, as if she suffered from heat stroke, only the heat wasn't coming from the sun but Zach. It poured over her in waves, singeing her from the inside out, as his mouth drank from hers and his hand closed over her breast. She'd forgotten what it felt like to be loved by Zach. It was like being swallowed by a firestorm—wild and hungry and all-consuming. His kisses chased every thought from her head.

His mouth never left hers as he carried her to the bedroom. Once there, he spread her out on the bed, his face awash in eagerness and something else—amazement. She didn't understand it. He was far more magnificent than she was. His skin was smooth, like polished gold, his arms strong and muscular. She tugged the shirt from his body, marveling at the splendid perfection of him. Whorls of dark hair covered his chest and slowly tapered down to his abdomen, where thick muscles bunched. She couldn't help but explore those muscles, loving the way they strained and rippled beneath her fingertips.

He was incredible, and he was hers. After all these years, he was still hers.

Her hand ventured lower. She unbuttoned his jeans, deliberately ran her thumbnail over his zipper. Muttering an oath, he grabbed her wrists and pinned them over her head. His mouth slid down her throat—hot, demanding. The silky feel of it flushed her system, made her skin purr and her body throb.

He carved a burning trail toward her breast, and she trembled in his arms. It had been so long since he'd loved her this way. So long since she'd allowed herself to dissolve in his arms and let the current carry her.

His lips slid down toward her navel, and he had no choice but to release her arms. As soon as he did, she buried her fingers in his hair and pulled him closer.

He peeled the swimsuit from her body, exposed her to his heated gaze. "You taste like the sea," he muttered as he flicked his tongue over her belly.

Pleasure whipped through her. "You don't like the sea."

"I like it just fine on you." He glided up toward her breast again.

"Maybe you should join me for a midnight swim sometime."

Shadows played across his back, outlining the thick tendons that stretched over his shoulder blades. "I'm sure you could persuade me if you set your mind to it."

Her fingers traced the length of his spine. "I'm always up for a good challenge." She loved the strength, the sharp leanness of him. Loved how delicate she felt when she was pressed against him.

Then his mouth closed over her nipple. Her mind went blank. She couldn't think, could barely breathe. She just wanted to feel, to lose herself to passion, to drown in this one moment and forget the past, for once stop questioning the future.

His need bulged against her inner thigh, branded her with its heat. She arched into him as a short burst of air escaped her lips. Desire hollowed out a place in her heart only he could fill, a gaping crevice that begged for completion.

He was holding back; she could tell. It was evident how badly he needed this, but he was taking his time, desperately clutching the tenuous string of self-control, trying to savor even as everything inside him screamed to devour.

She didn't want to be savored. She wanted to be consumed. Clasping a handful of his hair, she pulled him up, brought his lips to hers. With eager fingers, she pushed down his jeans and wrapped her legs around him, surrounding him with her heat. He groaned as a shiver quaked through him. Instinctively, his hips dug into hers. She welcomed him, urged him without words to enter her, but he pulled back.

A whimper of disappointment rose to lodge itself in her throat. Laughter rumbled next to her ear.

"You never were very good at being patient."

Frustration slow-danced with need, made her blood simmer. "And you were always too damn good at it."

He chuckled and drew her earlobe into his mouth. Frissons of pleasure poured through her. His hand ventured down her body, stroking the curve of her backside, the length of her leg. His fingers felt like coarse silk, rough and soft at the same time. He was driving her insane.

Hoping to get even, she rubbed against him until he grunted and shuddered. Need hardened every fabulous inch of him. Victory coursed through her. Any minute now he would cave to the persistent ache begging to be appeased and claim her the way only a man can claim a woman.

"I was right. You really are a siren."

"And you think way too much."

She covered his mouth with hers, cutting off his next breath. She knew the precise second his control snapped. A pained growl shook his chest and he wedged himself more firmly between her legs. Then he was inside her, possessing her. Her world spun and crashed. Each thrust was like the aftershock of an earthquake, fierce and mind-shattering.

Her body surged and bucked, rapture submerging her in blinding sheets. He cried out her name, convulsed against her, sending warm tremors skittering along her flesh. His pulsing heat inside her made her own body violently contract around him, then go limp and boneless.

Afterward, she lay spent in his arms, trying to remember how to breathe. Sex had always been intense between Zach and her—explosive, totally mind-blowing. If only they were as good together in other areas besides the physical, their marriage might have fared better. Would things go smoother the second time around or were they heading down the same dead-end street again?

"What now?" She didn't want to shatter the mood so soon, but the question slipped out before she could stop it.

A beat of silence followed. "I haven't got a clue." His gaze was riveted on the ceiling, his expression unreadable. "Why don't we just take it one day at a time?"

She could live with that. Life was easier to deal with in small chunks. She closed her eyes, snuggled closer. Peace was a funny thing. It crept upon you when you least expected it, spread its golden branches inside you. Before you knew it, hope took root in your heart. She prayed this time she could contain it, that it wouldn't grow to smother her.

Slowly, sleep rolled over her—a numbing mist that closed around her mind and sent her floating toward the realm of dreams, where the only sensation was a tender echo of contentment.

Dawn swept in, a diamond-flecked haze that flooded the room with light. For once, Zach awoke without any help from Will—his own personal alarm clock. Becca slept soundly in his arms, all delicate curves and fragrant heat. She fit beside him perfectly, completed him like the missing piece of a jigsaw puzzle. The part of him that had died along with their marriage had spun back to life last night, and he found himself smiling up at the ceiling like an idiot.

Damned if he wanted to get up. He wanted to lie here all day, with nothing to do but run his hands over Becca's sexy-as-sin body. He wanted to remember what it had felt like to be young and totally infatuated, before life had interfered.

Carefully, he brushed the hair from her face. He'd always loved to watch her sleep. Loved how soft and wild she looked. He would have given anything to see her dreams, to be able to make them all come true.

But he couldn't, and that pissed the hell out him and made him feel like the worst kind of loser. A man wasn't a man if he couldn't give his wife what she needed. Now, lying here in this bed with nothing but his conscience to listen to, he asked himself if that was the real reason he'd walked out on her. Every time he'd looked in her eyes, he'd seen everything he'd failed to give her, and that truth had burned like a knife-wound.

Maybe Becca had a point. Maybe he really did want to *fix* everything. That was what he'd always been—a fixer, the one everyone called in a crisis, the one with all the answers. He didn't know how to function otherwise, didn't know how to handle a problem he couldn't set right.

So he'd run. Like a goddamn coward.

She stirred beside him, moaned as her eyelids eased apart. "Why did morning have to come so soon?"

"We don't have to get out of bed just yet. The kids are still asleep."

A smile stretched across her lush mouth. "Good, 'cause I don't think I could move right now."

"Are you sure?" He nuzzled her ear, let his lips trail over her cheek. "I'm pretty sure I could convince you."

"You always were overconfident."

"With good reason." His mouth closed over hers, and her next argument was forgotten. She went liquid in his arms, warm and boneless. Desire spiked in his veins—as biting as it was seductive. They'd made love a second time in the middle of the night, and still he ached for her.

Her arms formed a loop around his neck. She deepened the kiss, and flames ignited in his blood. He wanted her to touch him, to close her fingers around him, to ride him till the sun set for the last time. As if reading his thoughts, her fingers lazed downward. They tightened around him, started stroking him, and every thought blasted from his head. Her caress was the sweetest agony.

With a regretful groan, he pried himself loose from her grip and immobilized her on the bed beneath him. "I'd forgotten how much trouble you are," he muttered between kisses.

"You wouldn't have me any other way," was her husky reply. "I must say I'm impressed with your stamina." She arched into him, kissed the side of his neck.

"It's been a while." He ran his tongue over her ear. "Two years to be exact."

The hand she was sliding down his back froze midway. He sensed the tremor of shock that coursed through her. "You didn't— There was no one else?"

He lifted himself high enough to gaze down at her startled face. "Why do you look so surprised?" Didn't she know what she'd done to him, the fundamental way she'd changed him? From the first time he'd touched her, every other woman had paled in his eyes. "How could I possibly want anyone else after having you?"

Moisture pooled on her lashes. "I always thought I was the only one who felt that way." The awe resonating in her voice both touched and unhinged him. She pulled his head down, fused her lips with his as her body combusted beneath him.

Then Will's banshee cry shattered the blessed silence.

Becca stiffened in his arms, then sighed in defeat. "I told you," she moaned. "Morning came too soon."

Chapter Twenty-One

The sun gradually climbed high in the sky, and the day grew increasingly hot. No breeze stirred today. The harbor was calm and motionless, the trees hardly swaying. An occasional cloud floated lazily overhead, as if it had no particular place to go and was in no rush to get there. The sand sizzled beneath their feet, making sandals a necessity.

They spent the day on the beach again, with Tess and Patrick fused to their side. Rebecca sensed a certain awkwardness hovering between her and Pat after his outburst the previous day, but overall, he hid it well.

Still, she couldn't help but ask, "Is everything all right? You looked really worked up yesterday."

Pat shifted uncomfortably in the sand, leaning back on his bent arms. "Yeah. Sorry again about that. That was Dan on the phone, the DA."

"Can't he just leave you alone?" Tess's voice held just enough bite to let them know this was a sore spot with her. "You're on vacation for God's sake."

"He's got his sights on the mayor's office," Pat explained. "Been thinking of running for quite some time, but he needs an edge. This case he's been hounding me about stretches far and wide. Could be just the boost he needs to shoot straight to the top. Problem is, he expects me to do all the legwork."

"Legwork's not always that bad," Zach tossed in, his gaze drifting over Rebecca's legs in a way that had her skin tingling.

Thankfully, Pat didn't notice Zach's teasing smile or the scalding stare Rebecca directed her ex-husband's way. "It is when it leads nowhere," he replied. "You don't understand what I'm dealing with here. I'm talking about a global network of criminals who've been at this for decades. They're virtually untraceable, untouchable." Rebecca could've sworn she caught a note of admiration in his voice.

"Enough talking about work," Tess admonished. "You're here to relax."

"Yeah, you're right." But Pat's features failed to slacken. His shoulders remained stiff, his back ramrod straight. "I really needed to get away. I get claustrophobic in the city sometimes. Unlike my lovely wife here, I'm a small-town boy through and through. Grew up in Oak Bluffs." A nostalgic mist rolled over his face. "Everything's simple there, with your homemade ice-cream shops and your mom-and-pop restaurants and the sea every which way you look. That's why I got this place. Reminds me of home."

Amy suddenly hopped toward them. Strawberry blond ringlets bounced around her pretty face, forming a striking contrast with her honeyed skin and dark brown eyes. She took her father's hand, begged him to go swimming with her. Pat muttered a protest, then stood with a grunt and obediently followed his daughter. Warmth ran lazy circles around Rebecca's heart at the sight of man and girl melting into the harbor to a chorus of joyful giggles.

Then Zach decided to distract her while Tess was busy yelling something at her son. He ran his palm down the length of her leg, and the heat raged out of control, spread to flood her system. The second Tess's head swiveled their way, he withdrew his hand, the picture of innocence.

"Are you overheating?" Tess asked her. "You look flushed."

"I'm fine." She directed a quelling look at Zach, who watched her with a knowing, totally infuriating grin. "But a swim might not be such a bad idea," she added just to get even.

When she emerged from the water a few minutes later, she didn't bother wrapping herself in a towel. The look on her ex-husband's face as she paraded toward him, dripping wet, was priceless. She stretched out on a towel and allowed the sun's rays to dry her, all the while sensing Zach's blistering stare.

"You're an evil woman," he whispered when the neighbors were out of earshot.

Laughter exploded from her. "It's no less than you deserve. You've been undressing me with your eyes all day."

"No I haven't. That string bikini leaves very little to the imagination. Patrick's been checking you out, too," he grumbled.

She sprang to a sitting position. "He has not." Unease skittered through her. "The guy's married."

"He'd have to be dead not to notice you in that number."

Suddenly self-conscious, she grabbed a towel and draped it over her damp body. A victorious smile bounced across his full mouth, and she couldn't help but wonder if his assertion was just a clever ruse to get her to cover herself up.

"Aren't you going to go for a swim?" she taunted.

"Maybe tonight." The unmasked implication in his voice turned her bones to rubber. Heat inundated her cheeks.

Zach ran his palm over her face. "I've always loved the way you could do that."

"Do what?"

"Blush. It's more potent than that bikini."

The man was killing her. His feathering caress, the way his eyes drank in the sight of her left her weak and molten inside.

Relief gushed through her when Tess came to sit beside them again. Now he'd have no choice but to behave.

"What a perfect day," the neighbor chirped.

Rebecca hummed her approval, closing her eyes for a second to chase the image of Zach's sexy grin, washboard stomach and perfectly chiseled chest from her mind.

"I forget how blue the sky is sometimes." Tess wrapped her arms around her legs and stared into the sea. There was a calmness about her that Rebecca envied.

Noah and Jason both raced out of the water, clambered onto the sand. Tess shot to her feet and swathed her son in a towel, planting a heartfelt kiss on the top of his head.

That familiar tightness blossomed within Rebecca, a gentle throb pulsing around a wound that refused to heal. Longing lumped in her throat, and she looked at Noah, who watched the scene with feigned indifference. Still, she caught a flicker of something beneath the apathy, an unspoken ache that mirrored her own. Following Tess's lead, she grabbed a towel and approached her nephew.

Noah shoved her arm away before she could cover him. "I'm okay," he spat, startling her with the sheer force of his words. Without sparing her another glance, he shook off the water and took off in search of his sister.

She turned to Zach and found him studying Noah, who was now wrestling with Kristen over a pail. It hadn't taken the boy long to pick a fight. Zach met her gaze, and she realized he'd reached the same conclusion. His expression dripped with the same helplessness unfolding inside her.

"Go play with Noah and the girls," Tess, who hadn't noticed a thing, crooned. Jason instantly complied. Pat dutifully joined them and began building sandcastles with his children. It was a scene right out of a commercial promoting one family getaway or another.

Except for Noah, who lingered a short distance away, watching them with barely contained resentment. Then, his features alight with the same mock innocence that had graced Zach's face minutes ago, he ambled toward them and stepped smack in the middle of their creation.

Jason jumped up. "You did that on purpose," he cried, blinking to chase away tears.

"Did not." Noah crossed his arms over his narrow chest.

"You did. I saw you," his friend insisted.

"Liar."

"You're the liar. You're just jealous 'cause my castle is better than yours."

Noah shoved him. Hard. The boy lurched backward and fell in the sand. Noah flung himself on top of Jason, hands fisted, body wired. Punches began to fly.

All four adults rose simultaneously and ran to stop the fight. They pried the children apart, everyone speaking at the same time.

"How could you?"

"What were you thinking?"

"You could hurt each other."

"You're supposed to be friends."

Tension spread like a black cloud to darken the peaceful afternoon. The lighthearted camaraderie was shattered. Tess was livid. Pat couldn't believe Noah had acted so poorly. Bolt barked up a storm. Kristen began to cry, and Amy sought refuge in the comforting folds of her mother's sarong. Only Will continued to smile and gurgle, oblivious to the commotion around him.

When the dust settled, Rebecca and Zach apologized to the neighbors, then gathered up the children and retreated into the house, where they could scold Noah in private.

It was like trying to squeeze compassion out of a rock. The boy was firm, resolute. He'd broken the sandcastle by accident. Jason had provoked him. It was all Jason's fault, and so forth.

Zach's exasperation was palpable. "Go to your room," he ordered, "and don't come out until I say you can."

The boy stomped away in a huff.

"And no video games," he called out after him. "I want that Game Boy."

Noah turned a pair of flaming eyes Zach's way. Realizing he wasn't going to win this one, he retrieved the device and slapped it in his uncle's waiting palm. Then, with a last mutinous look directed at Zach, he raced up the stairs and slammed the bedroom door shut with the force of a hurricane.

"I don't know what's up with that kid." Zach looked tired, beaten. "He's gotta get a handle on his anger."

She recalled the look on Noah's face when Tess had kissed Jason, the resentment in his eyes as he'd watched Pat build that sandcastle with his kids. "He didn't do it out of anger," she said. "He did it out of grief."

Zach's brows narrowed. "How do you figure that?"

"Seeing Jason with his parents made him hurt, so he returned the favor." Hadn't she been guilty of the same thing, back when her own dreams had died a slow, devastating death? The only way she'd known to deal with her pain was to push everyone she loved away—her best friend, her husband. Anger was just a shield, a barrier erected to conceal a deep well of sorrow.

Zach's frustration ruptured, and his face fell. "What am I supposed to do about that? How do I make him stop hurting?"

"You can't. He needs to deal with it in his own way, at his own pace. Some people have the ability to accept life's blows and move on. Those who don't, retreat into themselves." In Zach's troubled eyes she saw everything sorrow had cost her, everything she'd sacrificed for the simple luxury of wallowing in her misery. "And in the process they destroy everything that matters to them," she whispered.

He studied her for what felt like an eternity, and even though she was now fully clothed, she felt more exposed than she had in her swimsuit earlier today.

"You really do understand him," he finally uttered, and there was a hint of reverence to his words.

"Yeah, I do." She squeezed his shoulder reassuringly. "Let me talk to him. Maybe I can help."

"Be my guest." He ran his fingers through his hair until it spiked at the ends. Weariness rearranged his features in a mask she barely recognized. "I'm all talked out."

Zach watched Becca walk away, feeling oddly deflated. Kristen and Will played quietly in the living room, so he decided to join them. He dropped onto the couch, his mind riddled with troublesome thoughts he couldn't subdue. The last time he'd felt this useless, his marriage had fallen apart.

The stakes were even higher now. Noah's future was on the line. Right now he used his fists to deal with his grief. Later on, new, far more dangerous options would present themselves: booze, drugs, maybe even an act of crime or two. Zach needed to get the situation under control, and fast.

The question was how? How could he get through to his nephew?

Maybe Becca would have better luck. She understood the kid far better than he ever could. Then again, Zach saw more of himself in Noah than he cared to admit. There was something familiar about the boy's unfaltering stoicism, even as he shattered inside. Another iceberg with a volcano bubbling at the core. One of these days the ice would crack, and the pain would have no choice but to bleed out. Then what?

With a dejected grunt, he propped his elbows on his knees and linked his fingers. His head felt heavy, weighed down by the amalgamation of all his worries, so he placed his forehead on his fists for support. He stayed like this for quite some time, until a small body crept beside him. Hair brushed his biceps as a silky cheek dug into his arm. He raised his chin to find Kristen snuggled at his side, watching him shyly. A tentative smile ghosted over her lips.

Something warm and sweet coated the walls of his throat. He lifted his arm and clumsily draped it over her narrow shoulders. The girl relaxed, went limp against him, burrowed deeper.

And that made everything better somehow.

Noah slumped in his bed, his fists clenched, his heart pounding so hard he thought it would burst right out of his chest. His uncle didn't understand anything. All he did was yell at him, and he was sick of it. Why were adults so annoying? Why did there have to be so many lousy rules? What right did Jason have to tell him he was jealous of his crappy sandcastle? Who cared about a useless pile of dirt, anyway?

If his dad were still alive, they would have built a castle ten times bigger than Jason's. They would have made Jason's castle look like a dumb shack. Pain tightened inside him. His breathing grew rough, choppy, and hissed between gritted teeth. Was this what it felt like to have an asthma attack?

He wanted to hit something. Badly. Instead, he grabbed a pillow and flung it across the room. It nearly hit the door as it swung open, and Aunt Becca entered. Her gaze followed the arc the pillow made before it plunked at her feet.

"Are we having a pillow fight?" She was trying to be funny, but Noah's lips didn't as much as twitch. He was too busy dreading the lecture he was sure to get any minute now.

"What do you want?"

She looked nervous, uncomfortable, kinda like he always felt on the first day of school. "I thought maybe we could chat a little. Just you and me." She came to sit beside him on the bed, and he cringed.

"Why?"

"Why not?"

He could think of a few reasons, the fact that she couldn't stand him for one.

It hadn't always been that way. He remembered a time long ago when she'd played with him. He'd really liked her then. But the memories were old, fuzzy around the edges. He couldn't get any images, just a warm, funny feeling in his tummy. He wanted to ask her why she'd stopped liking him, but the words remained trapped in his throat.

"What happened out there today, kiddo?"

Here comes the lecture.

He shrugged, fingering his father's ring, which he'd worn on a chain around his neck ever since Will had found it in the canoe.

"Jason got on my nerves."

"It wasn't very nice of him to say you were jealous of his castle, was it?"

Surprise lanced through him. Maybe she did understand after all. "He was being a jerk."

"Friends do that sometimes. Your mom and I used to fight all the time when we were little."

He raised stunned eyes to her face, and she quickly added, "Not with our fists. We fought the way girls fight. One time I was mad at your mom because she called me carrot head, so I wrote a love note to the most popular guy in school and signed her name to it. Then I put it in his desk. She was mortified. Never called me carrot head again."

He wanted to smile, but he couldn't. His chest hurt too much whenever he thought of his mom. Tears stung his eyes, but he held them back. There was no way he'd let his aunt see him cry.

"What I'm trying to say is that it's all right to get mad at your friends. Just be careful because you never know when you'll lose them. And then you'll be left with nothing but regrets."

"Is that what happened to you?" He bit his lower lip. He shouldn't have asked that. Now she'd get angry.

"Yeah. That's exactly what happened to me," she whispered.

Then she was quiet for a very long time. With each breath he exhaled, Noah grew more and more agitated. He needed to say something, anything, to break the awful silence. "Why did you stop being my mom's friend? Was it because of Kristen and me? Did you hate us that much?"

He wasn't quite sure what to make of the expression that pinched her face. She seemed shocked, but at the same time she looked like she wanted to bawl. Noah sank farther into the bed. He should have kept his big mouth shut. He never knew when to be quiet.

"Why would you ever think something like that? How could I possibly hate you two?"

His stomach twisted uncomfortably. "I heard Mom talking to Dad once. She didn't know I was there. She was crying. She said you stopped being her friend because you couldn't bear to be around us."

Her face collapsed. Her eyes suddenly glistened, like raindrops in the sun. "I stopped being your mom's friend for the same reason you hit Jason today. Because I couldn't have what she had."

Their gazes locked. Noah saw his own pain reflected in the droop of his aunt's brows, in the stiff line of his lips, and for the first time he understood.

Rebecca had always loved to watch the sun set. There was something hypnotic about the way the pink swirls set the sea aflame.

Dusk was the only time fire and water could blend so seamlessly. It was undeniable proof even complete opposites could find a way to coexist and create something beautiful.

The night was cool, the breeze brisk as it feathered over her cheeks. On the outside she looked serene, at peace with the world around her. On the inside, anxiety bubbled, threatened to overflow. Noah's words reverberated in her mind, a sharp, unforgiving blade that stabbed into her and brought a strange weakness to her limbs.

"Did you hate us that much?"

She closed her eyes. The beautiful sunset suddenly felt sinister—a tiny death, a day gone that could never be recaptured, mistakes that could never be undone.

How had things gone so wrong? At one time she'd been completely infatuated with Noah. She'd held him when he was just a few days old, inhaled the fresh scent of newness only newborns possess. For the first two years of his life she'd been the model aunt. She'd fed him, changed him, played with him. She'd lived for his smile, his gentle hugs, the sound of her name on his lips. He hadn't been able to say Rebecca, so he'd called her Ecca instead.

Then she and Zach decided to have children of their own, and everything changed. Bitterness slowly seeped in, corroding the bond she and Noah had shared until it crumbled. She mourned the death of that bond now, would have given anything to have it back. Remnants of the tenderness she'd once felt for Lindsay's eldest child still echoed inside her. If she could reconnect with that old feeling, push down the walls she'd built around it, maybe...

"You look like you're miles away." Zach's voice sliced through her grim thoughts. He gently gripped her arms, then leaned his chin on her shoulder. Something inside her slowly stirred to life.

"Not miles, years." The sun tested the water, slid farther into the sea. "I was just remembering when Noah was first born. What it felt like to hold him."

His body tensed, his grip tightening. Memories of happier times often made the pain more difficult to bear. "You were his favorite. Lindsay was so jealous."

"Lindsay? Jealous of me? I don't think so."

"I know my sister. Believe me when I tell you she was green with envy."

"Why? She had everything." Everything Rebecca had ever wanted—beauty, grace, a child.

"Her firstborn cried whenever she took him out of your arms. You always had a way with kids. She was awkward with him, nervous. But you...you took to him like a fish to water. You always knew what he wanted, what he needed. It was uncanny."

Had she truly lost so much of herself to anguish? "How did I mess things up so badly?" She wasn't sure whether the question was directed at him or to the blazing sky.

He didn't answer. Instead, he turned her into his embrace and softly covered her mouth with his. This kiss was sweet and slow, like sugar melting on her tongue. It was a kiss that spoke of second chances, new beginnings.

Then the kiss deepened, grew desperate and demanding. Rebecca's skin began to tingle. She pulled him closer, wondering how she'd ever survived two years without him. It was as if the best part of herself had fallen into a deep sleep and was just now reawakening.

His arms encircled her back and drew her hard against him until she felt each splendid muscle carved into his solid chest, each pulse of his heart, each shiver of desire. Like ice on a hot day, the pain that had held her captive for so long slowly began to thaw. This kiss wasn't about physical need, although there was plenty of that.

It was about healing. Redemption. Hope.

The sun plunged deeper. Red flames danced along the surface of the sea. Soon it would be completely submerged, its brightness swallowed by blackness. But tomorrow it would rise again, peel away the smoky fingers of night and soar high in the sky.

Hand in hand, Zach and Rebecca walked back into the house, where their own radiant dawn awaited them.

Chapter Twenty-Two

Shadows swathed the beach house, a gray fog dusted with starlight. Zach guided Becca inside, unable to keep his hands off her, craving her kiss, her touch. Everything about this woman sang to him. No matter how many times he made love to her, it never took the edge off. It just made him yearn for her all the more. She was the missing part of himself, the one he'd been stupid enough to think he could live without.

Now he knew what an idiot he'd been. He might as well have attempted to live without his heart, which now thundered beneath his ribs as it sputtered back to life.

He didn't bother to wait until they reached the bedroom. Slowly, deliberately, he slid the straps of her dress from her shoulders, let the garment fall in a wrinkled heap at her feet. Moonbeams spilled in from the windows, caressing her skin and making it glow like alabaster.

His eyes drank in the sight of her. Fiery curls fell in satin sheets to brush the tips of her breasts. Her gaze was deep and molten, as potent as her kiss. The tightness in his groin grew painful.

She raised her arm, extended her hand to him.

Please don't touch me. I'll be lost.

But she did. And he was.

She peeled the clothing from his body, and a burning energy licked the underside of his flesh wherever her fingers ventured. Before long they both stood naked in a trembling puddle of moonlight. He bracketed her face with his hands, trailed his thumb across her cheek and over her lips.

"I can't bear to lose you again," he whispered.

She trembled against him. "You won't."

In that moment, when darkness crowded around them and crickets released their mating calls, when the ocean's night song escalated and drowned out the whistle of the wind, when Becca's mouth latched onto his and washed away his doubts, he believed her.

Heat flared inside him, surrounded him. Her scent intoxicated him, that subtle blend of lavender and sage sprinkled with a hint of sun and sea. He crushed her to him until not a sigh of air separated them. She went boneless in his arms, and somehow he had to find the strength to support them both even as his own knees weakened. He realized he could do it this time; he could be strong enough for both of them.

His lips never leaving hers, he swept her off her feet and pinned her to the wall. A soft gasp tickled his mouth as she wrapped her legs around him. His body lurched, sought out her liquid warmth, even as his brain warned him to take it easy. He was sick and tired of always striving for control. For once in his life he just wanted to be.

She didn't seem to mind. In fact, he was pretty sure she wanted him to lose control. The way her hips moved against his was undeniable proof of that. There was only so much stimulation a man could take.

He ran his hands over her torso, thrilled as her generous breasts spilled over his palms. She moaned and cupped his butt, increasing the pressure in his crotch. Desire tore through him, and he nearly cried out from the agony of it. Before he knew it, he was inside her. Heat swallowed him. Submerged him. Spun him around until he was sure he'd drown. His lungs refused to expand to admit any air. His heart grew so huge it blocked his windpipe. All the blood in his body sank to the part of him that was fused with her. They moved in perfect rhythm, in tune with the wind and the sea. His temples throbbed, his body stiffened, Becca shuddered and called out his name.

Then pleasure ripped through him. A torrent of emotion rushed in to sweep him away. He let the tide carry him, the night caress him, her gentle breath lull him until the fight leached out of him.

And for the first time, that was okay.

It was dark out, past midnight, he guessed. Noah liked to get up when everyone else was asleep. It made him feel older, free to do whatever he wanted. He'd always liked the night, until his parents got killed. Now it had become something sinister, a time when bad things happened, when the shadows came alive and threatened to gobble him up.

Stop being such a wimp, he told himself as he crept out of the room he shared with his dumb sister and crybaby brother. He was still angry about the scrap he'd had with Jason, couldn't bring himself to fall asleep. He figured playing a few games on Falcon World would help calm him down. It wasn't hard to find his aunt's laptop. She'd left it in the living room, on the oak table. Oak was easy to recognize because it had all those lines running through it. That's what his dad had said once. Noah never forgot anything his dad told him.

It helped that his uncle wasn't sleeping in the living room anymore. He was sharing Aunt Becca's bed now. What was up with that? Did that mean they were back together? Not that it mattered one way or the other. He was just curious.

He booted up the computer, logged on to the wireless network his dad had put in last year so he could stay in touch with the people he worked with whenever they were down here, then typed in the address for Falcon World. There were other kids on, probably from faraway places where it was much earlier.

"I've been W8ing 4 U."

The unexpected message from Night-Owl shocked him. "Didn't think you'd be up this late."

"Y do U think I call myself Night-Owl?"

Noah sent his friend a laughing face to tell him he thought his joke was funny.

"How's your vacation?"

"Sucks. My friend Jason pissed me off. He's 8, so sometimes he acts VD." *Very dumb.*

"Bet you whipped his butt."

"Yup. But now I'm grounded. Stuck in my room all f**king day."

His stomach clamped with anger at the thought of how his uncle had ordered him upstairs, taken away his Game Boy. It made him happy to know he was breaking Uncle Zach's dumb rules. It also helped to talk to Night-Owl.

"The only thing parents R good 4 is punishing their kids."

"Not yours. They let U play all U want, stay up till midnight."

There was a long pause. Then Night-Owl answered. "My parents R dead."

Noah's heart folded with a painful thump. The need to confide in someone—anyone—was a painful blister in his gut. "Mine 2."

"What happened?"

"Some AH broke in and shot them." His chest grew so tight he had trouble breathing. The images came again, hot and suffocating. "I still remember his face." It was the first time he'd admitted this to anyone, but it needed to be said, and Night-Owl was the easiest person to say it to.

"You saw the killer?"

"Yeah."

"What'd you do?"

A sob spread around his heart, but he struggled to keep it inside. He was afraid if he started crying he'd never be able to stop. The weight of his guilt crushed him. He touched his index finger to the keyboard and typed one word. One word that threatened to make the tears come. "Nothing."

Part Three

Revelations

Come away, O human child!
To the waters and the wild
With a faery, hand in hand,
For the world's more full of weeping than you
can understand.

William Butler Yeats, "The Stolen Child"

Chapter Twenty-Three

Noah was gone. Rebecca had searched the house twice, then scoured the beach, to no avail. Her pulse thundering, she raced back into the beach house and woke Zach, who lay sprawled on the bed, a peaceful expression on his face. She hated having to worry him, but she had no choice.

Where could Noah have run off to?

Zach groaned and parted his lids. "Where's the fire?"

"It's Noah. I can't find him."

The haze of slumber instantly cleared. Zach shot up in bed, his expression murderous. "He took off?"

"I don't know. He wasn't in his room when I got up. I searched the whole house and the beach."

"Did you check with Pat and Tess?"

Rebecca nodded. "Tess hasn't seen him. Pat wasn't around. He went fishing. He left at the crack of dawn."

He rubbed his eyes, clambered out of bed and yanked on his shorts. "How about Kristen? Did Noah tell her where he went?"

She shook her head and followed him out of the room. "She says she didn't hear him get up."

When they got downstairs, Kristen was sitting on the couch, her arms crossed over her chest, her bottom lip set in a pout. Will was fussing, tugging at his ear as he chewed up a notepad he'd gotten from a nearby end table.

"Kristen," Zach said, "do you have any idea where your brother may have gone?"

Her bottom lip trembled. Moisture pearled at the corners of her lashes. "I didn't see him. I don't know." A teardrop trailed down her rosy cheek.

Zach sighed long and hard. "When I get my hands on that kid..."

"Don't be mad at Noah." Kristen hopped onto her feet. "You'll make him sad. I don't like it when Noah's sad."

Rebecca approached her niece and placed a comforting arm around her shoulders. "We're not mad, sweetie. We just want to find him." Dread tingled in her gut. What if they were too late? What if he'd gone swimming by himself? What if...

Zach seemed to reach the same conclusion. Suddenly, he bolted out the back door and sprinted toward the water. The waves were rough today, loud and choppy. Foam pooled at the shore, only to be violently sucked in again.

Despite a healthy tan, his face looked ashen. She caught up in time to hear him say, "It's gone," and followed his gaze to where the canoe had been tethered.

All that remained was an empty wooden post. She hadn't noticed that before. "He didn't!"

Zach ran antsy fingers through his hair. "Then how do you explain the missing canoe?"

"Maybe he went to the Seashore." They both turned to find Kristen standing behind them, her arms clasped behind her back, her knees jerking restlessly.

"The seashore?" Zach watched his niece steadily.

The girl pointed east, where the National Seashore acted as a barrier between Chatham Harbor and the Atlantic Ocean. A bramble of trees sat nestled among golden dunes beneath an overcast sky. "Daddy used to take us there all the time in the canoe. Noah likes the dunes at the cove."

Clomping across the beach, Tess approached them, with her daughter's hand clasped protectively in hers and Jason following a safe distance behind. "Did you find him?"

Rebecca and Zach shook their heads simultaneously. "But we have an idea where he might've gone." Zach stared pensively at the breathtaking stretch of land at the other side of the harbor. "Doesn't look too far. I could probably swim there."

Rebecca's heart spun and crashed. "You'll drown."

He skewered her with a blistering glare. "Thanks for the vote of confidence."

"You don't swim."

"Just because I *don't* swim doesn't mean I *can't*." He ventured a few feet into the water. Rebecca gripped his arm.

Pain and urgency flashed in his cobalt-blue eyes. "I have to find him, Becca. I have to find my sister's son." His voice cracked, and something inside her broke.

"Take the dinghy," Tess interrupted. "The motor's broken, but you can still row."

"Thank you," Rebecca told her. "You're a lifesaver." She turned to Zach. "I want to come with you."

"I don't need a lifeguard."

"I'm worried about Noah, too. I'll go stir-crazy waiting for you to come back."

Obstinacy slid into compassion. "What about Kristen and Will?"

"I'll watch them," Tess offered.

Rebecca could've kissed the woman. She squeezed her hand in a gesture of appreciation. "Thank you," she said again. "Thank you so much."

"Don't mention it. I've got kids. I know what you're going through right now."

Kristen crept up to Zach and tugged at his shorts. "Bring my brother home. Please."

Zach fell to his knees, drew her into a bone-crushing hug. "I will," he promised.

The rowboat was old, its faded cedar hull in desperate need of another coat of varnish. Still, it hopped along the waves with remarkable ease.

The wind roared like an angry beast awakening from a nightmare. Thick clouds pooled in the sky, painting the day gray. Around them, water frothed and thundered, cold and hungry. Year after year, erosion ate away at the National Seashore, often causing large chunks of land to sink into the sea, and that brought the harsher Atlantic tides crashing into the once-peaceful Chatham Harbor.

Zach sat with his back to the stern and labored ahead. With each thrust of his arms, he propelled his body forward, focused on the rhythm of the oars as he plunged them into the greedy mouth of the harbor. Images surged within him, flashes from the past that suffocated his mind as mercilessly as the clouds fisting around the sun.

He fought them, stubbornly crammed them back into the darkened corners of his psyche. He couldn't let the memories devour him.

Becca was seated across from him, silent and thoughtful, her gaze trained on his face. He ignored her probing stare. With determined strokes, he continued to carve a thin path through the white-capped swells. The rowboat quaked menacingly each time a wave struck it. An oily feeling spread through him, coating the walls of his stomach and rising to fill his mouth, but he tamped it down.

He had to stay in control, had to get to Noah. Nothing else mattered.

Still, memories were nothing if not persistent. They chiseled away at his resolve and crawled through the cracks—waves crashing against the hull, icy water slapping his flesh, a vicious riptide dragging him under...

He shook the disturbing thoughts away and rowed harder.

"Are you all right?" Becca's voice shredded a hole through the thickening fog in his head. Slowly, it dissipated.

"I'm fine. I just hope Noah is, too. If he fell overboard—"

"He's a great swimmer."

"So was I. Once."

Twenty-five years ago these very waters had nearly claimed him. His father had taken him out in a rowboat similar to this one. The ocean had been calm at first, deceptive. Then it had grown restless. Violent waves had risen to pound angry fists against their small, pathetic craft. Unable to withstand the assault, the boat had capsized.

Instantly, the sea had wrapped frigid tentacles around him, pulled him deeper. He'd fought the brutal current, but no matter how hard he'd tried, he couldn't reach the surface. Above him, the sun's weak rays had speared through the impenetrable blackness. The light had hovered mere feet over his head, as inaccessible as the sky.

Fire had ignited in his lungs while darkness slid in to blur the edges of his vision. Then a strong hand had gripped his arm and pulled him out.

His father.

Cool, salty air had trickled down his throat to extinguish the flames. He still remembered the delicious taste of it, the way it had ballooned in his chest and chased the dizziness away.

That day he'd realized even a skilled swimmer was no match for the sea once it decided it wanted you.

He tried to keep it together when the dinghy lunged into the fierce waters of the Atlantic—where another fragment of land had recently fallen away—told himself they were almost at the Seashore.

"Zach, please tell me that's not what I think it is." Becca's sun-kissed skin went bone white.

He followed her gaze, and his worst fear came crashing down on him. In the distance—drifting on the waves—was the canoe. It looked empty. The urgency escalated to a physical ache. He pumped the oars with increased fervor until the boat lanced forward at astonishing speed. They reached the aimless craft within minutes.

As he'd suspected, there was no sign of Noah.

A small sob escaped Becca's lips. "Where is he?"

Zach shook his head and scanned the depths below. "Damned if I know. But I'm going to find him."

And with that promise hanging in the air between them, he plunged headfirst into his worst nightmare.

Chapter Twenty-Four

The sea was cold, deep and silky. It closed its wet mouth around him, then spit him out as if it didn't like the taste of him. The undertow was manageable today. With a few swift strokes, he was able to break through the surface. He dove in repeatedly, searching the darkened depths for a glimpse of a scraggy head, a pair of thin arms, a scrap of blue and yellow fabric. Murky water surrounded him, speckled with sand, hampering his visibility.

He wasn't sure why the hell he was doing this. Noah could be anywhere. The canoe could have been drifting for hours. Still a desperate, totally irrational energy drove him, kept him searching. He needed to convince himself his nephew wasn't in there, that he hadn't been swallowed by the sea. Needed it with a compulsion that all but consumed him.

His lungs began to burn. He didn't know how long he'd stayed under. A hand gripped his arm. Not his dad's this time, but Becca's. She'd jumped into the water after him. Together they floated toward the weak sun.

"You'll never find him this way," she told him in a breathless whisper. "We need to check the shore."

The crazy energy continued to vibrate in his veins, but he couldn't find his voice to argue with her. Instead he got back into the rowboat and yanked her out of the water. That was when he saw the cove—a tiny cut on the curved arm of the Cape. It dug into sand and stone, surrounded by dense shrubbery and a cluster of tall dunes.

Becca noticed it about the same time as he. "Look. Didn't Kristen mention a cove?"

With a brisk nod, he angled the boat north and set course for it.

It didn't look far. Not far at all. Then why was it taking so damn long to get there? It was the current. It swirled, fast and cold, around them, pushed them back even as he rowed harder. For a second the clouds completely blocked out the sun, and a chill skated down his back on thin legs of ice. Across from him, Becca shivered. The smell of salt and seaweed riding the breeze tickled his nostrils, made his throat sting.

Becca rubbed the goose bumps from her arms. On any other occasion he would have been more than happy to warm her. But right now he had to pour all his strength into reaching that cove. A seagull circled above, and its shrill, baleful cry urged him on.

"He has to be there." Her voice was gruff, thick with worry and the tears she refused to shed.

Determination steamrolled through him and flattened his fears, even as they snarled at being ignored. He couldn't lose himself to what ifs. He had to stay in the here and now, and that meant concentrating only on the next stroke, on the next foot the boat vanquished, on the next breath of oxygen he drew into his lungs.

Green meshed with blue and gray as they approached land. Zach maneuvered the boat through the narrow entrance, where the sea grew calm and the breeze stopped howling. Around them, wild tufts of grass spilled over sand like a straggly mop of hair. Dunes soared, almost as high as the trees. They quickly disembarked, and he carefully dragged the rowboat to the shore.

"How will we ever find him?" Discouragement tugged at Becca's mouth and brows. "He could be anywhere."

Zach scanned the deserted landscape, allowed determination to flood his system and drench his blood with adrenaline. "Then we'll just have to look everywhere. Even if it takes all day."

Noah liked to walk along the dunes. Liked the way the tall, powdery mountains tickled his bare feet. His dad had always said not to climb the dunes, that they were there to protect the beach, but he climbed them anyway. Anything that was fun seemed to be bad, and he was sick of it. Sick of always being told what to do and what not to do.

Uncle Zach was probably spitting out razorblades by now, but Noah didn't give a rat's ass. Served him right for grounding him. Not that he'd worry. His uncle didn't care about him. All he cared about was getting his way.

Today Noah had every intention of being his own boss. So, if walking on the dunes made him happy, then he'd sure as hell walk on the dunes.

It looked like it was going to rain. Gray clouds twirled over his head like strings of smoke from his grandpa's pipe. The air was damp and thick. Still, he enjoyed being outside, away from everyone and their dumb rules. Out here he didn't have to deal with his sister's constant whining, Will's screaming, Jason's dumb sandcastles. He didn't have to wonder why Aunt Becca was suddenly pretending to like him, while Uncle Zach seemed to have forgotten how. But most of all he didn't have to think of the confession he'd made last night or the sudden desire he felt to spill his guts to anyone who'd listen. As if admitting what a chicken-shit he was would make everything all right. Stupid, that's what he was. Stupid to have said anything to anyone, even Night-Owl.

He heard the barks then, turned and saw the harbor seals—a whole family of them—lying on a shelf of moss-covered rocks. Excitement flared in his chest, chased the bad thoughts away. He'd never seen so many seals this close to shore before. They were an awesome sight, gray with brown spots, their long whiskers twitching as they sniffed the air.

He had to get a closer look. He just had to. This was way too cool. He took off at a run, scaling dune after dune, heading for the rocks. He'd all but made it to the edge when the ground suddenly rolled out from under him. With a girlish scream, he tumbled down a steep slack, right before a shower of sand fell to block out the sky.

Rebecca heard the scream and stilled. The sound echoed off stone and brush, which convinced her she hadn't imagined it. "Noah?"

Barely a second later, Zach sprinted to her side. "Did you hear that?"

She nodded. "I think it came from those dunes."

Without another word, they headed in that direction.

"Over there." Zach pointed to a navy blue patch in the sand. It looked like a pair of sandals.

Noah's sandals.

So he was here. The question was, where?

"Noah!" she called out again, louder this time.

The only reply was the sound of the wind and a chorus of barks and grunts from beyond the dunes. She turned to Zach, her expression questioning.

"Harbor seals," he told her. "Must be perched somewhere on the other side."

They clambered up the dunes to get a better look. A recent storm had caused severe erosion, and the slipface was steep, towering above the shore like a cliff. Every so often the sand shifted, rose in swirls to be carried out to sea. The seals sat on a patch of mossy rocks a few feet from the bank.

"Noah!" Zach belted out, then lunged to the ground and raced across the beach. The seals scattered, dove beneath frothy waves. Rebecca climbed down and took off at a run after him.

Zach dropped to his knees and began digging in the sand at the foot of a vertical slope so sharp she wondered how the dune didn't collapse in a spray of dust. She realized what he was doing, and terror frosted along her spine. She finally reached him, kneeled beside Noah, who lay half-buried in the sand, and helped Zach dig him out.

The boy was in a state of panic. Gasping, he began to thrash wildly the moment they freed him.

"Are you hurt?" Zach cradled his nephew's face. "Can you breathe?"

Noah nodded. "I couldn't move. Couldn't get out." Tears carved thick tracks down his dirt-smeared cheeks.

Her hand rose to her mouth to stifle a cry. She wasn't sure whether it was one of shock or relief. All she knew was that she wanted to hold him, to shelter him in her arms the way she had when he was a baby. Right there and then, she buried her fears, her grief, her anger on that windswept shore. Buried them so deep they'd never see the light of day again.

She reached for Noah, pulled him close to her heart while she stroked the sand from his hair. "Oh, baby," she crooned. "You're safe now. You're safe."

Her own tears fell to dampen his head as he curled against her— so small, so fragile, like the infant she'd once rocked in her arms. In that moment the last seven years slipped away as surely as the sand rolling off the dunes. Suddenly, he was that round-faced toddler with the ready smile once more. He was the baby who, at one time, had preferred her to his own mother.

Zach slouched back on his haunches, his shoulders slumping even as his face tightened with disapproval. "What were you thinking, Noah, running off like that? You could've been killed. If Kristen hadn't told us about this place—" He paused, blew out a mouthful of air.

The boy was trying really hard to stop crying. She could tell by the stiffness in his limbs, the slight tremors that coursed through him.

"Why'd you do it? Why'd you take off without telling us?" Zach persisted.

Rebecca shook her head in silent warning. This wasn't the time to antagonize the child. He was too shaken.

Zach did what men do best; he ignored her. "We went half crazy with worry."

Noah ripped his body from her embrace. "Why?"

"Why?" Zach shook his head in pure bafflement.

"You don't give a damn about me. I just annoy you. You keep sending me to my room so you don't have to look at me." The tears came again, fast and violent. "Nothing I do is right. Ever."

Zach's face crumpled, and all the emotions he fought to conceal broke free. "That is the dumbest thing you've ever said." His inflection simmered with a potent combination of shock and frustration. "I send you to your room because I do care. I care too damn much. You've got so much anger inside you it's eating you up, and I don't know how to stop it."

The boy hugged his knees again, as if to protect himself from the deluge that threatened to overtake him. Or maybe he was just struggling to hold himself together and keep from shattering.

"We're family," Zach told him. "Families don't always get along, but they care about each other, watch out for each other, no matter what. You got that?"

Noah shook his head with a fierceness that matched the turbulent assault of the waves on the coast. "I don't have a family anymore. I don't deserve one."

"Of course you do," Rebecca reassured him. "Everyone deserves a family."

"No!" The vehemence with which the word was spoken was like a physical blow. "I screwed up. Don't you get it? I'm the reason they're dead."

Confusion slammed into her. She tried to stroke her nephew's damp hair, but he scampered out of her reach. "Don't touch me!" He was frantic. She barely recognized his voice. It was sharp and piercing, like an alarm. An alarm she would do best to heed.

Then his eyes rose to her face, wet and miserable, and her heart splintered into a million fragments of helpless sorrow.

"I saw him." He mumbled the words. "The man who killed them."

Zach was speechless. His gaze met and held hers.

"I thought everyone was asleep, so I got out of bed and went down to play on the computer. I saw the guy break in, saw the gun. He was dressed in black."

Noah's whole body shook from the force of his sobs. She wasn't sure there was enough of him to contain such agony. "I should've yelled out, warned them. But I was too scared, so I hid behind the stairs. Then I heard my mom scream."

Zach ran his palm down his face. "Why didn't you tell us?"

"I thought you'd hate me." A ragged gasp, followed by another sob.

Incredulity seeped in to soak Zach's features. "Scratch what I said before. *That* is the dumbest thing you've ever said." His Adam's apple bobbed as he swallowed past the pain. "I could never hate you. You're my sister's son. I love you like you're my own. Hell, you are my own."

Noah's cries settled into a low whimper. "But I could've saved them and I didn't."

Zach reached out and gripped his nephew's arms, gave him a brisk shake. "Hiding was the smartest thing you could've done. Probably kept you alive. You think you could've taken on a guy with a gun and won?"

The boy shrugged. "I don't know. Maybe."

"No maybes. You did the right thing. Your parents wanted you safe. They would've given their lives in a flash to keep you that way. So would I." He pulled his nephew hard against his chest, held him like the whole world was about to end. "You did the right thing," he said over and over again, as if wanting to ensure it sank in. Moisture sparkled in Zach's eyes as he held the boy in the protective loop of his arms and allowed him to cry out his grief.

Rebecca's stomach muscles bunched. As hard as she tried, she couldn't find her voice, so she just watched them. Watched as the clouds momentarily parted and sunshine spilled down to halo their heads. Watched as Noah's body went limp against his uncle's and his fists clenched around a handful of Zach's shirt. Watched as the man she loved fought to contain the turmoil churning within him so as to comfort this lost, guilt-ridden boy.

After a heartbeat that felt like an eternity, they broke apart. Noah mopped away his tears with the back of his hand. "Sorry I cried on you," he said, embarrassed.

Zach shrugged in a manner befitting his nephew. "No big deal. I was already wet."

The boy's lips twitched, but they failed to curl into a smile. "Are you gonna tell anyone? What I told you?"

"Why don't we worry about that later?" Zach filled his lungs with air, released it nice and slow. "Let's get you back to the house first, clean you up. You look like hell."

The three of them stood. Rebecca and Zach flanked their nephew, each taking hold of one of his hands. Then they advanced, a strong, united front, over the dunes and across the beach to the boat.

"Where's the canoe?" Noah asked.

"Probably halfway to China by now." Zach's lips quirked at the corners. "Thankfully, the dinghy's still here 'cause I, for one, have absolutely no desire to swim back."

"You can swim?" Noah's surprise was unmistakable.

Zach looked offended. "Why does everyone keep saying that to me?"

Rebecca couldn't help but smile, despite the worrisome thoughts that nagged at her.

Together they dragged the boat into the sea and climbed in. Seconds later, they drifted onto the vast ocean and floated toward home beneath an unpredictable sky, warmed by the intermittent rays of a fickle sun.

Chapter Twenty-Five

"Noah saw the bastard?" Pat's back went ramrod straight. Blatant interest twisted his features. "Are you shitting me?"

Zach had pulled Liam's old buddy aside while the kids were swimming and the women busy supervising them. "He told us a couple of days ago. This is good, right? We can nail the son of a bitch now."

Pat looked skeptical. "It's a break, no question about that. But kids aren't always the most reliable witnesses."

Zach's fists tightened, but he fought to keep his frustration under control. "It's more than we had a week ago. He saw the guy's face. What more do you want?"

"A goddamn picture would be nice."

"Then set up a session with a sketch artist. See if Noah can flesh this guy out for us."

Pat shook his head. "In my experience, when a child witness is involved, a sketch is pretty useless."

Zach didn't get it. A few days ago the guy had been all gung-ho about catching Liam and Lindsay's killer, and now he was stonewalling him. "Still worth a shot," he persisted.

A beat of silence followed. "Sure. I'll see what I can do. Maybe book something next week in Boston. I'm just telling you not to get your hopes up."

Noah raced out of the harbor, shot a questioning look their way. Zach couldn't help but sense the kid knew what he and Pat were discussing. Then Becca ran up to him and lovingly swathed him in a towel. This time, the boy didn't push her away.

Progress, Zach thought.

Ever since that day at the Seashore, they seemed to have made some kind of breakthrough. They'd gone from butting heads to actually acting like a family. A family he needed to protect, even if that meant forcing Noah to look fear in the eyes and beat it into submission. Truth was, the kid wouldn't find peace until the monster who shattered his world was caught. And Zach had every intention of ensuring that happened.

"Do you mind if I question him?" Pat asked. "Find out exactly how much he knows?"

Zach's gaze found and held Noah's, who still watched him curiously. "Be my guest. Not sure how open he'll be to the idea, though. He's convinced himself that he's to blame for his parents' death, that he could've saved them. It's embarrassing for him to admit he saw the killer and did nothing."

"What could he have done? He's just a kid."

"That's what I told him. But I get how he feels. I'd probably feel the same way in his shoes. It's hard to see someone you love hurting and not be able to do a fucking thing to stop it." He understood that kind of helplessness, the toll it takes on you. He'd experienced its crippling effect with his mother, with Becca, and now with these kids. But there came a time when a guy had to take back some of the control life stripped away from him. This was Noah's chance to do just that.

"I'll talk to him," he told Pat. "See if I can convince him to speak to you."

Pat nodded. "There's no point booking a sketch artist if Noah doesn't want to describe this guy."

"He will." Zach's tone was firm, resolute. "He has to. It's the only way for him to move on."

"I won't do it." Noah turned to face Zach, his body wired. "You can't make me!" He looked like a coiled snake, wrapped tight, ready to spring.

Zach took a step forward. Drizzle hung around them, a wet mist that refused to dissipate. Kristen was already in bed, wiped out from another full day of swimming. Becca was in the living room, attempting to soothe an inconsolable Will.

Fed up with his brother's caterwauling, Noah had slunk out onto the back porch, where Zach had followed him and broached the subject of Pat.

"He's the assistant DA," he told his nephew. "He can help nail this son of a—" He caught himself, bit back his anger.

"You can say it. I'm not a kid anymore. Son of a bitch is too nice for him anyway. How about shitfaced asshole?"

It was his own fault, really. How could he expect his nephew to watch his mouth when he could barely watch his? "Insults aside, Pat can work with the police to catch this guy. Isn't that what you want?"

"I'd rather shoot him dead, the way he shot my parents."

"You don't mean that."

"Yeah, I do. It's what he deserves." The conviction on his nephew's face chilled him.

"Maybe so, but it's not your job to do it. But you can help the police do theirs." Suddenly weary, he lowered his body onto one of the matching wicker chairs until his eyes were level with Noah's. "Talk to Pat."

"He'll think I'm a wuss. He'll tell Jason."

"No he won't. Whatever you say to him will be confidential."

A snort punctured the night. "Yeah, right."

"This is your chance, Noah. Your chance to help your parents." He knew it was low to play on his nephew's guilt, but it was the only way to get through to him. The boy wouldn't heal until he felt vindicated. If Noah helped nail this bastard, he'd reclaim the self-esteem he'd lost on that godforsaken night when—how had he put it?—the shitfaced asshole had crushed his sense of security to bits.

Noah hunched his shoulders, blinked to hold the tears at bay. "Won't bring them back."

"No. But it might help you let go."

"I don't want to let go." Bravado melted away. Only naked honesty remained.

"You don't have to let go of the good stuff, just the pain."

"The pain helps me remember."

Zach reached out, squeezed the boy's shoulder in a gesture of understanding and affection. "I'll make you a promise right here and now. As long as I'm alive, you'll never forget your parents. I'll make sure of it."

Noah nodded. Dampness pooled in his eyes, glinted silver in the moonlight. Then he did something that shocked the air from Zach's lungs and made his heart grow so damn tight it hurt. He hugged him.

Noah huddled in a chair in Jason's kitchen, repetitively tapping a spoon on the smooth wooden surface of the small table. Not oak, he noted, something else. His other hand played with the silver ring hanging from his neck. Across from him, Jason's dad waited for him to stop stalling.

"Noah, I know this is hard." Mr. Jenkins covered his hand with his, took the spoon away. "But I need you to tell me exactly what you saw."

He shifted in his chair, then raised his shoulder. "I saw a guy open the front door and walk in."

"Did you hear anything prior to that? Him picking the lock, maybe?"

"Just a click, like he had a key or something. Then he was inside."

"Were the lights on?"

183

"No."

"Then how did you see his face?"

"The blinds were open. Streetlamps were on outside."

"Did he see you?"

Noah shook his head. "I was in the shadows." The butterflies in his chest linked their wings, closed around his heart until it had trouble beating. "I saw the gun and hid behind the stairs."

"Can you describe the gun for me?"

He fought not to fidget. "Aren't cops supposed to figure this stuff out from the bullets or something?"

Mr. Jenkins' lips shook a little at the corners. "Just trying to see how much you remember."

"So this is some kind of test."

"Does that bother you?" Mr. Jenkins' eyes cut into him like lasers.

"No. I'm good at tests." The hand that no longer held the spoon curled into a fist. "It looked like a gun. Dark gray, maybe black, I don't know."

"Was it big or small?"

"Small with a long barrel. The barrel looked different from the rest of it, had these squares on it. I remember 'cause it made me think of Checkers."

Mr. Jenkins scribbled something in the notepad he held. From across the table, Noah caught a glimpse of what he'd written: *Norrell silencer.* Didn't mean anything to him, but Jason's dad looked interested...and confused. "You were able to see that much detail hiding behind the stairs with only the streetlights on?"

Noah shrugged. "Guess I got really good eyes." Truth was, he'd followed the guy to his dad's office, watched him press that checkered barrel to his mom's head.

"Did the gun make noise when it went off?"

The butterflies grew fangs. "Just a popping sound." Then blood staining his mom's shirt. Rivers of it streaming from his dad's chest, his dad's mouth...

Noah's hand closed around the ring, nearly ripped it off the chain.

"Can you describe the shooter for me?"

He surprised himself by finding his voice. "Tall, round around the edges. Looked a bit like a turtle."

"A turtle?"

"Yeah. Eyes far apart, big nose, not much hair."

"Did you notice anything specific, like a tattoo—"

Something sparked in his memory. Something he'd forgotten. "He had a birthmark on the back of his neck. Dark red, like a burn."

Mr. Jenkins' expression changed, grew pinched and serious, and Noah realized he'd said something important. "Did you get a good look at it?"

"Yeah. It was shaped like a heart. I remember thinking it was weird for a guy with a gun to have a heart on his neck. Maybe a skull, but not a heart."

"What happened when he went into the den?"

"What do you think?" *He shot my parents, genius. Shot them dead while I hid like a total coward.* The words whirled inside his head, took tiny nips out of him.

"Did you see or hear anything?"

The fridge stopped buzzing. Somewhere in the distance a faucet dripped. "I don't know. I think my dad gave him something."

"What did he give him?"

"I don't know." He didn't want to answer any more questions, didn't want to remember. But Mr. Jenkins wouldn't let him be. He kept pushing and pushing.

"Did they speak at all?"

"I told you I don't know." The shadows were closing in on him, suffocating him. "Can we please stop now?"

"Tell me what you heard, Noah, and this will all be over."

"Please. I can't— I don't—"

"Think, damn it, think!"

The door burst open, and Uncle Zach came rushing in. "Take it easy, Pat. We can hear you all the way outside."

Mr. Jenkins tossed his pencil on the table. It made a clunking sound, then rolled across the shiny surface. "Just trying to get to the truth, like you asked."

His uncle gathered him off the chair and held him hard against his side. It felt good, all that strength pouring into him, keeping him on his feet even as his knees wobbled. "Not this way."

Jason's dad closed the notebook and leaned back in his chair with a heavy sigh. "Sorry. Guess I got a little carried away."

Uncle Zach said nothing. He just led him out of the kitchen, through the back door and into the bright day. The shadows retreated. But they'd be back. Memories, same as nightmares, never really went away. They hid like snakes in the grass, waiting to pounce on him when he walked into a familiar room, played a favorite game, watched a friend build a sandcastle. They were part of him now.

Still, there was one thing he didn't get. Why did his parents' faces keep getting fuzzier and fuzzier, when their killer's ugly mug seemed to grow clearer by the day?

"You fucked up." His employer rarely swore, so Raymond knew this was bad. Perhaps even bad enough to get him discharged, permanently.

"I downloaded everything. If the information wasn't on there, then I was right. Birch didn't make a copy."

Static filled the line. "This has nothing to do with the files. It's about the kid. He saw you pop his parents."

For a second Raymond heard nothing but the annoying buzz in the untraceable cellular phone his boss had given him when he'd first hired him. Then the words took shape, sharpened. "Impossible. I'm always thorough, never leave witnesses behind. You know that."

"Not this time."

"How can you be sure?" Dread crusted along his spine, made ice chips congeal in his blood. A lifetime of being invisible, of blending into the crowd, and he was about to be exposed by a nine-year-old. It couldn't happen. He wouldn't allow it.

"I've got my sources."

"Want me to take care of him?"

A long, aggravating pause. "No, I want you to hang low. Your cover's blown. He knows what you look like."

That wasn't good enough. He needed this problem fixed. Now. "You can't expect me to just sit on my ass—"

"That's exactly what I expect."

"But what if he talks?" Sweat beaded on Raymond's forehead. His hands grew so damp the phone nearly slipped from his grasp.

"I won't let that happen. The plan's back on track. Meet me at the safe house tomorrow morning at seven."

"What are you going to do in the meantime?"

The phone line crackled, drowning out the roar of Raymond's heart as he waited for his boss to answer. "Damage control." The words rose above the hum, buzzed in his ear. Then, without warning, static melted into silence.

Chapter Twenty-Six

The night was deep and silent as Rebecca slipped into the children's room to check up on them. Will had taken an exceptionally long time falling asleep again. He'd been restless, more fussy than usual, and she couldn't help but worry. This whole mothering thing was new to her. She still couldn't tell the difference between a hungry cry, a teething cry or a something-is-seriously-wrong cry, which made her paranoid. How did mothers do it? How had Lindsay?

For now the baby slept peacefully enough, though not in his usual spot. At some point since she'd laid him down, he'd climbed out of his playpen and crawled into bed with his older siblings. The three of them huddled together in the king-sized bed, like little pixies trapped in a cloud. Concern slid into affection, wrapped in a ribbon of possessiveness.

They were hers, and they needed her.

No one had ever needed her before. It was crazy, the way children made you feel important, indispensable. They changed everything. You suddenly found yourself wondering what would happen to them if you weren't around. Who would make them breakfast, brush their teeth, give them a hug when they needed it? Who would guide them and teach them what it meant to be a better person? Who would love them the way only a mother could?

Because that was what she'd become to them now—their mother—whether she'd asked for it or not, whether she was ready for it or not.

Zach crept up behind her, wrapped his arms around her middle. His touch was as familiar as the sun, yet new somehow. Things were different between them, better than they'd ever been before. This time they were partners, equals in every sense of the word. She no longer felt like the ugly stepsister dancing with Prince Charming. For once in her life, she honestly believed she deserved him. They hadn't been able to build a life on the burning flames of passion alone, but maybe they could build one on love, understanding and mutual respect.

"I finally get it." His warm breath brushed her ear and sent a pleasant tingle skating down her neck.

"Get what?"

"Why they call them angels." His voice was thick and sweet, like candy melting in the sun.

She studied the children's peaceful expressions and knew exactly what he meant.

Then Will stirred, scrunched up his little face, and let out an ear-splitting scream. Bolt scampered into the room, happy for any excuse to bark. Both Noah and Kristen jackknifed in bed, their hair ruffled, their eyes glazed with sleep.

Rebecca swept the wailing baby in her arms as Zach chased the dog from the room. She hastened out after him, with the toddler wrapped securely in her embrace, leaving Kristen and Noah to drift back to sleep.

Small fists flailed as an inconsolable Will fought to free himself from her grasp.

"What's wrong with him?" Zach took the baby from her, attempted to soothe him.

"I'm not sure. He was restless all evening."

"Must be teething again. I'll give him some Tylenol. That'll help settle him down."

Nearly an hour later, Will finally succumbed to exhaustion and fell asleep. "Let's keep him in the room with us tonight," Zach proposed. "Keep an eye on him."

Rebecca couldn't have agreed more. They placed the dozing toddler between them, flanked him like bodyguards. Then, soothed by the gentle rhythm of his breathing, they, too, yielded to the numbing pull of sleep.

Noah spent a good hour tossing and turning, then decided it was useless. Will had snapped him out of a deep dream, and now he was wide awake. Beside him Kristen snored like a warthog. Not that he knew for sure that warthogs snored, but if they did, he was willing to bet that was the sound they'd make. Careful not to wake his sister, he hopped out of bed and fled the room. The house was really dark, so quiet it hurt his ears, same as when he was underwater and pressure built around his eardrums. The eerie silence almost made him miss Kristen's warthog snoring.

A floorboard creaked beneath his feet, and he nearly flew out of his skin. He stood statue-still, waited to see if his aunt or uncle had heard the noise. No one stirred. With feather-light steps, he slunk down the stairs. It was hard to find his aunt's laptop without turning on the lights, but he managed all right. He carried it to the kitchen, flipped open the screen and pushed the on button. Within seconds the machine came alive.

As usual, he logged on to Falcon World. This time it didn't surprise him to find Night-Owl waiting for him.

"I was hoping you'd be here," Noah wrote.

"I like the night," his friend replied. "What R U doin up so late?"

"Couldn't sleep. My dumb baby brother was screaming again."

"Babies are a real PITA." *Pain in the ass.*

"N/S." *No shit.*

"Guess what?" Night-Owl typed. "I'm coming to Chatham. I'll be staying with my aunt up at Minister's Point."

Excitement glided down Noah's spine, curled in his tummy. "That's where I'm at. What street?"

"Ministers Lane. The gray house with the blue shutters and the fake rooster on the roof."

"I think I know it. Went biking there once. When will U be here?"

"Tomorrow at 1. Wanna drop by? Ralph wants to meet U."

"You're bringing him along?"

"Yup. He gets lonely without me." A short pause, then, "Do you have a pet?"

"A dog."

"Don't bring him with U. Ralph will freak."

Noah sent Night-Owl a laughing face.

"And don't tell anyone you're coming. It's our little secret."

"Do I look stupid to U?"

"Tell U tomorrow."

He rolled his eyes, even though Night-Owl couldn't see him. "LMAO." *Laughing my ass off*, he wrote sarcastically.

"CU tomorrow," was Night-Owl's response.

For the first time in days, a smile spread across Noah's face. "CU."

Fog hovered over the sea like a drowning cloud. Raymond's motor boat cut a steady path through the blue-gray mist, angled toward the mountains, where his boss's craft sat moored. Behind him, a fat sun rose to salute the day. Raymond knew this place well. He came by every few months to drop off the special packages his employer dispatched him to collect. Here they remained, sometimes for days, until his boss could make the necessary arrangements to transfer them. Paperwork needed to be done, photographs taken, identities changed. Raymond didn't know where they ultimately ended up, and he didn't care.

He was just the middleman.

The day would be bright, clear and warm. He could tell by the way the sun steadily ate away at the fog. He anchored his boat, left the key in the ignition in case he had to make a quick getaway, then skillfully scaled the low cliff. Beyond it, acres upon acres of land stretched. There was a narrow trail that would lead him straight to his destination, so he took it. This tended to be a little more challenging in the winter months, but his employer needed the cloak of invisibility this remote location offered. Neighbors could be such a nuisance. Raymond had learned that the hard way.

Within minutes the house he sought came into view. It was quaint, picturesque, something one might expect to see in a painting of the countryside—the ideal shroud for the devil's workshop. The air was sweet, redolent with the aroma of fruit ripening beneath a thin cover of dew. The only sound was that of crickets and of a spotted sandpiper greeting him as he passed. He found the key hidden in the usual spot, a flowerbed now overrun with weeds, and fished it out. Then he let himself in.

The place looked deserted, but he knew his employer was here. He'd seen his boat anchored below. Raymond didn't bother announcing his presence. He just waited. As the minutes stretched, he grew restless, nervous. Damage control, his boss had said. Raymond was smart enough to understand he was part of the damage that needed to be controlled. So he'd hedged his bets, made a life-altering call late last night. If it came down to him or his employer, he'd feed the bastard to the wolves in a heartbeat.

A loud clang startled him. From the back room, machinery droned with steady precision, like a well-oiled assembly line. Raymond followed the sound. Rusted vats framed him as he searched for the source of the noise. Then he saw it, a mammoth of a contraption, lifting monstrous steel arms and plunging them deep within its own dark center. The sight mesmerized him. He'd never seen the machine in operation before. Curiosity and boredom propelled him up the metal stairs, where a low platform hung. He stared into the empty bowels of the crusher, waiting for his employer to make an appearance, wondering why he'd suddenly decided to turn the device on.

Then it struck him, the culmination of all his fears, seconds before he heard someone call out his name. He turned, aware that—despite all his planning—he'd walked straight into the belly of the beast. The black barrel of a gun yawned before him. He panicked, scrambled for the 9mm SIG strapped to his belt. But it was too late. The gun exploded, glinted silver in the semi-dark room. A spray of bullets slammed into him. Blood squirted from the wounds in his chest, thick and sickening.

Pain made his body spasm. Pain and an unbearable heat. Regret swamped him. The only consolation was the knowledge that his murderer would burn in hell alongside him. As he fell backward, right into the steel-toothed mouth waiting to chew his carcass to bits, his last thought was of the terrible mess he'd leave behind.

Chapter Twenty-Seven

Sometimes, when Zach watched the kids splashing around in the waves, running across the spit of a beach that bordered his dad's summer home or tossing a ball at the dog, he almost forgot everything they'd been through. Kids were so resilient. They found hope and a reason to smile even as the world collapsed around them. Unlike adults, they instinctively knew how to compartmentalize. He wished he did, too. Wished he could stop worrying about what tomorrow would bring or thinking of the son of a bitch who'd taken his sister from him.

At night, in Becca's arms, he almost did. A man could live an entire lifetime in just one minute holding the woman he loved. On those occasions when her fragrant skin brushed his or her hair feathered across his chest, soft as silk, their entire future slid into focus. He could see them raising the kids, growing old together, holding hands as they watched the sun set for the last time.

But the second night spilled into dawn, the doubts returned, sharper than before. He wanted to believe they'd get it right this time, but a part of him couldn't help but wonder what would happen the second a crisis came along. Would they crash and burn again? Would he be able to comfort her the way she needed to be comforted? Would she cave under the pressure and retreat into herself? Would he run away?

And what about the murderous bastard who still roamed the streets, gloating because he'd gotten away with a double homicide? He needed to be put behind bars before he could hurt anyone else, make another child an orphan. But Noah didn't want to remember, and Pat still hadn't gotten back to him about that appointment with the sketch artist.

Bolt's yapping snapped him out of his thoughts. The kids chased the beagle around the backyard, laughing each time they made him bark. The Jenkinses' door burst open, and Amy and Jason ran over to join the fun.

Hot on their heels was their mom. "Morning," she greeted.

"Looks like a nice day," he said, making small talk.

"Sure does. Better pile on the sunblock."

Zach leaned his elbows on the railing. A cool breeze rolled off the harbor, slid fine fingers through his hair, but failed to soothe his nerves.

"Is Rebecca around?"

"She's inside with Will. He's been acting up a lot these past couple days."

"I noticed. Probably teething, poor thing."

A cottontail darted across the yard, and the dog went wild. From the surrounding shrubs, a group of sparrows suddenly took flight.

"Is Pat up?" he asked. "I got something to talk to him about."

"Pat's gone back to Boston."

He directed an assessing stare Tess's way. "Hope everything's all right."

"Oh, yeah. Just some break in the big case he hasn't been able to get out of his head." The bitter note in her voice was unmistakable. "Maybe they'll finally put this thing to bed so we can all take a break."

"Will you be heading out, too?"

"I'll stay till the end of the week as planned. Then I'll drive back." She crossed her arms over her chest, propped her back against the wall. "Thank God he left me the car, at least. This is one of those rare times when I'm actually glad he got that ridiculously overpriced boat. I hate being stranded."

It seemed Pat's job, like his fishing, was a sore spot for Tess.

"Did he mention anything about the sketch artist before he left?"

She shrugged apologetically. "Not really. Sorry. He's been really preoccupied lately."

From the house, Becca emerged with a now-quiet Will perched on her hip. "Hi, Tess."

Tess brightened at the sight of her friend, and Zach couldn't blame her. There was something very vital about Becca, a light that shone from within that reached out and lit a fire deep inside you. For a while that light had dimmed. Now it was back, more radiant than the sun.

"How is he?" Tess asked, gazing at Will with doe-eyed affection.

"Better. But I'm still worried." Becca ran a loving palm over the baby's damp head. The kid had obviously cried himself into a sweat. "Maybe we should take him to the clinic."

Zach wasn't convinced. Will had been pulling these fits on him for weeks. "Aren't you jumping the gun a little? He's got a couple of molars coming. You'd be screaming, too, if your gums were about to be split open."

Tess and Becca exchanged a conspiratorial look, and he read the unvoiced thought that sped through their minds. *Men.*

He smiled and shook his head. *Women.*

The sudden roar of a motor slashed the air, and he turned his gaze toward the harbor, where a boat chugged steadily toward them. His first thought was that Pat had returned. Then he recognized the miniature yacht and realized with a sinking sensation exactly who was at the helm.

Martin.

What the hell was he doing here?

Martin anchored the boat, then used a motorized dinghy to zip to the shore without wetting his designer shorts. Bet they'd cost as much as this house. The closer he got, the more the greasy feeling in Zach's stomach spread. The jerk looked like a Ralph Lauren ad, with his white Polo opened at the neck, his surfer tan and his dirty blond hair fused to his scalp with enough gel to snare an entire swarm of flies. Not a single hair on his head moved, even as his clothing flapped in the wind.

Martin's face lit up like a Christmas tree when he saw Becca, and he gave her a wave befitting a politician. Becca waved back and smiled. If Zach had felt like shit before, he felt even worse now.

"Looks like you've got a visitor," Tess said. "Isn't that Liam's brother?"

"In the flesh." Zach grunted his frustration.

Becca inched up beside him. "Behave," she whispered. Her breath scraped his ear—soft, seductive. That familiar tingle coiled deep in his gut, made him wish everyone would disappear so he could have her all to himself, just for a minute or two.

No such luck. Before he could catch his breath, Martin invaded their space like a goddamn elephant. Becca gave him her most luminous smile. The kids practically tripped over themselves in their rush to greet him. Even the dog proved himself a traitor, nearly peeing from excitement.

Zach didn't get it. The guy was as fake as imitation leather, but everyone seemed to worship the ground he walked on. Was he the only one who saw through his plastic grin?

Martin gave him the benefit of that grin now. "Enjoying the sun?"

Zach managed a stiff nod. "Looks like you are, too. No multi-million-dollar deal to land this week?"

"Nope." Martin flashed a set of perfectly aligned, impossibly white teeth. "Have a few days off. I was on my way back from my place at the Vineyard, so I thought I'd drop by and visit my little buds here." He slapped Kristen and Noah on the back affectionately. "Hope you don't mind."

Zach gritted his teeth and fought real hard not to answer that question.

193

Thankfully, Becca answered for him. "It's always nice to see you, Martin. It's been a while."

"It sure has." Martin reached for her hand, then brought it to his lips like some smarmy Casanova. "I didn't think it was possible, but you've gone and done it."

Confusion tugged at her full mouth. "Done what?"

"Grown even lovelier."

Zach nearly choked on a snort. Did women actually buy this load of crap?

Becca beamed, and he had to fight to keep from rolling his eyes. *Guess they do.*

"Martin, you know Tess," she quickly introduced the neighbor in an effort to downplay her embarrassment. Becca never could take a compliment without turning every known shade of red.

"Yes, of course." Martin clasped Tess's hand in his. "Pat's wife, right?"

"That's right."

Martin displayed those blinding teeth again. "Must be the water. The ladies here are positively radiant."

Now it was Tess's turn to blush.

Oh, brother.

Zach took Will from Becca and propped him on the railing in front of him. He needed to keep his hands busy so he wouldn't be tempted to wrap them around Martin's slick throat. Will fussed for a second, then thankfully settled.

Kristen tugged at Martin's shorts. "Can you take us on a boat ride?" She unleashed the full force of her liquid blue gaze. "Pleeeease!" Unable to contain her eagerness, she jumped on the balls of her feet. "I wanna see dolphins and whales."

"Maybe later, pip-squeak." Martin ruffled her wispy blond hair. "I think I'm suffering from heat stroke right now."

"Why don't you come inside?" Becca offered. "I'll get you something cold to drink."

"Why thank you. I never turn down a chance to have a drink with a pretty lady."

Becca's cheeks flushed with color again. Zach wondered how cocky the flirtatious bastard would look without his front teeth. He was tempted to find out.

Instead, he swallowed his irritation and grudgingly watched Martin follow his blushing wife into the house.

Becca invited Martin to stay for lunch; he'd come all this way after all. The kids were ecstatic and talked Martin's ear off. They seemed determined to share every detail of their stay here so far.

Zach cut into his steak and tried to look pleasant for Becca's sake. She'd warned him about a dozen times to behave. He was determined to prove to her that he could be civil. Even with the likes of Martin Birch.

"So are you still writing for that magazine?" Martin asked Becca between mouthfuls of sweet peas and mashed potatoes.

"Uh hum." She dabbed at the corners of her mouth with a napkin. "*Women Today*. I write an article a month."

"What about that book you started? Did you ever finish it?"

How did Martin remember that? Becca hadn't talked about it in years. In the early days of their marriage she'd toyed with the idea of writing a novel. Then things had gotten complicated, and she'd abandoned the whole project.

"No." Embarrassment bled across her cheeks.

"Why not?"

She carved tracks in her mashed potatoes with her fork and averted her gaze. "Life got in the way."

"Life always gets in the way," he told her. "That's no excuse to give up on your dreams."

A light came into her eyes, and Zach wished he'd been the one to put it there. "You're right. It's easy to give up sometimes. But we shouldn't, should we?"

Martin wagged his head. "Nope. Life's too short not to make the most of it."

She gave Liam's brother a grateful smile, and a rock fell to settle in Zach's gut. Suddenly, he couldn't take another bite. His resentment for Martin snowballed inside him until he thought he'd burst. Not because the man had said the wrong thing, but because he'd said the right one. The truth was, Zach had never known exactly what Becca wanted or needed. When she'd given up on the book, he'd assumed she'd grown bored, so he hadn't hassled her about it. Now he realized what she'd really needed was a kick in the pants.

And when they'd failed to conceive, what had he done? He'd tried to placate her, to downplay the significance of the misfortune that had befallen them. But that had only made her grow angry and bitter. He was a goddamn idiot. She hadn't needed someone to tell her everything would be all right. She'd needed someone to share her grief. Unfortunately, like Noah, grief wasn't something he handled well. He wasn't the kind of guy to sit and cry in his beer. He had to take action, solve the situation. That was just the way he was made.

Back then, leaving her had seemed like the answer. Now he wasn't so sure.

Will let out another scream and tossed a handful of peas on the table. He'd complained throughout most of the meal. His eyes looked tired, his skin pink and clammy. Right there and then, Zach wondered whether Becca was right and that something was wrong with the kid.

Becca stood and gathered the weeping toddler in her arms. Concern instantly pleated her brows. "I think he's running a fever."

Zach shot to his feet and joined her. He slid his palm across Will's head. The kid was burning up. "You're right. We need to have him checked out. Noah, Kristen, go change. We're going to the clinic."

Fire blazed in Noah's eyes, and Zach knew the boy would put up a fight. "I wanna stay with Uncle Martin."

"Me, too." Kristen happily joined her brother's act of mutiny.

"I don't mind staying with them," Martin tossed in, thoroughly undermining him.

Even Becca decided to jump ship. "There's no use dragging everyone along. We could be there for hours."

But Zach wasn't ready to surrender just yet. "I'm not sure that's such a great idea."

"Why not?" Martin looked offended. For the first time his artificial smile faltered. "You don't trust me to look after my own niece and nephew?"

"Of course we trust you." Becca tried to soothe his bruised ego. "Zach's just being a little overprotective."

"You really think you can handle these two on your own?" Zach asked him, trying not to sound too condescending or smug.

"You handled the three of them on your own for weeks." An unmistakable challenge resonated in the other man's voice. "I sure as hell can do it for a few hours."

"Uh, boys?" Becca interrupted, looking seriously distressed. "I hate to break it to you, but we really don't have time for this. The baby's about to self-combust." She angled an admonishing stare Zach's way. "I'll grab his diaper bag and meet you in the car."

And that was the end of that.

The ride to the clinic was strained, the silence more slicing than the blades of light slanting across the windshield. Will had fallen asleep in his car seat, and Rebecca couldn't help glancing back at him every minute or so. It comforted her to see the steady rise and fall of his chest, the repetitive twitch at the corner of his mouth. Fear and compassion tightened the steel clamp wrapped around her heart. She'd waited too long, should have trusted her instincts and brought him in sooner...

"He'll be all right," Zach reassured her. "Probably just a bug."

"He looks so weak." A drowning sense of failure submerged her. "Lindsay would've realized something was wrong—"

"You can't be sure of that. Stop beating yourself up. You told me you were worried. I'm the one who was being bull-headed."

She stared at the glistening blacktop as Zach's silver Audi sped across the road, faster than it should've, and shook her head in denial. "It's a woman's—a mother's—job to know these things." Problem was, she wasn't meant to be a mother, and just when she was beginning to forget that undeniable fact, something like this happened to remind her.

"That's a load of crap." His features grew stormy, so intense her stomach folded. "You're not a doctor. Or a fortune-teller, for that matter. You're doing the best you can. We both are."

"What if that's not enough?" Tall trees shivered as they scraped a hazy sky, blurring at the tips.

"It is." Zach clenched the steering wheel so tight his knuckles blanched. "It has to be."

Chapter Twenty-Eight

It was almost one o'clock, and Noah couldn't find Uncle Martin anywhere. Just as well. It would be a lot easier to sneak away with no one around keeping an eye on him. He tiptoed to the back door, swung it open as quietly as he could, then froze at the loud bark that followed. Bolt stood behind him, happily wagging his tail.

"Shhh. I'm not taking you for a walk, so be quiet. Okay?"

The dog kept right on yapping. "Stay," Noah commanded in his I-really-mean-it voice.

Bolt dropped his butt to the floor and swept the tiles clean with his tail, all the while watching him with a dumb look. A warm tingle spread through Noah, so he reached out and petted the puppy's head. "I'll take you for walk later," he said. "Promise." With those parting words, he darted outside and circled the house to where his bike sat perched.

In a few minutes he'd finally get to meet Night-Owl face-to-face. The idea thrilled him. Having an older friend was really awesome. He could say things to Night-Owl. Things he couldn't say to anyone else. Night-Owl never judged, always listened and understood.

What luck that he happened to be right here in Chatham, and only a block away!

Excitement setting off small explosions inside him, Noah mounted his bike.

"Where are you going?" The question nearly knocked him out of his socks. His heart took off at a gallop.

It's just Kristen, he told himself in an effort to ease the wild roar of his pulse. "None of your business."

"I wanna come, too."

His sister could be a real pain sometimes. "You can't."

"But I want to." Her bottom lip shook. Any minute now she'd start to bawl.

"Go back inside. Keep Bolt company."

"Why?"

"Because I said so." He pumped the pedals, intending to high-tail it out of there, but his tires were flat. Crap. Now he'd have to walk. Easier said than done with Kristen dogging his every step. He had to get her off his back...and fast. "All right," he lied, "you can come along. But only if Uncle Martin says it's okay. Why don't you go ask him and meet me back here?"

Kristen's face glowed. "Don't leave without me," she warned, right before she took off at a dash.

The minute the door slammed shut behind her, Noah made a beeline for the woods. It would be faster this way. The house he sought was just beyond these trees. The forest was alive, filled with sighs and rustling sounds—the breeze whispering through the leaves, a rabbit making a desperate run for its burrow, a jumpy squirrel hiding beneath the brush. Still, he heard the distinct snap of a twig, the crunch of dirt and grass beneath someone's feet, and tossed a nervous glance over his shoulder.

No one there.

He quickened his pace, kept plowing ahead. In the distance waves crashed over the shore, quick as a whip.

Before long he reached the other side, relaxed as rock and soil turned to sand beneath him. Then he saw the house—tall and gray, with blue shutters and a spinning rooster on top—and anticipation filled all the empty spaces in his chest. Night-Owl was just a short climb away. Noah took off at a run.

When he stood at the front door, a twinge of guilt assaulted him. Maybe he should have told someone where he'd gone. Even if he'd wanted to, no one had been around, he reasoned. He probably should have left a note. A note would have done the trick.

Too late now.

He grabbed the knocker and slammed it hard against the dark blue door.

He waited a few seconds, knocked again. When no one answered, he decided to try the handle and was surprised to find the door unlocked. He took an uncertain step forward. "Night-Owl? Are you here? It's Raptor."

He walked farther inside, noticed the house was empty. Maybe he'd gone to the wrong place. He ran Night-Owl's description through his mind. No, this was the right house. His friend was probably just running late. But why was there no furniture in sight?

A door squeaked, followed by the sound of a floorboard creaking behind him. Noah spun on his heels.

"You came." The man's voice was as familiar as his face.

Confusion leaked in to snuff out excitement. "What are you doing here?"

"We had a play date, remember?"

Was he missing something? This guy didn't belong here, in Night-Owl's house, waiting for him as if he was expecting him. Then it struck him like a baseball bat to the head. "You're Night-Owl?"

"I always knew you were a bright one."

"But you're supposed to be twelve." Something was wrong. He felt it, saw it in the funny way the man was looking at him, like an owl watching a mouse.

"I was. Once."

Noah approached him, even as something inside him wanted to recoil. "Why did you pretend to be a kid?"

"Because I needed to get close to you. Needed you to trust me."

None of this made any sense. "Why?"

"You ask too many questions." The man reached into his pocket, pulled out a bottle and a white rag.

Noah's stomach pitched, then crashed into his gut. "What are you doing?"

The smile that had once been friendly turned ice cold. "What I should have done months ago."

Before Noah could make a run for it, the door slammed open, and Kristen came stomping in. "You left without me," she whined. "But I followed you. You can't trick me. I'm too smart."

Every protective instinct inside him flared to life. His gut told him something bad was about to happen, that the shadows were hungry again, and he'd led Kristen right to them.

"Kristen, get out of here!" he yelled as a strong arm snaked around him. The rag covered his face, cut off his next breath. It smelled strong, sweet and rotten at the same time. His ears began to ring. The whole world spun like a merry-go-round gone wild.

Then everything faded to black.

They'd been at the clinic for over an hour. Rebecca sat at Will's bedside, stroking his hair as she waited anxiously for the test results. The nurse had taken blood, a urine sample, a throat swab. The doctor had checked his mouth, ears, nose, and dutifully listened to his heartbeat. Will, who'd taken offense at being poked and prodded, had cried up a storm. Eventually, he'd exhausted himself and fallen asleep on the examination table.

"I hope they figure this thing out soon." Zach leaned against the doorjamb, looking restless and irritated. "Wonder how things are going with Martin."

So that was the reason he was in such a rush to get out of here. "I'm sure everything's fine. Try to relax."

His brows narrowed. "I can't."

She'd never truly understood his intense dislike for Liam's older brother. It was completely out of character for him. Zach was nothing if not diplomatic, yet with Martin he seemed to regress to such primal aggression it made her think of a caveman guarding the entrance to his cave.

"I don't get it." She couldn't help herself. She had to ask. "Why do you hate him so much?"

He answered without hesitation. "He's too slick, and he smiles too much." The fact that he didn't even bother denying it spoke volumes.

"Are you sure it's not because of what happened at our wedding?"

The heated expression on his face could have melted snow. "He hit on you. Any reason something like that would make me hate his guts?"

"He was drunk. He didn't know what he was doing." The baby stirred, and she soothed him with a gentle pat on the chest.

"A man's true character shows when he's drunk," Zach continued, oblivious to Will's unrest. "He did what he didn't have the guts to do sober."

"And you've held a grudge for ten years." She shook her head, amazed.

He shrugged, scanned the corridor at the sound of footsteps approaching. "It's not a grudge, just a healthy dose of hostility."

The baby's brows relaxed as peace found him again. Rebecca linked her fingers and lowered them to her lap, where they remained in a nervous tangle as she studied the man she'd known practically her whole life. A man she was just beginning to see.

In this painfully silent room, where the walls were an impeccable white and the air smelled faintly of antiseptic, the blindness lifted, and she finally understood something fundamental. If a silly pass had the power to inspire a decade of resentment, then Zach's feelings for her surely ran deeper than she'd always believed, which meant their relationship hadn't been one-sided at all. In her increasingly hectic reality, that was something big. Something to grab hold of, to build on.

For the first time in her life she didn't feel alone, and that made her strong enough to face anything. Still, her stomach pitched when the doctor returned with the test results—a small-framed Asian woman with jet-black hair pinned up in a bun and a practiced smile sure to comfort the most irate patient.

Rebecca shot to her feet and bridged the distance between them. "What's wrong with him?" She didn't mean to sound panicky, but she couldn't stop fear from spilling into her voice. Like it or not, she'd already begun to feel like a mother, and worrying was part of the deal.

"He'll be fine," the doctor reassured them. "He just has an ear infection. Thankfully, you caught it in time. There's no damage to the eardrum."

Rebecca wanted to knock herself over the head. "That's why he's been tugging on his ear. I should've figured—"

"Don't be so hard on yourself," the woman soothed in a lyrical voice. "It's painful but easily treated." She pulled out her prescription pad. "Is he allergic to penicillin?"

"I don't know." She looked to Zach for guidance.

"No. He's taken it before."

"Good." The doctor scribbled something illegible down, then tore off the sheet and handed it to her. "Five ml, twice daily for ten days. Keep giving him Acetaminophen or Ibuprofen for the fever. It should last another day or two."

Rebecca took the slip of paper and nodded.

"You should have him checked again when the treatment is over," the doctor added, "just to make sure."

"We will." Zach came to stand beside Rebecca, draped an arm over her shoulder. "Can we take him home now?"

"Go right ahead. Feel free to bring him by again if the symptoms persist beyond forty-eight hours, but I doubt they will."

Relieved, Rebecca lifted Will off the examination table and cradled him—still sleeping—in her arms. It felt good to hold him. So good her heart nearly broke from it. Then, with Zach's protective arm still wrapped around her, they stepped out of the stark white building, directly into the blazing sun's welcoming embrace, where dark fears dulled and sweet promises sprang to life.

Rebecca knew better than anyone that promises were rarely kept. Too many things existed that had the potential to shatter them—an illness, an accident, a trigger-happy burglar. For a few minutes she'd almost forgotten that. It took a phone call to remind her. They'd just finished filling Will's prescription at the drugstore, not to mention acquiring an impressive supply of Tylenol, when Zach's cell began to buzz. The second he answered it, she knew from the murderous look on his face that something was terribly wrong.

"Well, they couldn't have gone far. Did you check the beach?" Silence. Deep, silky, aggravating silence. "How about Tess and Pat's place?"

Zach's knuckles blanched from the death grip he had on the phone. "Keep looking. We're on our way."

She pressed Will to her side with one hand, gripped Zach's arm with the other. "What's happened?"

Anger, hot as hell, flamed in his eyes. "That dipshit Martin's gone and lost the kids." He sliced her with his gaze. "Still think he's a prince?"

Chapter Twenty-Nine

Zach stormed into the beach house, his blood pumping fast and furious through his veins. The place was empty except for Martin, who sat on the couch holding his head like the goddamn idiot he was.

"Why the hell aren't you out there looking for the kids?"

The blood leached from Martin's face. "I have been. They're nowhere. It's like they just up and disappeared."

"Kids don't just disappear. You were supposed to be watching them."

"I was. I was only gone a minute. A client called, so I went to my boat to get my briefcase—"

Zach ate up the distance between them and grabbed the worthless piece of shit by the collar of his designer shirt. "I don't give a damn about your clients. I left those kids with you because you told me I could trust you." He lifted Martin to his feet and shook him, hard.

Becca gripped his biceps. "Don't do this, Zach. Please."

The tremor he caught in her voice sobered him. Although he wanted nothing more than to flatten Martin, he released him and took a step back. "If anything happens to those kids, I'm going to finish what I started."

For the first time, Liam's older brother looked beaten. He slumped against the arm of the sofa, his hair an awkward bramble of spikes, the plastic grin gone.

All the commotion upset Will, who began to fuss again.

Becca ran her palm down the baby's back and pressed him to her chest, holding on to him like a lifeline. "Martin, please tell us what happened," she asked over the toddler's downy head.

The scorching pain in her eyes took tiny nips out of Zach's soul.

"I told you," Martin sputtered. "I got a call. Went to my boat for just a sec. When I got back, they were gone."

"Did they say anything before they took off? Mention a place, a friend?" Becca was grasping at straws.

"No."

"Did you talk to Jason and Amy? Maybe they know something—" The desperation he caught in her voice made Zach want to pummel the negligent bastard all over again. He reached out, ran his own palm down her back to comfort her.

"They said they didn't see anything. Neither did Tess." Martin's tone rang flat, frustration gnawing away at the edges.

"When's the last time you saw them?" Zach probed.

"A couple of hours ago, give or take."

"And you waited till now to call us? What the hell were you thinking?"

Indignation thinned Martin's mouth. "I was busy looking for them."

"Did you search the woods?"

"Yes. Several times." Defeat no longer rearranged Martin's features. Defiance now smoldered in his gaze. "There was no sign of them."

As if her legs could no longer support her, Becca dropped into the couch, still clutching the baby. Will, who obviously didn't appreciate the death-grip she had on him, complained and wrestled free.

"Then there's only one thing to do." Tears pooled in her eyes, but failed to flood her cheeks. "We need to call the police."

Evening fell like a black cloak to cover the sky, and they were still no closer to locating the children. The authorities had spent the better part of the day scouring the area, but their efforts had turned up nothing. They'd promised to resume the search at first light, but that did little to comfort Rebecca. Noah and Kristen were out there, somewhere in the dark night—alone, frightened, maybe even hurt.

She pictured their sweet faces, and her gut clamped. She felt empty inside, as if someone had reached into her chest cavity and torn out her heart. Now all that was left in its place was a jagged wound that pulsed and throbbed with each breath she drew into her lungs. The need to find them, protect them, slashed through her. She'd thought she'd lost them before—when Kristen had gone to visit Voula and Noah had taken the canoe to the Seashore—but this was different. This was real.

The kids hadn't just wandered off. If they had, they would have found them by now. Something was wrong. She felt it.

Her throat was swollen, thick with the tears she refused to shed. She wouldn't cry for them. Crying would mean she'd given up, that she didn't think she'd ever see them again.

Zach and Martin were still out searching. She was itching to join them, but she couldn't. Someone had to stay at the house and watch over Will.

Sharp-toothed anxiety shredded her insides and left her all the more hollow. She should have known not to take happiness for granted. She'd forgotten how ephemeral it was.

An illusion.

Whenever she got a taste of it, it was snatched away.

She walked onto the porch and lowered her body onto the steps. Above her, stars sizzled, blind to the darkness that now enfolded her like a death shroud.

The impenetrable stillness only made her thoughts screech louder. The wound in her chest throbbed. These children had irrevocably changed her. She'd learned to hold them, to smile at them, but she'd failed to tell them she loved them. Now she might never get the chance.

In the distance she made out two blurry silhouettes. Seconds later, Zach and Martin cut through the shadows and approached her. Something cold and clammy tightened around her middle. They were alone.

"Still no sign of them," Zach told her, his face a flat, unreadable mask. He was doing it again—hiding his emotions. Disappointment twined with sadness. The Iceberg was back.

Martin looked broken. Without a word, he heavily mounted the stairs and entered the house. Zach turned his back to her and stared at the unnaturally calm ocean. She could almost see the thoughts churning in his head.

"We'll find them," she reassured him in a gravelly voice she barely recognized.

His hand twitched, the only indication he'd heard her. "I knew I never should've left them with Martin."

"You can't possibly blame yourself for this." But she knew he did. That was just the way he was made.

She stood and narrowed the distance between them, but refrained from touching him. Over the years, she'd learned to give him space when he was feeling this way. He needed room to beat himself up properly.

"I think maybe you were right all along," he said. "Maybe we really *are* cursed." She'd told him that once, weeks before their break-up.

She shook her head, even though he wasn't looking at her. "I don't believe that anymore. That was just my grief talking." She closed her fingers around his arm, despite her better judgment. "We're going to find them, Zach," she said again because she needed to convince herself the words were true.

Muscles bunched beneath her fingers. Tension rippled through him, a sharp current of electricity that thrummed against her palm.

Please don't give up, she whispered silently. *Not this time.*

The darkness seemed to deepen. It congealed around them as a cloud drifted across the nearly full moon. Without as much as a sigh, Zach pried his arm from her grasp and vanished into the house, leaving her with nothing but the wind to embrace her.

Never had dawn taken so long to come. Each dark hour had stretched into infinity. When the sun finally clawed its way out of the sea to part the gray curtains of mist that still hovered over the waves, Rebecca experienced an irrational sense of relief. None of them had slept that night except for Will. The penicillin had already kicked in, and, feeling better, the baby had finally succumbed to exhaustion.

Zach had lain in bed with his arm slung over his eyes, silent and unmoving, but she'd known he was every bit as conscious as she. He'd oozed tension from head to toe. Every inch of him was tight and hard, chiseled in stone.

She wanted to inch closer, to draw comfort from his solid body, but, afraid of invading the frosty barrier he'd erected around himself, she crawled out of bed and made her way downstairs instead.

She found Martin in the kitchen, inhaling a mug of coffee. He hadn't bothered to shave. Stubble shadowed his cheeks. His hair stood out at strange angles and fell in wisps over his forehead. He wore the same clothes he'd worn yesterday—a white Polo over a pair of beige shorts. The shirt was wrinkled, the shorts creased, and that somehow made him look more human.

Rebecca couldn't help the clutch of compassion that gripped her. Zach had every reason to blame Martin, but she could empathize with the man. She couldn't begin to imagine how lousy he felt, knowing the kids went missing on his watch. The truth was, it could have happened to any one of them.

"Is there enough coffee for two?" she asked.

He jolted at the sound of her voice. "Yeah. I made a whole pot. I figured we'd need it today."

She poured herself a healthy dose of the dark brew, then spiked it with a splash of milk.

"I never should've taken that call," he told her.

She joined him at the table and took a hearty swallow, in desperate need of the caffeine boost.

"I cleared my schedule," he insisted. "I wasn't expecting to have to work. But then this client phoned me out of the blue and—"

"It's okay, Martin. You don't have to explain yourself to me. I'm not interested in blaming anyone. All I care about is finding Noah and Kristen."

Pain radiated from her chest at the mention of their names. Their faces flashed before her eyes again. She'd once thought nothing could be more devastating than mourning the children she'd never have, but she'd been wrong. Those children had been nothing more than an idea in her head. Noah and Kristen were real. They had faces and souls and smiles that could melt ice cream on a winter's day. And she missed them. Missed them with a fervor that burned straight to the marrow of her bones.

"Do you think we will?" he asked her.

"We have to."

He reached across the table, covered her hand with his in an effort to give—or perhaps receive—comfort. "What if we don't?"

Rebecca placed her other hand over his and squeezed. The coffee suddenly tasted unbearably bitter on her tongue. "I can't go there, Martin. Not even in my head. If I do, I'll never climb back out again."

Martin's gaze fell to their joined hands. The look on his face told her he understood. "Then I won't, either."

Zach felt like a wreck when he clambered out of bed that morning. His muscles were taut, his neck strained, and a vicious headache pounded behind his eyes. Inside him a firestorm raged, hot and insistent, incinerating everything it touched. He didn't think it was possible to feel any worse...until he entered the kitchen and found Becca holding hands with Martin.

Fury ignited in his veins. The bastard had cost him his kids, and now he was making a move on his wife. Right there and then, he regretted not having beaten him to a pulp yesterday. His hands fisted at his sides, but he managed to roll his anger into a tight ball and swallow it. It left an acrid taste in his mouth, so he went and poured himself some coffee.

From the corner of his eye, he caught a flicker of movement. Becca had pulled her hand away from Martin's. "How are you feeling?" she asked him.

"How do you think?" He didn't mean to be short with her, but he was infinitely annoyed with everyone at the moment, his ex-wife included.

"Did you sleep at all?" she persisted.

"Sure. If you consider staring at the ceiling all night sleep." He approached the table and crashed into the chair beside her. "Are the cops here yet?"

"No," Martin rasped.

Zach directed a withering look his way. "Why the hell not? They said they'd be here at sunrise."

Becca rubbed her eyes, distressed. "Give them a chance."

Zach was about to tell her exactly what he thought of the cops' efforts so far, when the doorbell rang.

Today they'd brought the dogs. Becca had gathered up some of the kids' belongings, and a handful of German Shepherds now combed the surrounding woods, hoping to pick up the scent. Zach had tagged along because he couldn't bear to hang around just twiddling his thumbs the whole damn day. He needed to do something, even if all he could do was follow the cops around and make a nuisance of himself.

So far, nothing had turned up. He wasn't sure whether that was a bad sign or a good one. At least they hadn't found their bodies, which meant they could still be alive. That hope was all he clung to now.

The hours stretched, endless threads of time that snaked toward another dusk. The hot sun beat down on them, harsh and unrelenting. Zach plowed ahead, so charred inside he felt nothing but a soft throb of emptiness beneath his ribs and a burning sensation in his gut. Fatigue clawed at him, but the adrenaline pulsing through his bloodstream kept it at bay. He couldn't imagine ever sleeping again. Not until Noah and Kristen were found.

"I don't think they're out here," Lieutenant Mason, the officer in charge, said.

"They have to be." Zach's pace matched the lieutenant's. "Kids don't just disappear. If they didn't come this way, then they took to the sea. That would be pretty hard to do without a boat, unless..." He chased the thought from his brain. They couldn't have drowned. Not both at once.

"The Coast Guard is checking things out at its end. Something's bound to turn up."

He wanted to believe the lieutenant, but the sizzling wound in his gut wouldn't let him. It just grew bigger, rawer with each hour that passed. "Tell me the truth," he said to the other man. "What are the chances we'll find them alive?"

Lieutenant Mason's somber expression said it all.

"That's what I thought." The wound turned gangrenous. Zach knit his brows against the pain. Straightening his back, he forged ahead, trekking between the shivering trees.

A cacophony of barks broke the eerie silence. The dogs sniffed at the ground, mere feet before the woods ended and another stretch of beach began. Lieutenant Mason sped ahead, with Zach close on his heels.

"Stay back," the officer warned him, then crouched to study the ground.

"What is it? What did they find?"

"Footprints. Two sets from the looks of it. Judging from the sizes, they could very well belong to your kids." The dogs sprinted out of the woods and up a steep incline toward a house. Zach and the cops quickly followed.

The back door was unlocked, but Lieutenant Mason didn't enter. Instead, he whipped out his cell phone. "I need a search warrant for—" He turned to one of his detectives. "Get me the address to this place."

"You gotta be kidding me." Zach's frustration bubbled and overflowed. "My kids could be in there and you wanna wait for a search warrant—"

Lieutenant Mason raised his index finger to silence him. The detective returned and handed him a piece of paper with the address, and he relayed the information to whomever he was talking to on the phone. "That's right. On Ministers Lane. And make it quick."

"This is bullshit."

Mason skewered him with a pointed stare. "I have to do things by the book. This is private property. Unless I actually hear someone scream for help, I can't enter without a warrant."

"Yeah, well I can." Shoving his way past the lieutenant, Zach bulleted into the house. "Noah, Kristen, you in here?"

The place was deserted. No furniture filled the hollow spaces, no frames decorated the walls and a thin carpet of dust blanketed the floors. Still, maybe the kids had come here to play, locked themselves in a room...

Lieutenant Mason and his crew reluctantly trailed behind him, weapons raised. "You're compromising the investigation," Mason accused. "Go back outside."

"You can forget about it." He raced to the foot of the stairs. "Noah, Kristen! Answer me." He was about to sprint upstairs, when two detectives grabbed him and hauled his ass outside.

The lieutenant's expression was lethal. "Don't make me arrest you."

"You honestly expect me to sit around like a goddamned idiot waiting for some stupid piece of paper when my kids could be inside that house hurt or worse?"

"Yes." Mason's tone didn't falter. "That's exactly what I expect."

She sat at the edge of the shore, her arms wrapped around her waist, staring at the whitecaps as if they held the answer she so desperately sought. A few feet back, Will rolled in the sand, his mood greatly improved now that his ear no longer tortured him.

Rebecca wasn't nearly as lucky. A million thoughts plagued her, none the least bit comforting. In her hand she clutched Kristen's Ventolin. She'd found it in the children's room that morning, which had only added to the questions, the worry.

What if Kristen had another attack? What if it was already too late?

She tamped down the anxiety, wiped the disturbing thoughts from her mind. She couldn't think this way. She had to believe the kids would be fine. Otherwise her heart would fracture into a million fragments of grief, and she'd fall apart. What good would she be to them then? This time, she had to stay strong. Retreating into self-indulgent misery wasn't an option.

Still, acid tears dampened her lashes, and she quickly blinked them away. Bolt ambled up beside her and whimpered. Lathering her face with a wet tongue, he tried to lick her anguish away. With a gasp that was half surprise, half sob, she hooked her arm around him and pressed him to her side, soothed by his warmth.

There was something immeasurably calming about a dog. The way it looked at you with sad eyes that never judged. The way it gave you a soft body to hold on to, even as the ground slowly rolled out from under you.

"What happened to them, boy?"

The puppy replied with a short bark.

She released a shaky sigh and scratched him. Bolt's ears twitched. With an excited wag of his tail, he tore out of her embrace and vaulted into the bordering woods. He looked back at her, barked a few more times, then gazed out at the distant trees again. For a second she thought he was trying to tell her something. Then a squirrel dashed down from one of the trunks, and she shook her head in defeat.

Placing the pump back in her pocket, she dug her heels into the sand and stood.

"You've been out here for hours." Tess's voice startled her.

Rebecca slanted a glance her way. "I don't know what else to do with myself. I'm going stir-crazy."

"Where are the men?"

"Zach's out with the search party. Martin went back home to pick up some things. He hadn't planned on staying more than a day when he first showed up." The wind rustled through the trees, caressed her face with invisible fingers. "Have you spoken to Pat?"

"I tried calling him several times. Can't seem to reach him. Something big is going down. Knowing Pat, he'd going to want to be right smack in the middle of it, whatever it is." Tess looked drawn. Her skin was paler than usual, and fine lines creased her forehead. "Why don't you come inside? It's almost suppertime. You haven't eaten a thing all day. I've got a nice pot of soup simmering on the stove."

"I don't think I could eat. My stomach's shrunk to the size of a raisin."

Tess wrapped her arm around Rebecca's. "But Will's probably getting hungry."

She was right, of course. Rebecca nodded heavily. She pulled free from Tess's grasp and lifted the toddler, who squirmed in protest. "I should probably get him washed up first."

"I'll go whip together some sandwiches." A smile fluttered over the neighbor's lips but failed to mask the dark concern in her gaze. "Drop by whenever you're ready."

Rebecca nodded meekly, then slogged toward the house. Beneath a green canopy of trees, Bolt continued to watch her with imploring brown eyes, full of gentle sadness.

"I'm cold." His sister shivered and pressed her lips together, now a frightful, purplish shade of blue. A real nasty cough clattered in her chest.

Noah drew her closer, tried to warm her with his body. They both wore nothing but T-shirts and shorts, and this place was cool and damp and smelled like rotten vegetables. He'd never had much use for vegetables, even the non-rotten kind.

They'd spent the night on the hard cement floor with nothing but each other for warmth. The room was bare, dirty. Above a row of huge wooden barrels, dust-speckled light poured in from a tiny window.

Noah's head felt heavy, full of cotton, like his mouth. A swarm of bees buzzed in his tummy. He didn't want to die here in this damp, smelly room. He wanted to go back home, to hang out on the beach with Uncle Zach, to feel one of Aunt Becca's flower-scented hugs again, even though he always pretended he didn't like them. The bees suddenly stung, made an ache spread in his chest. He hadn't realized until now how safe he felt with them. Almost as safe as he'd felt with his parents.

"I wanna go home," Kristen echoed his thoughts, her mouth curling into a pout. Noah prayed she wouldn't start bawling. "I don't like it here." Her breathing grew ragged.

He had to distract her before she got really upset. She didn't have her asthma pump with her, and if she had an attack here...

He didn't even want to think about it.

"Aunt Becca and Uncle Zach will find us," he told her, not sure if she'd buy it when he didn't even believe it himself.

"Why did he bring us here, Noah? I thought only bad guys took kids."

Noah looked around the small room, empty except for the neatly stacked barrels beneath the window. On the floor beside them sat two bottles of water, two half-eaten sandwiches and a bag of stale chips.

"Guess he's a bad guy." He felt like a complete idiot for ever trusting Night-Owl. His dad had been right. Why hadn't he listened? "Dad knew."

Kristen looked at him with wet, curious eyes.

"He warned me." Noah felt his own eyes sting. "This is all my fault."

"It's okay, Noah. You didn't know. I liked him, too."

Warmth expanded inside him. His sister could be pretty annoying sometimes, but deep down where it counted, she was all right.

He had to do something. It was up to him to protect her. The window drew his attention again. It was small, but so were they. They could use the barrels to climb up, crawl out...

He shot to his feet and ran to the other side of the room. Carefully, he began to scale the barrels.

"What are you doing?"

"Getting us out of here." The barrels nearly slid out from under him, so he grabbed the metal frame that held them in place to keep from falling.

Kristen crawled over to him, crouched at the bottom and watched him with a funny mix of hope and fear in her eyes. Noah reached the window and tried to unlatch it.

"Is it open?"

He pushed it, but it wouldn't give way. "It's painted shut." Using what little fingernails he had, he peeled away the paint. One by one, the chips fluttered to the ground like snowflakes. He shoved the glass again.

Nothing. It didn't budge an inch.

That was when he noticed the nail. It was old and rusted. He began to jiggle it, thinking if he played with it, it might come loose. From the looks of it, someone else had had the same idea because it moved around easily.

"Noah." Kristen's voice was frantic. "I think he's coming."

Keys jingled in the lock, and Noah's stomach did a belly flop. As fast as he could, he scurried back down, praying the barrels wouldn't collapse beneath his weight.

With a reassuring look directed at his sister, he jumped to the ground seconds before the door swung open.

Chapter Thirty

Rebecca managed to swallow a couple of spoonfuls of soup, but that was the extent of her appetite. The sandwich still sat on her plate, untouched. Thankfully, Will had eaten a decent supper and was now amusing himself exploring Tess's house, carefully monitored by Jason and Amy.

Beyond the windows, twilight stretched. The painful void in Rebecca's chest pulsed. Another day was drawing to a close, and the children had yet to be found.

Tess watched her with a somber look, her hands clasped nervously over her bent knees, as she sat across from her in the living room. "Zach should be back soon," she told her.

Rebecca nodded feebly. "If they'd found them, we would have heard by now."

"You don't know that for sure."

"Zach would have called." Her tone was flat, monotonous. Despair was creeping in. She was familiar enough with the feeling to recognize it. Only this time she wouldn't recover from it. It would eat her alive and spit her out in pieces.

"I never knew," she admitted to Tess. "I thought the absence of love was the worst thing a person could endure, but it isn't. Love is far, far worse." She bit her lower lip until she tasted blood. "What am I going to do, Tess? Now that I've known them, how do I go on without them?"

Tess reached out and clutched Rebecca's trembling fingers. "Don't think like that. It isn't over yet."

Rebecca wanted desperately to believe her, but every minute that passed fueled her worst fears. "How am I going to get through another night, knowing they're out there somewhere on their own? What if they're hurt?"

Tess tightened her grip on Rebecca's hand but didn't speak. There was nothing her friend could say that would provide any real comfort. It would be like trying to mend a broken bone with a Band-Aid.

"Don't touch that!" Jason yelled, following Will into the living room. Pat's prized figurine collection had caught the toddler's eye, and he wanted to get his pudgy hands on one of the porcelain figures—an angel with golden wings. Jason ran to block him. Will, who didn't appreciate the interference, let out an indignant yowl.

Rebecca pulled free from Tess's grasp and rose. "I should take Will home. He's about due for his next dose of penicillin."

Tess nodded and followed Rebecca as she went to retrieve the toddler. "Will you try to get some sleep tonight?" The concern lacing the neighbor's words was thick, almost tangible.

Rebecca's lips curled into a meek smile that trembled at the corners. She didn't even have the energy to answer.

"Hold on a sec." Tess quickly disappeared into the kitchen. When she returned, she clasped a small bottle. "Sometimes I have trouble sleeping," she told her. "The doctor prescribed these. They're a mild sedative." She placed the pills in the palm of Rebecca's hand. "I think you need them more than I do."

"I really shouldn't—" Her last experimentation with sleeping pills had been a disaster.

"Take them, just in case," Tess insisted. "You won't do these kids any good if you're too tired to stand on your own two feet. You need to rest."

With an uncertain nod, Rebecca pocketed the bottle. She was too tired to argue. "Thank you, for everything," she told Tess. "You've been a great friend." And with that, she lifted Will and left the warm bosom of Tess's home to return to her own, where another sleepless night awaited her. There was no way she was going to take a single one of those sedatives. The last time she had, it had destroyed her marriage and nearly killed her.

Pills numbed not only the senses, but the mind, and she was determined to stay sharp and alert no matter what. She would hold herself together, bite down on the pain and somehow find a way to believe that the universe wasn't out to steal every pathetic ounce of happiness she was blessed enough to find.

When Zach got home that evening, adrenaline coursed through him like a drug. He'd never been the kind of guy who punched holes in walls, but right now that was exactly what he wanted to do. He wanted to pummel every object in sight. Helplessness ate away at him, laced with a potent dose of fear. The cops had waited too long. They should've brought the dogs yesterday, searched through the night. Now, whoever had nabbed the kids had a thirty-hour head start and they had nothing. Nothing but questions.

Becca trudged down the stairs, her hair tied in a loose knot at the nape of her neck. Her complexion was pale and drawn. The light had gone out of her eyes, replaced by a flat look that left him suddenly spent.

She's withdrawing into herself again.

Her expression blackened the second she realized he was alone. "You didn't find them." Her tone rang flatter than her gaze.

Zach stared at the blank wall behind her. He couldn't bear to look at her, couldn't bear to see the pain and disappointment on her face. "No."

"Why didn't you call me?"

He wasn't sure how to answer that, so he just shook his head. "Where's Martin?" he asked, changing the subject.

"He went back home to pack up some things."

He snorted in a way that reminded him of Noah. The thought of his nephew poured lemon juice over the gaping wound in his abdomen. "I knew it wouldn't be long before the jerk jumped ship."

"You're not being fair. He didn't even have a change of clothes with him. He said he'd be back to help as soon as he could."

"You should have told him to forget about it. We don't need his brand of help."

Fatigue and exasperation tugged at her lips and brows, and she didn't bother to acknowledge his bitter comment with a reply. "Did the police find anything?"

She waited for an answer he was hesitant to give. How could he tell her Lieutenant Mason's theory without crushing her hopes, adding another layer of worry to the multitude already weighing her down?

Her patience finally snapped. "Zach, please talk to me. I'm dying here."

Sadness scraped the walls of his throat. "They found tracks out in the woods." He forced himself to meet her dampened gaze. "They belonged to the kids. The dogs led us to a house up on Ministers Lane. It was empty." It had taken over an hour for the warrant to arrive, while they'd sat on the back steps with the sun bearing down on them, sweating inside and out. "The owners put it on the market over a year ago. Lieutenant Mason and his crew tracked them down and questioned them. Their alibi checks out. They were nowhere near the house yesterday afternoon."

"I don't understand. If the kids were playing in an abandoned house, why didn't they come home?"

"The cops believe someone else was in there. There were traces of a man's shoes imprinted in the dust, signs of a struggle." He swallowed to wash down the bitterness that spread through his mouth. "Lieutenant Mason is convinced whoever was in the house took the kids."

Becca shook her head and covered her mouth with her fingers. "Is

215

this all speculation or fact?"

He ran his own hand over his face, felt the stubble scratch his palm. "Does it really matter? It makes sense. If they'd wandered off, we would've found them by now."

"I don't understand any of this." She wrapped her arms around herself, seeking warmth or comfort, he couldn't be sure which. "First Liam and Lindsay, now Noah and Kristen."

"Maybe it's all linked."

Her head snapped up. "What are you saying?"

"Noah confesses to seeing the guy who killed his parents, then disappears. Pretty convenient, don't you think?"

Fear came into her eyes, sharp enough to slice him in two. "You think the killer took them? Oh, God." Hysteria shook her voice, and he wanted to smack himself for speculating out loud. All he needed now was to push her over the edge. But she pulled herself together, gathered her thoughts enough to ask, "How could he possibly know?"

Guilt slammed into him. "Because I pushed Noah into talking to Pat, urged Pat to book a session with a sketch artist. Maybe Pat went ahead and shared what he knew with the Boston PD—"

"Don't tell me you're trying to take responsibility for this." Her tone was hot enough to melt steel. "You're doing it again. Trying to control everything. To shoulder the blame."

"It's all I know how to do," he answered honestly. "What got us into this mess in the first place. If I'd only let sleeping dogs lie—"

"Stop. Just stop." She closed her lids to block out the sight of him. "We'll blame the sick bastard who took them. That's who we'll blame." She bridged the distance between them, waited for something he was unable to give.

He went as far as to lift his arm, but as much as he ached to pull her to him and reassure her everything was going to be all right, something held him back. Maybe it was his sense of inadequacy. He didn't know how to be the man she needed, never had. With a short, exasperated breath, he let his arm drop to his side.

She studied him. The broken look on her face stabbed him, dead-center, in the heart. "It's happening again," she whispered so softly he barely made out the words. "You're pulling away from me. I'm losing you."

Her statement bowled him over. She was afraid of losing *him*? Maybe he wasn't the man she needed, but she was all he'd ever wanted. He'd die before he let her go again. This time when he reached out, he wrapped his fingers around hers and drew her close. Her heat singed him, thawed the splinters of ice in his bloodstream. Her bottomless eyes drew him in, swallowed him like quicksand, and his lungs suddenly felt heavy, full of mud.

He slid his palms up her arms. "I sucked at being a husband," he confessed. "Turns out I suck at being a father as well."

She shook her head in protest, and he silenced her by pressing his finger to her lips. "But I'm in this for the long haul. In good times and in bad. For better or for worse. Isn't that what we promised each other? I forgot that for a while. But I remember now."

He gripped her shoulders, gave her a nice, hard squeeze. "I need one more promise from you, though. You've got to stay with me this time because I can't bear to watch the pain bury you again."

Clutching his shirt for support, she nodded feebly and curled up against him. Her softness, her tender heat sapped all his energy. The overwhelming urge to collapse in a heap on the ground with her tucked safely in his arms seized him. But he kept standing, infusing her with whatever strength he had left. Stress and despair hollowed out a space inside him he was desperate to fill, so he crushed his mouth to hers. He needed to believe that all wasn't lost, that some hope still remained. He wanted to chase away the crippling numbness that had clung to him for days, to feel alive again, if only for a few minutes.

She went limp in his arms, and he lifted her off her feet and carried her to the couch where they'd made love for the first time, before things had gotten so complicated. He just wanted to hold her, kiss her, press her to him and know she was still his. He was drowning again, grasping at an elusive lifeline, struggling to stay afloat any way he could.

He couldn't think, could barely breathe. He just wanted to feel, to bury himself in the one woman he just couldn't teach himself to live without. There was a limit to how much loss a man could handle, and he'd reached his. This was his way to strike back, to tell fate it wouldn't take another damn thing from him.

With a fire in his blood that bordered on desperation, he peeled the blouse from her shoulders, kissed her creamy skin, tossed her sweater on the floor...

Something fell out of the pocket and plunked to the ground, distracting him. He shot a cursory glance at the heap of wool at the foot of the couch, and stilled. It looked like fate had taken him up on his challenge, happily turned around and kicked him in the teeth yet again.

Next to Becca's gray sweater—rolling ominously toward him—was a small bottle of pills.

Chapter Thirty-One

The look on Zach's face when he saw the tranquilizers said it all. Rebecca scurried off the couch, cursing herself for ever being stupid enough to let Tess talk her into taking the bottle.

She leaned over to retrieve it, but Zach beat her to it. "What's this?" The cold accusation in his voice froze her solid.

"Sedatives," she admitted warily. "Tess insisted I use them to help me sleep. I just took the bottle to get her off my back. She can be very persistent."

He didn't believe her. She saw it in the stiff set of his shoulders, the thin line of his lips. There was a hard glitter in his eyes that hadn't been there before.

Seconds later, he echoed her thoughts. "I don't believe this. I'm such an idiot." His fingers tightened around the bottle before he pitched it on the table. His anger was tangible. She could feel it fisting around her, taste it in the thickening air, hear it in the deafening silence pulsing between them.

He jumped to his feet, the muscles on his back rippling beneath his shirt. He refused to meet her gaze. "This was a mistake," he spat at her. "I knew we'd end up right back where we started."

Her own anger flared. She'd had enough of being continuously reeled in only to be tossed aside. "You're really full of shit, you know that?"

Shock momentarily sliced through his fury. "I'm full of shit? *I'm* full of shit?"

She wanted to punch him. Badly. Almost as badly as she'd wanted to kiss him earlier. "One minute you're jumping my bones, the next you're telling me it's a mistake. Make up your mind, because I've had about as much as I can take. You either want me or you don't."

"Is that what you think this is about? Wanting you? Good God, Becca, wanting you was never the problem. The problem is that I'm too damn selfish to let you go."

His statement floored her. Anger dissipated until only weakness remained. "If you want me so darn much, why have you spent the last two years pushing me away?"

The dam broke, and a sea of anguish shone in his midnight blue gaze. "Because I'm bad for you. This relationship never seems to work. Things always go south, and I just don't know how to fix them." His anxiety was finally catching up to him, and his voice splintered under the pressure. "I've failed you over and over again. Now I've gone and failed my sister's kids, too."

It all became clear then. Every question that haunted her turned to dust and rolled away. He hadn't walked out on her because of her failures but because of his own. The weight of his responsibly crushed her. "You've failed no one. No matter how strong you are, no matter how hard you try, you can't stop life from happening. You can't live in a bubble, and neither can the people you love. Believe me, I've tried. Pain still finds you. The only difference is that you have to bear it alone."

Their eyes locked, and raw honesty passed between them. "I wasn't going to take the pills," she told him with as much passion as she could muster, and this time she almost sensed he believed her.

He took a step toward her, his expression alight with a burning intensity that incinerated her flesh and left her bare, exposed. She wasn't sure whether he planned to shake or embrace her, and she never found out. He stopped when he kicked something half concealed by the sofa. The blow knocked the object against the leg of the couch, and it shattered. His attention diverted, Zach fell on his haunches and picked up the broken pieces of porcelain. "Where did this come from?"

Rebecca bent over for a closer inspection. One of Pat's figurines, the angel Will had been fixated on, stared back at her with deadened eyes. "From Tess's house. Will must have snatched it when I wasn't paying attention." Regret slid through her. How was she going to tell her friend and neighbor that they'd broken one of her husband's prized possessions?

Maybe she could glue it back together. She fell to her knees next to Zach and proceeded to amass the pieces of the broken angel, then stopped short. Kristen's innocent ramblings from a few nights ago came back to her.

"Amy's dad said the children are disappearing because the angels are broken."

Broken Angels.

The words scrolled through her mind. Why did they sound so familiar? Then it came to her. That was the name of the organization she'd seen on the pictures she'd pitched in the trash.

Like a curtain, the fog in her mind parted, replaced by a spark of understanding. She thought of Voula and what she'd told her: *"I think Liam may have gotten himself into some kind of trouble. He was acting very strangely before he died. He told me if the kids were here and anyone came knocking on my door, I shouldn't let them in, even if I recognized them."*

"You were right," she whispered. "It's all linked."

Zach raised a pair of questioning eyes her way.

"Liam and Lindsay's murder, Pat's case, the kids going missing...all linked." The shards she'd collected clunked to the ground as she bounded to her feet. "When you had those photos developed, did you download all of them on Noah's iPod?"

Confusion pleated his brows. "As many as I could. Why?"

"I need that iPod." She ran to boot up her laptop, frowned when it wasn't where she'd left it. "Have you been using my computer?"

"No. Becca, you're not making any sense." He followed her around the house while she searched for her laptop. She finally found it in the kitchen.

"Just get me Noah's iPod. I'll explain everything in a sec."

He lingered while she waited for the screen to come alive, then hastened from the room when she gave him a pointed look.

He returned a few minutes later and handed her the device. Her blood pumped thick and scalding through her veins as she attached it and proceeded to copy the files. Then she began inspecting each and every one of them until she came across the one she sought.

The image was blurry, the resolution low, but she made out the words just the same.

Broken Angels.

A list of names and contact numbers followed. She opened file after file until she found the birth certificates. Then there were pictures of children she didn't know, gazing up at her with frightened eyes.

"What the hell is this?" Zach had been glancing over her shoulder, his body stiffening with each document she opened.

"I'm not sure. But it's important."

"Son of a bitch." Tension spilled from Zach's limbs like a current of pure electricity. "They're forgeries. Fake birth certificates. Passport pictures."

Her pulse stumbled and crashed. "What for?"

"My guess—to smuggle children out of the country...or into another one."

"Human trafficking?"

He nodded ominously. "And from the looks of it, Liam put enough evidence together to hang the scumbags." He clicked on the first document. "Take a look at this."

One name in particular stood out. Her gaze settled on it, and her stomach plunked all the way to her toes. "Oh, God."

The expression on Zach's face reflected the same staggering

disbelief rioting through her. "The goddamned bastard killed them. He killed my baby sister."

Everything inside her shriveled. "And now he's got Noah and Kristen."

Rage contorted his features, underscored by a wild rush of determination. "Not for long."

They heard the front door swing open. Zach must have forgotten to lock it when he'd gotten home tonight. Seconds later, Martin stepped into the kitchen, caught sight of their troubled expressions and froze. "What's happened?"

"It's Neil Hopkins," Rebecca blurted out. "He has the kids."

Neil wasn't normally one to make mistakes. He liked his affairs tidy, all loose ends tied up, nice and snug. These past few months, however, he'd messed up. Badly. There was one rule he'd always made it a point to live by—never shit in your own backyard.

But that was precisely what he'd done when he'd targeted Noah Birch.

He never should have probed the kid for his Falcon World user name when he'd seen him at the Birches' Christmas party, never should have approached him online. But the boy was perfect, exactly what the Broken Angels wanted—healthy, strong, with a dark, brooding look their clients valued. Neil knew the kind of kids a certain depraved brand of people favored...because his father had taught him.

Couldn't say the old man never gave him anything.

He killed the motor and anchored his boat next to Raymond York's. He'd have to remember to get rid of that hunk of junk, but there was no rush. Raymond was a lone wolf. No search parties would be called, no missing person's report filed, so the boat was of little consequence.

Right now, getting the kids ready for the drop-off, which was scheduled to go down at midnight tonight, was far more pressing. The documents were finalized, secured in a manila envelope in his briefcase. Beside it sat a couple of Happy Meals. No one could ever accuse him of not being a good host.

He grabbed the briefcase and the paper bags, used his motorized dinghy to zip to the shore, then scaled the small bluff and took the familiar path to his childhood home. The winery came into view, a white-washed gingerbread house, capped by a red roof. The sunny yellow shutters shone gray in the moonlight, the walls draped in shadows, making the usually cheerful structure look unnaturally sinister.

He used his key to let himself in and hastened to the plant, where rusted vats and metal tanks hunkered like weary soldiers in the dark.

He could almost hear them whisper familiar words of welcome as he slid between them. His digital camera swung from his shoulder, its task completed. The twenty-four-megapixel Nikon was top of its class, nothing like the antiquated device his father had used. When Neil closed his eyes at night—which was becoming less and less frequent— he could still see that long, probing black lens boring into him, could still feel the light of the flash spilling over his naked flesh in blinding sparks. Each degrading click had taken a bite out of his dignity, left him a little emptier.

He shoved the memories aside, buried them deep in a place within him no one knew about, then gave himself a quick, mental shake. There was no use dwelling on the past. He was the one in charge now, the one with the camera. But unlike his dad, he only took headshots. Shots he could later use to forge passports for the children he recruited for the Broken Angels. What they did with the kids afterward was their business. He wanted no part of it.

All he cared about was the money, the power and prestige it could buy. Nothing restored dignity better than cold hard cash. Some said that Italian leather shoes and designers suits didn't make the man, but Neil disagreed wholeheartedly. As far as he was concerned, appearances were everything, and he was willing to do anything to preserve his. No one would strip him of his self-respect ever again. Success—any way he came by it—was his God-given right after what he'd endured at his father's hand. It was justice, pure and simple, and the irony pleased him tremendously.

He paused briefly when he passed the grape-crusher, where Raymond York had at last found his peace. The mammoth of a machine now lay quiet, as still as the souls it had claimed. Ages ago another man had fallen into that particular piece of equipment, drunk on his own wine. The crusher had been off at the time—a situation Neil had promptly rectified. That was the last the world had ever seen of Neil Hopkins Senior. Not that anyone had missed him. Like Raymond York, Neil's dad hadn't been a man who'd cultivated friendships. A single father, he'd chosen to rot away on this vineyard, alone with his one son.

And that son had been more than happy to see him reduced to pulp.

The smell of burgers and fries was starting to turn his stomach. How did kids digest this stuff? He could feel his arteries clogging from the mere stench of grease rising from the bags. He turned the corner, bypassed a stack of barrels and made his way down the metal stairs to the cellar where the children were being kept. He deeply regretted having had to snatch the girl as well. Normally, he never took more than one child from any given family. Not because he was particularly sentimental, but because it wasn't worth the risk.

This time he hadn't had a choice. He couldn't very well leave another witness behind, especially since Kristen was acquainted with him. Sometimes sacrifices had to be made, rules broken. That was life.

At least she'd bring in a decent profit. The blond ones always did. The asthma was a problem, though, and could end up taking a chunk out of his commission.

Overall, he was pleased by how well he'd pulled the whole thing off. He hadn't known the exact location of the Ryler summer home, but it had been easy enough to find. He was an expert at research, had all the right contacts in place. That a vacant house sat mere yards away had been sheer luck. The only luck he'd had in this whole wretched situation so far.

He deposited his briefcase on the cement floor, then fished out his keys. Hunched at the foot of the stackable barrel racks, the kids watched him with sad, frightened eyes. This was the part of his job he hated most. The way they all looked at him, like he was some kind of monster about to swallow them whole. He knew that look well, had worn it once himself.

"I brought you supper," he told them, right before he placed the bags at their feet.

"We don't want your stupid food." Hatred gleamed in the boy's eyes, bright enough to cut through the fear. "We want you to take us back home."

"I can't do that."

The girl began to cry. A worrisome wheeze resounded from her chest. He couldn't very well have her gasping for air when he delivered her to his contact. That might be a deal-breaker.

"Does she have her pump?" he asked Noah, who had his arm wrapped in a protective clasp around his sister.

"What do you think, asshole? If you don't take us home, she could die."

Wouldn't be the first child he lost in transit. These misfortunes were just part of the trade. "Keep her calm. Get some food in her. We'll be taking a little boat trip real soon."

And with that, he left them to huddle in the damp room, surrounded by the nauseating smell of grease and the faint, underlying odor of fermented grapes.

"Neil Hopkins? Liam's old boss?" Martin's shock sent a frisson of unease rippling through the room. "Why?"

Zach struggled to keep murderous thoughts from consuming him, failed. "Because the sick son of a bitch is part of a child-trafficking ring. And Liam knew about it."

Martin ventured farther into the house, all false pride stripped from his face. His hair was a mess, his collar crooked, the beige

Dockers he wore soaked to the knees. For a second Zach almost felt sorry for the jerk. "Are you going where I think you're going with this?"

Becca rubbed the tension from her eyes, or maybe she was just trying to squelch the tears that beat beneath her lids. "We think he's behind Lindsay's and Liam's deaths, and that he came after the kids because of what Noah saw."

"You guys aren't making any sense."

That's right. Martin didn't know. "Noah saw the man who shot his parents. He told Pat Jenkins about it," Zach explained. "We figure Neil Hopkins somehow got wind of it and decided to finish what he started that night."

Suddenly weary, Martin propped his butt at the corner of the kitchen table. "Have you told the cops?"

Becca shook her head. "Not yet." She grabbed the mouse, clicked it a few times. "I just e-mailed Tess the evidence Liam collected. She'll forward it to Pat." With a sudden burst of energy, she shot to her feet. "I should call Lieutenant Mason."

"Bad idea." Zach's tone was firm, resolute. "The guy's got a righteous streak a mile long. He'll just make us wait till he gets all his ducks in a row, especially if a search warrant is required. At this time of night, that could take hours. I doubt the kids have that long. Pat's our best bet."

"I'll call Tess then. See if she can reach him." Running on adrenaline, Becca left the room in search of the cordless phone. Both men stared after her.

"How she holding up?" Martin asked.

"Better than I expected. She's keeping it together." Zach took Becca's place at the keyboard and continued to examine the documents, hoping to find some kind of lead that would tell him where the sick bastard had taken the kids.

"This is huge." Martin's expression darkened the more he scanned the files.

No shit.

There had to be something in here. An address, a location. There were several drop-off points listed, but no safe house. Where did Neil Hopkins harbor the kids before he delivered them?

"What if he's already handed them over?" Martin's words were like a swift uppercut to the midsection. Once Hopkins passed the kids on to these Broken Angels, they would be virtually impossible to track down. The trail seemed to end with Hopkins and the handful of contacts he had. What happened to the kids afterward was anyone's guess.

"I spoke with Tess." Becca joined them at the table. "She says Pat hasn't been answering his phone, but she promised to do everything in her power to reach him. She said she'd leave a message with the DA's office, but there's no telling when he'll get it." Worry lines bracketed her mouth. "Maybe we should call nine-one-one."

"Forget it." Zach refused to cave in. "They'll only hold us back. No way I'll sit tight while the cops dick around." This afternoon he'd gotten a pretty good idea of how the system worked. "We'll just have to figure this thing out on our own."

Thankfully Becca didn't argue with him. Instead, she leaned over his arm to stare at the screen. "Did you find anything?" The urgency in her voice matched the tension snaking through his limbs.

"Not yet, but I will. There's gotta be something here."

Zach clicked on another file, and a picture flashed onto the monitor. A picture of a little girl with blond hair and familiar blue eyes. His stomach folded shut. Thoughts of Kristen doused him in cold waves, followed by a rush of anger so sharp it left him shredded inside. He had to find them. Had to find his kids. This time failure wasn't an option.

"Take a look at that." Becca pointed to the far-left corner of the screen. "Zoom in."

"What is it?"

"I'm not sure yet." She snatched the mouse from him, enlarged the image. "It looks like the corner of a barrel. The kind you use to store wine. Didn't Hopkins tell us he grew up on a winery?"

The conversation came back to him. "Yeah, he did."

"That's where he takes the kids." Hope sparked in her eyes. "We find that winery, we find Noah and Kristen."

Martin squeezed in for a better look. "Could be anywhere from here to Napa Valley."

Zach wagged his head. "Has to be nearby. He wouldn't risk boarding a plane. That's not his job. He's just the recruiter."

Becca opened up the Internet browser and typed in the words *Hopkins* and *winery*. Several files appeared on the screen. She quickly scrolled through them. There didn't seem to be anything of interest until she landed on an obscure article, several pages down. It looked like an archive from a community paper in Martha's Vineyard, dating back to the seventies.

Neil Hopkins Sr., owner of Martha's Cellar, a local winery just East of Chilmark, was found crushed to death in his plant this morning. Authorities believe the inebriated man died instantly, after falling into the grape crusher while the machine was in operation. His son, Neil Hopkins Jr., was devastated by the accident and refused to give a statement.

"This is it." Life trickled back into her voice. "This is where he's keeping them."

She typed in Martha's Cellar as the search string and pressed Enter. Another list of sites flashed onto the monitor. Becca opened each and every one of them until she found what she was looking for. "I got the address." Her attention spun to Martin. "Does your boat have a navigation system?"

He nodded. "Top of the line."

Zach scoffed. "Figures."

"Instead of acting like a smart-ass, you should be thanking your lucky stars I don't cut corners."

Becca was already up, whizzing through the house like a woman on speed. "Are you two going to sit around taking cheap shots at each other all night or are you coming?"

They both rose simultaneously. "What about Will?" Martin asked.

"I'll drop him off next door. Tess will watch him." Without another word, she rushed upstairs to retrieve the baby.

Zach turned the full force of his attention on Martin. "Just because you're giving us a ride, don't think all is forgiven." Understanding sizzled between them.

Martin's expression grew feral. "Don't worry. I've learned not to expect any goodwill from you." He shook his head without an ounce of shame. "Ten years later and I'm still wondering what she sees in you."

That hit a little too close to home. Zach took a threatening step forward. "It's eating you alive. That after all is said and done," he elaborated, "I'm still the one she wants."

They stared at each other, neither daring to blink, engaged in a contest of wills that had spanned a decade.

Becca returned with Will fussing in her arms, a diaper bag slung over her shoulder. "Let's go," she commanded, oblivious to the fact that she was the object of one man's unrequited desire and the other's unwavering devotion. "What are you waiting for? Time's running out."

Outside, the bleached face of the moon glared down at them, fierce and menacing.

Chapter Thirty-Two

The sharp caress of the wind made moisture pearl on Zach's skin. He tasted salt on his lips, peppered with the unmistakable flavor of an incoming storm. The sea churned, ice cold and restless. Like black glass, it reflected the moon.

Zach stood at the helm next to Martin, his gaze fixed ahead. He tried not to think of the bottomless beast raging beneath them. Becca sat a few feet back, shivering.

He reluctantly approached her and draped a heavy arm over her shoulders to warm her. "You all right?"

"I'm fine. I just can't stop thinking about the kids. They need us, Zach." Her eyes shimmered like aged whiskey, deep and intoxicating. "They need us and we're not there."

"Won't be long now," Martin called above the roar of wind and surf.

Becca didn't look reassured. "What if we're too late?" The question squeaked out of her.

"We won't be." Zach didn't know where this unshakable faith came from, but there it was, hanging between them, a beacon of hope cleaving the darkness.

Her hand clenched around something she held.

"What's that?"

"Kristen's asthma pump. She left it behind."

His own fears rose to smother him. "She'll be all right." He had to believe that or he'd lose it. "Noah will keep her safe."

A weak smile played at the corners of her mouth. "He's so much like you it scares me."

His own lips trembled. "Yeah, me too." The moon disappeared behind an invisible cloud. Seconds later a fine drizzle began to fall. "Why don't you go below deck and warm up? There's no use all of us getting soaked."

She nodded. "Come with me."

"No. I have to stay up here." He needed to feel he was doing something, even if all he could do was stand vigil.

"Afraid I'll get us lost?" Martin tossed over his shoulder.

"Or fall overboard," Zach shot back.

"I think the probability of that happening increases exponentially if you stick around."

"All the more reason for me to stay."

Becca shook her head and rose. "I'll leave you two to your petty squabbles. My fingers are just about ready to fall off."

As soon as Becca disappeared below deck, Martin shot Zach a resentful stare. "She's too good for you," he told him without a hint of remorse.

"Maybe so, but she's mine." Zach's tone was unmistakably proprietary. "And I'm keeping her this time."

Martin flinched.

The wind howled as the boat gained speed. Zach returned to the helm to watch the hull slice through the waves. "I'm curious. How come you never made a move on her when we broke up?"

Martin was silent for a long time, and Zach wondered if he'd heard him. Then he finally answered in a steady voice that belied the stiff set of his jaw. "I know how to hedge my bets. I never stood a chance with her. She'll always be hung up on you—any fool can see that—and I'm not the kind of guy who can settle for second best."

Everything suddenly made sense. "It's just killing you, isn't it?"

Martin angled a quizzical look his way.

"That Liam and Lindsay named me guardian instead of you." The miniature yacht hit an unexpected swell, and Zach grabbed hold of the hull for support. The fine drizzle turned to a downpour. Impenetrable blackness rolled in from the north to shroud the sky. "That's why you've been sniffing around us like a dog in heat."

Martin chuckled, but the sound held no amusement. "You've got me all figured out, don't you?" He shook his head, steered the boat westward. "Did you ever stop to consider that maybe I've been *sniffing* around because these three are all I've got left of my kid brother?" His hands tightened around the rudder, but his expression gave nothing away. "I was never really there for Liam. I always had some big deal to close, the next plane to catch. I thought I had all the time in the world to make it up to him. I was wrong."

He aimed a steely glare Zach's way. "You may not think much of me, but I'm no idiot. I make it a point to learn from my mistakes. I'm going to be a part of these kids' lives, whether you like it or not."

It looked like Martin had finally grown a backbone, and resentment briefly morphed into respect. Before Zach could analyze the touchy-feely moment, the misty outline of land caught his eye. Anticipation and anxiety dueled along his nerves. "Let's find them first." His stomach muscles gathered in a tight knot. "We'll work out the details later."

It was night again. Noah could tell by the dark wall that stretched beyond the window. The moon had disappeared behind the clouds, and it looked like someone had thrown a black cape over the building. He listened for the sound of footsteps, but all he heard were crickets and rain. The hamburgers remained untouched in the paper bags. Kristen had dug out the toy—a small, stuffed bear—and now hugged it to her chest.

Her breathing had gotten worse.

At the top of the barrel stack, Noah stood working the nail again, as he had most of the day. His fingers had begun to bleed. Thankfully, Neil Hopkins hadn't noticed when he'd brought them the stupid burgers.

"We're never going back, are we?" Tears leaked from the corners of his sister's eyes, and she rubbed them away with her fists. It was late, and they were both exhausted. "We're never going back home. Like Mom and Dad. Do you think Mr. Hopkins took them, too? Will he bring us to them now?" she asked between a cough and a wheeze. "Bring us to Mom and Dad. I miss them." Her words were choppy, her breath short. Panic was setting in, and she was babbling.

Noah didn't answer. He just kept working the nail. The tips of his fingers burned. A sob expanded in his chest, but he swallowed it. Kristen couldn't see him cry. She'd totally freak out if she did.

"It's dark outside. Why is it so dark?"

"It's night."

"It wasn't so dark before."

"That's because the moon was out." Now it had disappeared behind the clouds. Rain pelted the glass.

"I d-d-don't like the dark." Her next breath hissed out of her. "It s-s-scares me."

He hated the dark, too. It suffocated him, like when he sometimes slept with a blanket over his face. The thought of being trapped in the dark forever, with nothing to see or smell or hear, terrified him.

"Do y-you think Mom—" she coughed, "—and Dad are scared of the dark?"

The tears punched at his eyes, lumped in his throat. "'Course not. Mom and Dad weren't scared of anything."

"Even dying?"

Noah's stomach kicked him in the ribs. Kristen's eyes had grown so big and so deep, it hurt to look into them. "They're not dead," he lied, feeling beaten, like an old man. "They're just sleeping."

She hugged herself, squeezed that silly pink bear. "They're never going to wake up, are they?"

He wanted to tell her what she needed to hear, but the lie wouldn't come this time.

Tears spilled over her cheeks. "Are we g-g-going to die, too?"

"No." The word tore out of his chest. "Do you trust me?" She gave him a weak nod. "Good, 'cause I'm getting us out of here."

Kristen stood on wobbly legs and began to climb up the mountain of barrels.

"Careful," he told her.

When she reached the top, she surprised him by wrapping her thin arms around his neck and sliding in for a hug. "I love you, Noah."

His throat suddenly felt scratchy, as if he'd swallowed a mouthful of sand. "Yeah, me too."

Then the nail slid free. With a swell of triumph, he shoved at the window until it burst open and a cool mix of wind and rain rushed in to soak their faces.

"You did it!" Kristen's wide smile filled him with pride.

"Told you."

After pocketing the nail, he clutched her by the waist and lifted her to freedom. They were in some kind of basement because the ground was at the level of the window. Kristen didn't have far to fall. The black, hungry night instantly swallowed her as she crawled away. He began to climb out after her, but his chain snagged on the latch and broke. His father's silver ring clattered to the ground. He couldn't leave it. He had to go back for it. It was all he had left of his dad.

"Be right there," he called to his sister, then scrambled back into the room to look for the ring.

He found it hidden behind the metal rack and grabbed it. Just as he began to scale the barrels again, the familiar jingle of keys reached his ears. "Kristen, don't wait for me. Run!" he cried at the top of his lungs, hoping she listened this time. Then he raced up the rack to the window.

He never made it. A hand gripped his shirt, pulled him down. The ring slipped from his grasp as the barrels collapsed beneath him. His last sight before he hit the ground was of the pale moon cutting a scar across the bloated black belly of the clouds. His last thought was of Kristen, alone and frightened, lost in that night.

Chapter Thirty-Three

"How are we going to find this place?" Rebecca could barely feel her legs, a result of cold and fatigue. They'd set anchor in the cove below, next to another two motor boats—one of which they hoped belonged to Neil Hopkins—and were now snaking their way up the surrounding hills with nothing but a couple of flashlights to cut through the gray gloom.

"There's a trail up ahead." Zach quickened his pace, crouched, then directed his weak beam to the ground. "I see prints. About the same size as the ones we found in the house. Someone's been here. Recently."

When she approached, she saw the faint outline of a man's shoe etched in the mud. The rain hadn't washed it away yet, which meant Zach was right.

Martin caught up with them. "Are you sure this is a good idea? There were two boats down there. What if he's not alone?" He mopped the rain from his face with his palm. "Maybe we should wait for that ADA, Jenkins, to send back-up."

"No damn way." Zach's sharp tone sliced the night. "By the time Pat gets anyone out here, Hopkins and the kids could be long gone. I'm not willing to risk it." The moon cut through the haze to paint his face silver. His skin was smooth and hard, like polished rock. "Back-up will come when it comes. Till then, we keep looking."

Dampness beaded on Rebecca's flesh, sent a chill skittering along her spine. She tasted salt on her tongue, mixed with the cloying tang of overripe fruit. "But what if Martin's right and he's not alone? They may be armed, and all we've got are these flashlights."

Zach wouldn't be swayed. "We'll cross that bridge when we get to it. Right now all I care about is finding the kids." There was fire in him. Fire and determination.

He wouldn't quit on her this time. She saw that now. He had purpose, conviction. He'd fight for what was his, battle the demons, plow through the carnage of their lost dreams and breathe new life into them. No matter what it took. He wasn't the same man who'd insisted she give up trying to conceive, the one who'd taken off at a run when she'd refused to do as she was told.

She realized then these children had changed him, too. They'd reached deep inside him and fixed what was broken, the same way they had with her. They were the glue that would hold them together, restore their hope, teach them what it meant to be whole.

That was what children did. Amidst the haze of sleepless nights and chaotic days, they gave you clarity, made sense of the madness, filled all the hollow spaces in your heart. Now that she'd experienced the fullness that came with loving a child, she could never go back to the emptiness again. It would kill her.

Zach raised his hand to her cheek, swiped at it with his thumb, and only then did she realize she was crying. "Hey, it's going to be all right. We'll find them."

She nodded, the lump in her windpipe so thick it crushed her voice.

Martin, who'd walked ahead of them, suddenly stopped. "I think I see something."

Rebecca scrambled up the path to where Martin stood. To their right, where the trees thinned and a trembling moon cut a patch through the clouds to cast its waxing glow, a tenebrous structure hunkered amidst unkempt shrubs.

"Is that the winery?" It was so dark she couldn't be sure.

Zach came to stand beside them. "Sure looks like it. Come on, let's go." He grabbed her by the elbow, urged her forward. "Time to take back what's ours."

Neil lifted Noah off the floor, fighting the urge to slap him. Liam always said the kid was trouble. Because of the brat's unwillingness to do as he was instructed, barrels now inundated the cellar. Some had burst open, and wine trickled across the floor to pool around his feet. But that was the least of Neil's worries. He struggled to look out the window for the girl, but all he saw was the yawning night.

No child had ever escaped him before. Over the years he'd perfected his craft, and things always ran like clockwork.

But not this time.

Everything had gone wrong from the get-go. That was what he got for breaking his number one rule. *Never target someone you know.* That was the code he'd always lived by. But he'd gotten overconfident, strayed from the path, and now he was paying the price.

The boy struggled as Neil dragged him out the door and up the staircase. "Where are you taking me? Let me go! I have to find my sister."

"I'd help you, but there's no time. Someone is waiting for us." Just south of the Vineyard, on a deserted chip of land drowning in the Atlantic, a boat sat moored, eagerly anticipating Noah Birch's long-overdue arrival. Once there, Neil would swap the kid and the documents for a briefcase filled with cash. The payment would need to be renegotiated, of course, now that he no longer had the girl.

A pang of disappointment assailed him. He could've used the extra cash, especially now that he had to find himself another middleman. He couldn't keep doing what he'd done yesterday. Pick-up duty was risky. He needed someone he could trust to handle that particular aspect of the operation. Someone who knew as little as possible about Neil and his connection to the Broken Angels. Raymond York had been perfect, almost always doing exactly as he was told, never bothering to ask tedious questions.

Frustration made him tighten his grip on the boy's biceps as he yanked him through the plant. "You shouldn't have helped your sister escape. She'll die out there on her own."

The thought was some consolation. At least she wouldn't live to expose him. Martha's Cellar sat on an impressive expanse of land, hidden by a vast maze of trees, on the quieter southwestern side of the Vineyard. No one even remembered the winery was here, so there was no chance someone would wander by and find Kristen Birch wheezing in the shrubs. The girl was as good as dead.

A shudder shimmied up Noah's arm. "Let me find her. Please." Neil understood how much it cost the boy to beg.

"Sorry. We can't be late." Regret traveled through him. "I'm really going to miss our chats, Raptor."

Noah's small frame hardened to stone. "My dad was right when he told me not to trust you. The meeting at Ringgold Park. It was a trap. That's why my dad grounded me."

Neil felt a crazy rush of pride, as if this kid belonged to him now. In a way, he did. "I always knew you were a bright one."

Just like your father.

It still amazed him how Liam had pieced it all together. Somehow he'd realized someone was preying on his kid and had asked Adrien Gorski to create a spyware program for him that could track his son's chats. When Neil had invited Noah to meet him at Ringgold Park, Liam had shown up instead. Thankfully Neil had sent Raymond to collect the boy, so his cover hadn't been blown. Still, Liam had been far from dissuaded. On the contrary, he'd grown even more determined, engaging in a one-man crusade to bring the stalker down.

Neil hadn't been worried at first. For years he'd evaded the Feds and their ever-increasing Internet crime squads. There was no way the chats could be traced back to him. His IP address was secure. Or so he'd thought. He must have said something on one of the chats, or maybe inadvertently at the office, because Liam had put two and two together.

Neil would never have known how close his employee had gotten to exposing him if he hadn't intercepted a phone call from Gorski.

"You were right, Liam," the tech-guy had said. *"It wasn't easy, but I managed to trace the chats back to Hopkins and Associates. Night-Owl is someone you know."*

Neil had erased the message, but Liam must have gotten in touch with Gorski, because soon after he began a dogged investigation into the life of his own boss.

Ungrateful little prick.

That was what he got for giving Birch a job right out of law school, making him partner...

"The man who shot my parents, did you send him?"

The question froze him solid. Apparently, the kid had not only inherited his father's acumen but his deductive abilities. "Enough questions." Neil shoved the boy forward just as the sound of breaking glass shattered the stillness.

Someone was here. Fear laced with dread lanced through him.

No, not now.

A few more minutes and he'd be home free.

Maybe a vagrant had wandered by, seeking shelter from the rain. People normally didn't come this way, but he couldn't rule out the possibility, especially given the lousy luck he'd suffered recently. He changed his course, circled around a stainless-steel tank toward the back door.

But Noah had heard the sound, too, and reached the same conclusion. "Help!" he screamed. "He's got me. He's taking me to his—"

Neil clamped a firm hand over the boy's mouth and half carried, half dragged him out the back door. He wished he had the use of both his hands, but the other was securely fastened around his briefcase. The kid was strong, nearly impossible to hold, especially now that he believed rescue was imminent.

Neil wrapped his arm—the one clutching the briefcase—around the boy's middle and lifted him off the ground. Then he carried him into the woods, where towering trees sheltered and concealed them. Above their heads, a thick cover of clouds conveniently slid in from the west to block out the moon again.

Chapter Thirty-Four

Noah's voice bounced off wood and metal to fill the cavernous space like a death knell. The unexpected sound of it sent a sharp jolt through Zach. Urgency searing his veins, he reached his arm through the window he'd shattered with his flashlight, not caring when the jagged glass tore through his forearm, and unlocked the door. A heartbeat later he was sprinting across the faded wooden floorboards. On either side of him, empty shelves reached scaly arms toward a water-damaged ceiling.

"Noah!" His voice traveled through the gingerbread-style house, reverberated off glass and steel.

No one answered.

Becca tumbled in after him, dogged by Martin. "Are they here?" Her strained tone matched the tight look on her face.

Zach was too distracted to reply, his attention riveted on the door looming behind a rundown counter. A door that would probably give them access to the plant that stretched behind this peaceful façade like the back end of a spider. Judging from the cobwebs that clung to the walls and ceiling, it was a fitting analogy. The building smelled of mold and neglect and of something else. Something he couldn't identify. All he knew was that it made his stomach twist and bitter bile rise in his throat.

Following his gut, he breached the back room. An impenetrable maze devoured him, cluttered with large white bins, stainless steel tanks and old equipment that had rusted from lack of use. Fluorescent lights buzzed overhead, casting an eerie white glow over the place.

"What's that smell?" Becca came to stand beside him.

"Blood." The color drained from Martin's face, giving him the look of a ghost.

Becca's face crumpled. "The kids—"

"He wouldn't hurt them," Zach reassured her as he scoured the plant, with Becca and Martin hot on his heels. "They're worth more to him alive. And I just heard Noah call out for help. He's here." His chest clenched at the vastness that surrounded them. "We need to split up. Martin, stay with Becca. You two search up here. I'll check out the cellars."

Becca clutched his arm. "I don't think you should go alone."

"There's no time to argue. Go." He turned to Martin. "Watch out for her."

Then, leaving the woman he loved in the care of a man he'd never trusted, he lunged down the stairs.

The night was cold and wet, like the drooling mouth of the giant reptile he'd drawn in his comic book. Noah's heart flapped out of control as his dad's old boss lugged him into the darkness. Shadows gathered around them, baring blackened teeth.

"Let me go," he screamed, but his pleas fell on deaf ears. Neil Hopkins had stopped listening the moment the glass shattered.

Uncle Zach and Aunt Becca had come for them. Noah was sure of it. He needed to get away, find them before something bad happened to Kristen. But the man's grip was tighter than a python's.

Scary-looking trees hunched over them. They looked mean and hungry. A cold wind swept between the trunks, flecked with rain. Noah shuddered. "Put me down."

Something icy brushed his arm. A chill raced down his back. Hopkins was beginning to pant. He wouldn't be able to carry him much longer. Noah was heavy, and the creep was old and out of shape. A minute or two later, the man stopped to catch his breath. Remembering the rusted nail he'd shoved in the pocket of his shorts, Noah dug it out, then plunged it into his captor's hand.

Neil Hopkins' scream made the trees shake. It was louder than thunder, louder than Will. The thought of his brother made tears pool in his eyes. He missed the little pest. He missed Kristen, too. With a surge of strength, he pried himself free from Hopkins' grasp and stumbled into the woods. He had to get back to the building, find his sister, find his aunt and uncle. Then the nightmare would end. But the shadows were deep and determined, the forest a complicated maze, like the ones in the activity books his mom used to get him.

He was good at mazes, but this one made no sense. The grass was long, and bristly weeds snagged his legs.

Behind him, the air rustled. Neil Hopkins had recovered, and he was raging mad. His screams rode the wind as he trampled the wet grass in search of him.

With a broken sob, Noah plunged deeper into the woods.

Rebecca stopped mid-step. "Did you hear that?"

Martin's grave expression was all the answer she needed. His features reflected the same crippling fear that afflicted her. "It sounded like a scream."

"I think it came from outside." They weaved their way between pumps and presses, grape conveyors and tanks, until they found a narrow passageway, where the light receded and the stench of mildew thickened. At the end of the corridor, a door gaped. From beyond, the night beckoned them, cold and bottomless.

Her pulse matched the tempo of her heels as she raced down the hall and flung herself into the vast web of trees that bordered the plant. Martin matched her pace, vigilant and on guard beside her.

They began to search the woods, but it seemed fruitless, despite the rows of grape-bearing vines that enfolded them. Acres and acres of land stretched as far as she could see. They tried to stay on the paths, avoiding the tangled mass of weeds that snaked across the ground on either side of them. The more they searched, the more convinced she became that they needed help. They couldn't do this alone. Maybe Pat could get a search party out here.

"Give me your cell," she told Martin. She knew he always carried it with him. He did as she asked, digging the phone out of his coat pocket and placing it in the cradle of her palm.

She punched in the Jenkinses' number, hoping Tess had managed to reach her husband and that help was on the way. The phone chimed annoyingly, and she snapped it shut in frustration. "No service."

"Let's keep looking. The scream came from somewhere nearby. We wouldn't have heard it otherwise."

Martin was right. The kids had to be close. But the night was exceptionally dark, the shrubs thick and impenetrable. Brambles of neglected grass scraped their legs as they struggled to advance.

When they came to a wide clearing, something soft lumped under her feet. Rebecca grabbed the flashlight from Martin and angled the beam toward the ground. Whatever she'd stepped on was small and pink. She swooped down and retrieved the object. "A teddy bear."

Martin squeezed in for a closer look. "Kristen's?"

She shook her head. "I don't recognize it."

Then she heard the wheeze. If she hadn't stopped for the toy, she would have mistaken it for the whistle of the wind. But now the sound was shrill and clear and released a torrent of ice-splinters in her bloodstream.

"Kristen?" she called, her voice an odd blend of hope and terror.

The only reply was a gasp, punctuated by another wheeze. She quickly followed the sound to an alcove of hunched trees. Nestled between their peeling trunks, Kristen lay still on the ground, laboring to breathe, her skin an eerie blue shadow, glistening in the rain.

A violent wind swirled up to swallow them. The child shivered. Rebecca dove through the trees and scooped the girl off the cold ground. Her heart pounding a ferocious beat in her throat, she pulled the pump out of her pocket and administered the drug.

"Come on, baby, breathe it in." Anxiety tripped through her system. A sob swelled to crush her lungs until she, too, had trouble drawing breath.

Martin crouched down beside her. "Is she breathing?"

"Barely. I just hope it's enough for the drug to work." She pulled off her sweater and wrapped it around the trembling girl. It was damp from the rain, but it would have to do. "We need to get her to the hospital."

"There's one in Oak Bluffs. I can get you there in no time flat."

"But Zach, Noah—"

"I'll come back for them. I promise."

Rebecca gazed down at Kristen's ashen face and nodded. She had no choice. Kristen needed her. Decisively, she gathered the unconscious girl in her arms and stood. "Let's go."

Chapter Thirty-Five

There were several cellars, all stacked with tall racks, oak barrels and dust-encrusted bottles—some full, some empty. It looked like none of them had been disturbed in years. Hell, decades. The stench of aged fruit spiced with mildew pummeled Zach's nostrils. He closed the door of the last cellar he'd searched and moved on. The next room was locked, but the wood was old and mold-infested. With a few hard kicks, it splintered and burst open. Zach crashed inside, carried by the swift thrust of his kick. He found himself in some kind of makeshift office. A scuffed desk sat at the far-left corner, next to a metal filing cabinet. On a shelf over the desk, over a dozen hard drives stood side-by-side, perfectly lined up. He didn't have to guess what information they stored. He'd seen their sick contents first-hand. This was where Liam had uncovered the truth, where he'd found the evidence he'd compiled.

And gotten himself and Lindsay killed.

Idiot.

If Zach had his brother-in-law in front of him now, he would've punched him. He should've gone to his buddy, the ADA, instead of taking matters into his own hands. Then again, wasn't Zach guilty of the same thing?

Doubt poked at him, but he shoved it away. He'd taken a risk coming to the vineyard alone, with only Becca and Martin as back-up, but he'd had no choice. The kids were counting on him. There was no way he'd allow a bunch of red tape to jeopardize their lives.

With that bolstering thought in mind, he shot down the hall again, continuing his search of the premises.

He wanted to call out to his kids, but he wasn't sure who was listening, so he kept quiet. The only thing he had going for him was the element of surprise. Of course he'd probably just blown that with the racket he'd made tearing the door down.

At the end of a winding hall he came to another room. The door was open this time. The place was a mess. A rack had been overturned, and barrels littered the floor. Some had burst open from the impact, spilling a sticky burgundy substance he assumed was wine. It sure smelled like wine. Or sour grapes.

A cold wave of air rolled in from the open window. Zach approached it. Wrapped around the latch was a familiar chain. "Noah?" he yelled into the night. The stomach-curdling liquid curled around his feet. He swept another cursory look through the stifling cell and saw a spark of silver bathed in red. He bent over and retrieved it, then wiped the band clean with his thumb. The ring, too, was familiar. It had once belonged to Liam. Noah had been wearing it around his neck when he disappeared.

A few feet away, drenched in wine, two Happy Meals squatted, partially crushed beneath a runaway barrel.

Fury suffused him, tempered by an odd rush of hope. This was where the bastard had kept the kids. In this damp room, with its stale air and hard, gray walls.

And from the looks of it, they'd escaped.

Noah's breath came hard and fast. His sides hurt from exhaustion and from the fall he'd taken earlier. The forest grew so dense he barely saw where he was going. It seemed like he'd been running forever. He thought if he got back to the building, back to the window he'd pried open, he'd find his sister. But the night was deep, the trees alive and furious.

I'm lost. No way out. Nowhere to go.

Tears throbbed behind his eyes.

I'll never see Kristen again, or Will, or Uncle Zach and Aunt Becca.

Wet tracks streamed down his face. The sky seemed to be closing in on him, like a black garbage bag blocking out the air. He gasped, choked on a sob.

Somebody help me, please.

The grass was sharp and vicious, clawing at his legs, taking nips out of his skin. Around him, a cold wind stirred, its breath foul. Noah tripped and fell to his knees. The sky opened up. Tears poured down over him, drenched him to the bone.

Not tears. Rain.

His teeth clattered. His body trembled. He was going to die.

Behind him, the forest cackled. Footsteps hammered the ground.

Get up. Run, you wuss. Get out of here.

But his legs wouldn't listen. They were too busy shaking. Uncontrollable sobs pummeled his chest.

Shut up. He'll hear you.

He tried to crawl away. The rough grass cut into his flesh, scraped his palms and knees raw.

Then a hand slithered around his waist, lifted him off the ground.

His arms and legs flailed. Before he could stop it, a sissy scream tore loose from his throat. The sound continued to echo around him, a loud whistle, as harsh as the night.

Chapter Thirty-Six

"Shh." Zach pulled Noah close, tried to shelter him with his body. "I've got you. You're safe now."

The fight melted out of him, and the boy turned to a boneless heap in his arms. "Uncle Zach?"

Zach hooked two sheltering arms around his nephew. Relief swamped him. After finding the trashed cellar, he'd circled the building to the open window and begun searching the surrounding woods, hoping the children hadn't wandered too far. He hadn't realized how difficult it would be to locate two small kids in this treacherous network of trees, with nothing but a flashlight to illuminate his way. If he hadn't heard the boy's sobs...

Helplessness rose to block his throat.

"It's Mr. Hopkins," Noah cried in a jumbled rush. "He's after me. I don't know where Kristen is."

"We'll find her," he reassured the boy. "Becca and Martin are with me. They're looking, too. The place looks big, but there are only a handful of paths you can take."

"The asthma," the boy implored. "She was having trouble breathing."

Dread thickened in Zach's veins, cold as ice. Desperation tangled his gut. He stripped off his coat and wrapped it around Noah. "We can't stay here." He put his nephew down and secured a firm hold on his hand. "Let's go find your sister."

Noah huddled close, and Zach felt a soft stab in his heart. The boy had never looked this small before. The bravado was gone. Undisguised fear shone in his eyes. That lost, beaten expression made all of Zach's protective instincts spring to life. Nobody would ever hurt his kids again. *Nobody.* He'd tear them apart with his bare hands.

He was about to urge Noah down the thin trail that led to the boat, in case Martin and Becca had found Kristen and taken shelter there, when something hard and cold dug into his neck.

"Don't take another step." The voice was cultured, familiar. "One move and I'll shoot you both."

The doctors and nurses at the Martha's Vineyard Hospital in Oak Bluffs were fast and efficient. The second Kristen arrived, they'd strapped an oxygen mask on her, infused with a very strong dose of Ventolin, then whisked her away on a gurney. Rebecca had tried to follow, but they'd forced her to stay in the waiting room. Her heart thumped a million beats a minute as she paced, waiting for news. Martin, keeping his word to return for Zach and Noah, had left almost instantly. She had yet to hear from him or Zach. She'd called Tess to check up on Will and give her an update. Tess still hadn't reached Pat, but she promised to keep trying.

Now all Rebecca could do was wait, and she hated it. Hated the questions reeling in her head, the knot of fear in her chest, the unabated tension crawling through her limbs. But most of all she hated the sense of helplessness that had gripped her. She should've been in there holding Kristen's hand or out there helping Zach find Noah. Instead, she was stuck in this stark room, alone with her dark thoughts.

"Why don't you sit down, dear?" The woman's voice jarred her out of her quiet musings and Rebecca turned to face the stranger. "You're wearing yourself out. Not to mention the floor." The lady's smile was warm, comforting. Liquid brown eyes met and held hers, filled with compassion and a glint of humor. Was she a hospital employee, a patient, someone waiting for news about a loved one?

"I can't." Rebecca crossed her arms over her middle, hoping to hold in the pain, to crush the anxiety that thrummed beneath her skin. "Not until I know my—" She'd been about to say niece, but stopped herself. "Not until I know my daughter's going to be all right." That was what she considered Kristen now, her daughter, her baby. She couldn't have loved her more if she'd felt her grow inside her.

Love was more than DNA. She understood that now. Love was holding a child in your arms while she fell asleep, comforted by your embrace. Love was nursing a baby through an ear infection, hoping a hug could lessen his pain. Love was staying awake at night worrying, defending a kid's honor, telling him you understood even when you didn't. Being a parent wasn't about getting it right. It was about doing what needed to be done, even when you were in way over your head.

"Dear, do you need something? A cup of coffee? Water?" The older woman with the kind face and the salt-and-pepper hair was still watching her.

Rebecca shook her head. "No, thank you. I'm fine."

If only the same could be said about her family.

Chapter Thirty-Seven

Neil urged Ryler and the kid through the woods to where his boat waited. Anxiety made his breath come in short, jagged gasps. He was getting too old for this. Maybe it was time to retire. He'd been thinking about that a lot lately. He had a house in the Cayman Islands, several offshore accounts set up. It wouldn't be difficult to disappear.

"It's over, Hopkins."

Neil shoved Ryler as they wended their way through the trees, just a few yards from the bluff. "Shut up. Unless you want a hole in the back of your skull."

The boy whimpered. Neil ignored him. The kid would be out of his hair soon enough.

"We found the evidence Liam collected," Ryler persisted. "It's in the hands of the ADA right now. Your cover's blown. Everyone knows what you are."

Neil's stomach caught fire. "Impossible. You're lying."

"Dates, names, drop-off points and pictures. Lots of pictures."

He wasn't lying. Neil's finger twitched against the trigger. There was no way Ryler could know what the files contained unless he'd seen them. But how? York had wiped the hard drive clean, fried the computer.

Unless there was another back-up out there. Something he'd overlooked.

Sweat misted over his face. A sharp pain lanced through him. He should have been more careful, destroyed the records, deleted the pictures. But they were his insurance policy. Over the years he'd kept detailed accounts of all his transactions, the people he'd dealt with, the places where drops had taken place. The Broken Angels knew that if he was to suddenly disappear or die mysteriously, all the evidence would be promptly turned over to the authorities and their smooth, nearly untraceable distribution network would be severely compromised. He'd left clear instructions, had scattered the evidence in several locations to ensure the Broken Angels didn't uncover it.

His biggest treasure trove, however, was here at the vineyard. This was where he kept all the pictures—every snapshot he'd ever taken of every child he'd ever relocated. They'd become trophies of sorts, something he could hold on to when his best years were behind him. In time the need to remember the faces of all the children he'd placed had morphed into compulsion. He wondered about them sometimes, asked himself what had become of them. Many—the ones who'd survived—would be adults by now. What if he crossed one on the street and didn't recognize him? What if someone came back with an ax to grind?

"If you let us go, Pat Jenkins may be persuaded to cut a deal with you." The man was relentless. "But if you hurt us, he'll make sure they lock you up and throw away the key."

No way he'd cut a deal...or go to jail. He had money, options. He just needed to make this last drop, collect his finder's fee, then make a run for it. It wouldn't be difficult to steer his boat north and head to Canada. He always carried fake ID on him, just in case. He could take a flight from there to the Cayman Islands, start fresh. There was enough money in his offshore accounts to ensure he lived out the rest of his life comfortably.

But first he had to get out of the States. For that to happen, he needed the cash his associate had promised him. Noah Birch was his ticket to freedom, and Zach Ryler was a thorn in his side.

They reached the bluff. His boat came into view, a hazy shadow in the damp night. Using the butt of his gun, he struck Ryler hard on the back of his head. The man instantly crumpled. He considered shooting him, then decided against it. The last thing he wanted was for the kid to freak out on him before the drop.

Ignoring Noah's terrified scream, Neil hooked his arm around the boy's waist and carried him down the bluff to his boat, where the vast sea rippled beneath the wind in silent welcome.

When Zach came to, he was momentarily stunned, disoriented. Rain poured over him, drenching him to the bone. A fierce ache pounded at the base of his skull. He peeled himself off the ground, flinching at the sharp throb that speared through his brain. Shaking the haze from his head, he stumbled to his feet and crested the bluff.

Dread and fury wrapped unforgiving arms around his ribs and squeezed. Neil Hopkins' boat was gone. And so was Noah.

Fighting a wave of dizziness, he sped down to the beach, where another boat still sat docked. Martin's yacht was nowhere in sight. What the hell was going on tonight? Where were Martin and Becca and Kristen? And where had Hopkins taken Noah?

He closed his eyes against the pain, forced himself to think. The man was desperate. He'd built his entire life on a house of cards that was about to collapse. What would a desperate man do?

Run. The answer sliced through his brain like a blade. Hopkins' next move was to cut his losses, grab as much cash as he could and get the hell out of Dodge. But for that to happen, he needed to sell Noah to the Broken Angels.

A list of drop-off points scrolled through his mind, one in particular—an unpopulated island just south of Chilmark. The location had marked him because it was the closest to Hopkins' vineyard. Zach was willing to bet a kidney that was where the son of a bitch was headed.

Urgency gnawing a hole through his gut, he sped across the beach, trudged through knee-deep water and jumped into the unfamiliar boat loitering there. He didn't know much about hotwiring boats, but damn it, he was about to learn. Or not, he thought when he noticed the key in the ignition. Now for lesson two, steering this thing.

It took him a few seconds, but he finally figured out how to lift the anchor and back out of the cove. Next thing he knew, he was cutting a strip through the choppy waves.

The irony wasn't lost on him. He'd spent nearly his whole life avoiding the sea like some lethal disease. And now here he was again, braving the snapping swells in search of his kid. He would've sailed through a fucking typhoon to get to Noah. He would've swum across if he'd had to. No one would hurt his boy. He'd die before he let that happen.

Determination rose to submerge him, more consuming than any ocean, more feral than the most violent storm. Neil Hopkins was going down, and Zach was going to be the one who drowned the bastard.

Relief doused Neil when he saw the other craft bobbing on the water, exactly where it was supposed to be. So his associate had stuck around, despite the fact that Neil was nearly half an hour late. That struck him as strange. He'd been half convinced his contact would be long gone. Still, he was too ecstatic to dwell on it. Finally, things were going according to plan. Everything was back on track.

He dropped anchor and went to retrieve the boy, whom he'd locked in a small cabin below deck. The kid's eyes were red and swollen from all the crying he'd done. He looked like someone had punched him. Neil hoped that wouldn't take another chunk out of his fee. Then again, most of the kids he placed with the Broken Angels looked beaten by the time the trade took place.

"Time to go." He'd used his tie to bind the boy's wrists. Noah Birch had proven time and time again that he couldn't be trusted.

"I'm not going anywhere with you." The kid tried to look tough, failed miserably.

"I've had enough of your insolence. Get up."

Noah didn't budge. He just sat there staring at Neil with blazing hatred in his eyes. Neil grabbed him by the arm and yanked him to his feet. This trade was going to happen, even if he had to fling the brat over his shoulder.

"Let go of me! You're hurting me."

Good. Maybe you'll finally learn to behave and do as you're told.

The rain had stopped. Now only a fine drizzle hung suspended in the air. Moisture beaded over Neil's skin—he wasn't sure whether it was the mist or his own perspiration—as he lugged the kid above board. Then, half dragging, half pushing his uncooperative captive, he mounted the neighboring boat.

"Sorry I'm late." Neil shoved Noah a few steps closer to the bow and approached the dark shadow standing at the helm. The man didn't turn around to face them. "I ran into some trouble."

"What kind of trouble?" The voice was low, raspy.

Neil's gut twisted in a series of painful knots. He should've kept his mouth shut. The Broken Angels didn't appreciate trouble. Of any kind. "Nothing I couldn't handle."

The man stared out at the churning waves. "So what have you got for me today?"

"A nine-year-old boy, in perfect health, as handsome as they come. Your clients will be very pleased."

"Send him over."

The boy tried to wrestle free, and Neil tightened the grip he had on him. "Not until I see the cash."

The man stood statue-still for the longest time. Anxiety pulsed in the air, sharp and electric. Then his associate spoke. "Do you doubt my intentions?"

"I didn't get where I am today by taking people at their word. Nothing personal."

Noah took advantage of the distraction and kicked Neil in the shin. Hard. Pain shot up his leg, quick and jolting. He stifled a cry, reined in his temper before he reciprocated and seriously hurt the brat. The last thing he wanted was to damage the merchandise.

Thankfully, his associate didn't notice the commotion. Instead he bent over and retrieved a briefcase. "It's all in here, like we agreed."

After securing Noah to a metal rail with the tie that still dangled from his wrists, Neil approached the other man. Something wasn't right. He could feel it. He slipped his free hand in his pocket, reveled at the cool feel of his gun against his palm. "Turn around and hand it to me."

The man slowly pivoted on his heels. Neil took a step back when he got a good look at him—not his contact, but a complete stranger.

"Who the hell are you? Where's Carlos?"

"He couldn't make it tonight. The Broken Angels sent me instead."

Neil's fingers twitched, and he prepared to withdraw his Glock at the slightest move. "How do I know I can trust you?"

"Trust is cheap." The man opened the briefcase and flashed several thick wads of hundred-dollar bills. "This suitcase isn't. Hand me the documents and the boy, and it's yours."

Wetting his lips, Neil studied the cash. "All of it?"

"Yes."

"Even though I don't have the girl I promised you?"

Something glinted in the other man's eyes—a hesitation, a flicker of doubt. "What happened to the girl?"

"She got away. Don't worry. She's as good as dead."

Another hard look. "Accidents happen. I'll just tell my superiors she died in transport and I threw her body overboard."

Why did Neil feel he had a rattlesnake uncoiling in his stomach, spilling venom? "I didn't expect you to be so...understanding."

"I'd like to keep doing business with you."

From the rear of the vessel, Noah let out an ear-splitting scream. "Help! Somebody help me! I've been kidnapped."

Neil rolled his eyes. The kid just wouldn't quit. "Shut up. There's no one out here but us."

The boy kept right on screeching.

"Let's get this over with," Neil told the other man. Letting go of his gun, he opened his briefcase and pulled out the manila envelope. "The paperwork is all in order." He handed his new associate the documents. "Now the cash."

The man kicked over the briefcase that held his finder's fee. The moment Neil's hand closed around the handle, the traitorous bastard reached for the weapon holstered at his waist. "Freeze." He pulled out a compact firearm—a SIG-Sauer from the looks of it. Neil knew his guns, and this one was of military caliber. He'd gotten a similar one for Raymond York.

He had to act fast. With lightning quick reflexes despite his advanced years, he whipped out his Glock and shot the son of a bitch in the shoulder—nerves made his hand shake and threw off his aim. Then he raced across the deck and practically threw himself into his boat. No shots rang out behind him. The man obviously didn't want to risk injuring the boy. Wasting no time, Neil wound in the anchor, gunned the motor and backed out. Next thing he knew, his vessel sprang forth, leaving froth and waves behind.

A spray of bullets rained over the waves. The man had inched his way to the stern and was shooting at him. One hand gripped his SIG, the other, his injured shoulder. Far away on either side of them, two ships lined the horizon, draped in mist.

What the hell was going on tonight? The tides seemed determined to sweep him away. But he'd worked too hard for too long to surrender now. Spinning around, he shot a few holes in the hull behind him. Last thing he wanted was for the traitor to follow him.

Then, still stunned by the betrayal, he steered his boat north and swiftly melted into the fog.

Chapter Thirty-Eight

Zach fought to control the unfamiliar vessel and stay on course. In the quickly receding distance he made out the hazy outline of land. At least he hadn't gotten lost. But would that be enough? He didn't know how long he had before Noah was carried away, his identity stripped from him, his future destroyed. Like so many others before him. The thought sickened him. So many children, so many faces. Those faces kept flashing across his mind—a repulsive slideshow.

At least Kristen had escaped, but where was she now? Had Becca and Martin found her or did she lie in the shrubs unconscious, struggling for breath?

Acid scalded his gut. Everything had spiraled out of control, and he was fighting to hold it together. Memories of the past month unspooled in his head...and heart. Maybe he didn't know shit about being a father, but he loved these kids with everything he had. Loved them so much he no longer knew how to function without them. They'd somehow crept under his skin and carved a permanent place for themselves within him. No one else could fill that space. It was theirs and theirs alone. And right now the large chunk of his soul that belonged to them throbbed with an emptiness that was painful.

The wind moaned as the boat picked up speed. Fog lined the horizon, eerie tendrils that rolled across the sea like the ghost of some long-extinct sea creature. To Zach's surprise, a boat sprang from the depths of its smoky belly. The night rumbled as the craft speared through the waves. Someone was in a real hurry to get away. He recognized the vessel. It belonged to Neil Hopkins.

Urgency flooded Zach's system. He couldn't let him get away, with or without Noah, so he did the only thing a man could do in this situation. He pushed the motor until it sputtered from the effort, then plowed right into the other craft. A thunderous crash rent the air as both boats came to a sudden halt. Wasting no time, Zach boarded the other vessel and launched himself on a flustered Neil Hopkins. The two men plunked to the ground in a twisted splay of limbs. The lawyer swiped his fist at him, but Zach managed to dodge the blow and land one of his own.

"Where's my kid?"

Hopkins didn't answer, so Zach hit him again, harder this time. Blood spurted from the bastard's nose. "What did you do with him?"

"You're too late." Fury tinged with satisfaction contorting his face, Hopkins cuffed Zach on the chin. "He's gone."

Zach had had enough. He dragged the bag of shit to his feet and kneed him in the gut. The lawyer doubled over, so Zach followed through with a swift uppercut to the jaw. "That's for my sister." He rammed his fist in the son of a bitch's plexus. "That's for my brother-in-law."

Just a few short weeks ago he'd told Noah that violence wasn't the answer. He'd been a goddamn moron. Sometimes violence was the only answer. It was the only thing scum like Hopkins understood.

"Now, I'll ask you again," he said between clenched teeth. "Where. Is. My. Boy."

"Put your hands up and turn around."

The unexpected sound froze Zach solid and filled him with confusion. Releasing Hopkins, he rotated his body and peered out to sea. A Coast Guard patrol ship rapidly approached, ghostlike in the gray gloom.

"I said put your hands up," the Coast Guard cried through a bullhorn again. Zach did as he was told and moved away from Hopkins toward the stern.

Seconds later, a swarm of law enforcement officials spilled into the sinking ship, rifles raised. Hopkins didn't seem to care. With the look of a man who had nothing left to lose, he pulled out a gun and tried to shoot his way out. Bullets whizzed past Zach's head. Before he had time to register what was happening, spasms shook Neil Hopkins' body, and he collapsed on the deck to swim in a sea of his own blood.

Panic screamed through Zach. "No, damn it." Ignoring the guns aimed at his back, he sprinted across the boat and sank to the ground next to the man who'd conspired to destroy his family. "He has to tell us what he did with Noah."

He grabbed the lawyer by the collar, shook him. "Wake up, you bastard." Pain laced with desperation lumped in his throat. Somewhere in the distance the rev of a helicopter punctured the dense shroud of night. "Wake up and tell me where to find my boy."

Then they were prying him off Hopkins, dragging him away. Zach struggled for freedom, the urgency inside him reaching a dangerous high. "Noah—" His voice broke. "Noah, where are you?"

"Right here."

The fight drained out of him at the sound of the familiar voice. "Noah?"

"Over here."

He slanted his head to the left and saw his nephew, standing next to Pat Jenkins on a second patrol ship that had just pulled up beside them. The kid looked drawn, shaken, but otherwise unharmed. Relief arrowed through Zach, cut him off at the knees. If they hadn't been holding him up, he would've surely smashed to the ground.

The Coast Guard escorted him to the patrol ship, where Pat hastened to greet him. "You all right?"

"I've been better."

Noah raced into his arms. The impact sent a jolt vibrating through him. Zach held the boy tight, blinking to crush the sting in his eyes. There was no feeling in the world like a hug from his kid. Especially after the night he'd just had.

"I thought he killed you." A bout of shaking overtook Noah's body. "Please, don't ever die, all right?"

Zach closed his lids tight to crush the amplifying throb in his temples. "I'm not going anywhere. By the time I'm through, you'll be begging to get me off your back."

The boy inhaled in broken gasps. "I don't care. You can take away my Game Boy, send me to my room." A sob thrummed in his chest. "I really want to go to my room."

"That can be arranged."

Then Noah sobered, ripped his body out of Zach's arms. "What about Kristen?"

Zach shook his head. He didn't know what to tell the boy.

"She's fine." Pat placed a reassuring hand on Noah's neck. "I spoke with Tess. Wasn't easy, I can tell you that. Reception here's a bitch. But I caught bits and pieces of the conversation. Rebecca called and told her that Kristen's at the Martha's Vineyard Hospital. She's stable."

Zach couldn't even begin to describe the emotion that overtook him. Exhaustion crashed over him in sheets. It was as if he'd been holding his breath for days, and he'd finally released it. "How did you find us?" he asked Pat.

"I've been trying to bring the Broken Angels down for years. Kept hitting one roadblock after another. Then a couple of days ago, out of the blue, I get an anonymous tip that a transfer's about to go down here. The Coast Guard and I have been staking this place out for over thirty-six hours. We caught the scumbag Hopkins came to meet, replaced him with one of our men, but Hopkins shot him and got away. We've been on his tail ever since he gunned it out to sea."

Zach folded his body onto a bench, drew Noah beside him. "Liam knew about Hopkins. That's what got him and Lindsay killed. I've got a ton of evidence he gathered. There's more at Hopkins' winery."

Pat's face lit up like a beacon. "I'll get my men on it."

Determination hardened his jaw. "It's about time these Broken Angels got what's coming to them."

Rebecca's body ached from stress and all the hours she'd spent sitting on a hard chair. The kind woman who'd spoken to her earlier had brought her some coffee. Shaking lightly, she raised the Styrofoam cup to her lips. Anxiety had taken its toll on her.

Thankfully, the doctors had reassured her that Kristen was stable. Rebecca sat beside her, holding her small hand in quiet reassurance while the girl slept beneath an oxygen mask far too big for her face.

She had yet to hear anything from Zach or Martin. Worry was a living thing. It grew inside her, squeezed out all rational thought and filled her with darkness. That darkness ate away at her now, one nip at a time, even as the night edged toward dawn. Just a few more hours and the sun would rise to streak the sky pink. A new day would begin. What it brought with it was still a mystery.

When the door swung open, she rocketed to her feet. Martin entered, looking haggard.

"Did you find them?"

Regret rearranged his features. He shook his head. "I searched everywhere—the winery, the woods. Both boats were gone."

Her heart sank. Worry bit into her with dagger-sharp teeth. Her knees wobbled, so she dropped back into the chair. "I don't understand. Where could they have gone? And why hasn't Zach called?"

Martin approached her, touched a comforting hand to her shoulder. "I'm sure he's got everything under control. You know Zach. He's a total control-freak." This time his voice didn't drip with bitterness. It was tender and genuine.

She appreciated his attempt to comfort her and lighten her spirits. "He'll call." Tears burned behind her eyes. She needed to believe everything would be all right. She voiced a silent prayer, swore she'd never ask for another thing if Zach and Noah were returned to her, safe and sound.

None of her prayers had ever been answered before. Eventually, she'd stopped praying altogether. But today something inside her shifted, and she was overcome with a soul-deep yearning to believe in something greater than herself, so she grasped at anything that offered hope.

As if a higher power had indeed heard her and answered her plea, Zach's wide frame filled the doorway. He looked like hell, and yet he'd never looked more beautiful to her. Shadows played across the strong planes of his face, darkening his eyes, accentuating the sharp slant of his cheeks and jaw. She stood on shaky legs and walked toward him, hesitant to trust what she saw.

"Noah?" The question squeaked out of her.

Zach turned to face the hallway, then yanked the boy to his side and urged him into the room. At the sight of her nephew's exhausted, dirt-dusted face, her legs nearly gave way, and she grabbed hold of the bed railing for support.

Then Noah did something that stole every last vestige of strength she possessed. He raced across the room and embraced her. She stood there holding him for the longest time, her heart drumming against her ribcage, the tears she'd held at bay for days flooding her cheeks. In a few long strides, Zach closed the distance between them and drew them both into the protective fortress of his arms. "It's over," he soothed. "Everyone's safe."

"And Hopkins?" The words were a low tremble in her throat.

He placed his chin on the top of her head, held her tighter. "Dead."

She jerked back. "You killed him?"

"I wanted to, but the cops beat me to it."

Confusion made her head pound. Then Zach explained everything. When he was done, both she and Martin watched him silently, their faces awash with shock.

"I'm still reeling from all this." Martin rubbed his eyes. "Hopkins, a kidnapper. How did he do it? Find the kids, get them to agree to meet him..."

Noah shook against her. "Falcon World."

Everyone gazed down at him expectantly.

"It's an online game," he told them. "He pretends he's a kid, chats with us." Tears pooled on his thick, black lashes. "I thought he was my friend."

Rebecca ran a comforting palm down the boy's back. "It's over now. He'll never hurt anyone again."

A beat of silence followed, then Zach turned to Martin and extended his hand. "You came through for us," he said. It was the closest to a thank-you he could muster.

Martin met his handshake. "These kids are my family, too."

Zach nodded. "I know."

No more words were spoken, but an understanding had been reached. The past was dead and buried, the future still unknown. But right there and then, they were all connected, a group of people bound by blood and love. Alone they were adrift. Together they stood tall and strong.

"Noah?" Kristen's gravelly voice shook them all out of their trance. "You came back."

The boy approached his sister, climbed up on the bed. "You can't get rid of me that easy." He stretched out beside her. "Someone's gotta watch out for you two babies."

"I'm not a baby," Kristen whined.

"Course you are."

"Am not."

"Are too."

And with those words, the darkness lifted and the world happily slid back into place.

Chapter Thirty-Nine

"Happy birthday to you. Happy birthday to you. Happy birthday dear Kristen..." Voula walked out of the kitchen carrying an enormous chocolate cake and singing the familiar song with the confidence of a seasoned pop star.

The guests joined the chorus while Kristen watched them with a shy smile. Noah and Jason joyfully sang their own version, louder than everyone else, "Happy birthday to you. You belong in the zoo. You look like a monkey and you smell like one, too."

Rebecca shook her head. Some things never changed.

True to her word, Voula had thrown Kristen a birthday party fit for a princess, especially after she'd heard about the ordeal the children had been through. The woman had been absolutely beside herself and had had quite a few choice words to say about Neil Hopkins.

Gazing around the brightly decorated room, Rebecca almost convinced herself it had all been a bad dream. Everything looked so normal. The children were laughing and teasing each other, Will was digging into the cake, even Bolt stood on his hind legs, hoping for an opportunity to lick off some of the icing.

This was it—home, family. This was what life was all about. She was no longer on the outside looking in. This time she was smack in the middle of it. Time had started moving again, and the future was ripe with possibilities, especially now that everything was official.

The hearing to establish guardianship had been held that morning. Judge McIntyre—a stern-looking woman in her early sixties, with silver hair that perfectly matched her piercing gray eyes—had questioned her and Zach for over an hour. As always, Zach had handled the interrogation with impressive aplomb. She, on the other hand, had fumbled through her answers.

"You and Mr. Ryler were married for eight years," the judge had stated. "But you never had children. Am I to presume you didn't want any?"

"Of course I wanted children," she'd muttered. "I've always wanted children. We tried. We couldn't."

"And two years ago you were divorced."

"Yes."

"And how, may I ask, do you intend to raise these children apart?"

Breath-smothering silence had followed. "Well, we're— What I mean to say is—"

"We've reconciled," Zach had answered for her. That had cinched it for the judge, and she'd promptly signed off on the guardianship.

Now, as Rebecca met Zach's gaze across the bustling room, she wondered what he'd meant by that. She knew they'd gotten back together for the sake of these kids, but had it grown into something more? Did he want to put everything on the line and try again? Did she?

The kids left a horrific mess behind—paper plates smeared with cake and icing, cups of grape juice knocked over on the pristine white tablecloth, heaps of discarded napkins. Still, Rebecca couldn't help but smile.

When the children scrambled out to play, Voula and Tess helped Rebecca clean up. The guys followed the kids outside. It seemed no one was ready to let them out of their sight quite yet.

"The food was incredible," Rebecca told Voula. "Thanks for doing this. Kristen's having a blast."

"You don't have to thank me. It's my pleasure. Like I said, these three are like grandkids to me. The first of many I hope." There was a twinkle in the woman's eyes, an excitement that piqued Rebecca's curiosity.

"Voula, is there something you're not telling me?"

Voula continued emptying plates in the trashcan, looking like a cat with a fat canary in her mouth. Even Tess noticed and crowded in to get the scoop. "I promised I wouldn't tell anyone," she admitted guiltily. "My daughter wants to wait till after the first trimester to spread the news, but if I don't say something I'll explode. She's pregnant!"

In the past, news like this would have knocked Rebecca off her feet, and not in a good way. But that didn't happen this time. Instead, she surprised herself by feeling an overwhelming joy for this kindhearted woman who'd longed for grandchildren with an ardency Rebecca understood all too well. She stopped washing the dishes and went to hug her. "That's wonderful news," she said and meant it. "I'm very happy for you."

"Congratulations," Tess added, putting aside the large platter she'd finished drying.

And just like that, one small change at a time, life continued its inexorable tumble forward.

"Things are moving forward," Pat said as he stretched out on a lawn chair. "The DA's office is working with Interpol and the OSCE to nail the bastards that did this to Noah and Kristen. Caught over a dozen of them already. All small fish unfortunately, but we're hoping they'll talk, give us something we can really sink our teeth into."

Zach nodded his approval. "Glad to hear it. It'll help me sleep at night to know these so-called Broken Angels won't be snatching another kid anytime soon." The children's faces were still imprinted on his mind. Every day he wondered what had become of them. Every night he saw their pleading expressions in his dreams. He'd reach out to help them, but they'd just as quickly turn to fog and disappear.

"I thought this kind of thing only happened in foreign countries." Martin came to sit beside them.

"A myth." Pat's features hardened to ice. "This sort of thing goes on under our noses all the time. Human trafficking is the second-largest illegal trade after drug trafficking. It's also the fastest-growing criminal industry with global revenues to the tune of forty-two billion dollars. The sad part is that most Americans don't have a clue. They think because they don't live in a third-world country their children are safe, but they're dead wrong. No one is safe."

Pat leaned forward, stared at the kids playing with carefree abandon and shook his head. "Usually, kids are shipped to the U.S. instead of out," he explained. "But every so often, like now, an organized group of thugs decides to use it as a source country. There's a very high demand for Caucasian children right here in the U.S. How many childless couples are willing to pay an arm and a leg to adopt?"

Zach knew the answer to that question better than anyone. He'd seen the way Becca's desperation for a child had torn her apart. If she'd voiced a desire to adopt, he would have done anything to make her wish come true, even pay through his nose.

"Then there's the sex trade, not to mention the organ trade," Pat continued, oblivious to the dark turn the conversation had taken. "The older children are either shipped to foreign countries, where they're sexually exploited or harvested for their organs."

Martin suddenly stood. "I think I need a beer." Seconds later, he vanished inside the house.

"Looks like you rattled him," Zach observed.

"Just saying it like it is. Can't turn a blind eye to what's happening. That's why so many kids are in danger."

Zach steepled his fingers and continued gazing at his kids with an odd blend of pride and possessiveness. "There's still something I don't get. How did Neil Hopkins manage to run a law firm and a kidnapping ring all at once?"

Naked interest flared in Pat's eyes. He really was obsessed with his job. "We think he had an accomplice," he told him. "Found bits and pieces of him in the grape crusher."

That sparked Zach's curiosity. He remembered another man who'd met his end in the grape crusher—Neil Hopkins Sr.—and he couldn't help but wonder if it was a coincidence. Something primal told him it wasn't. "Are you sure it was his accomplice and not some poor chump who stumbled into something he shouldn't have?"

"There was a 9mm SIG among his remains, matches the bullets we pulled from Liam and Lindsay. We also got lucky, managed to lift a partial print from the body. Dead guy's name was Raymond York, petty thief turned murderer. One of these days I'd really like to show his mug shot to Noah, see if he's the guy the kid saw that night."

From a distance Zach studied Noah, who now tossed a ball with Jason. "Not yet. Give him a chance to come to grips with everything that's happened. The guy's dead. There's no use dredging this whole mess up again." He wouldn't force Noah to do anything he wasn't ready to do, not ever again.

The ADA nodded. "If that's how you feel, I respect it."

Summer was drawing to an end, but you couldn't tell by the way the sun cut through the clouds to soak them in heat. Zach reclined in his chair and contented himself with watching Will roll in the grass, Kristen play in the sandbox, Noah grapple with Jason for the ball. A glowing warmth spread through him.

Kids messed you up; there was no question about that. But somewhere amidst the insanity, they carved a path straight to your soul and completed you. Right now that completeness washed over him, imbued him with certainty, and he understood exactly what he needed to do. The realization should have scared him shitless. Instead, it filled him with an electric anticipation that shot through his veins and made every inch of him vibrate.

Somehow he had to make this family solid—permanent—the consequences be damned.

Night fell, a translucent black veil embedded with diamonds. Rebecca was outside, picking up the toys the kids had scattered, with only the porch lights to illuminate her way. A cool breeze stirred, making the trees rustle and the evening come alive.

Zach crept up behind her and wrapped his arms around her waist. The act startled her, and she spun around to face him, her hand fisted over her heart. "How many times have I told you not to sneak up on me?"

"I didn't mean to frighten you. You just looked so...*huggable*."

"Huggable?"

"For lack of a better word."

"All right. Hug away." She stepped into his arms, rejoiced as they tightened around her. It was strange how her skin always thrummed when they touched. So many years later, he still had the same power over her that he'd had when she was an awkward, lovestruck schoolgirl.

Everything had changed, yet so much had stayed the same. The love she'd felt for him back then hadn't faded. It had only grown stronger.

"Are you looking forward to having a little more time to yourself?" His breath brushed her ear as he spoke, sending tendrils of heat skittering down her neck.

The kids were going back to school next week, and Zach was scheduled to resume work. "Not really. I'm going to miss having everyone around."

"I guess you'll just have to find something to do to keep yourself busy."

She shrugged. "I'm sure Will is going to make sure I don't get too bored."

"Yeah, but Will naps most of the afternoon." There was an unspoken implication in his voice, some conclusion he wanted her to draw.

She wrenched free from his grasp, even as her body uttered a silent protest, and glanced up into his beautiful face. "What is it you'd like me to do?"

"Oh, I don't know. Maybe finish that book you started ages ago...or start a new one."

His words took her by surprise. "I haven't thought of that in years."

"Maybe you should." He pinned her with a meaningful stare.

She tamped down her reservations and considered his suggestion. Did she really have a story to tell? Yes, she concluded, now more than ever, she did. She smiled up at him. "Maybe I will."

He bracketed her face with his palms. His warmth seeped into her flesh and set her cheeks afire. "Here's something else you should think about. I know you generally hate to make the same mistake twice, but I hope you'll make an exception this time." His eyes deepened to a midnight blue, dark and vulnerable. The emotion she caught within them made the ground drop out from under her, as did his next words, "Marry me again."

"There's nothing to think about. I made up my mind about that back when I was twelve."

He grinned, and his whole face sparkled. Almost as much as the ring he promptly slipped onto her finger.

"I still have my old ring."

"I want you to have a new one, a symbol of new beginnings, a fresh start." He trapped one of her curls between his fingers, slowly let it slide out of his grasp. "We're starting over. And this time we're gonna make it work."

She gazed down at the square-cut diamond, mesmerized. "It's beautiful. Why does it look so familiar?"

"It was my mom's. My dad gave it to her on their silver wedding anniversary. She would've wanted you to have it."

Emotion pooled in her throat. "I'm honored to wear it."

She wrapped her arms around his neck, slid in close. With a brisk yank, he flattened her to him until every splendid muscle on his chest dug into her breasts. The air squeezed out of her lungs and a gasp tumbled from her lips. Then his mouth found hers, sweet and hot and intoxicating. It turned her spine to rubber, made her insides twist and her pulse roar.

A long-forgotten feeling expanded within her. *Happiness.* She recognized it for what it was, reached out and grabbed it. This time she'd never let it go.

"I love you, Becca." His soft whisper scraped her ear and made the tender flesh beneath it tingle. "Always have. Always will."

She hadn't believed him the first time he'd voiced those words to her, a lifetime ago. This time she did. Believed him with a depth and intensity that shook her to the core. "I love you, too."

He nestled his chin in the crook of her neck. "How about we start the honeymoon early?"

"I thought we already had."

He answered by sweeping her off her feet and carrying her back into the house, where their family peacefully slept and the future waited to unfurl before them, an endless ribbon of time radiating with promise.

About the Author

Anne Hope is the author of contemporary, emotionally intense romances with a twist—a twist of humor, a twist of suspense, a twist of magic. All her stories, however, have a common thread. Whether they make you laugh or cry or push you to the edge of your seat, they all feature the redeeming power of love and the heart's incredible ability to heal.

Anne's passion for writing began at the age of eight. After penning countless stories about enchanted houses, alien girls with supernatural powers and children constantly getting lost in the woods, she decided to try her hand at romance. She lives in Montreal, Canada, with her husband, her two inexhaustible kids, a lazy cat and a rambunctious Australian Kelpie.

To learn more about Anne Hope, please visit www.annehope.com. Send an email to Anne Hope at anne@annehope.com or sign up for her newsletter at http://groups.yahoo.com/group/annehopeauthor.

Breaking his heart may be the only way to save his life.

Where Dreams Are Made
© 2008 Anne Hope

A woman running from the past...

Jenny Logan is alone, penniless, and indebted to a ruthless man who will stop at nothing to own her. All she wants is a chance to pursue her dreams and make a fresh start, but the past refuses to release her.

A man hiding from the future...

Daniel Frost, a scarred, reclusive toymaker, is trying to escape his memories. Burdened by guilt over a violent car accident that destroyed his family, he believes loneliness is the only way to atone for his sins.

Sometimes, today is all that matters...

One magical Christmas, Daniel's meddlesome grandfather secretly hires Jenny to act as his grandson's assistant, starting them both on the road to recovery. On a remote island where miles of sea meet miles of sky, two lonely people learn that love can heal even the deepest scars—but it comes at a price.

Warning: This title contains violence, sex, emotional intensity that may cause your mascara to run, and a dark, sexy hero who'll make you want to believe in Santa all over again.

Available now in ebook and print from Samhain Publishing.

CPSIA information can be obtained at www.ICGtesting.com
Printed in the USA
238586LV00002B/14/P